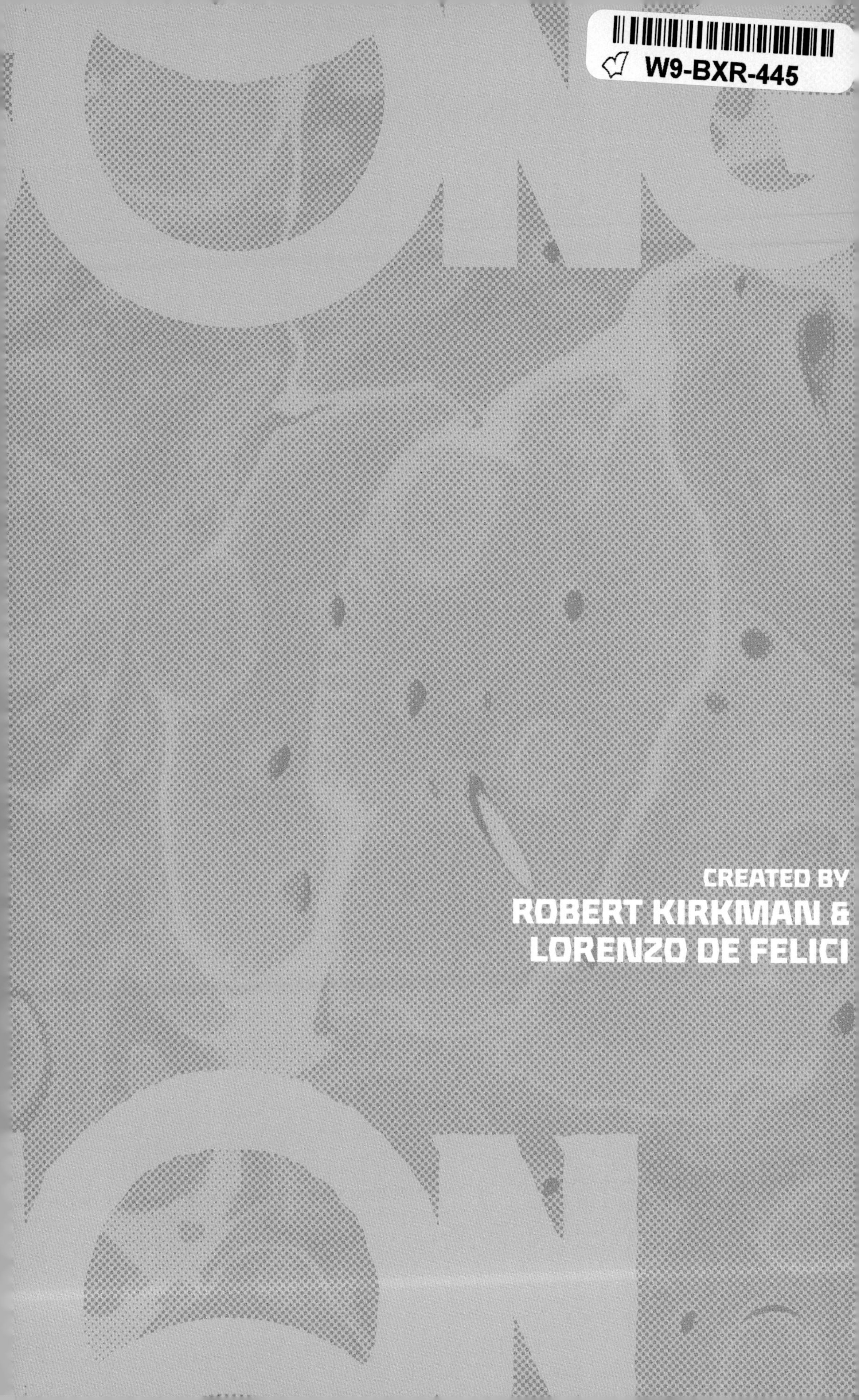

CREATED BY
ROBERT KIRKMAN &
LORENZO DE FELICI

ROBERT KIRKMAN
WRITER/CREATOR

LORENZO DE FELICI
ARTIST/CREATOR

ANNALISA LEONI
COLORIST

RUS WOOTON
LETTERER

ARIELLE BASICH
ASSOCIATE EDITOR

SEAN MACKIEWICZ
EDITOR

LORENZO DE FELICI
COVER

ANDRES JUAREZ
LOGO & PRODUCTION DESIGN

CARINA TAYLOR
PRODUCTION

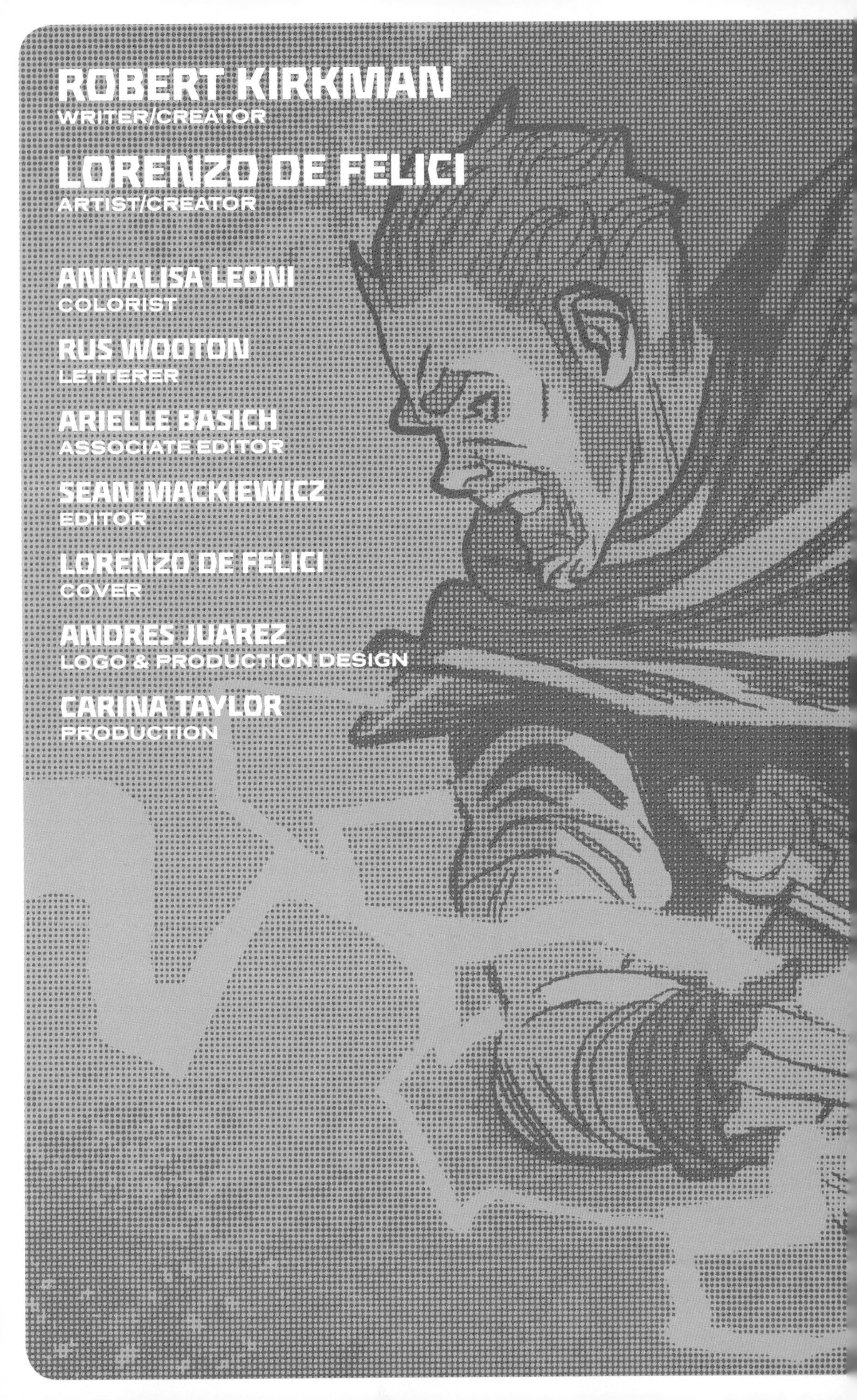

SKYBOUND

FOR SKYBOUND ENTERTAINMENT
ROBERT KIRKMAN *Chairman* • DAVID ALPERT *CEO* • SEAN MACKIEWICZ *SVP, Editor-in-Chief* • SHAWN KIRKHAM *SVP, Business Development* • BRIAN HUNTINGTON *VP of Online Content* • SHAUNA WYNNE *Publicity Director* • ANDRES JUAREZ *Art Director* • JON MOISAN *Editor* • ARIELLE BASICH *Associate Editor* • CARINA TAYLOR *Production Artist* • PAUL SHIN *Business Development Manager* • JOHNNY O'DELL *Social Media Manager* • SALLY JACKA *Skybound Retailer Relations* • DAN PETERSEN *Sr. Director of Operations & Events*

International Inquiries: ag@sequentialrights.com
Licensing Inquiries: contact@skybound.com
WWW.SKYBOUND.COM

IMAGE COMICS, INC.
ROBERT KIRKMAN *Chief Operating Officer* • ERIK LARSEN *Chief Financial Officer* • TODD McFARLANE *President* • MARC SILVESTRI *Chief Executive Officer* • JIM VALENTINO *Vice President* • ERIC STEPHENSON *Publisher* • COREY HART *Director of Sales* • JEFF BOISON *Director of Publishing Planning & Book Trade Sales* • CHRIS ROSS *Director of Digital Sales* • JEFF STANG *Director of Specialty Sales* • KAT SALAZAR *Director of PR & Marketing* • DREW GILL *Art Director* • HEATHER DOORNINK *Production Director* • BRANWYN BIGGLESTONE *Controller*
WWW.IMAGECOMICS.COM

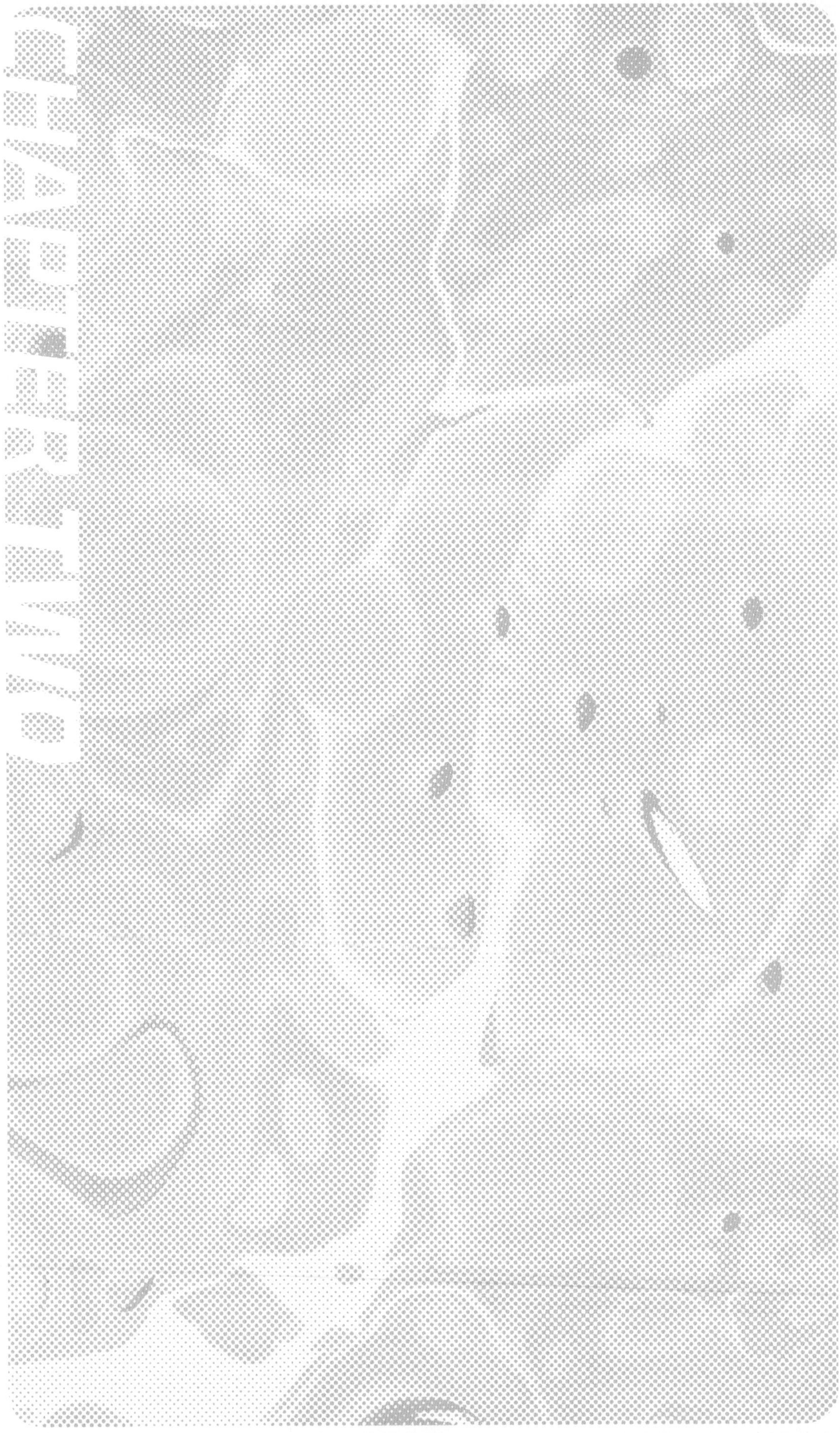
CHAPTER TWO

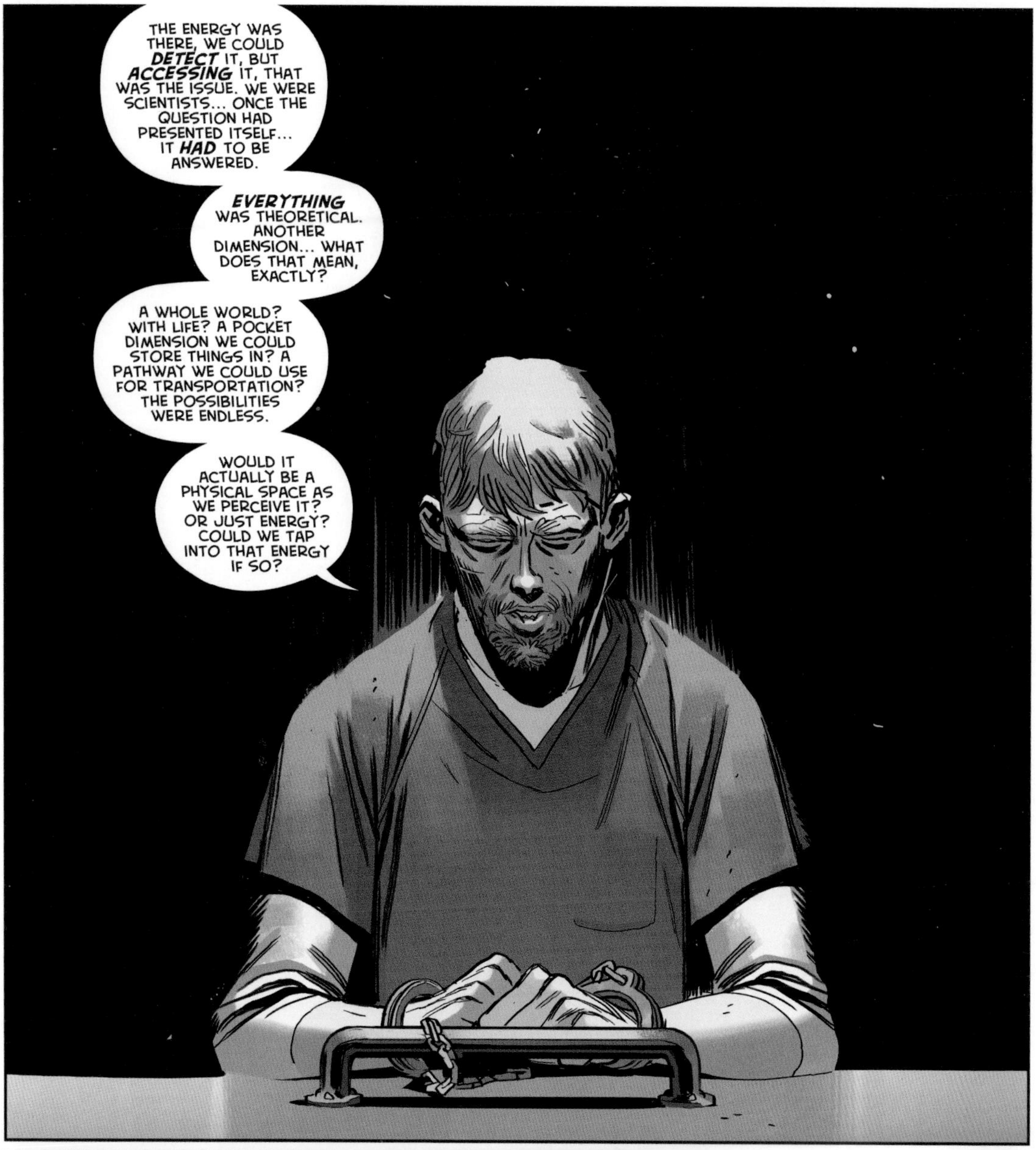
THE ENERGY WAS THERE, WE COULD DETECT IT, BUT ACCESSING IT, THAT WAS THE ISSUE. WE WERE SCIENTISTS... ONCE THE QUESTION HAD PRESENTED ITSELF... IT HAD TO BE ANSWERED.
EVERYTHING WAS THEORETICAL. ANOTHER DIMENSION... WHAT DOES THAT MEAN, EXACTLY?
A WHOLE WORLD? WITH LIFE? A POCKET DIMENSION WE COULD STORE THINGS IN? A PATHWAY WE COULD USE FOR TRANSPORTATION? THE POSSIBILITIES WERE ENDLESS.
WOULD IT ACTUALLY BE A PHYSICAL SPACE AS WE PERCEIVE IT? OR JUST ENERGY? COULD WE TAP INTO THAT ENERGY IF SO?

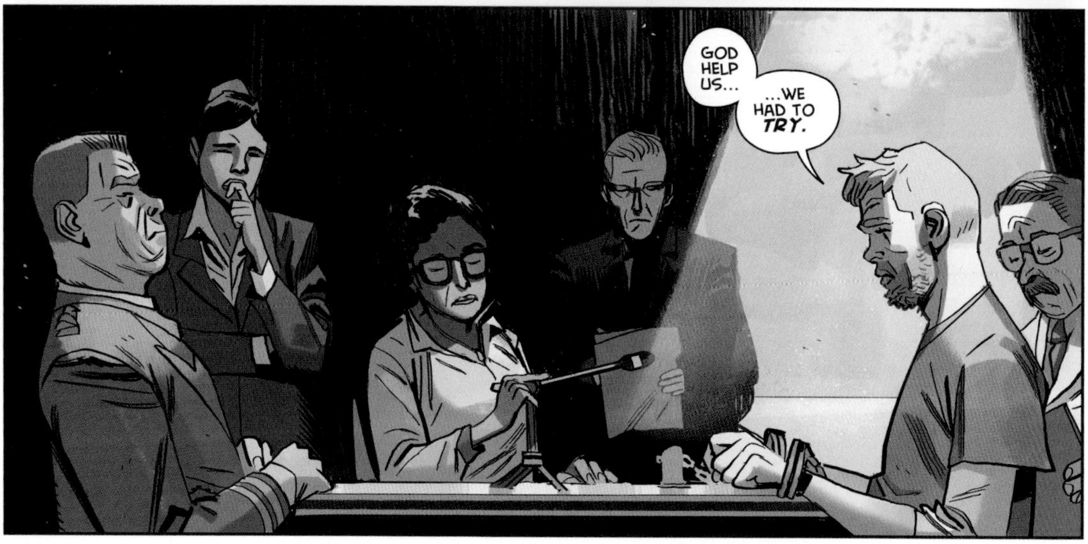
GOD HELP US...
...WE HAD TO TRY.

WE WERE AN INDEPENDENT THINK TANK, FUNDED BY GRANTS... WE STRUGGLED TO HOLD THINGS TOGETHER, BUT WE MADE IT ALL WORK.

WE BELIEVED IN IT. OUR WORK WAS MORE IMPORTANT THAN ANYTHING ELSE IN OUR LIVES.

BERNARD OSMOND WAS SOMEONE WE ALL LOOKED UP TO. HE'D FOUNDED THE THINK TANK.

HE'S THE ONE WHO DISCOVERED THE ENERGY SIGNATURE IN THE FIRST PLACE.

HIS DAUGHTER MARIE KEPT EVERYTHING RUNNING.

SHE SOMEHOW SPENT HALF THE DAY APPLYING FOR GRANTS AND STILL WORKED CIRCLES AROUND THE REST OF US.

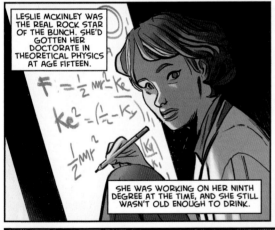

LESLIE MCKINLEY WAS THE REAL ROCK STAR OF THE BUNCH. SHE'D GOTTEN HER DOCTORATE IN THEORETICAL PHYSICS AT AGE FIFTEEN.

$$F = \frac{1}{2}mv^2 - Ke$$

$$Ke^2 = \left(\frac{1}{2} - K_y\right)$$

$$\frac{1}{2}mv^2 \quad \frac{Ky}{k}$$

SHE WAS WORKING ON HER NINTH DEGREE AT THE TIME, AND SHE STILL WASN'T OLD ENOUGH TO DRINK.

KATHERINE JONAS HAD A MIND TO RIVAL EINSTEIN.

SHE COULD USE THOUGHT EXERCISES TO EXPLORE AND SOLVE ALMOST EVERY ROADBLOCK WE ENCOUNTERED. IT WAS REMARKABLE.

THAT'S WHO WE WERE, THIS GROUP OF PEOPLE FROM DIFFERENT BACKGROUNDS, WITH DIFFERENT AREAS OF EXPERTISE, BRINGING OUR UNIQUE VIEWPOINTS TOGETHER TO TRY AND SEE ALL SIDES OF THIS OBJECTIVE.

TO PEER THROUGH A WINDOW INTO THE *UNKNOWN*.

THERE WAS NO GREED, NO EGO, NO SINISTER MOTIVE... WE WERE JUST... *CURIOUS*.

WE HAD *NO IDEA* WHAT WAS COMING.

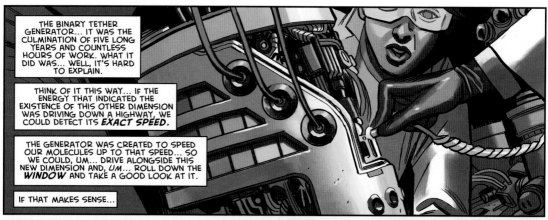

THE BINARY TETHER GENERATOR... IT WAS THE CULMINATION OF FIVE LONG YEARS AND COUNTLESS HOURS OF WORK. WHAT IT DID WAS... WELL, IT'S HARD TO EXPLAIN.

THINK OF IT THIS WAY... IF THE ENERGY THAT INDICATED THE EXISTENCE OF THIS OTHER DIMENSION WAS DRIVING DOWN A HIGHWAY, WE COULD DETECT ITS *EXACT SPEED.*

THE GENERATOR WAS CREATED TO SPEED OUR MOLECULES UP TO THAT SPEED... SO WE COULD, UM... DRIVE ALONGSIDE THIS NEW DIMENSION AND, UM... ROLL DOWN THE *WINDOW* AND TAKE A GOOD LOOK AT IT.

IF THAT MAKES SENSE...

THAT WAS MORE OR LESS HOW IT WORKED. IT WOULD CREATE A DISRUPTION FIELD IN THE IMMEDIATE AREA, PULL US TO THEM AND THEM TO US, SO WE COULD VIEW THE *OVERLAP.*

NEEDLESS TO SAY, IT WAS ALL THEORETICAL.

BUT IT WAS GAMED OUT TO THE POINT WHERE WE THOUGHT WE'D ANALYZED AND PREPARED FOR ANY POTENTIAL OUTCOME.

WE WERE SO CONFIDENT IN WHAT WE WERE DOING. THE ARGUMENT WASN'T *IF* WE WOULD ACTIVATE IT, BUT RATHER *WHEN.*

FINALLY, THE DAY CAME... A DAY WE'LL ALL REMEMBER, TEN YEARS AGO.

THE DAY WE TURNED IT ON.

THE POWER WENT OUT.

AT FIRST IT SEEMED LIKE ALL THE DEVICE DID WAS KNOCK OUT A PORTION OF THE CITY'S ELECTRICAL GRID.

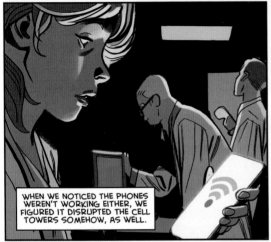

WHEN WE NOTICED THE PHONES WEREN'T WORKING EITHER, WE FIGURED IT DISRUPTED THE CELL TOWERS SOMEHOW, AS WELL.

POWER, PHONES, EVERYTHING WAS JUST... *DEAD.* EVEN THE WATER TO OUR BUILDING WASN'T WORKING.

EVENTUALLY WE NOTICED PEOPLE WERE STARTING TO GATHER OUTSIDE--SO WE JOINED THEM.

IN THOSE FIRST FEW MOMENTS WE DIDN'T NOTICE ANYTHING HAD CHANGED. THE STREET LOOKED THE SAME... THE AIR SMELLED THE SAME, AT FIRST. PEOPLE CAME OUTSIDE BECAUSE OF THE POWER OUTAGE. IT SEEMED... NORMAL, SAVE FOR *ONE* LARGE DETAIL...

...THE SKY WASN'T RIGHT.

WE STARTED TO SEE THINGS--FLASHES OF AN ODD BIRD IN THE SKY, A STRANGE INSECT-- NOTHING WE COULD GET A GOOD LOOK AT.

THE AIR, IT SORT OF... *SOURED.*

THAT'S WHEN I FIRST NOTICED THE SOUND... THE *OBLIVION SONG.* IT GOT SO QUIET, PEOPLE WERE SO WORRIED AND SCARED. YOU COULD HEAR THAT HUM, THAT... RUSTLE TO THE AIR THAT WAS UNLIKE ANYTHING HERE.

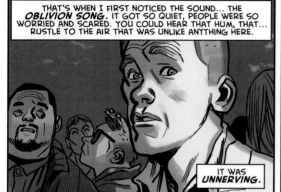

IT WAS *UNNERVING.*

THINKING BACK, IT SEEMED LIKE FOREVER. BUT IN TRUTH WE ONLY HAD A FEW QUIET MINUTES BEFORE THINGS GOT UGLY.

I'M SURE AT THE EDGES OF THE CITY THINGS ESCALATED FASTER--BUT WE WERE AT THE CENTER OF THE TRANSFERRED AREA.

IT TOOK TIME TO REACH US.

BUT WHEN IT FINALLY DID...

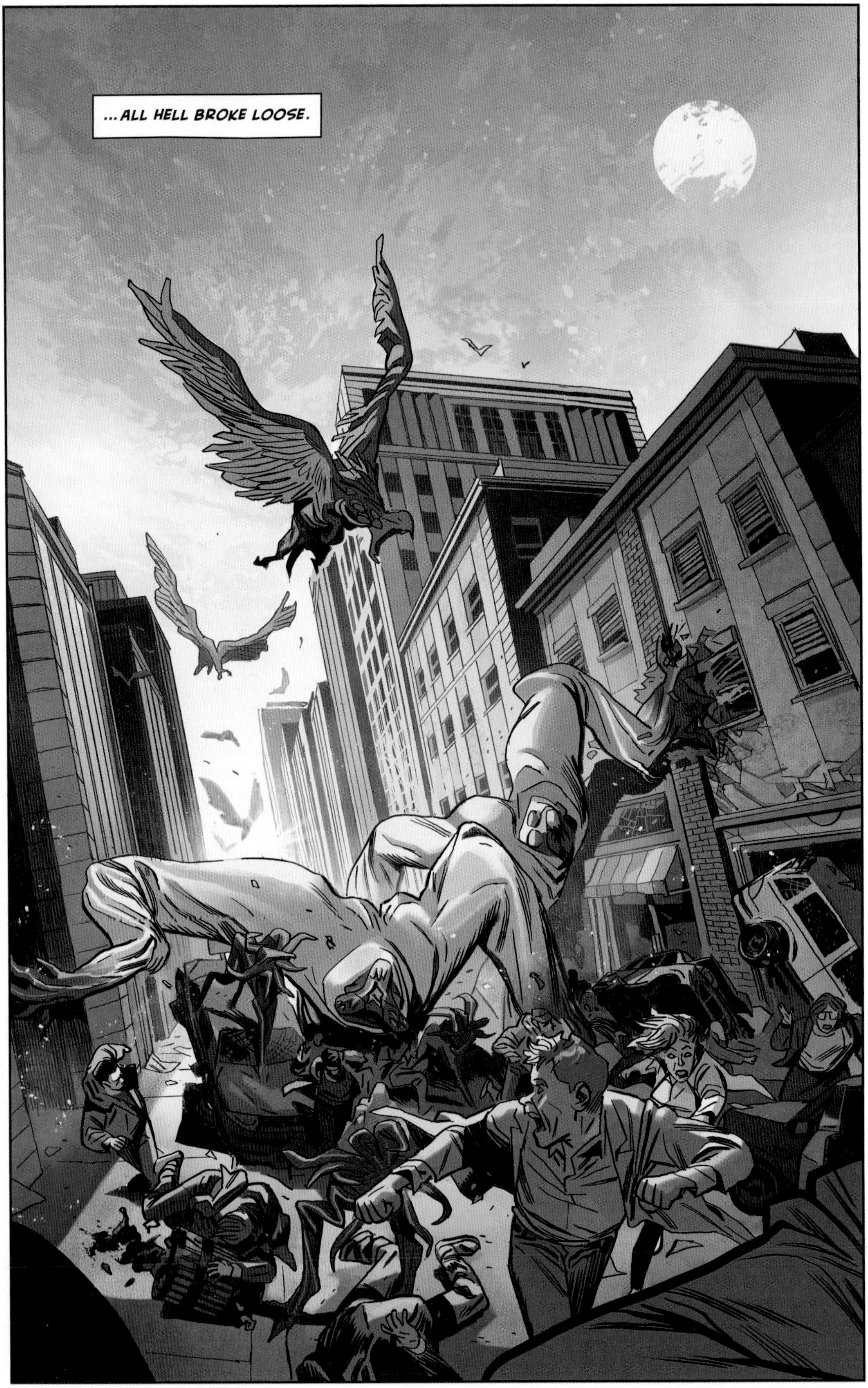
...ALL HELL BROKE LOOSE.

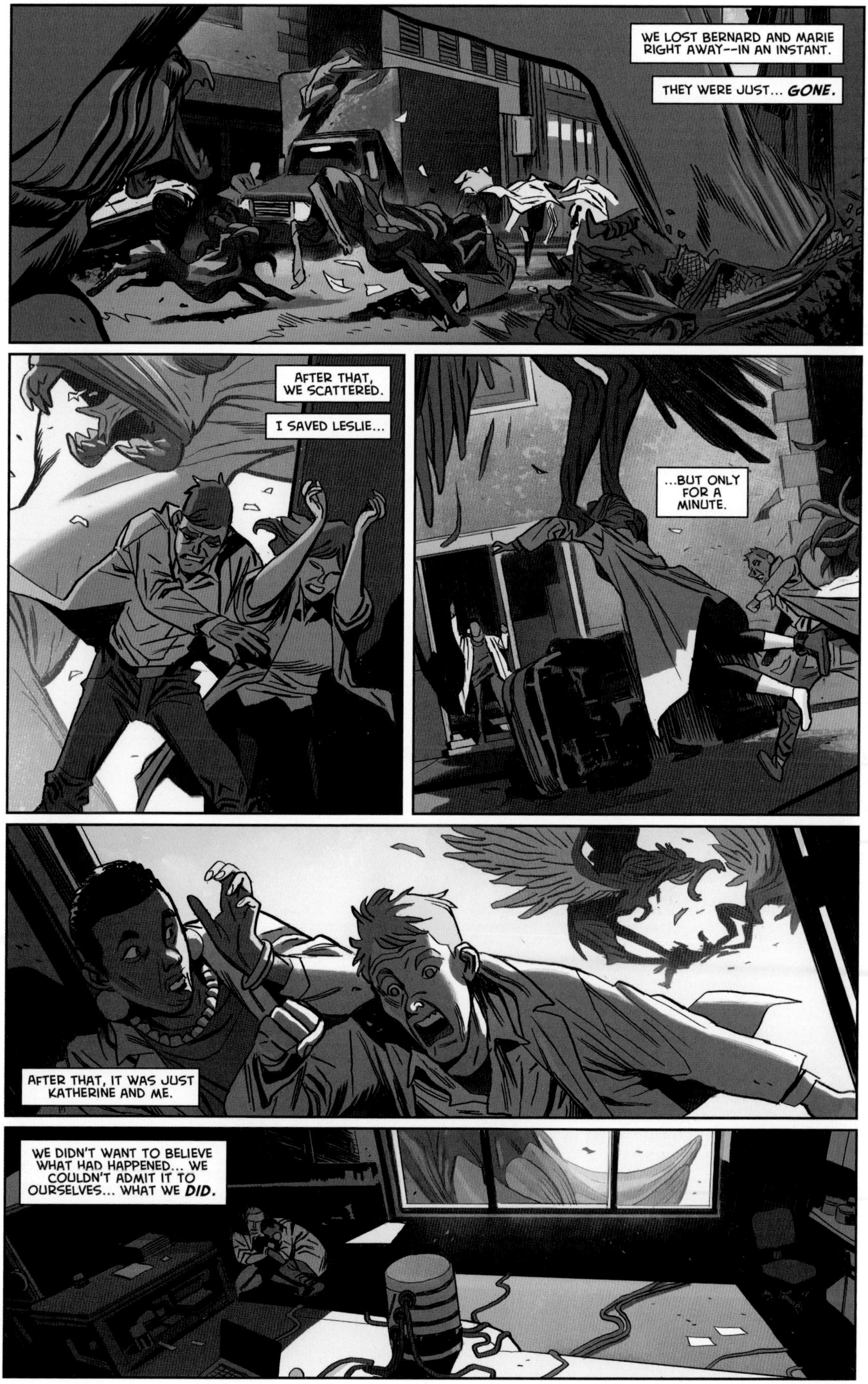
WE LOST BERNARD AND MARIE RIGHT AWAY--IN AN INSTANT.
THEY WERE JUST... GONE.
AFTER THAT, WE SCATTERED.
I SAVED LESLIE...
...BUT ONLY FOR A MINUTE.
AFTER THAT, IT WAS JUST KATHERINE AND ME.
WE DIDN'T WANT TO BELIEVE WHAT HAD HAPPENED... WE COULDN'T ADMIT IT TO OURSELVES... WHAT WE DID.

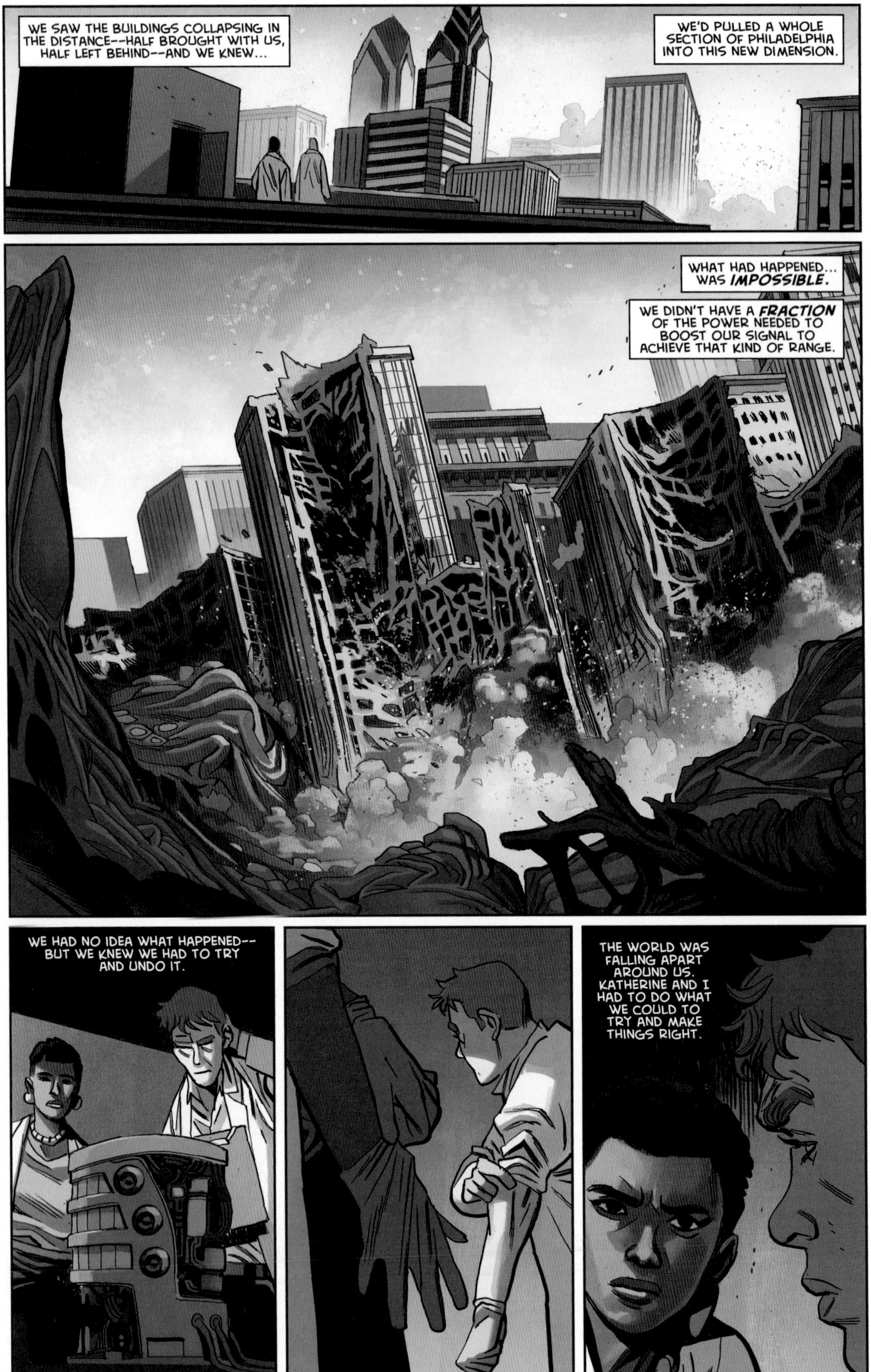
WE SAW THE BUILDINGS COLLAPSING IN THE DISTANCE--HALF BROUGHT WITH US, HALF LEFT BEHIND--AND WE KNEW...
WE'D PULLED A WHOLE SECTION OF PHILADELPHIA INTO THIS NEW DIMENSION.
WHAT HAD HAPPENED... WAS *IMPOSSIBLE.*
WE DIDN'T HAVE A *FRACTION* OF THE POWER NEEDED TO BOOST OUR SIGNAL TO ACHIEVE THAT KIND OF RANGE.
WE HAD NO IDEA WHAT HAPPENED-- BUT WE KNEW WE HAD TO TRY AND UNDO IT.
THE WORLD WAS FALLING APART AROUND US. KATHERINE AND I HAD TO DO WHAT WE COULD TO TRY AND MAKE THINGS RIGHT.

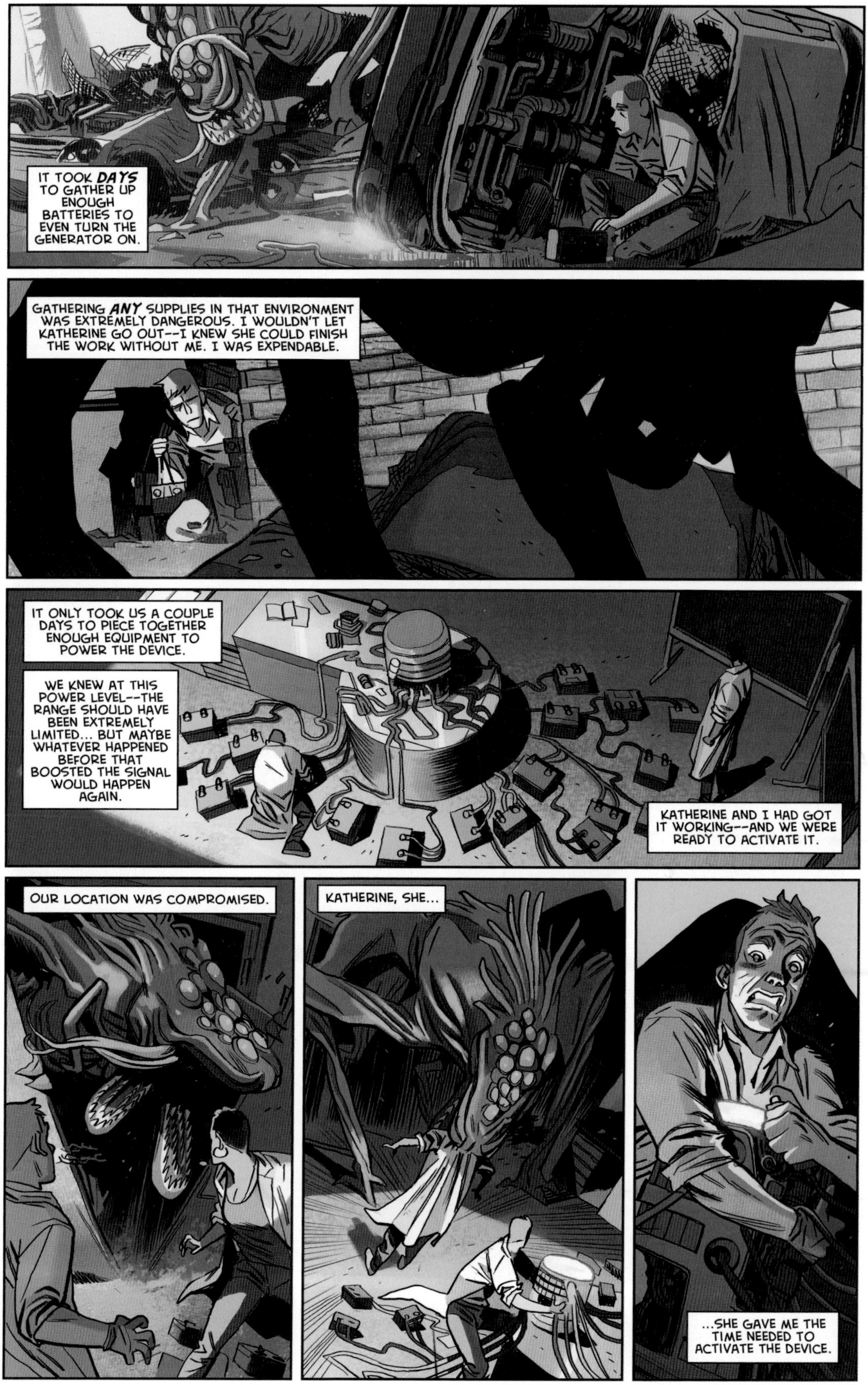
IT TOOK DAYS TO GATHER UP ENOUGH BATTERIES TO EVEN TURN THE GENERATOR ON.
GATHERING ANY SUPPLIES IN THAT ENVIRONMENT WAS EXTREMELY DANGEROUS. I WOULDN'T LET KATHERINE GO OUT--I KNEW SHE COULD FINISH THE WORK WITHOUT ME. I WAS EXPENDABLE.
IT ONLY TOOK US A COUPLE DAYS TO PIECE TOGETHER ENOUGH EQUIPMENT TO POWER THE DEVICE.
WE KNEW AT THIS POWER LEVEL--THE RANGE SHOULD HAVE BEEN EXTREMELY LIMITED... BUT MAYBE WHATEVER HAPPENED BEFORE THAT BOOSTED THE SIGNAL WOULD HAPPEN AGAIN.
KATHERINE AND I HAD GOT IT WORKING--AND WE WERE READY TO ACTIVATE IT.
OUR LOCATION WAS COMPROMISED.
KATHERINE, SHE...
...SHE GAVE ME THE TIME NEEDED TO ACTIVATE THE DEVICE.

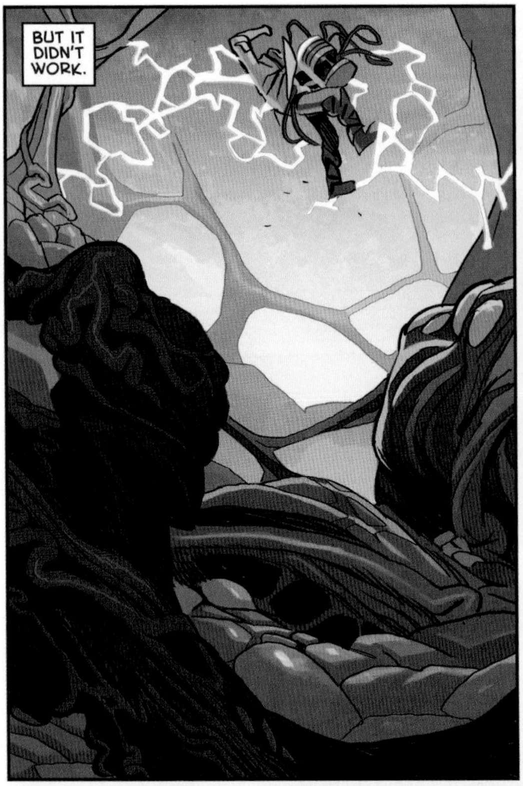
BUT IT DIDN'T WORK.

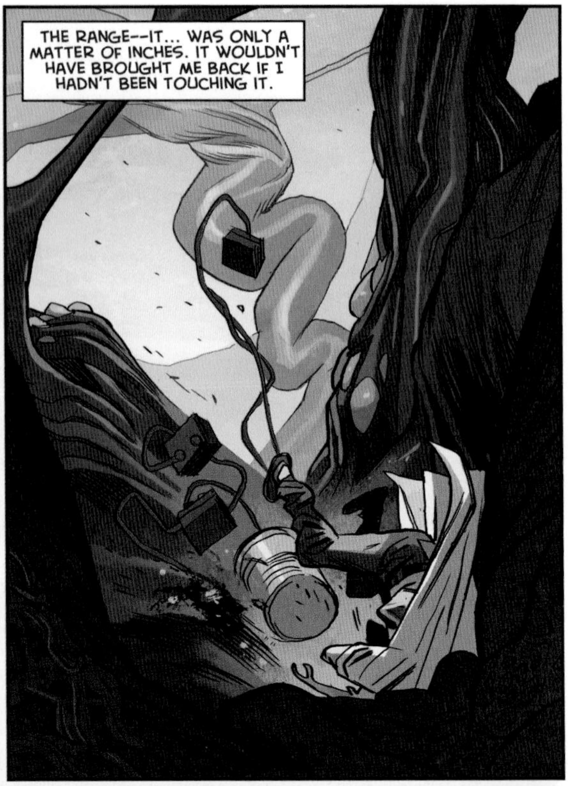
THE RANGE--IT... WAS ONLY A MATTER OF INCHES. IT WOULDN'T HAVE BROUGHT ME BACK IF I HADN'T BEEN TOUCHING IT.

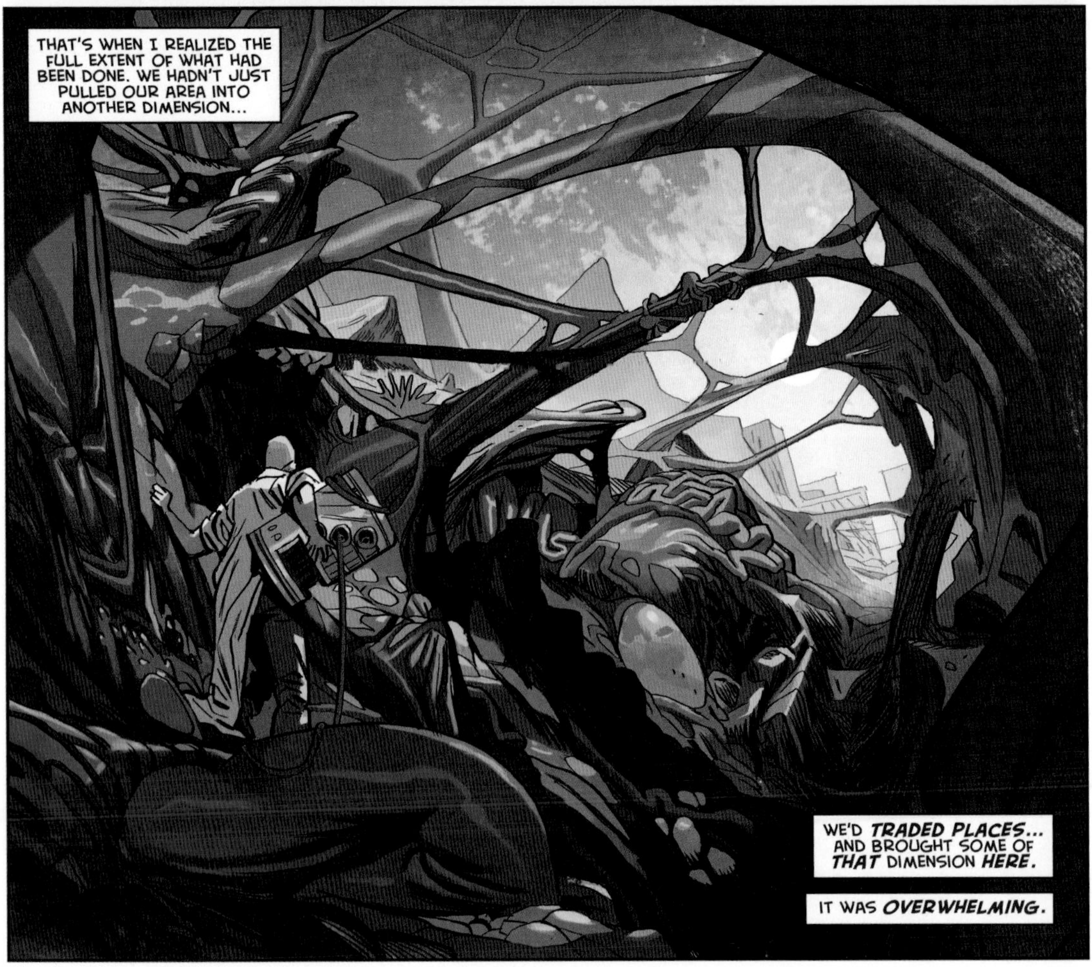
THAT'S WHEN I REALIZED THE FULL EXTENT OF WHAT HAD BEEN DONE. WE HADN'T JUST PULLED OUR AREA INTO ANOTHER DIMENSION...
WE'D TRADED PLACES... AND BROUGHT SOME OF THAT DIMENSION HERE.
IT WAS OVERWHELMING.

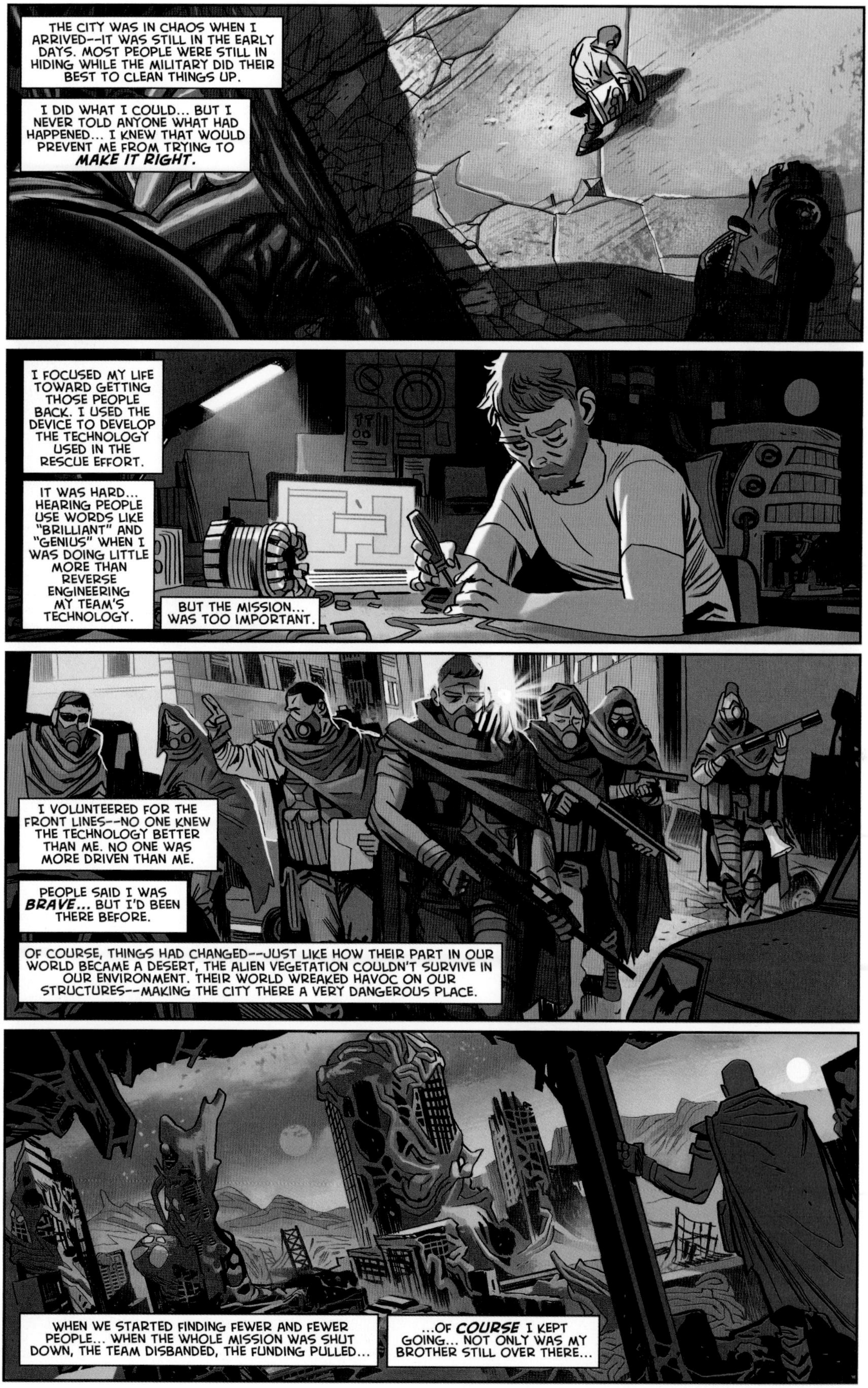
THE CITY WAS IN CHAOS WHEN I ARRIVED--IT WAS STILL IN THE EARLY DAYS. MOST PEOPLE WERE STILL IN HIDING WHILE THE MILITARY DID THEIR BEST TO CLEAN THINGS UP.
I DID WHAT I COULD... BUT I NEVER TOLD ANYONE WHAT HAD HAPPENED... I KNEW THAT WOULD PREVENT ME FROM TRYING TO ***MAKE IT RIGHT.***
I FOCUSED MY LIFE TOWARD GETTING THOSE PEOPLE BACK. I USED THE DEVICE TO DEVELOP THE TECHNOLOGY USED IN THE RESCUE EFFORT.
IT WAS HARD... HEARING PEOPLE USE WORDS LIKE "BRILLIANT" AND "GENIUS" WHEN I WAS DOING LITTLE MORE THAN REVERSE ENGINEERING MY TEAM'S TECHNOLOGY.
BUT THE MISSION... WAS TOO IMPORTANT.
I VOLUNTEERED FOR THE FRONT LINES--NO ONE KNEW THE TECHNOLOGY BETTER THAN ME. NO ONE WAS MORE DRIVEN THAN ME.
PEOPLE SAID I WAS ***BRAVE...*** BUT I'D BEEN THERE BEFORE.
OF COURSE, THINGS HAD CHANGED--JUST LIKE HOW THEIR PART IN OUR WORLD BECAME A DESERT, THE ALIEN VEGETATION COULDN'T SURVIVE IN OUR ENVIRONMENT. THEIR WORLD WREAKED HAVOC ON OUR STRUCTURES--MAKING THE CITY THERE A VERY DANGEROUS PLACE.
WHEN WE STARTED FINDING FEWER AND FEWER PEOPLE... WHEN THE WHOLE MISSION WAS SHUT DOWN, THE TEAM DISBANDED, THE FUNDING PULLED...
...OF ***COURSE*** I KEPT GOING... NOT ONLY WAS MY BROTHER STILL OVER THERE...

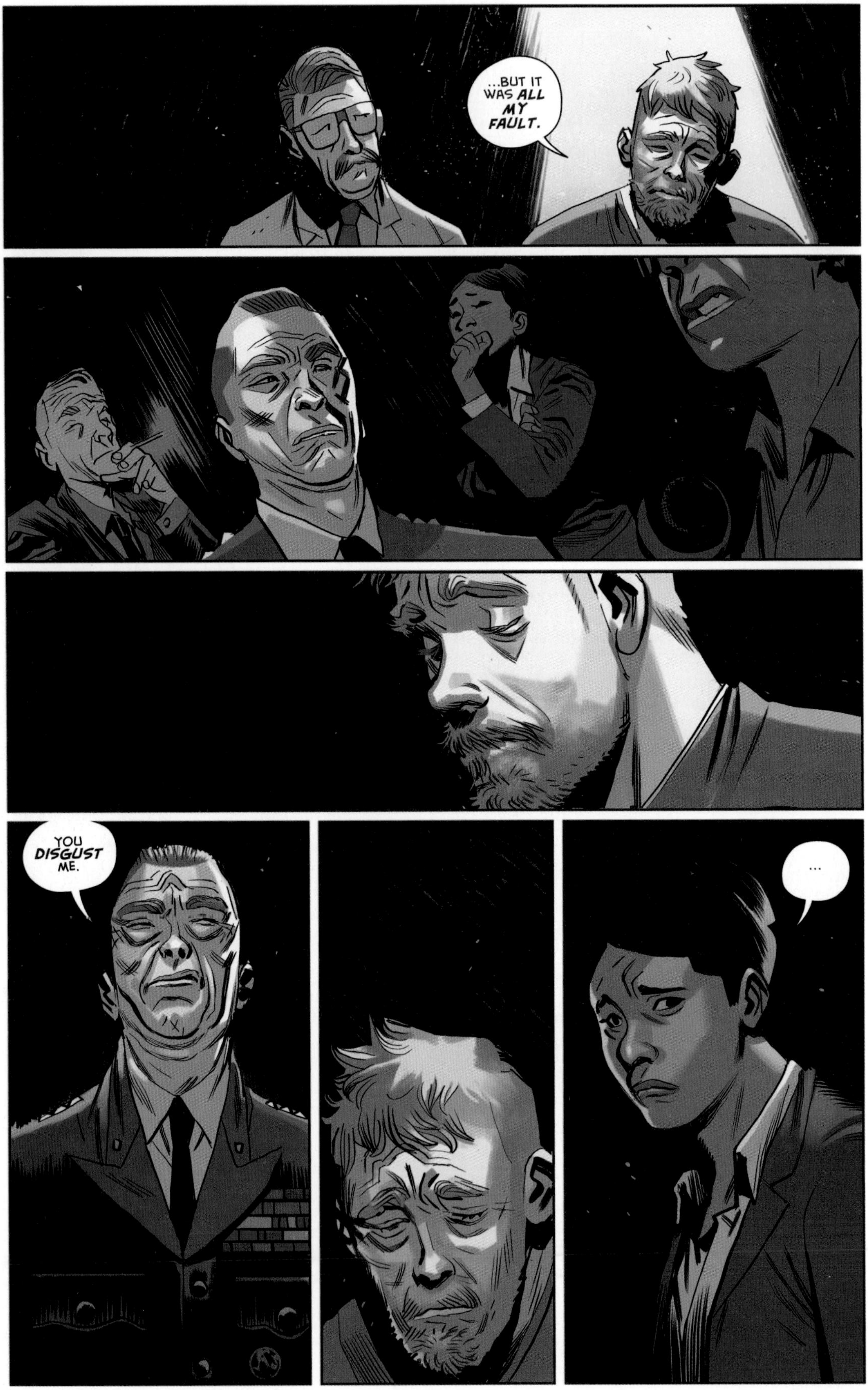
...BUT IT WAS ALL MY FAULT.
YOU DISGUST ME.
...

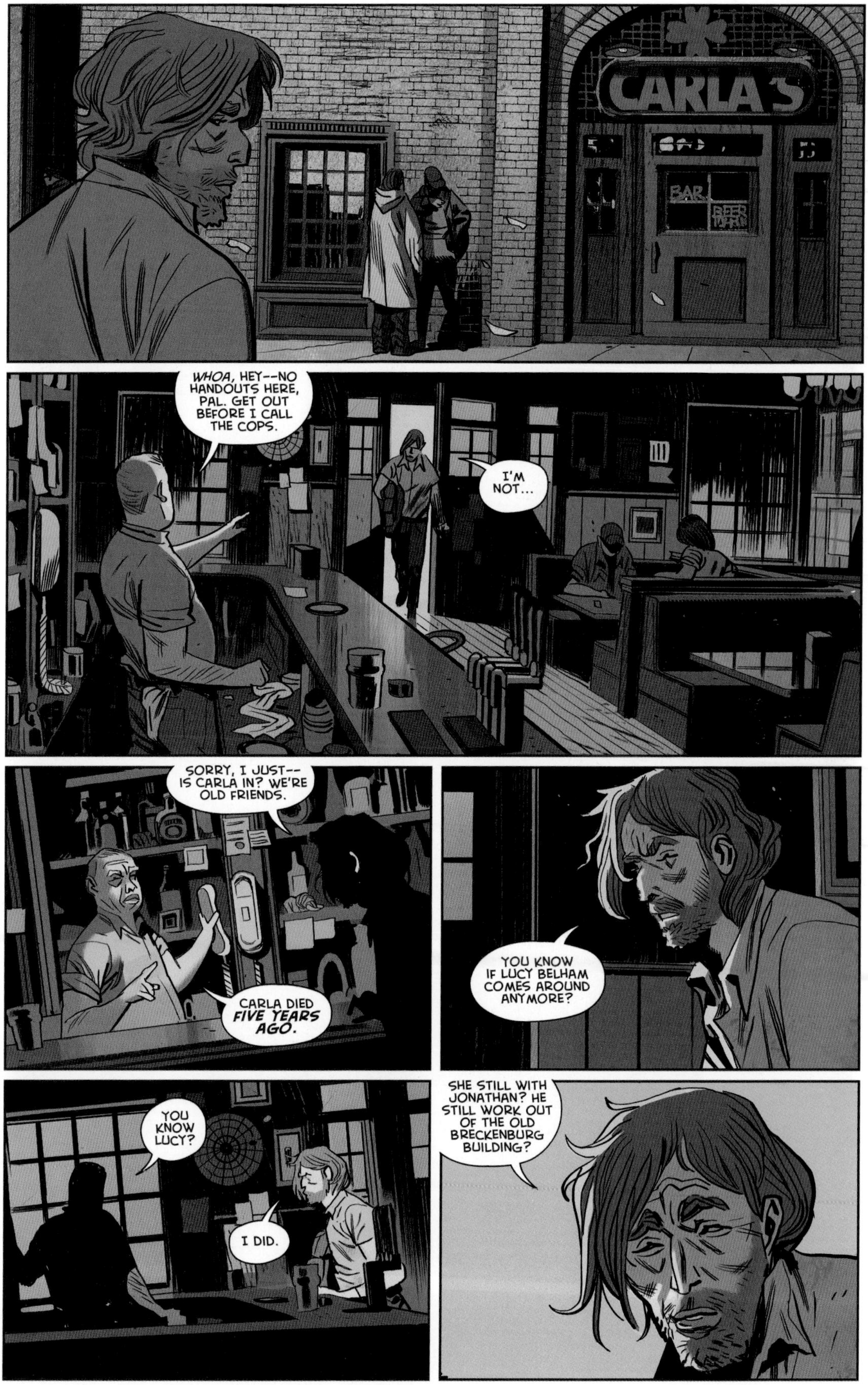
CARLA'S
BAR
BEER
WHOA, HEY--NO HANDOUTS HERE, PAL. GET OUT BEFORE I CALL THE COPS.
I'M NOT...
SORRY, I JUST--IS CARLA IN? WE'RE OLD FRIENDS.
CARLA DIED ***FIVE YEARS AGO.***
YOU KNOW IF LUCY BELHAM COMES AROUND ANYMORE?
YOU KNOW LUCY?
I DID.
SHE STILL WITH JONATHAN? HE STILL WORK OUT OF THE OLD BRECKENBURG BUILDING?

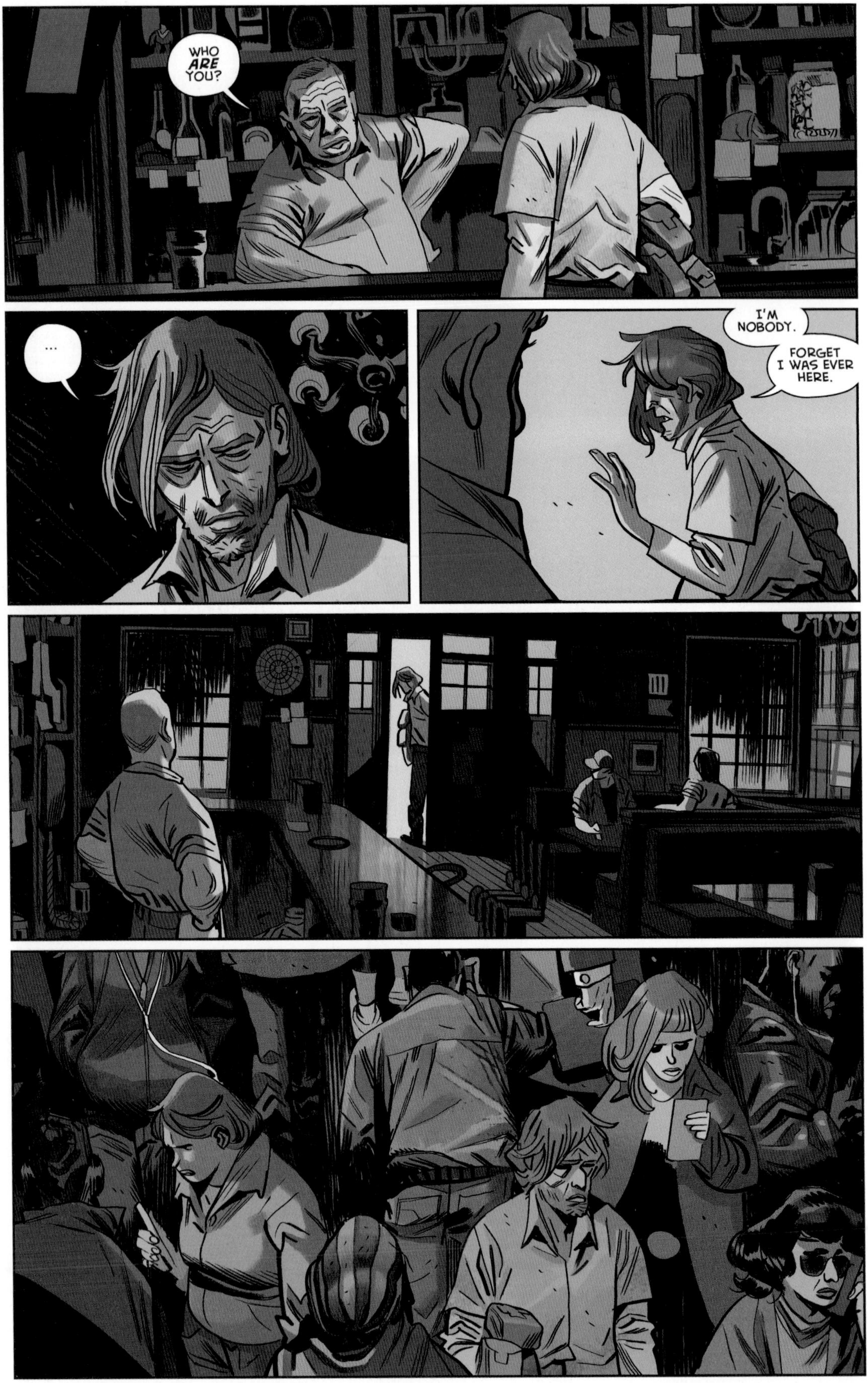
WHO ARE YOU?
...
I'M NOBODY.
FORGET I WAS EVER HERE.

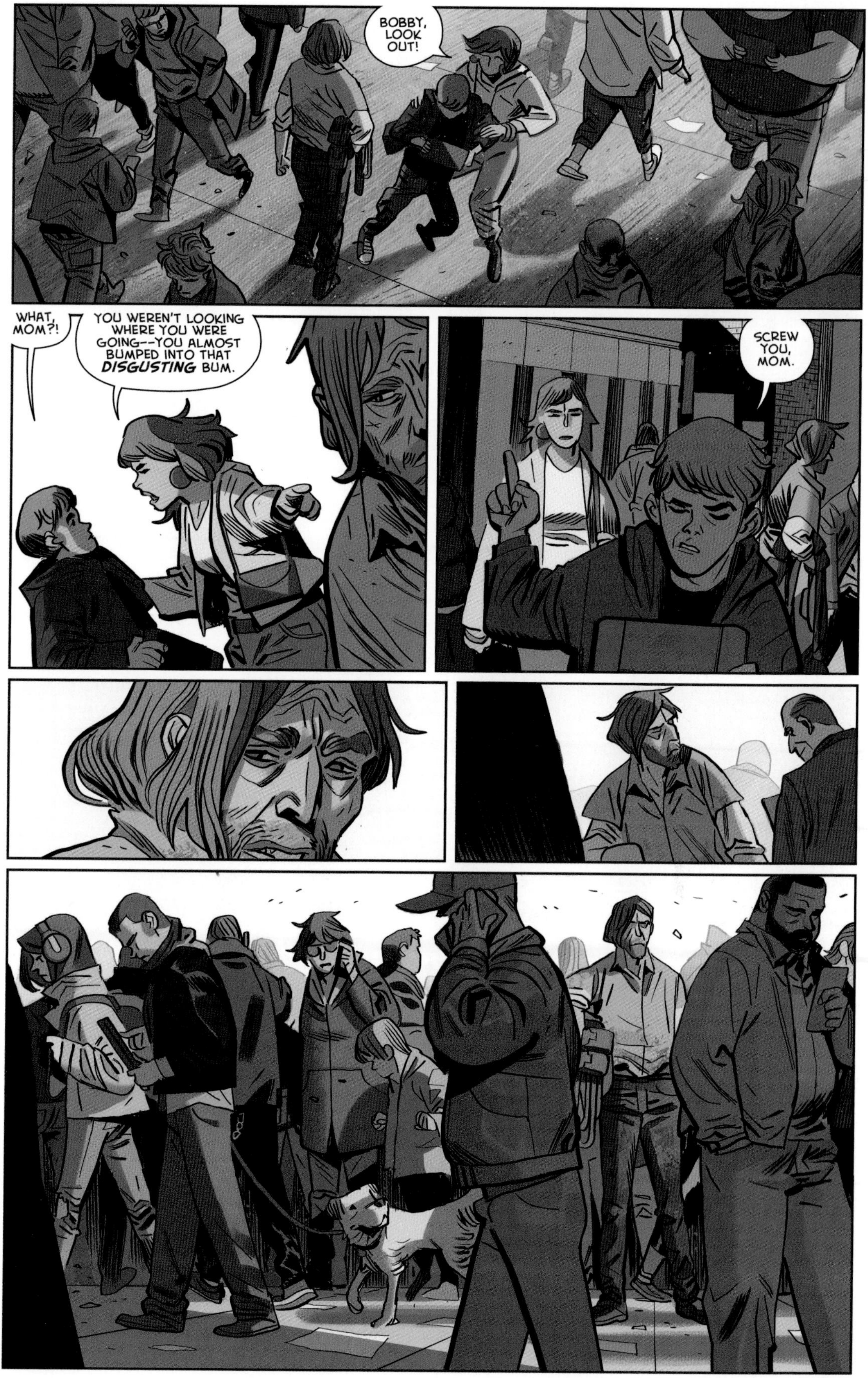
BOBBY, LOOK OUT!
WHAT, MOM?!
YOU WEREN'T LOOKING WHERE YOU WERE GOING--YOU ALMOST BUMPED INTO THAT DISGUSTING BUM.
SCREW YOU, MOM.

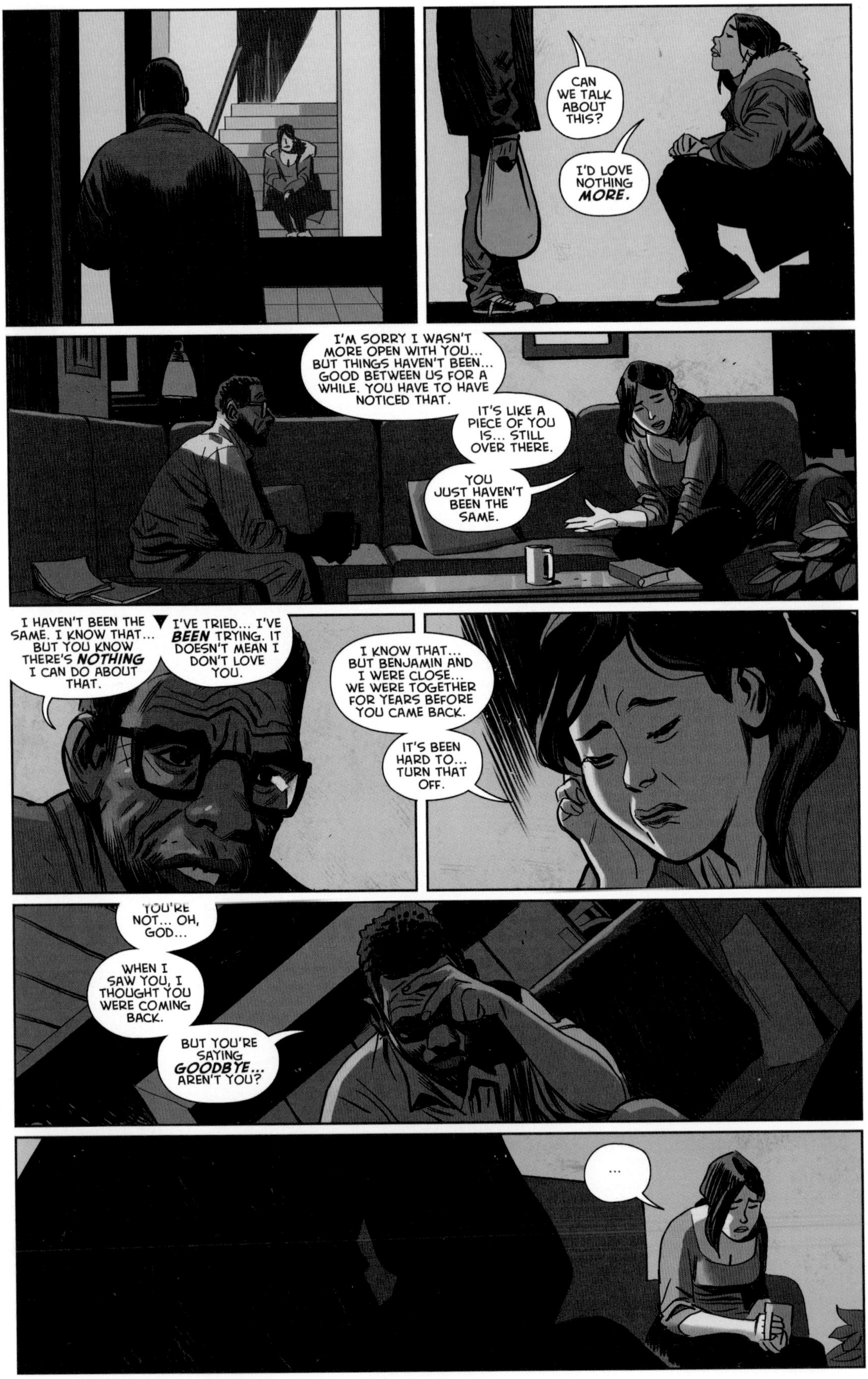
CAN WE TALK ABOUT THIS?
I'D LOVE NOTHING *MORE.*
I'M SORRY I WASN'T MORE OPEN WITH YOU... BUT THINGS HAVEN'T BEEN... GOOD BETWEEN US FOR A WHILE. YOU HAVE TO HAVE NOTICED THAT.
IT'S LIKE A PIECE OF YOU IS... STILL OVER THERE.
YOU JUST HAVEN'T BEEN THE SAME.
I HAVEN'T BEEN THE SAME. I KNOW THAT... BUT YOU KNOW THERE'S *NOTHING* I CAN DO ABOUT THAT.
I'VE TRIED... I'VE *BEEN* TRYING. IT DOESN'T MEAN I DON'T LOVE YOU.
I KNOW THAT... BUT BENJAMIN AND I WERE CLOSE... WE WERE TOGETHER FOR YEARS BEFORE YOU CAME BACK.
IT'S BEEN HARD TO... TURN THAT OFF.
YOU'RE NOT... OH, GOD...
WHEN I SAW YOU, I THOUGHT YOU WERE COMING BACK.
BUT YOU'RE SAYING *GOODBYE...* AREN'T YOU?
...

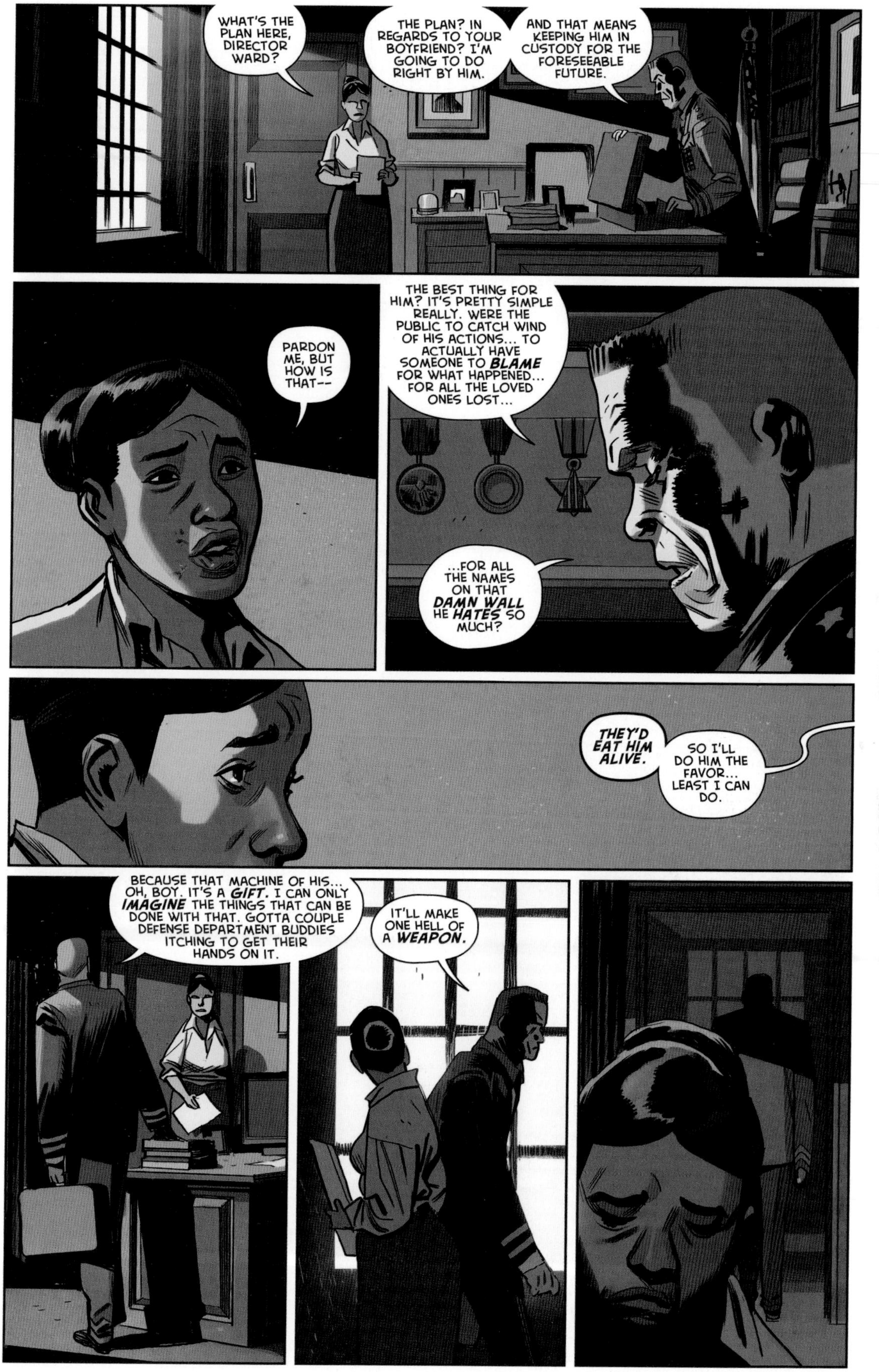
WHAT'S THE PLAN HERE, DIRECTOR WARD?
THE PLAN? IN REGARDS TO YOUR BOYFRIEND? I'M GOING TO DO RIGHT BY HIM.
AND THAT MEANS KEEPING HIM IN CUSTODY FOR THE FORESEEABLE FUTURE.
PARDON ME, BUT HOW IS THAT--
THE BEST THING FOR HIM? IT'S PRETTY SIMPLE REALLY. WERE THE PUBLIC TO CATCH WIND OF HIS ACTIONS... TO ACTUALLY HAVE SOMEONE TO BLAME FOR WHAT HAPPENED... FOR ALL THE LOVED ONES LOST...
...FOR ALL THE NAMES ON THAT DAMN WALL HE HATES SO MUCH?
THEY'D EAT HIM ALIVE.
SO I'LL DO HIM THE FAVOR... LEAST I CAN DO.
BECAUSE THAT MACHINE OF HIS... OH, BOY. IT'S A GIFT. I CAN ONLY IMAGINE THE THINGS THAT CAN BE DONE WITH THAT. GOTTA COUPLE DEFENSE DEPARTMENT BUDDIES ITCHING TO GET THEIR HANDS ON IT.
IT'LL MAKE ONE HELL OF A WEAPON.

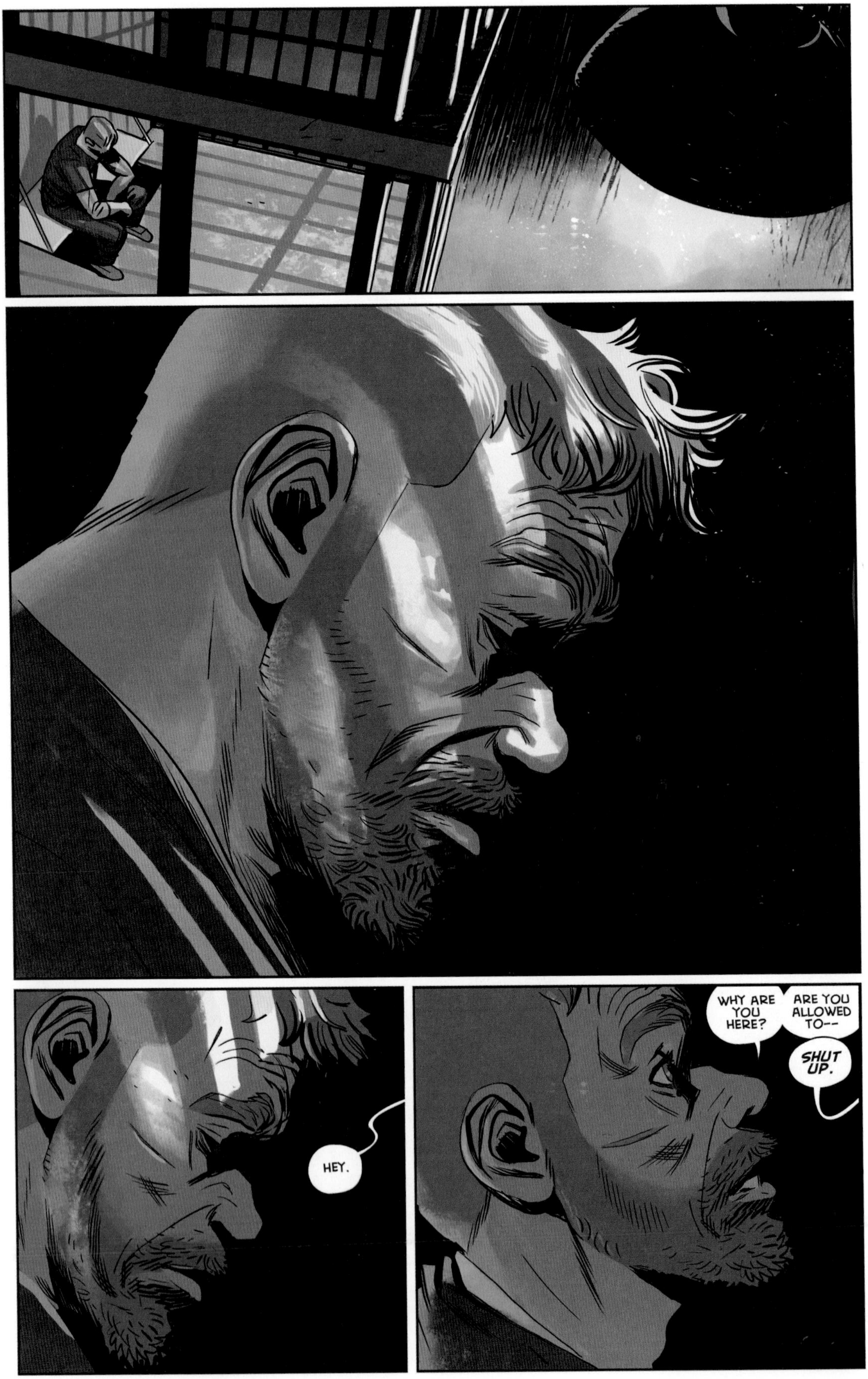
HEY.
WHY ARE YOU HERE?
ARE YOU ALLOWED TO--
SHUT UP.

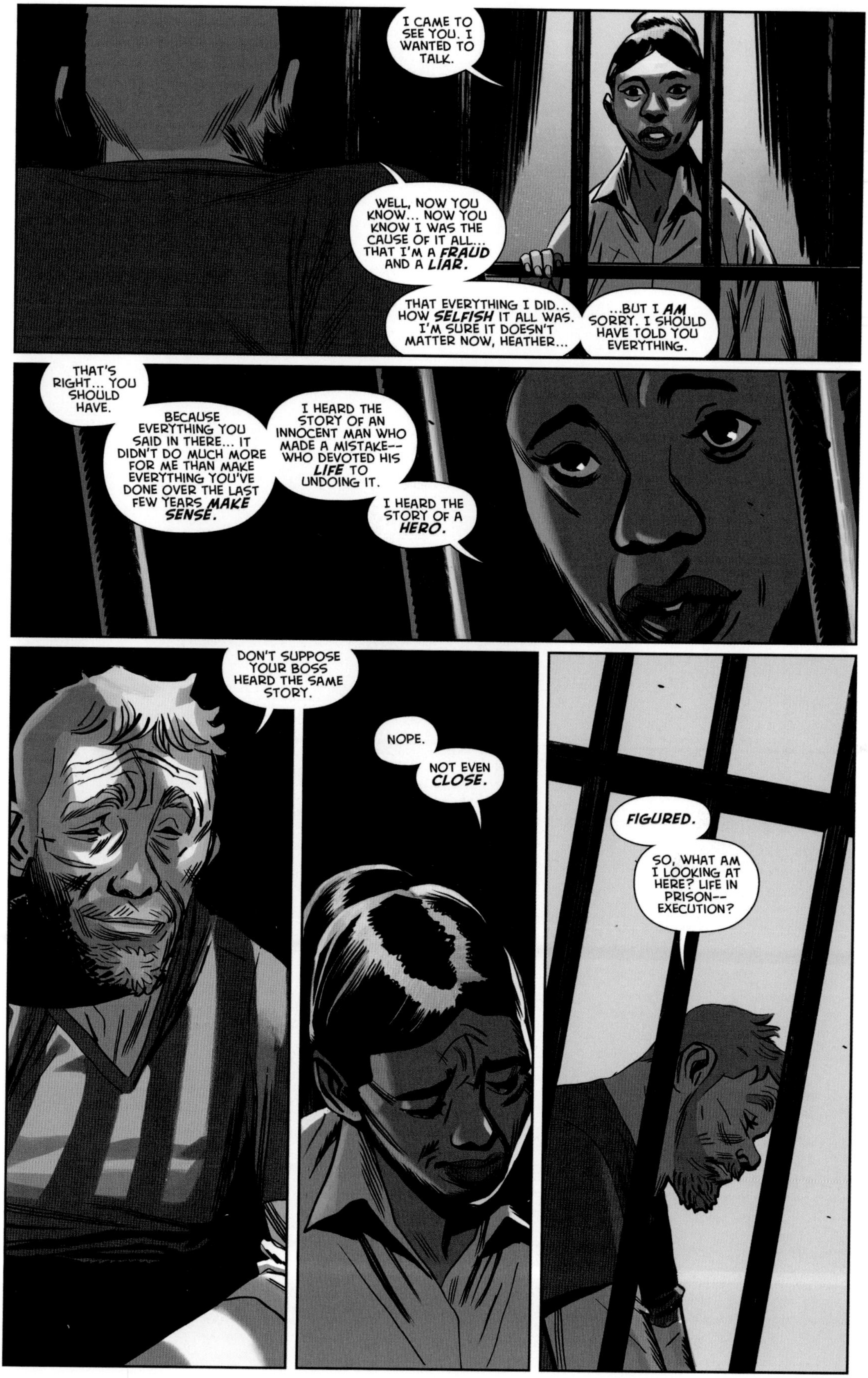
I CAME TO SEE YOU. I WANTED TO TALK.
WELL, NOW YOU KNOW... NOW YOU KNOW I WAS THE CAUSE OF IT ALL... THAT I'M A FRAUD AND A LIAR.
THAT EVERYTHING I DID... HOW SELFISH IT ALL WAS. I'M SURE IT DOESN'T MATTER NOW, HEATHER...
...BUT I AM SORRY. I SHOULD HAVE TOLD YOU EVERYTHING.
THAT'S RIGHT... YOU SHOULD HAVE.
BECAUSE EVERYTHING YOU SAID IN THERE... IT DIDN'T DO MUCH MORE FOR ME THAN MAKE EVERYTHING YOU'VE DONE OVER THE LAST FEW YEARS MAKE SENSE.
I HEARD THE STORY OF AN INNOCENT MAN WHO MADE A MISTAKE-- WHO DEVOTED HIS LIFE TO UNDOING IT.
I HEARD THE STORY OF A HERO.
DON'T SUPPOSE YOUR BOSS HEARD THE SAME STORY.
NOPE.
NOT EVEN CLOSE.
FIGURED.
SO, WHAT AM I LOOKING AT HERE? LIFE IN PRISON-- EXECUTION?

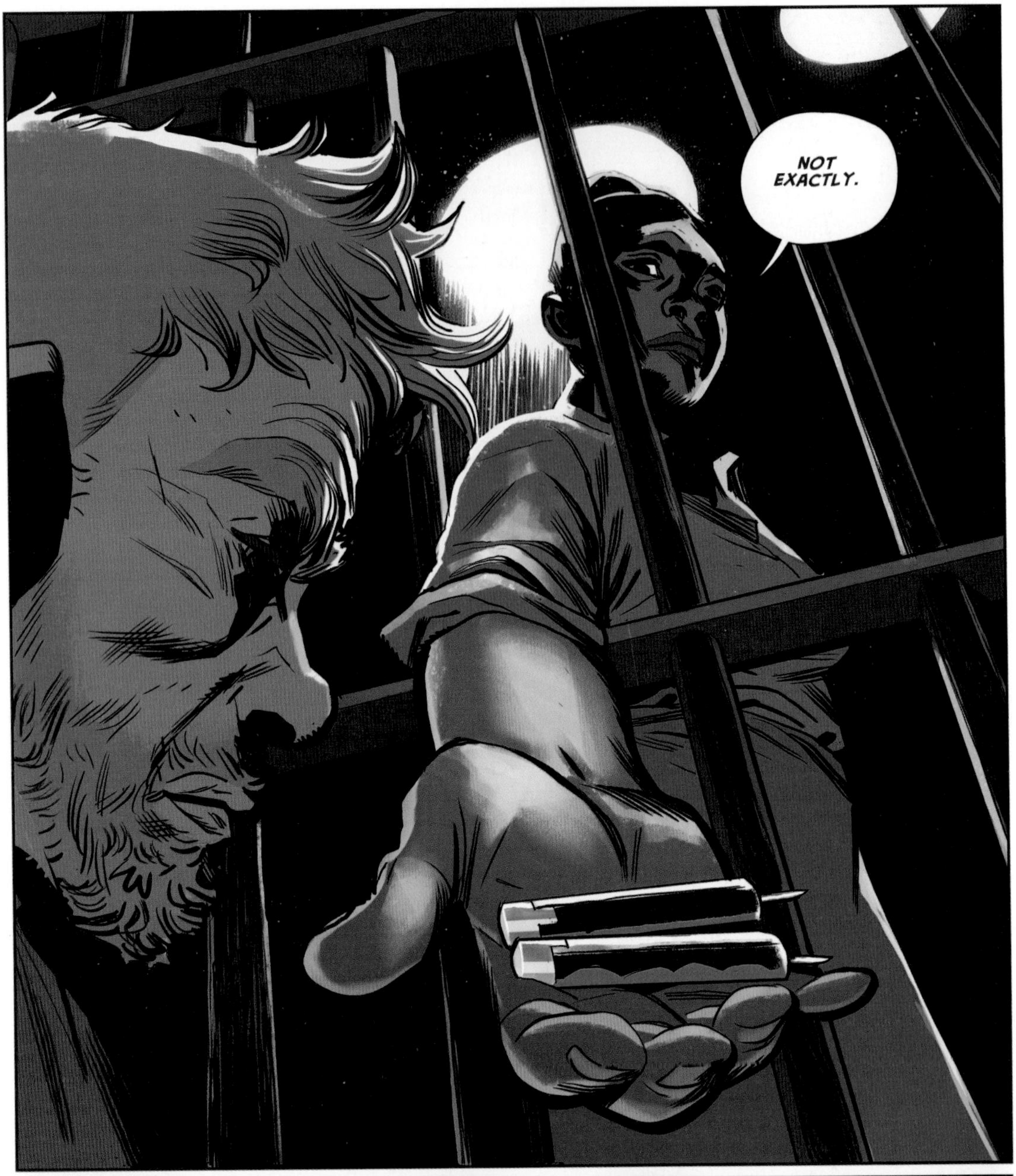
NOT EXACTLY.

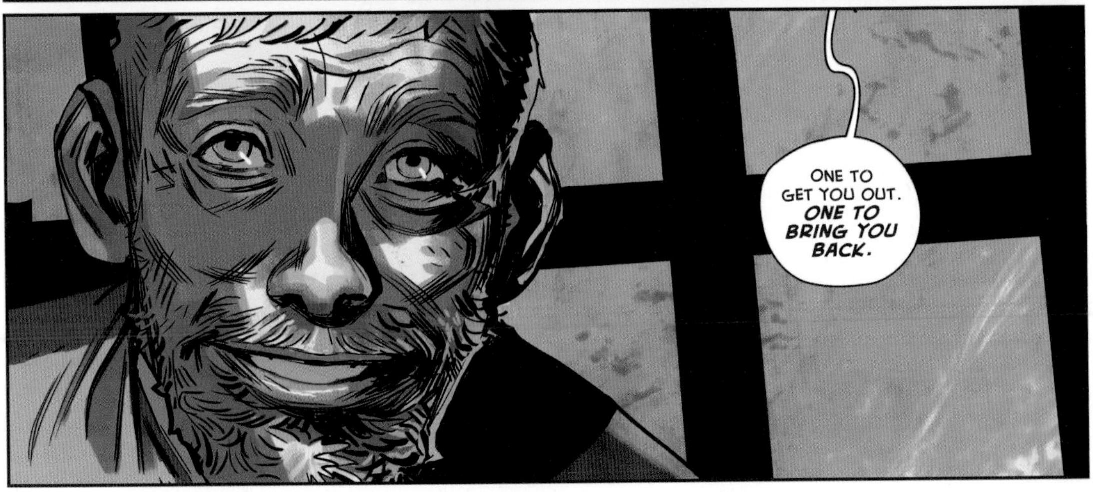
ONE TO GET YOU OUT. ONE TO BRING YOU BACK.

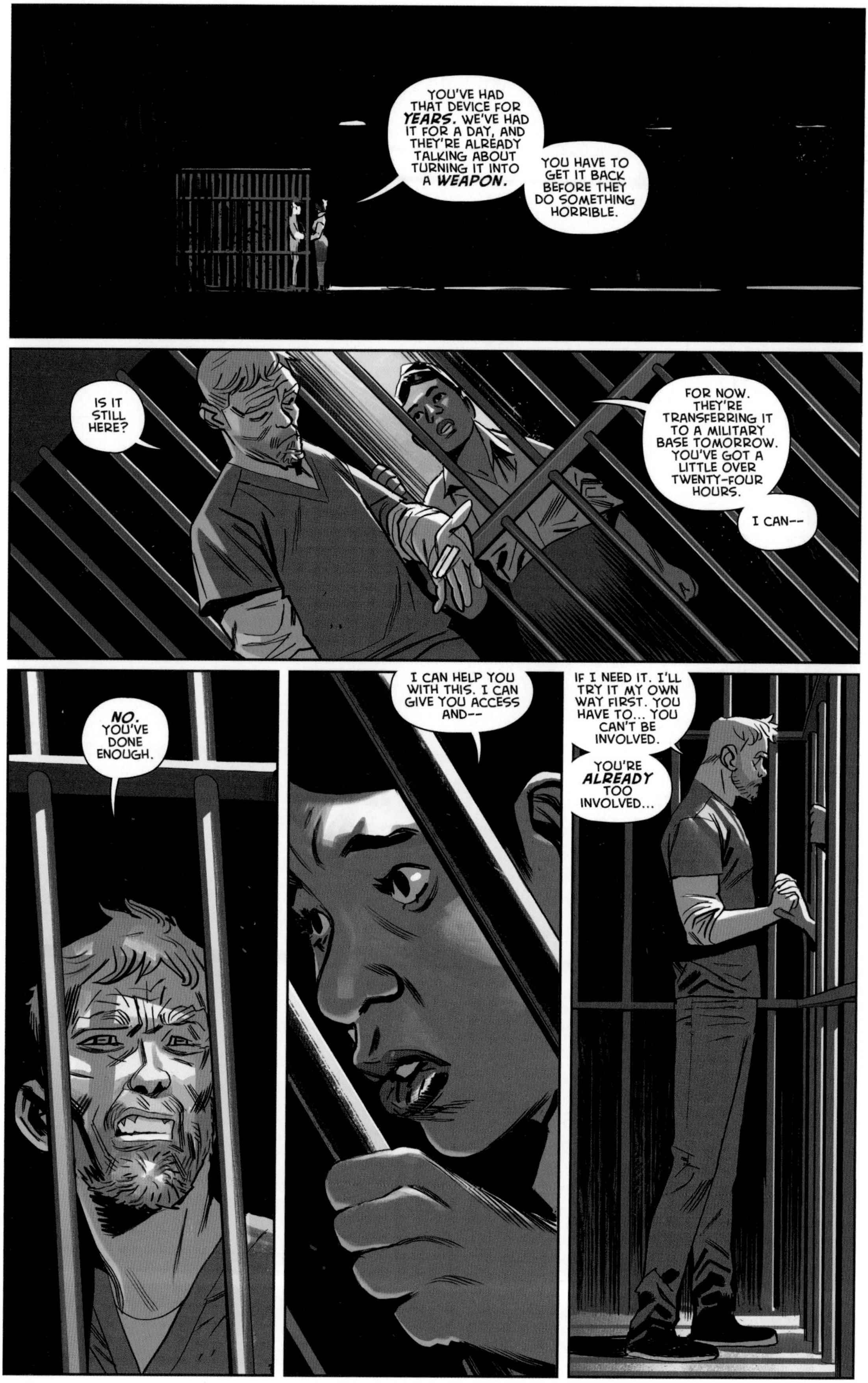

YOU'VE HAD THAT DEVICE FOR YEARS. WE'VE HAD IT FOR A DAY, AND THEY'RE ALREADY TALKING ABOUT TURNING IT INTO A WEAPON.
YOU HAVE TO GET IT BACK BEFORE THEY DO SOMETHING HORRIBLE.
IS IT STILL HERE?
FOR NOW. THEY'RE TRANSFERRING IT TO A MILITARY BASE TOMORROW. YOU'VE GOT A LITTLE OVER TWENTY-FOUR HOURS.
I CAN--
NO. YOU'VE DONE ENOUGH.
I CAN HELP YOU WITH THIS. I CAN GIVE YOU ACCESS AND--
IF I NEED IT. I'LL TRY IT MY OWN WAY FIRST. YOU HAVE TO... YOU CAN'T BE INVOLVED.
YOU'RE ALREADY TOO INVOLVED...

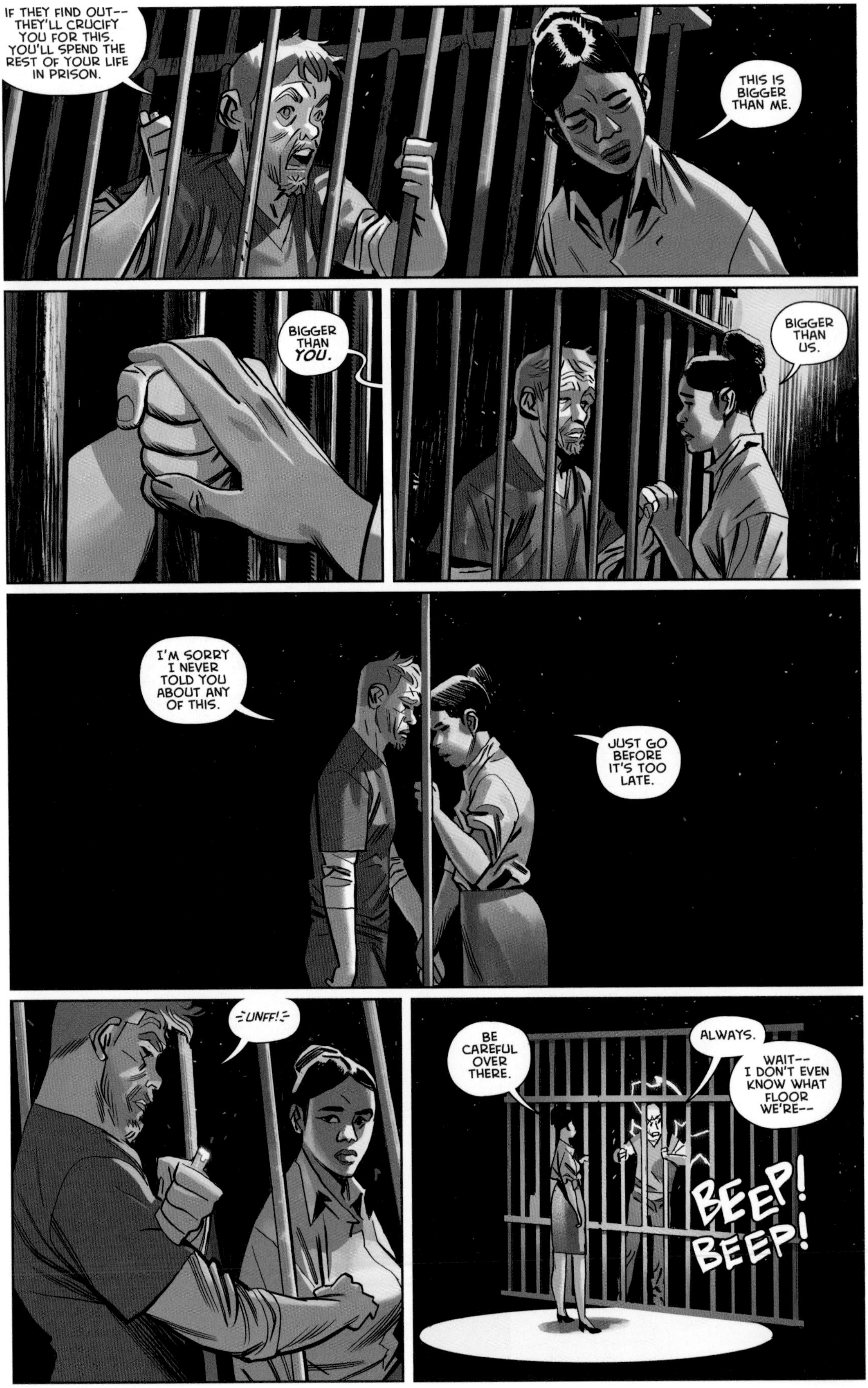

IF THEY FIND OUT--
THEY'LL CRUCIFY YOU FOR THIS. YOU'LL SPEND THE REST OF YOUR LIFE IN PRISON.
THIS IS BIGGER THAN ME.
BIGGER THAN *YOU*.
BIGGER THAN US.
I'M SORRY I NEVER TOLD YOU ABOUT ANY OF THIS.
JUST GO BEFORE IT'S TOO LATE.
=UNFF!=
BE CAREFUL OVER THERE.
ALWAYS.
WAIT-- I DON'T EVEN KNOW WHAT FLOOR WE'RE--
BEEP! BEEP!

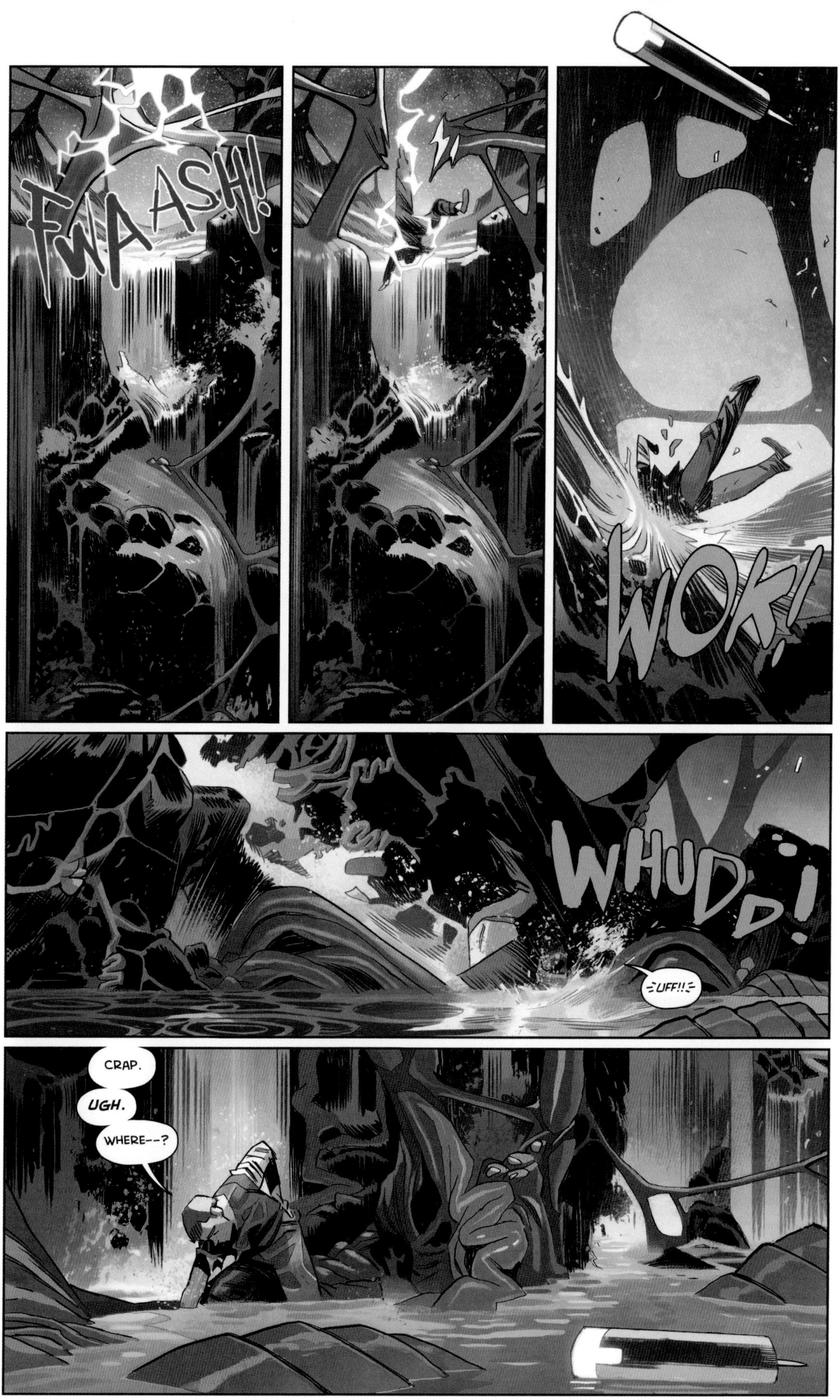
FWAASH!
WOK!
WHUDD!
UFF!!
CRAP.
UGH.
WHERE--?

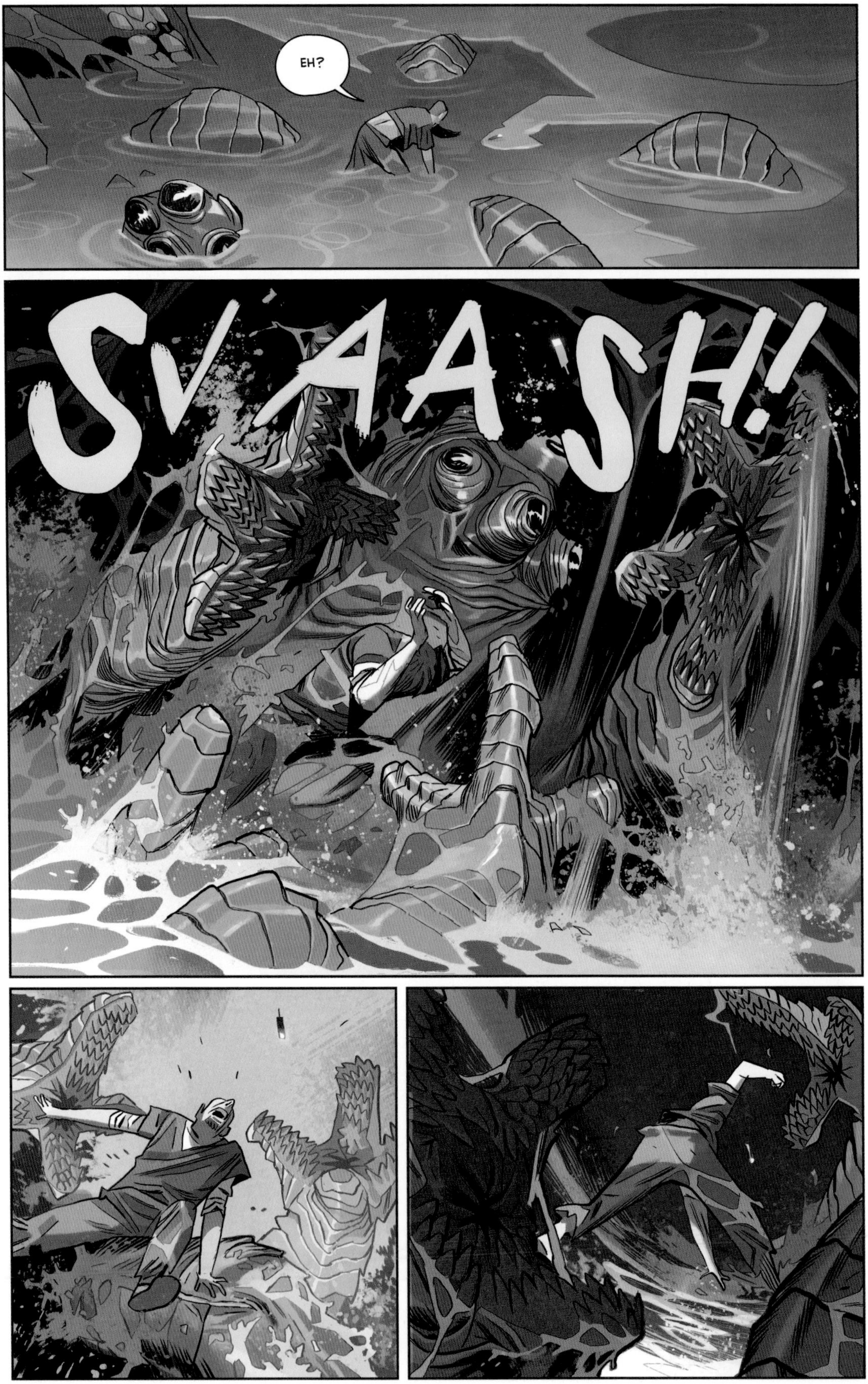
EH?
SVAASH!

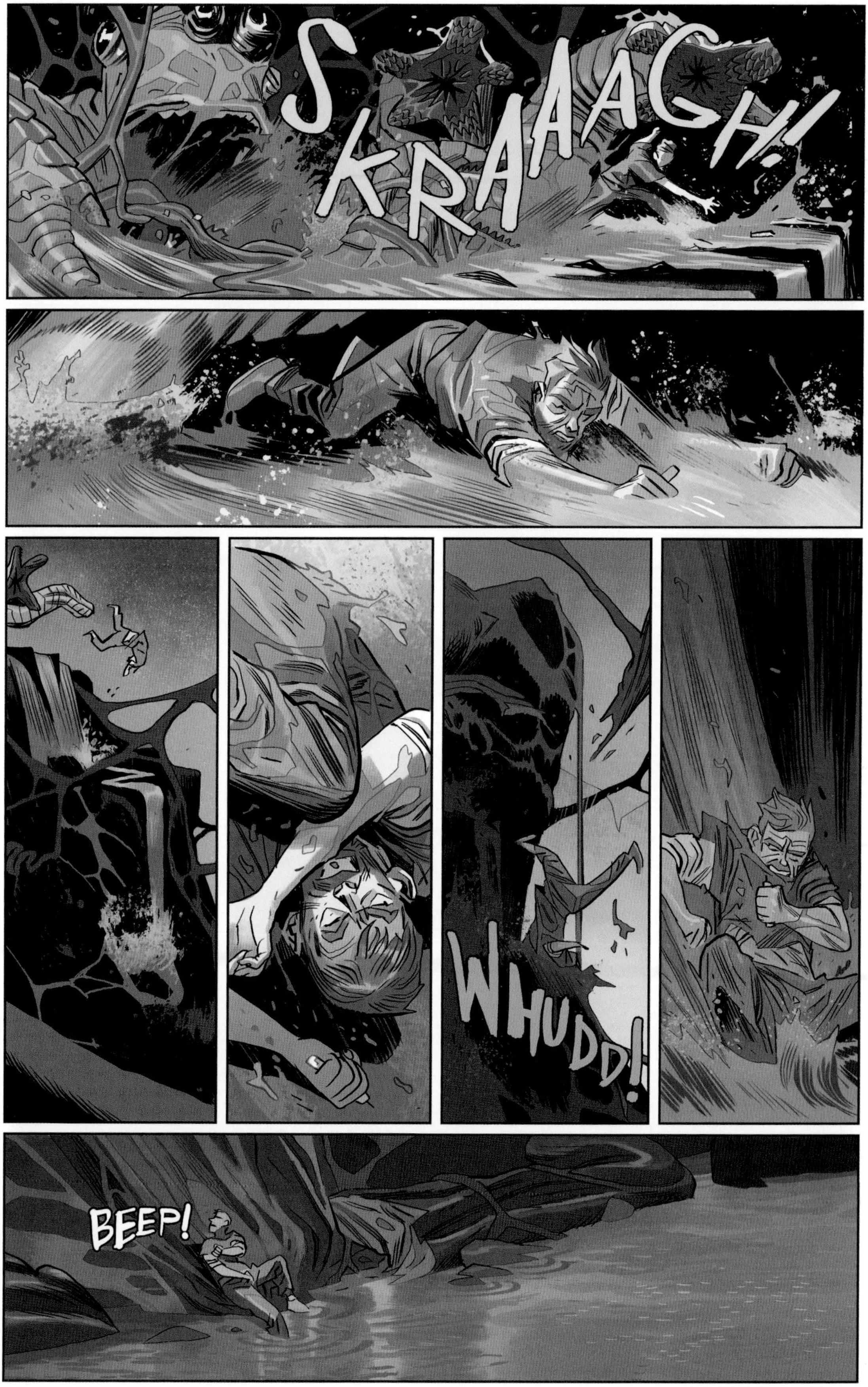
SKRAAAAGH!
WHUDD!
BEEP!

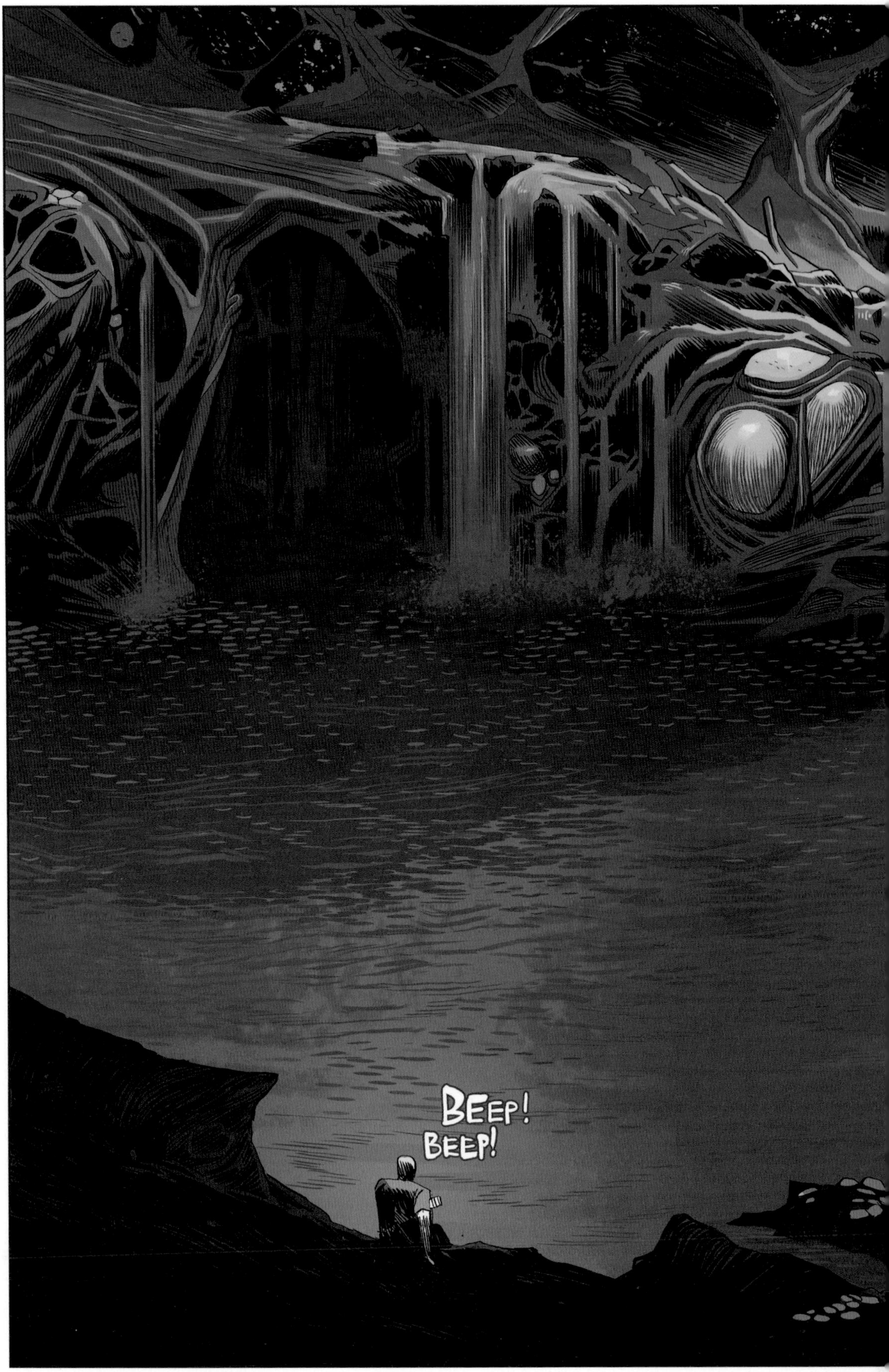
BEEP!
BEEP!

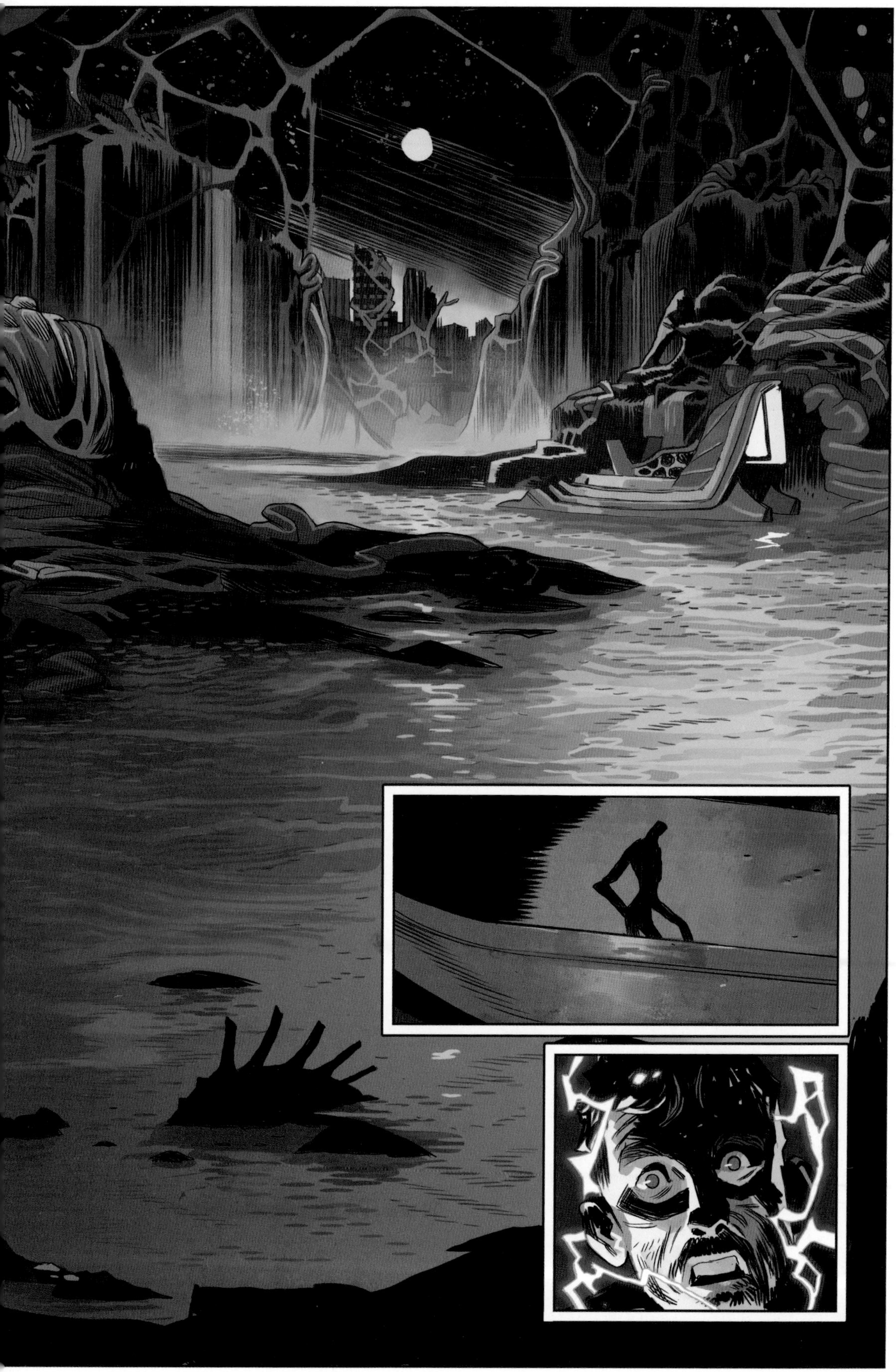

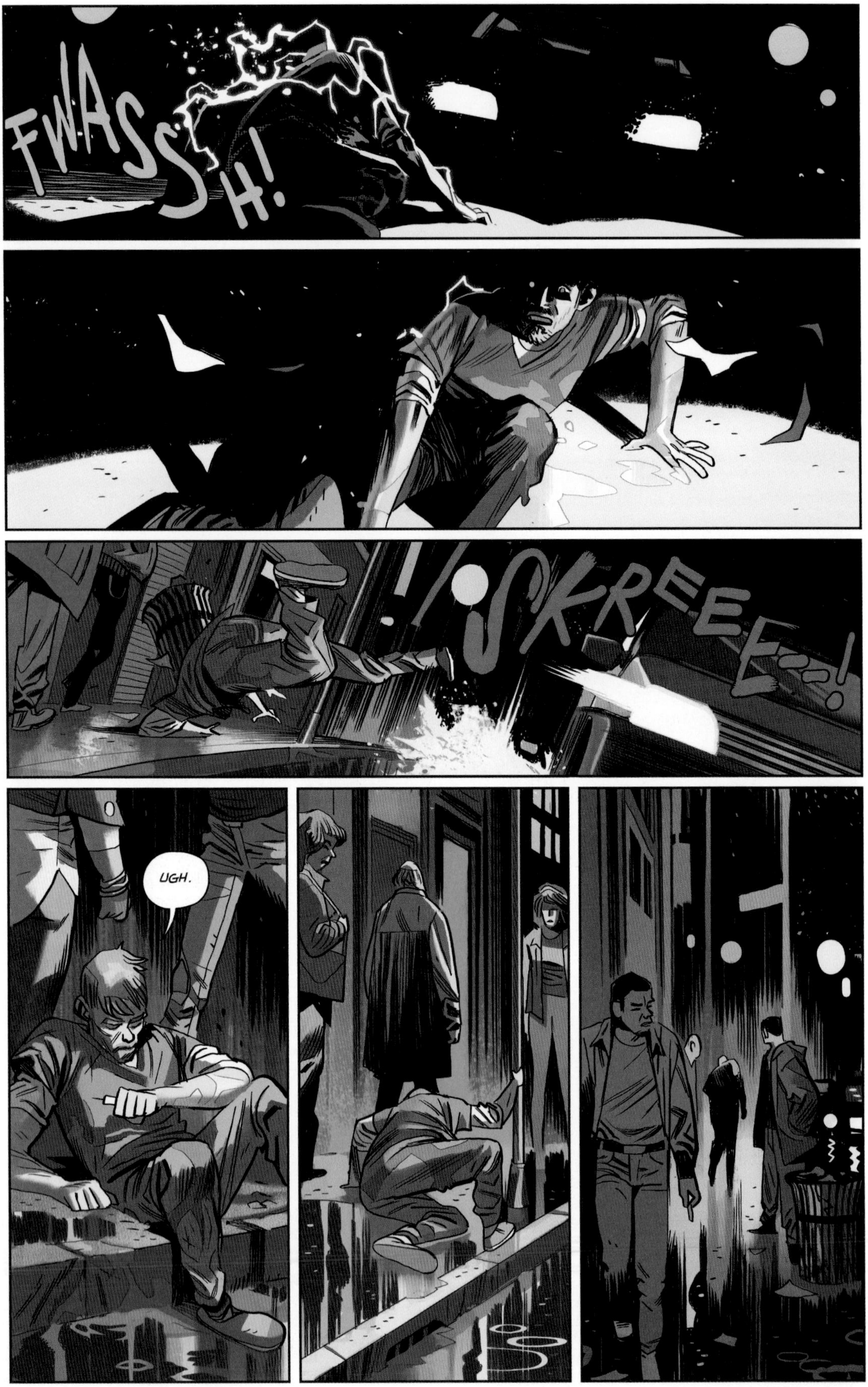
FWASSH!
SKREEE--!
UGH.

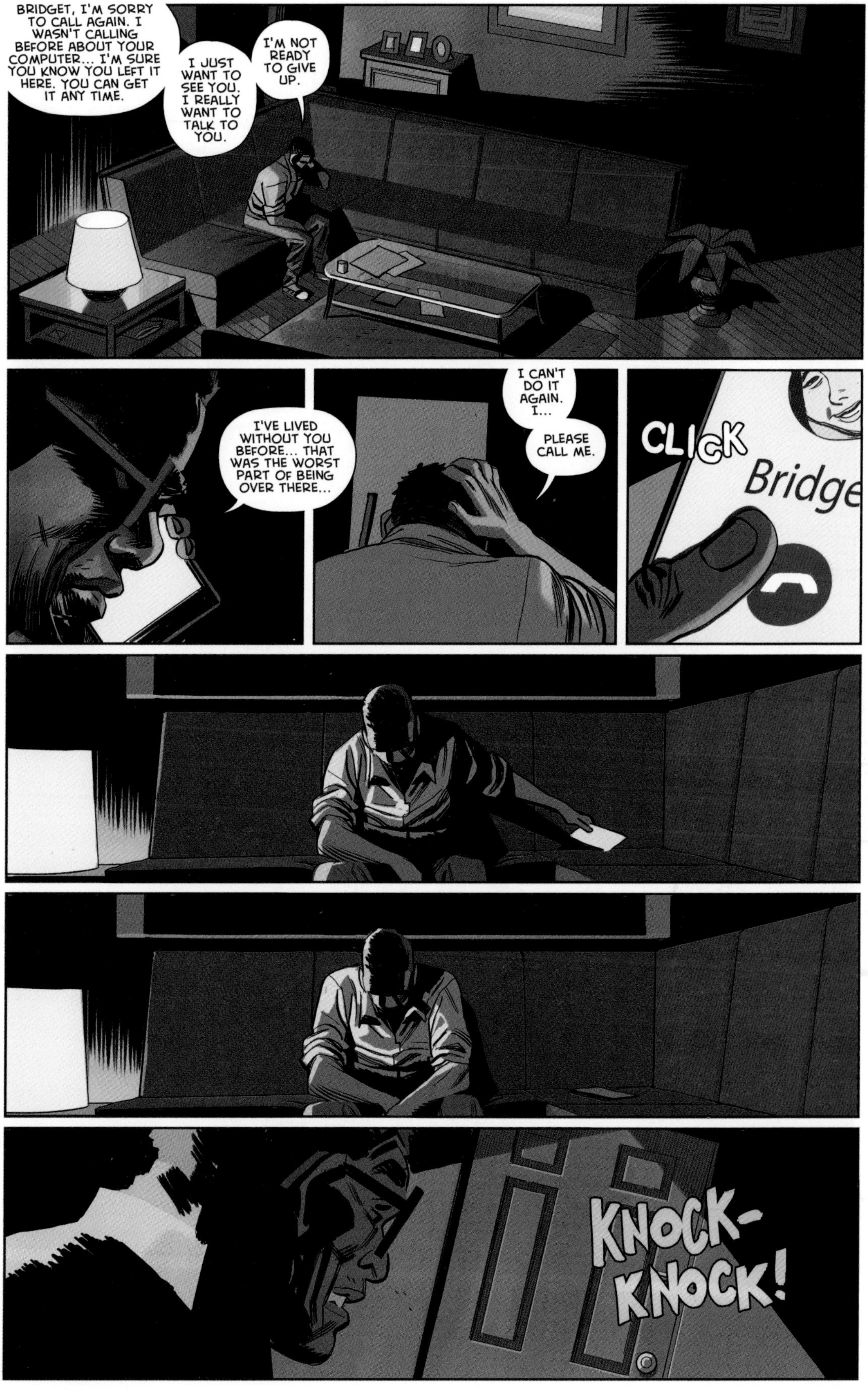
BRIDGET, I'M SORRY TO CALL AGAIN. I WASN'T CALLING BEFORE ABOUT YOUR COMPUTER... I'M SURE YOU KNOW YOU LEFT IT HERE. YOU CAN GET IT ANY TIME.
I JUST WANT TO SEE YOU. I REALLY WANT TO TALK TO YOU.
I'M NOT READY TO GIVE UP.
I'VE LIVED WITHOUT YOU BEFORE... THAT WAS THE WORST PART OF BEING OVER THERE...
I CAN'T DO IT AGAIN. I...
PLEASE CALL ME.
CLICK
Bridge
KNOCK-KNOCK!

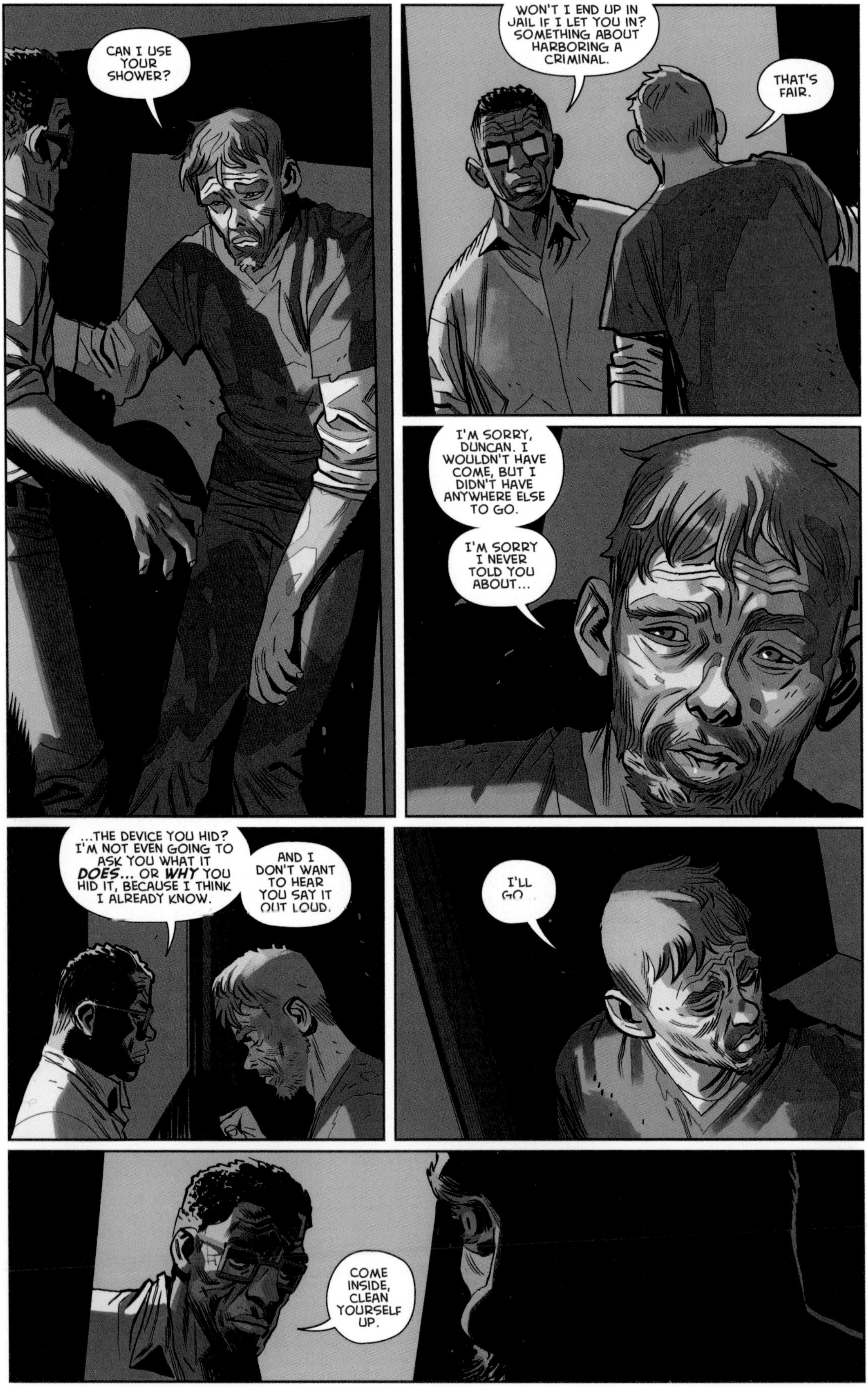
CAN I USE YOUR SHOWER?
WON'T I END UP IN JAIL IF I LET YOU IN? SOMETHING ABOUT HARBORING A CRIMINAL.
THAT'S FAIR.
I'M SORRY, DUNCAN. I WOULDN'T HAVE COME, BUT I DIDN'T HAVE ANYWHERE ELSE TO GO.
I'M SORRY I NEVER TOLD YOU ABOUT...
...THE DEVICE YOU HID? I'M NOT EVEN GOING TO ASK YOU WHAT IT DOES... OR WHY YOU HID IT, BECAUSE I THINK I ALREADY KNOW.
AND I DON'T WANT TO HEAR YOU SAY IT OUT LOUD.
I'LL GO...
COME INSIDE, CLEAN YOURSELF UP.

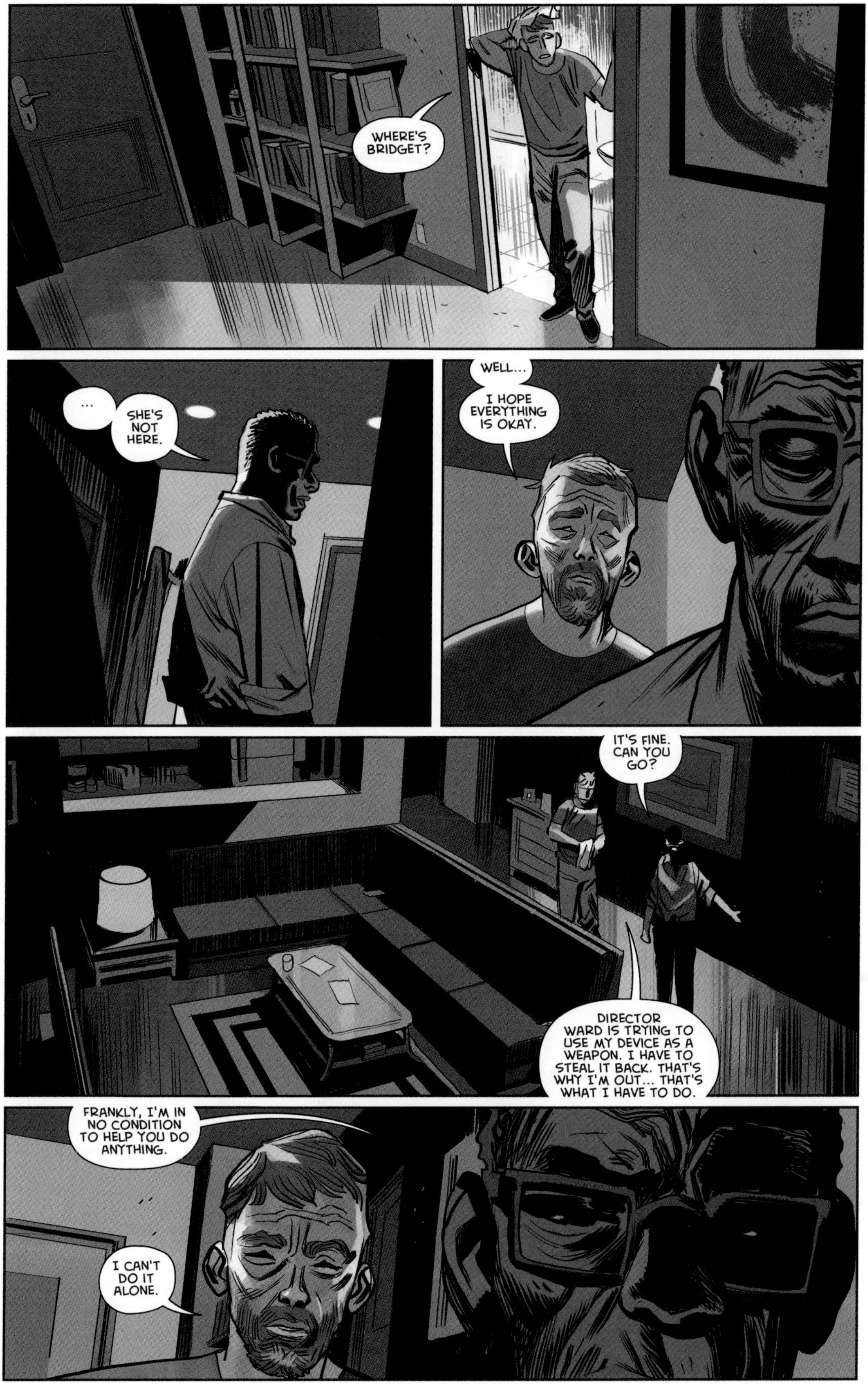
WHERE'S BRIDGET?
...
SHE'S NOT HERE.
WELL...
I HOPE EVERYTHING IS OKAY.
IT'S FINE. CAN YOU GO?
DIRECTOR WARD IS TRYING TO USE MY DEVICE AS A WEAPON. I HAVE TO STEAL IT BACK. THAT'S WHY I'M OUT... THAT'S WHAT I HAVE TO DO.
FRANKLY, I'M IN NO CONDITION TO HELP YOU DO ANYTHING.
I CAN'T DO IT ALONE.

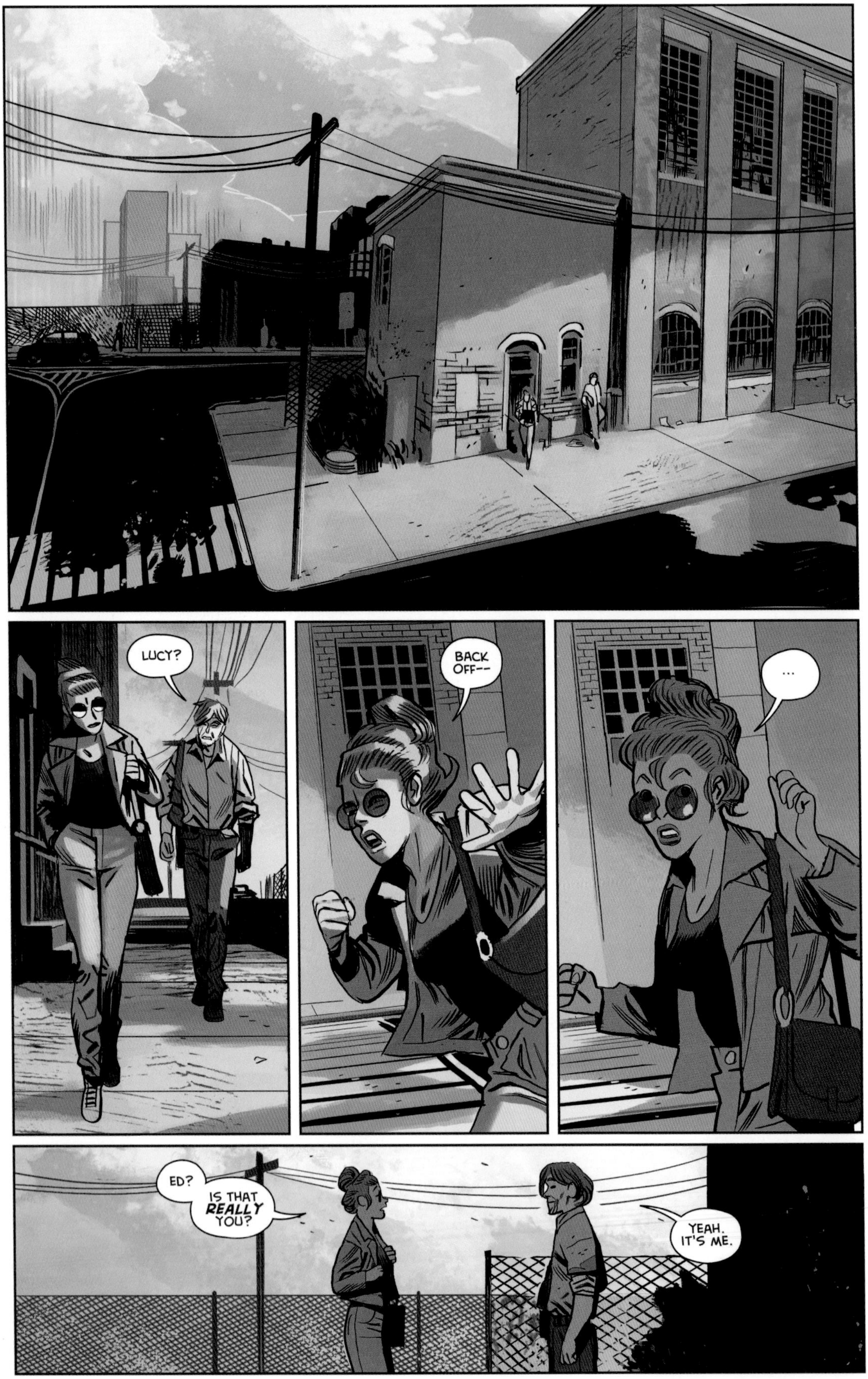
LUCY?
BACK OFF--
...
ED?
IS THAT REALLY YOU?
YEAH. IT'S ME.

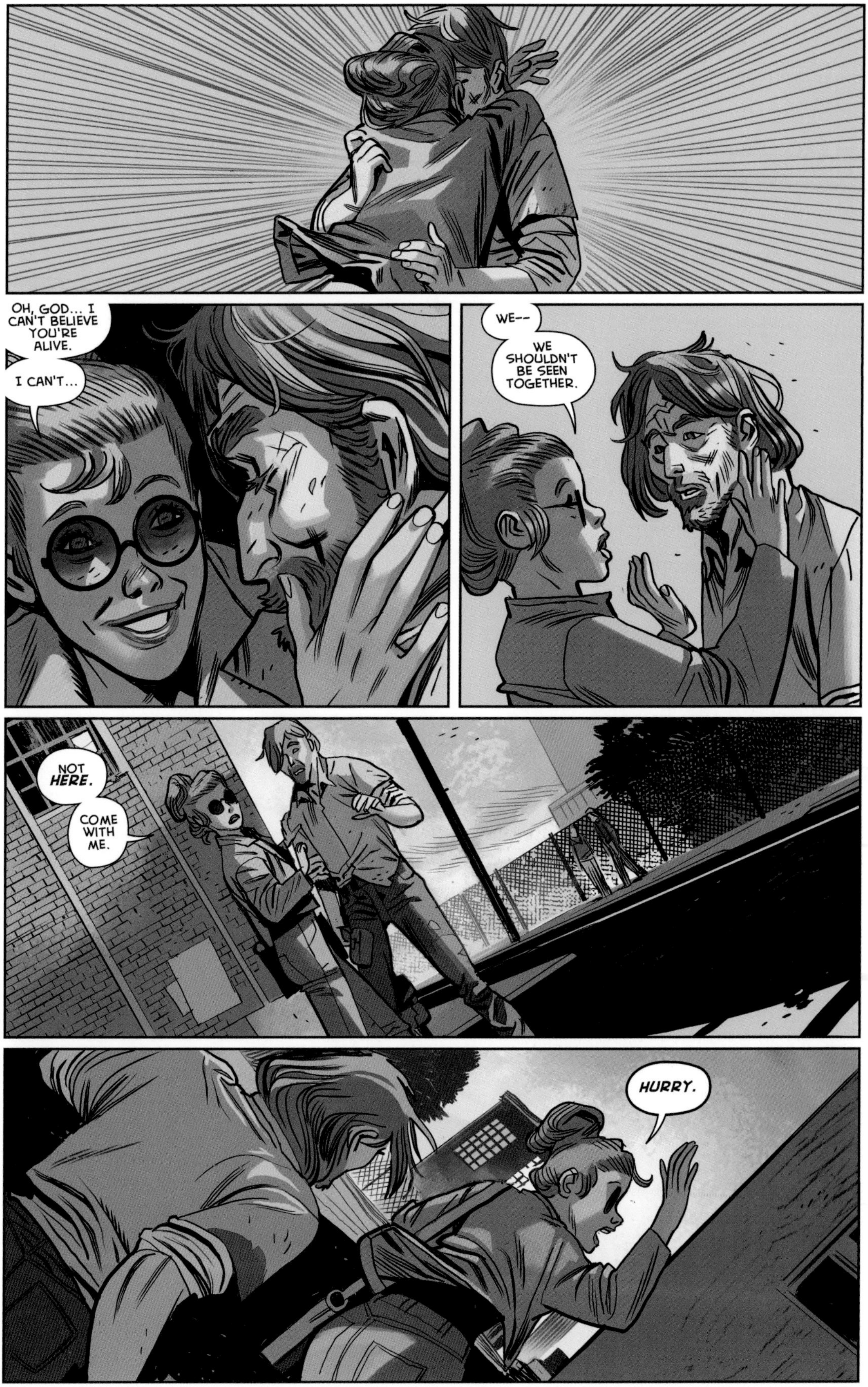
OH, GOD... I CAN'T BELIEVE YOU'RE ALIVE.
I CAN'T...
WE--
WE SHOULDN'T BE SEEN TOGETHER.
NOT HERE.
COME WITH ME.
HURRY.

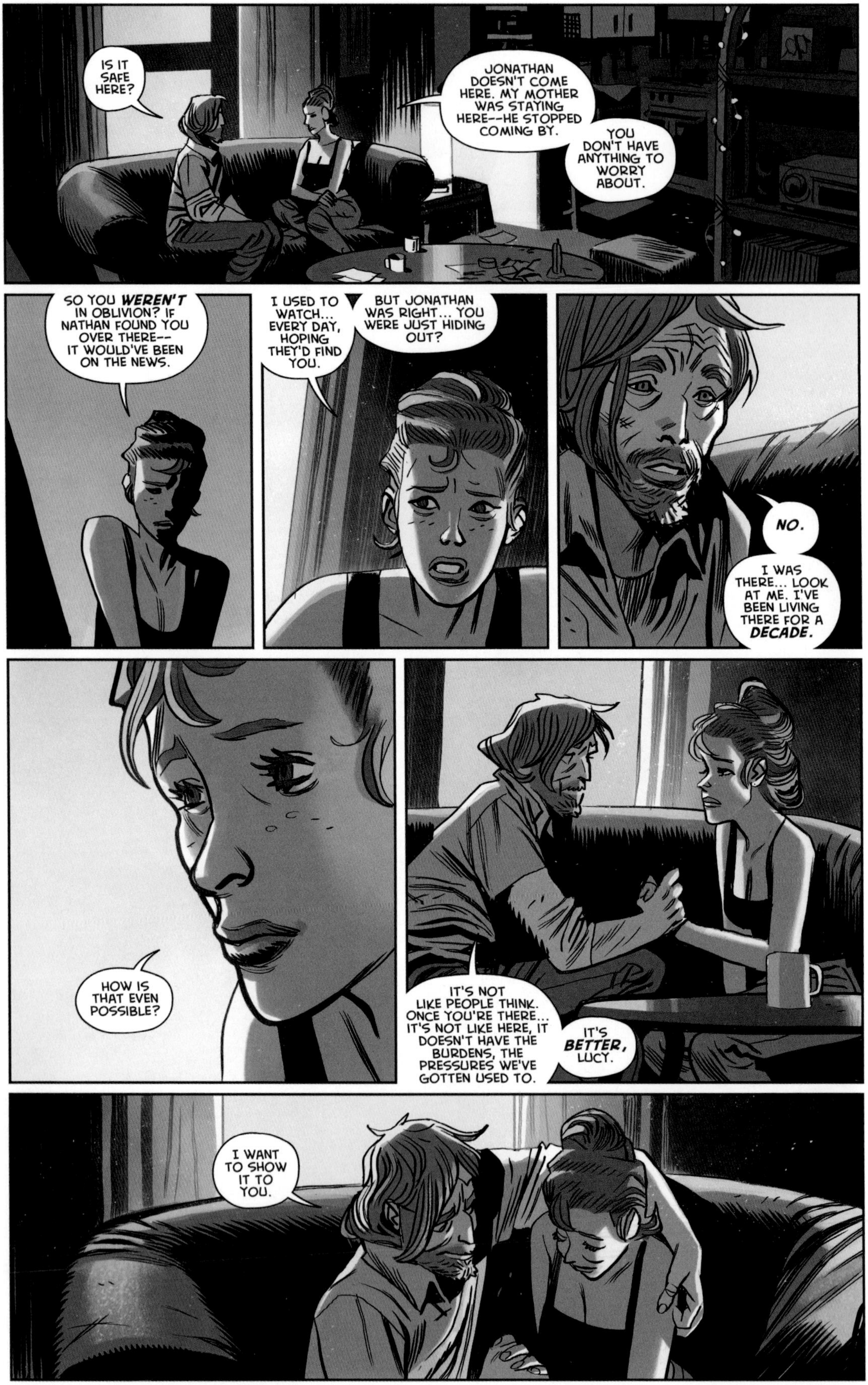
IS IT SAFE HERE?
JONATHAN DOESN'T COME HERE. MY MOTHER WAS STAYING HERE--HE STOPPED COMING BY.
YOU DON'T HAVE ANYTHING TO WORRY ABOUT.
SO YOU WEREN'T IN OBLIVION? IF NATHAN FOUND YOU OVER THERE-- IT WOULD'VE BEEN ON THE NEWS.
I USED TO WATCH... EVERY DAY, HOPING THEY'D FIND YOU.
BUT JONATHAN WAS RIGHT... YOU WERE JUST HIDING OUT?
NO.
I WAS THERE... LOOK AT ME. I'VE BEEN LIVING THERE FOR A DECADE.
HOW IS THAT EVEN POSSIBLE?
IT'S NOT LIKE PEOPLE THINK. ONCE YOU'RE THERE... IT'S NOT LIKE HERE, IT DOESN'T HAVE THE BURDENS, THE PRESSURES WE'VE GOTTEN USED TO.
IT'S BETTER, LUCY.
I WANT TO SHOW IT TO YOU.

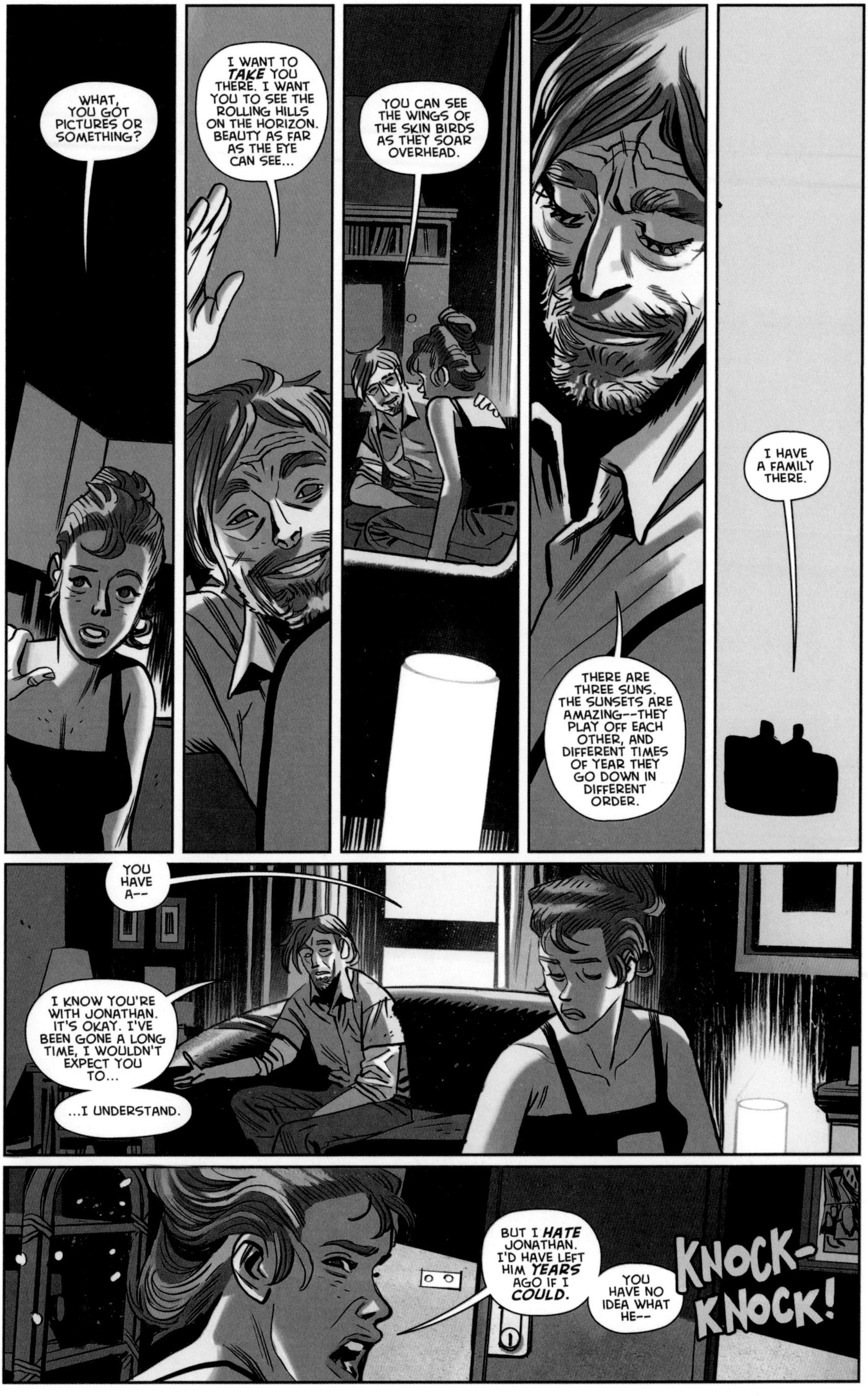
WHAT, YOU GOT PICTURES OR SOMETHING?
I WANT TO *TAKE* YOU THERE. I WANT YOU TO SEE THE ROLLING HILLS ON THE HORIZON. BEAUTY AS FAR AS THE EYE CAN SEE...
YOU CAN SEE THE WINGS OF THE SKIN BIRDS AS THEY SOAR OVERHEAD.
THERE ARE THREE SUNS. THE SUNSETS ARE AMAZING--THEY PLAY OFF EACH OTHER, AND DIFFERENT TIMES OF YEAR THEY GO DOWN IN DIFFERENT ORDER.
I HAVE A FAMILY THERE.
YOU HAVE A--
I KNOW YOU'RE WITH JONATHAN. IT'S OKAY. I'VE BEEN GONE A LONG TIME, I WOULDN'T EXPECT YOU TO...
...I UNDERSTAND.
BUT I *HATE* JONATHAN. I'D HAVE LEFT HIM *YEARS* AGO IF I *COULD*.
YOU HAVE NO IDEA WHAT HE--
KNOCK-KNOCK!

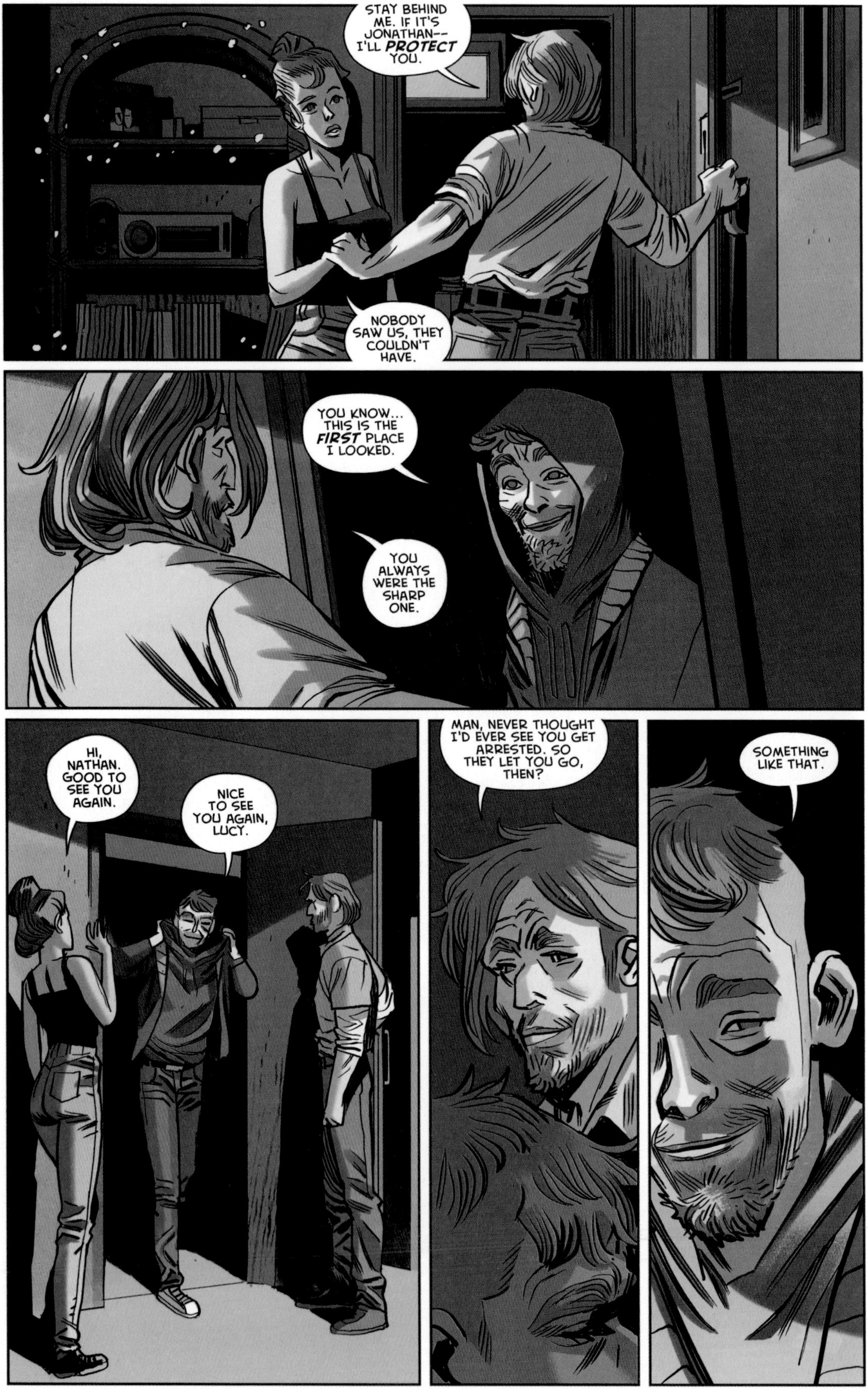
STAY BEHIND ME. IF IT'S JONATHAN-- I'LL *PROTECT* YOU.
NOBODY SAW US, THEY COULDN'T HAVE.
YOU KNOW... THIS IS THE *FIRST* PLACE I LOOKED.
YOU ALWAYS WERE THE SHARP ONE.
HI, NATHAN. GOOD TO SEE YOU AGAIN.
NICE TO SEE YOU AGAIN, LUCY.
MAN, NEVER THOUGHT I'D EVER SEE YOU GET ARRESTED. SO THEY LET YOU GO, THEN?
SOMETHING LIKE THAT.

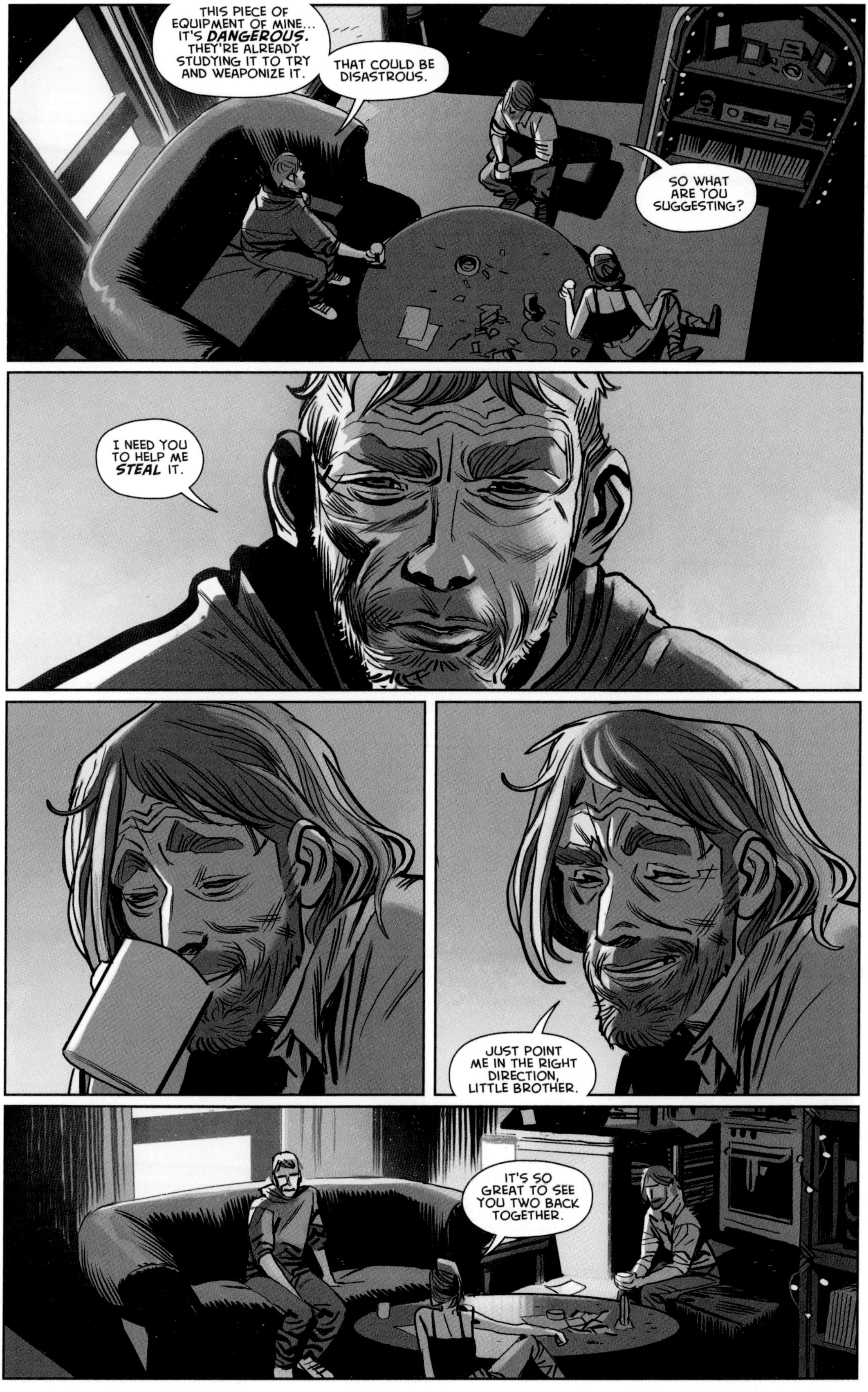
THIS PIECE OF EQUIPMENT OF MINE... IT'S DANGEROUS. THEY'RE ALREADY STUDYING IT TO TRY AND WEAPONIZE IT.
THAT COULD BE DISASTROUS.
SO WHAT ARE YOU SUGGESTING?
I NEED YOU TO HELP ME STEAL IT.
JUST POINT ME IN THE RIGHT DIRECTION, LITTLE BROTHER.
IT'S SO GREAT TO SEE YOU TWO BACK TOGETHER.

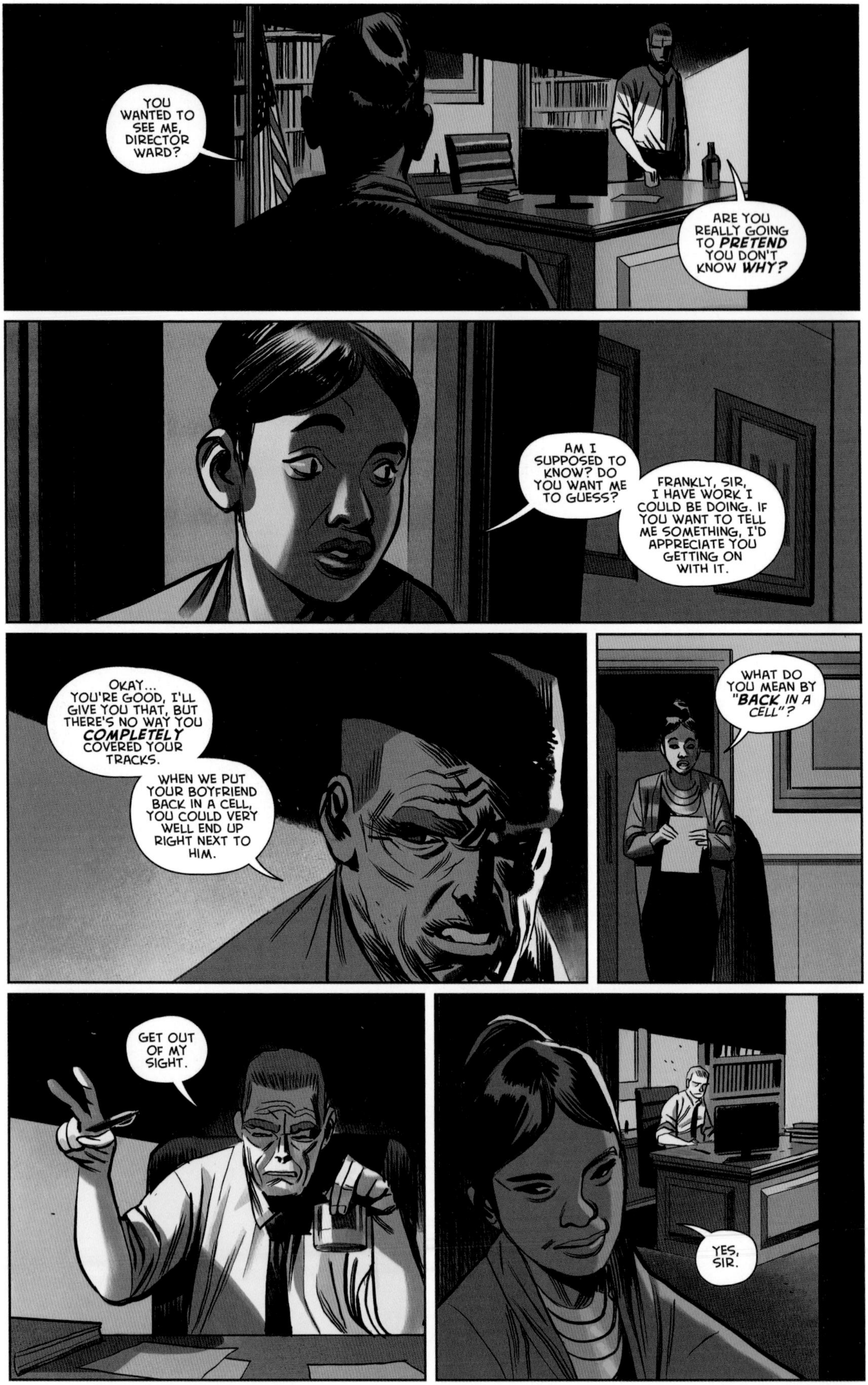
YOU WANTED TO SEE ME, DIRECTOR WARD?
ARE YOU REALLY GOING TO PRETEND YOU DON'T KNOW WHY?
AM I SUPPOSED TO KNOW? DO YOU WANT ME TO GUESS?
FRANKLY, SIR, I HAVE WORK I COULD BE DOING. IF YOU WANT TO TELL ME SOMETHING, I'D APPRECIATE YOU GETTING ON WITH IT.
OKAY... YOU'RE GOOD, I'LL GIVE YOU THAT, BUT THERE'S NO WAY YOU COMPLETELY COVERED YOUR TRACKS.
WHEN WE PUT YOUR BOYFRIEND BACK IN A CELL, YOU COULD VERY WELL END UP RIGHT NEXT TO HIM.
WHAT DO YOU MEAN BY "BACK IN A CELL"?
GET OUT OF MY SIGHT.
YES, SIR.

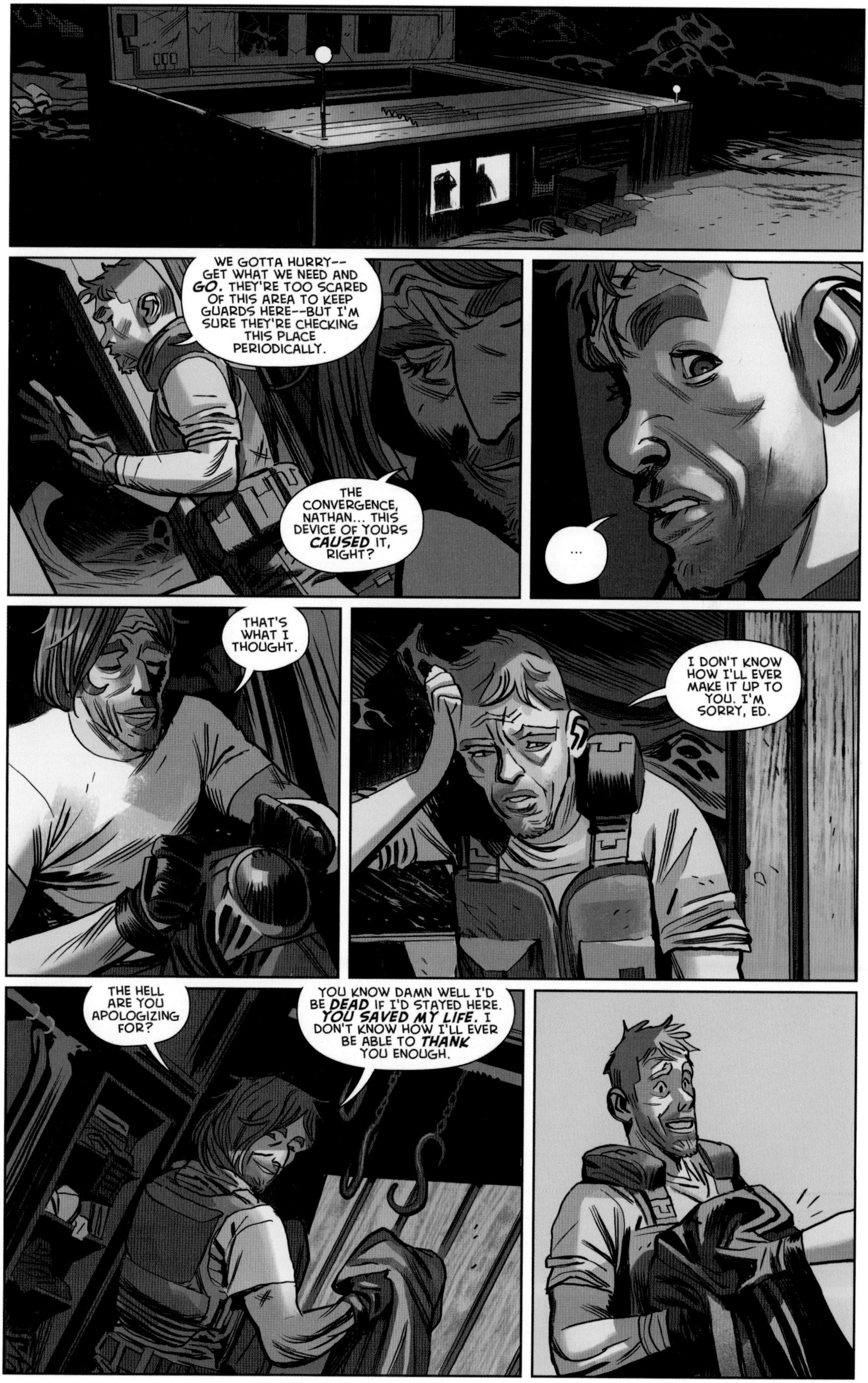
WE GOTTA HURRY-- GET WHAT WE NEED AND GO. THEY'RE TOO SCARED OF THIS AREA TO KEEP GUARDS HERE--BUT I'M SURE THEY'RE CHECKING THIS PLACE PERIODICALLY.
THE CONVERGENCE, NATHAN... THIS DEVICE OF YOURS CAUSED IT, RIGHT?
...
THAT'S WHAT I THOUGHT.
I DON'T KNOW HOW I'LL EVER MAKE IT UP TO YOU. I'M SORRY, ED.
THE HELL ARE YOU APOLOGIZING FOR?
YOU KNOW DAMN WELL I'D BE DEAD IF I'D STAYED HERE. YOU SAVED MY LIFE. I DON'T KNOW HOW I'LL EVER BE ABLE TO THANK YOU ENOUGH.

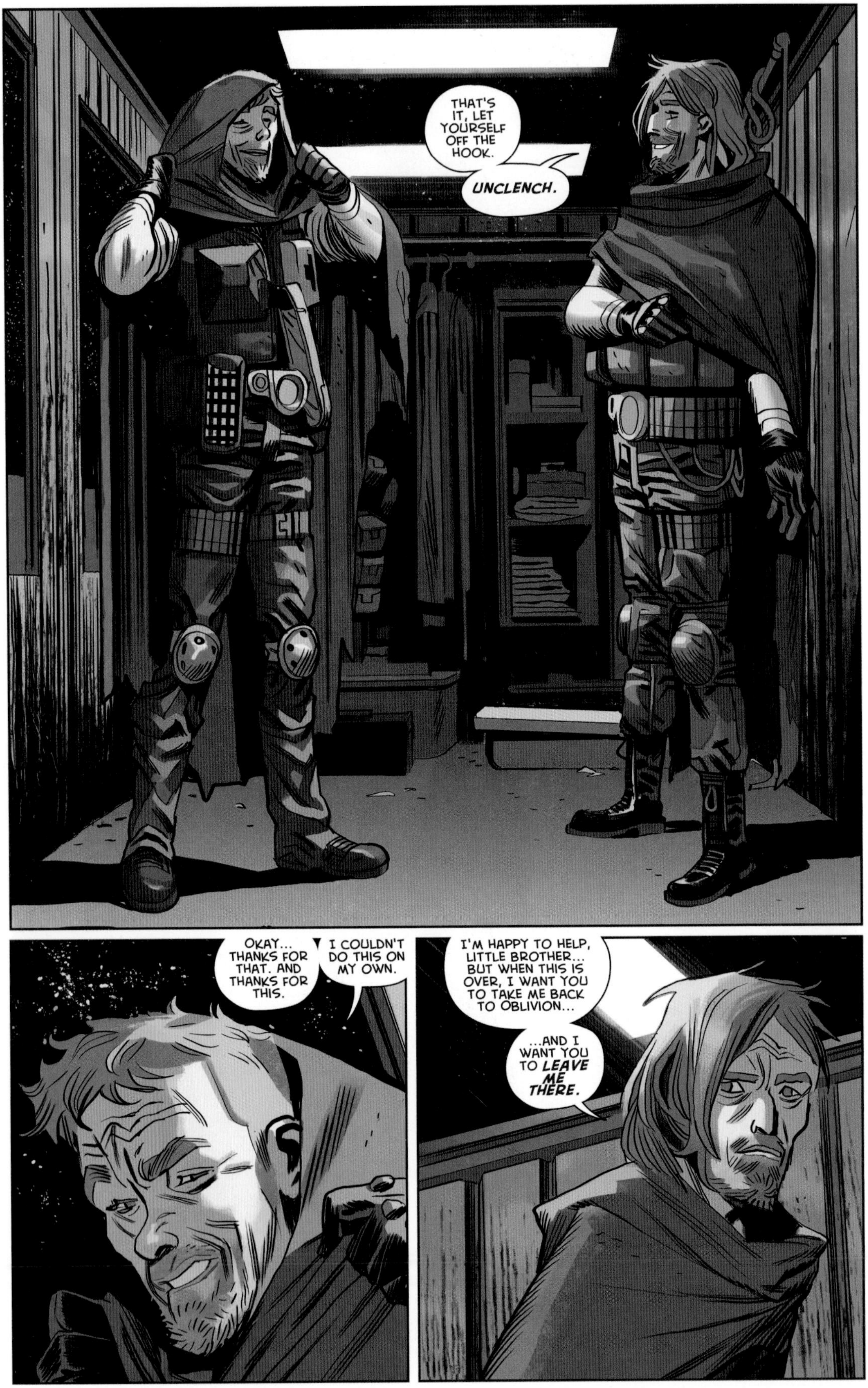
THAT'S IT, LET YOURSELF OFF THE HOOK.
UNCLENCH.
OKAY... THANKS FOR THAT. AND THANKS FOR THIS.
I COULDN'T DO THIS ON MY OWN.
I'M HAPPY TO HELP, LITTLE BROTHER... BUT WHEN THIS IS OVER, I WANT YOU TO TAKE ME BACK TO OBLIVION...
...AND I WANT YOU TO LEAVE ME THERE.

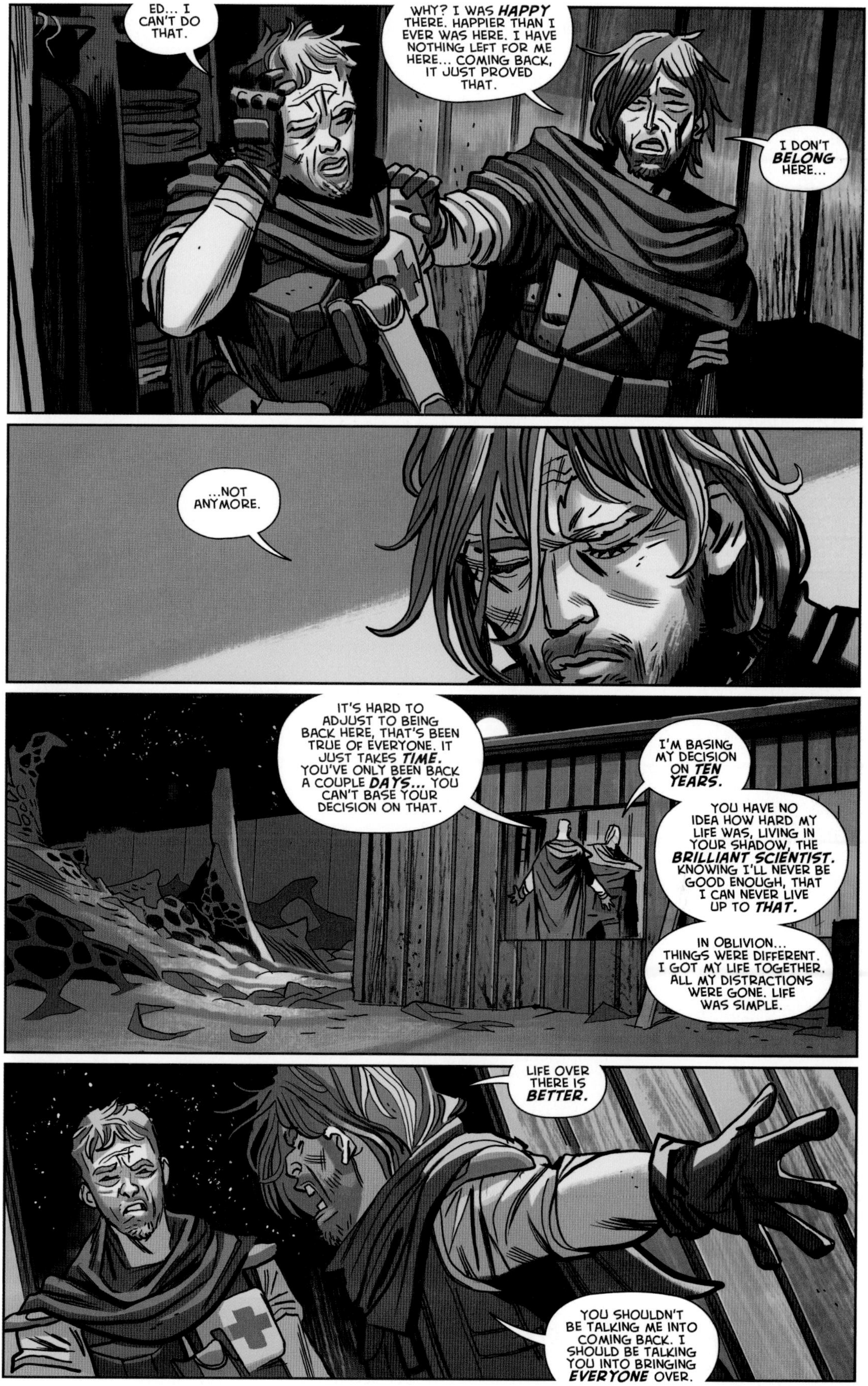
ED... I CAN'T DO THAT.
WHY? I WAS *HAPPY* THERE. HAPPIER THAN I EVER WAS HERE. I HAVE NOTHING LEFT FOR ME HERE... COMING BACK, IT JUST PROVED THAT.
I DON'T *BELONG* HERE...
...NOT ANYMORE.
IT'S HARD TO ADJUST TO BEING BACK HERE, THAT'S BEEN TRUE OF EVERYONE. IT JUST TAKES *TIME*. YOU'VE ONLY BEEN BACK A COUPLE *DAYS*... YOU CAN'T BASE YOUR DECISION ON THAT.
I'M BASING MY DECISION ON *TEN YEARS*.
YOU HAVE NO IDEA HOW HARD MY LIFE WAS, LIVING IN YOUR SHADOW, THE *BRILLIANT SCIENTIST*. KNOWING I'LL NEVER BE GOOD ENOUGH, THAT I CAN NEVER LIVE UP TO *THAT*.
IN OBLIVION... THINGS WERE DIFFERENT. I GOT MY LIFE TOGETHER. ALL MY DISTRACTIONS WERE GONE. LIFE WAS SIMPLE.
LIFE OVER THERE IS *BETTER*.
YOU SHOULDN'T BE TALKING ME INTO COMING BACK. I SHOULD BE TALKING YOU INTO BRINGING *EVERYONE* OVER.

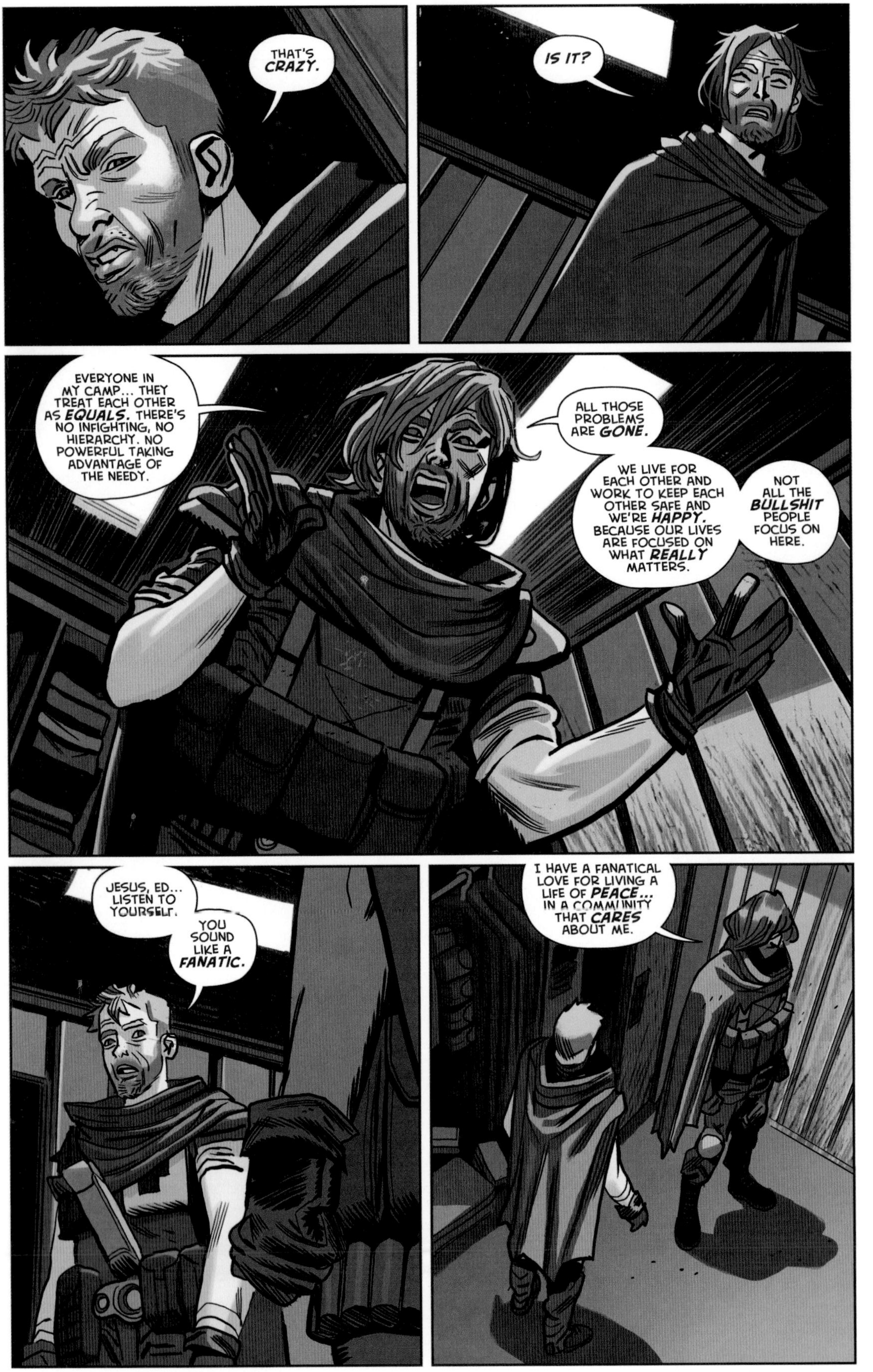
THAT'S CRAZY.
IS IT?
EVERYONE IN MY CAMP... THEY TREAT EACH OTHER AS EQUALS. THERE'S NO INFIGHTING, NO HIERARCHY. NO POWERFUL TAKING ADVANTAGE OF THE NEEDY.
ALL THOSE PROBLEMS ARE GONE.
WE LIVE FOR EACH OTHER AND WORK TO KEEP EACH OTHER SAFE AND WE'RE HAPPY. BECAUSE OUR LIVES ARE FOCUSED ON WHAT REALLY MATTERS.
NOT ALL THE BULLSHIT PEOPLE FOCUS ON HERE.
JESUS, ED... LISTEN TO YOURSELF.
YOU SOUND LIKE A FANATIC.
I HAVE A FANATICAL LOVE FOR LIVING A LIFE OF PEACE... IN A COMMUNITY THAT CARES ABOUT ME.

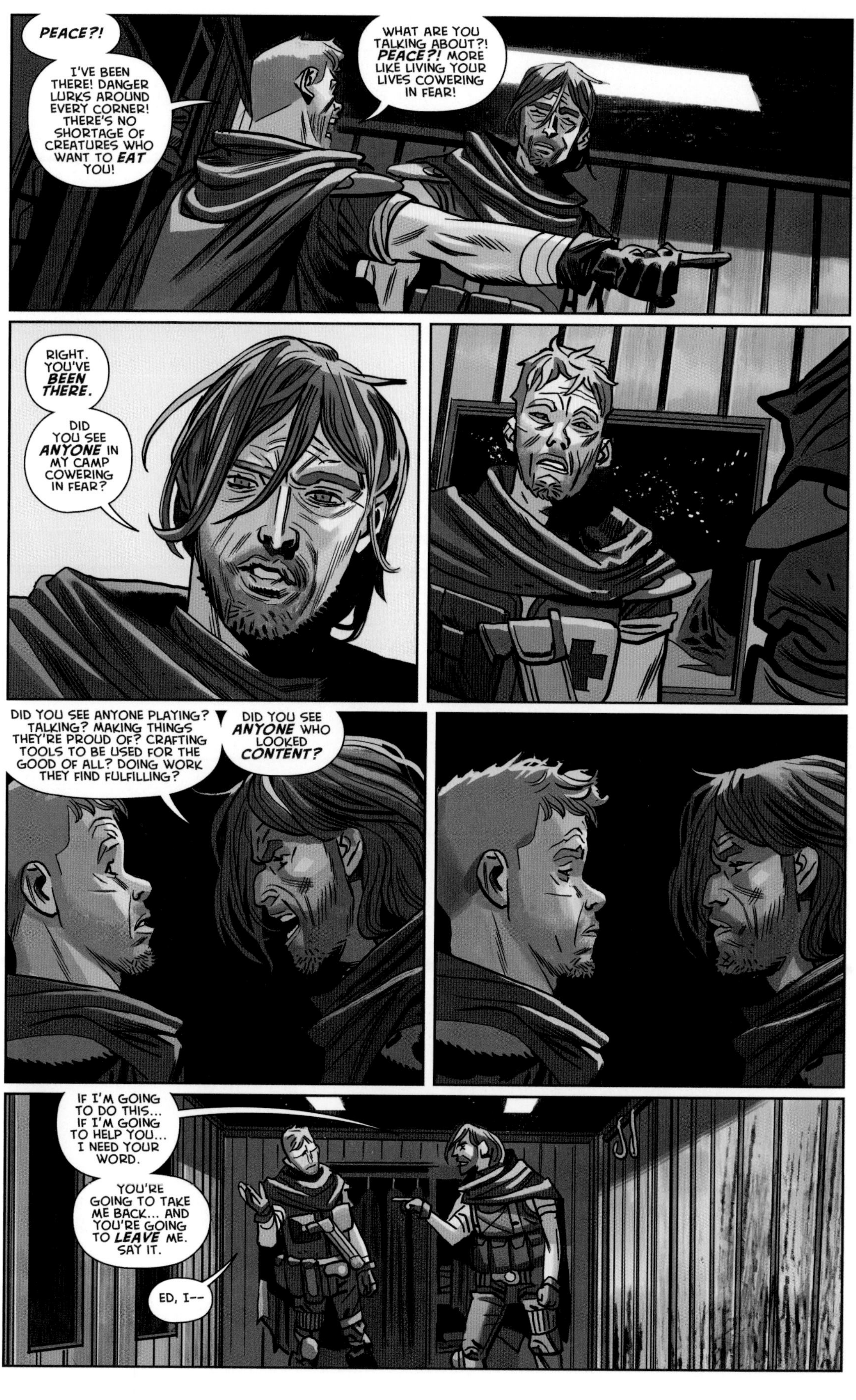

PEACE?!
I'VE BEEN THERE! DANGER LURKS AROUND EVERY CORNER! THERE'S NO SHORTAGE OF CREATURES WHO WANT TO EAT YOU!
WHAT ARE YOU TALKING ABOUT?! PEACE?! MORE LIKE LIVING YOUR LIVES COWERING IN FEAR!
RIGHT. YOU'VE BEEN THERE.
DID YOU SEE ANYONE IN MY CAMP COWERING IN FEAR?
DID YOU SEE ANYONE PLAYING? TALKING? MAKING THINGS THEY'RE PROUD OF? CRAFTING TOOLS TO BE USED FOR THE GOOD OF ALL? DOING WORK THEY FIND FULFILLING?
DID YOU SEE ANYONE WHO LOOKED CONTENT?
IF I'M GOING TO DO THIS... IF I'M GOING TO HELP YOU... I NEED YOUR WORD.
YOU'RE GOING TO TAKE ME BACK... AND YOU'RE GOING TO LEAVE ME. SAY IT.
ED, I--

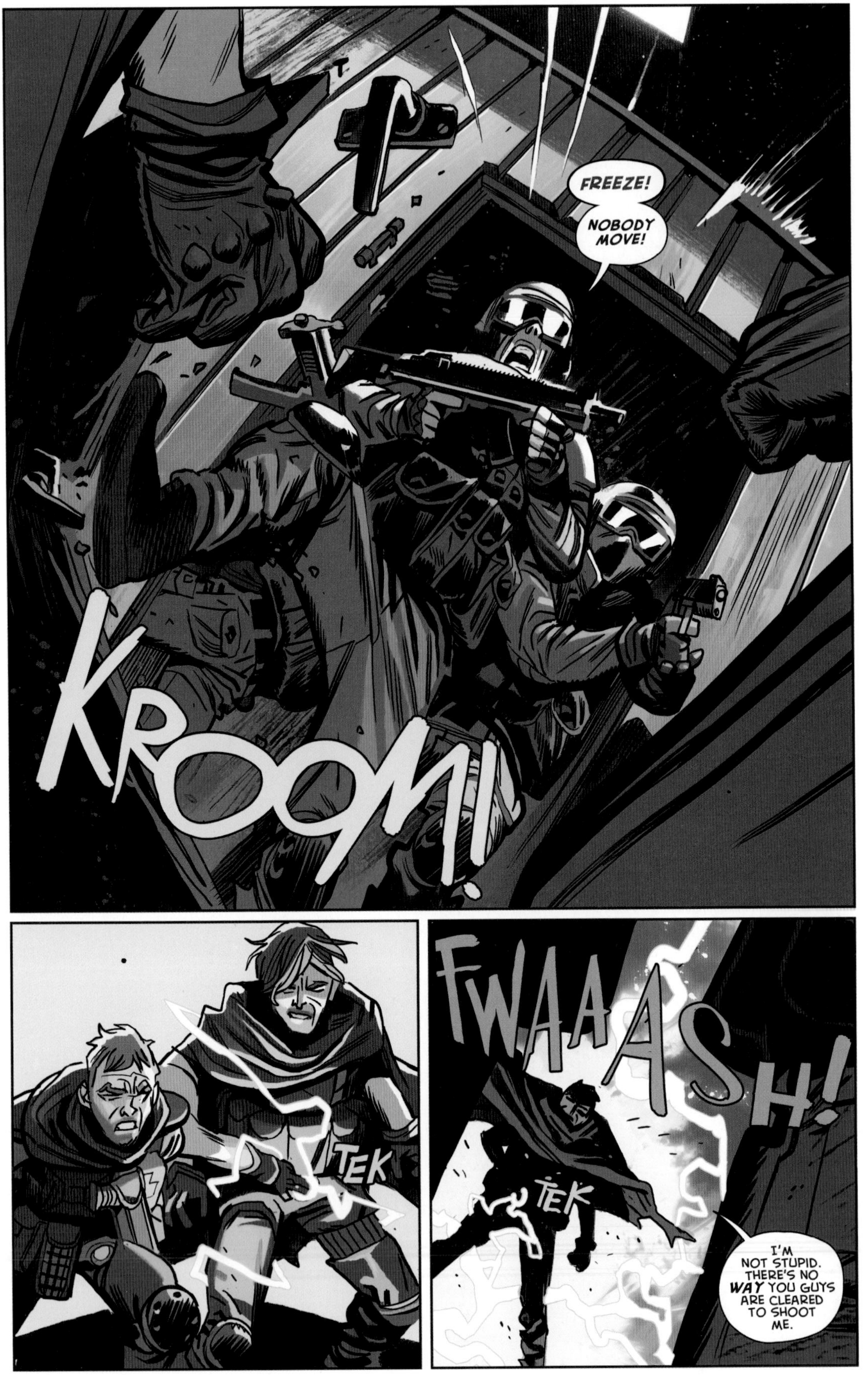
FREEZE!
NOBODY MOVE!
KROOM!
TEK
FWAAASH!
TEK
I'M NOT STUPID. THERE'S NO WAY YOU GUYS ARE CLEARED TO SHOOT ME.

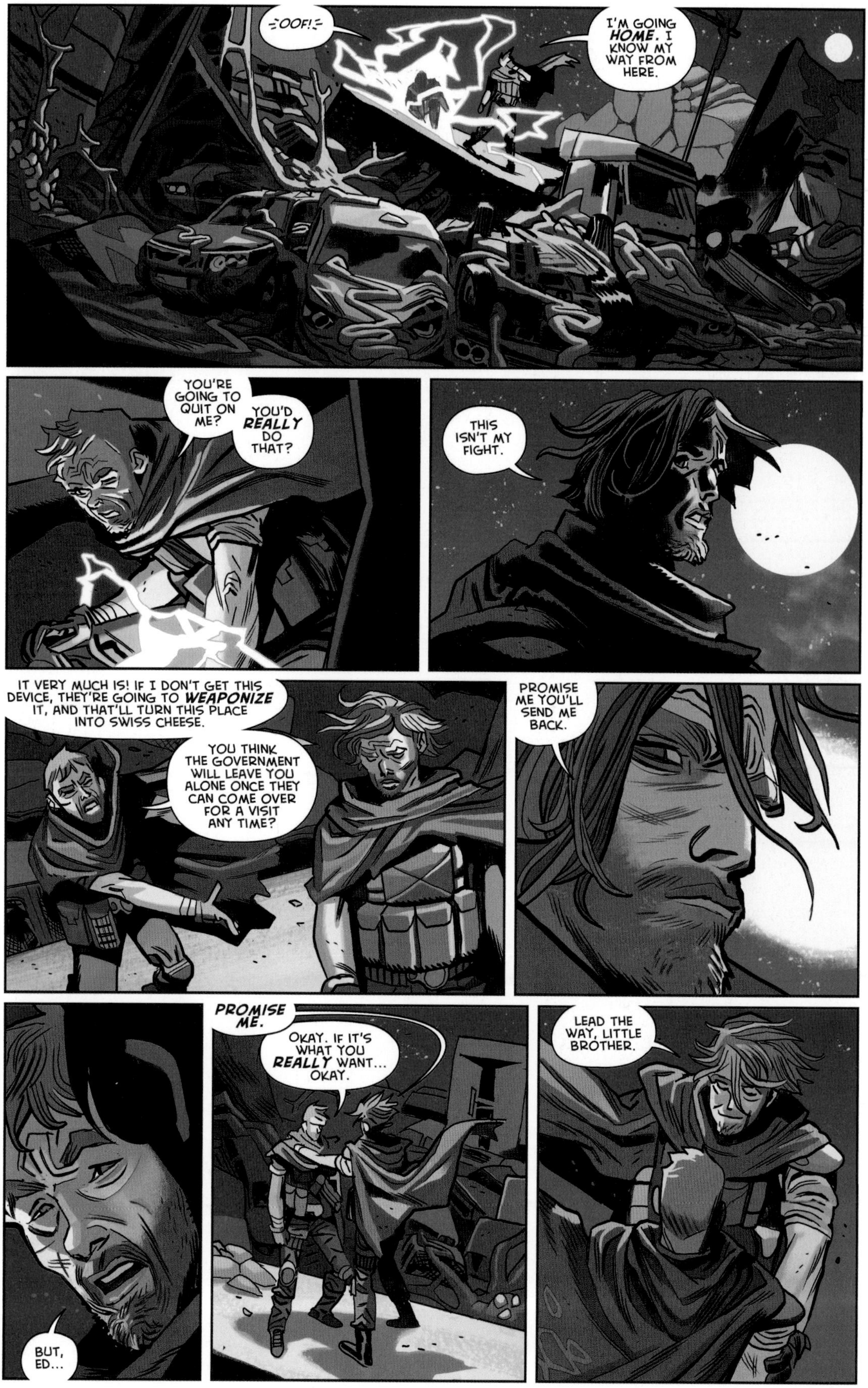

OOF!
I'M GOING HOME. I KNOW MY WAY FROM HERE.
YOU'RE GOING TO QUIT ON ME?
YOU'D REALLY DO THAT?
THIS ISN'T MY FIGHT.
IT VERY MUCH IS! IF I DON'T GET THIS DEVICE, THEY'RE GOING TO WEAPONIZE IT, AND THAT'LL TURN THIS PLACE INTO SWISS CHEESE.
YOU THINK THE GOVERNMENT WILL LEAVE YOU ALONE ONCE THEY CAN COME OVER FOR A VISIT ANY TIME?
PROMISE ME YOU'LL SEND ME BACK.
BUT, ED...
PROMISE ME.
OKAY. IF IT'S WHAT YOU REALLY WANT... OKAY.
LEAD THE WAY, LITTLE BROTHER.

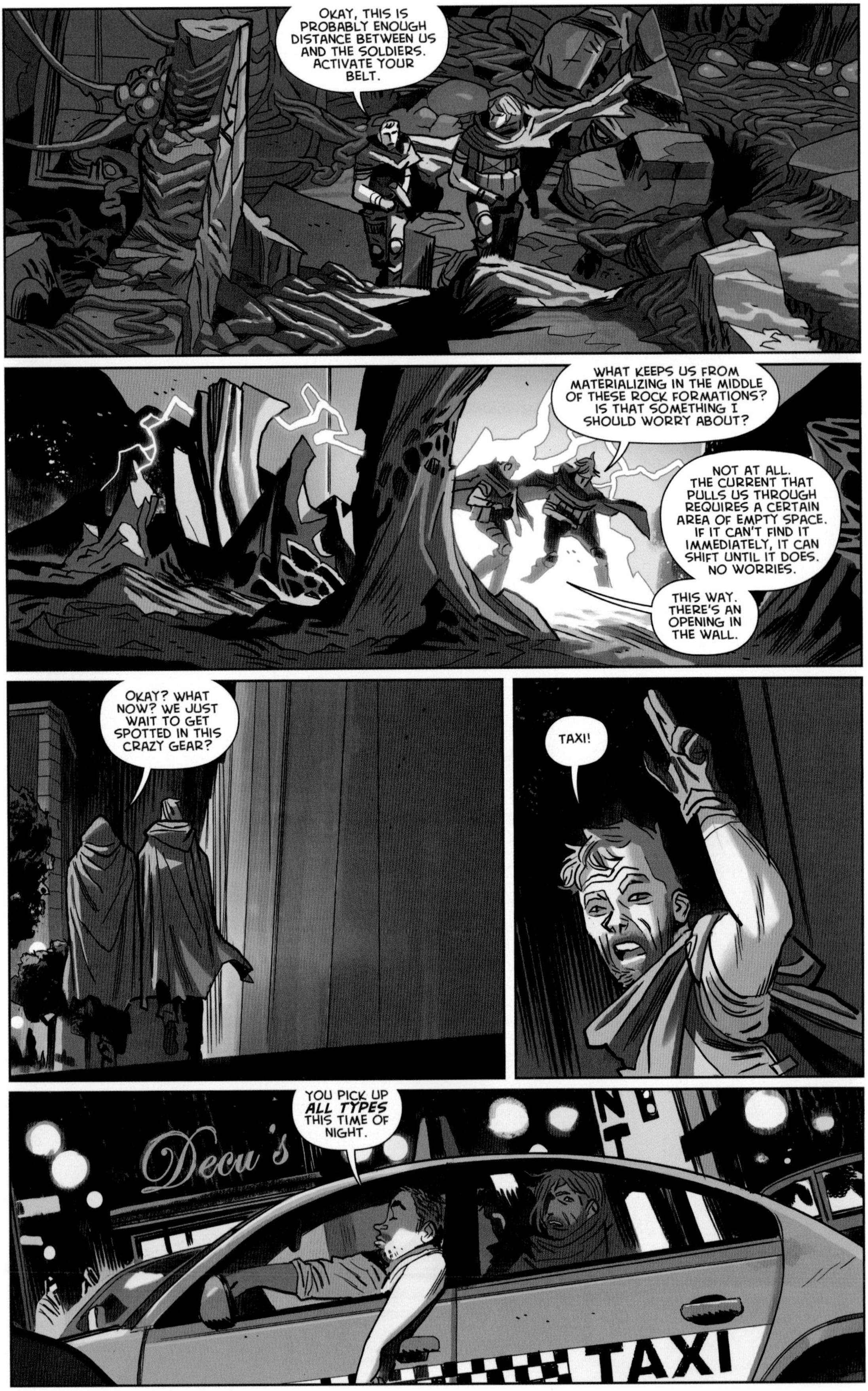
OKAY, THIS IS PROBABLY ENOUGH DISTANCE BETWEEN US AND THE SOLDIERS. ACTIVATE YOUR BELT.
WHAT KEEPS US FROM MATERIALIZING IN THE MIDDLE OF THESE ROCK FORMATIONS? IS THAT SOMETHING I SHOULD WORRY ABOUT?
NOT AT ALL. THE CURRENT THAT PULLS US THROUGH REQUIRES A CERTAIN AREA OF EMPTY SPACE. IF IT CAN'T FIND IT IMMEDIATELY, IT CAN SHIFT UNTIL IT DOES. NO WORRIES.
THIS WAY. THERE'S AN OPENING IN THE WALL.
OKAY? WHAT NOW? WE JUST WAIT TO GET SPOTTED IN THIS CRAZY GEAR?
TAXI!
YOU PICK UP *ALL TYPES* THIS TIME OF NIGHT.
Decu's
TAXI

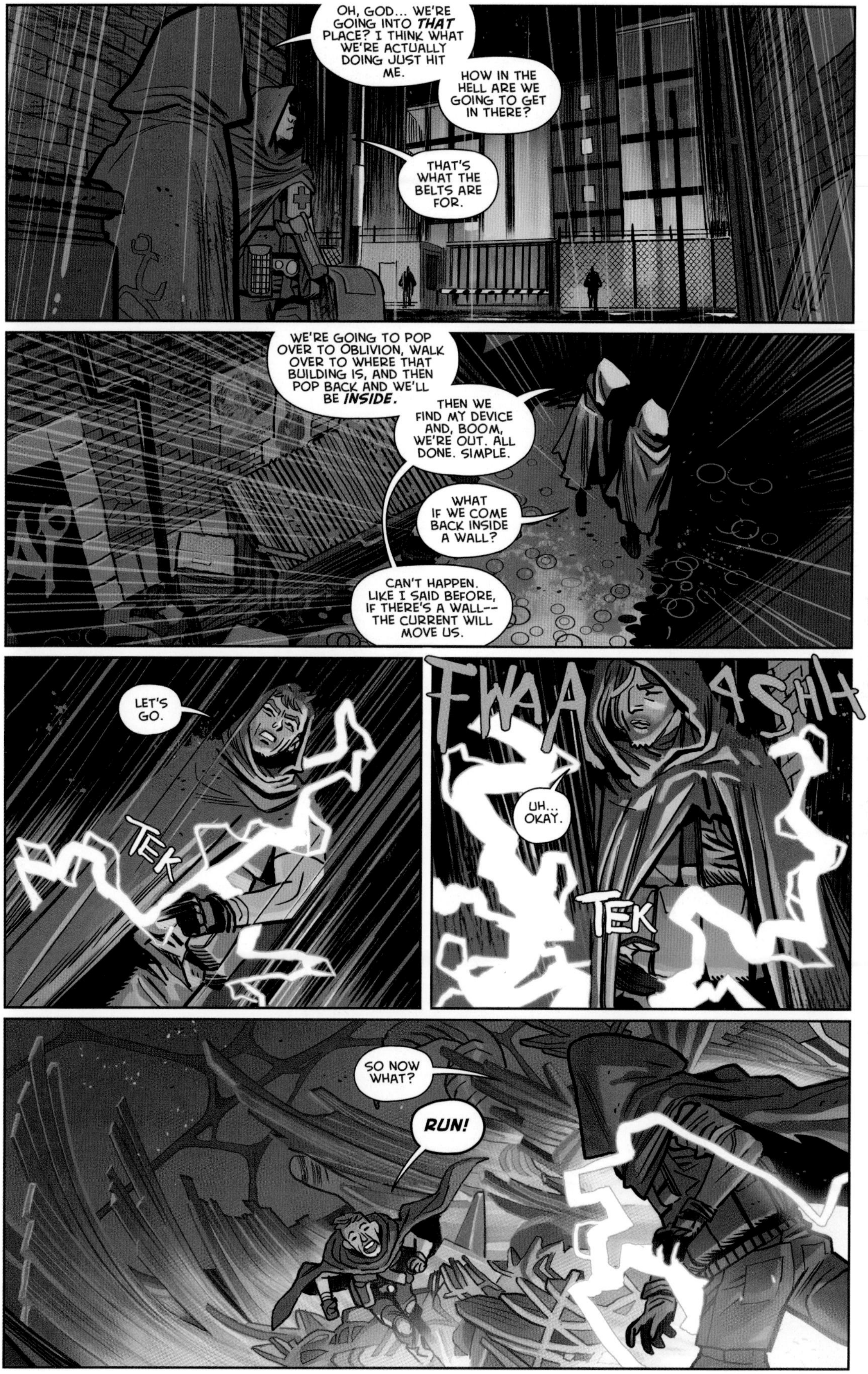
OH, GOD... WE'RE GOING INTO THAT PLACE? I THINK WHAT WE'RE ACTUALLY DOING JUST HIT ME.
HOW IN THE HELL ARE WE GOING TO GET IN THERE?
THAT'S WHAT THE BELTS ARE FOR.
WE'RE GOING TO POP OVER TO OBLIVION, WALK OVER TO WHERE THAT BUILDING IS, AND THEN POP BACK AND WE'LL BE INSIDE.
THEN WE FIND MY DEVICE AND, BOOM, WE'RE OUT. ALL DONE. SIMPLE.
WHAT IF WE COME BACK INSIDE A WALL?
CAN'T HAPPEN. LIKE I SAID BEFORE, IF THERE'S A WALL-- THE CURRENT WILL MOVE US.
LET'S GO.
TEK
FWAAASHH
UH... OKAY.
TEK
SO NOW WHAT?
RUN!

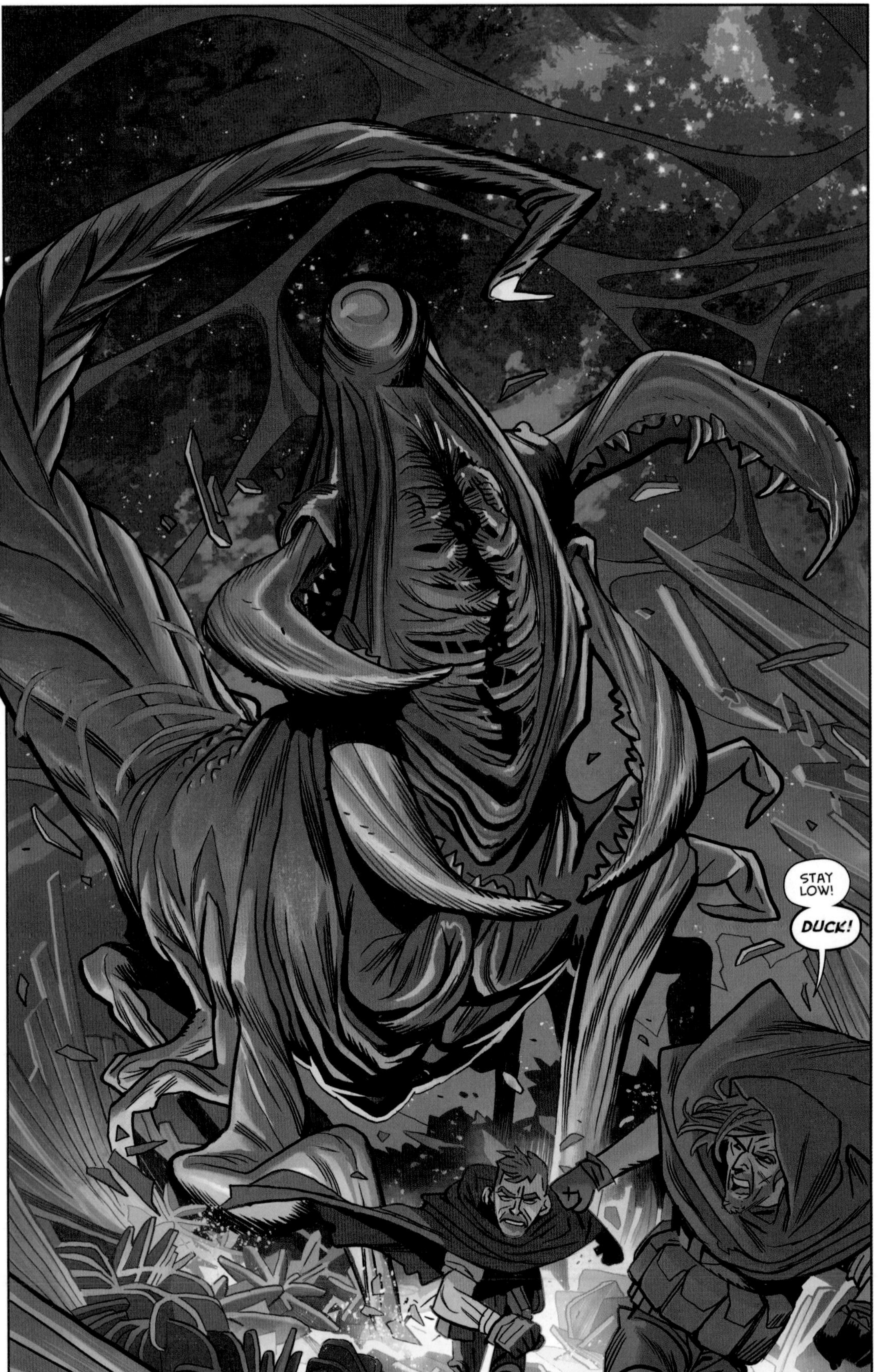
STAY LOW!
DUCK!

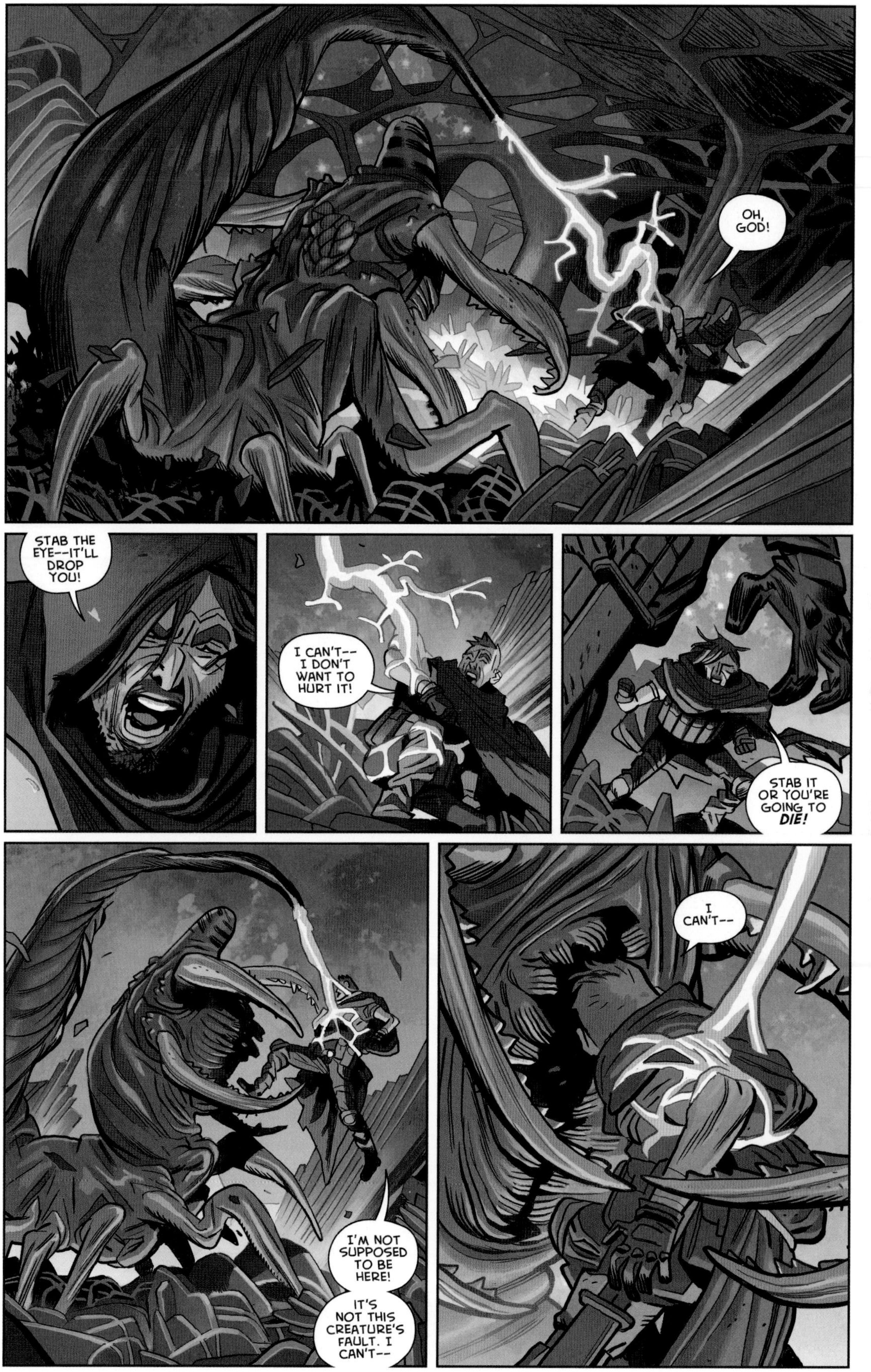
OH, GOD!
STAB THE EYE--IT'LL DROP YOU!
I CAN'T-- I DON'T WANT TO HURT IT!
STAB IT OR YOU'RE GOING TO *DIE!*
I'M NOT SUPPOSED TO BE HERE!
IT'S NOT THIS CREATURE'S FAULT. I CAN'T--
I CAN'T--

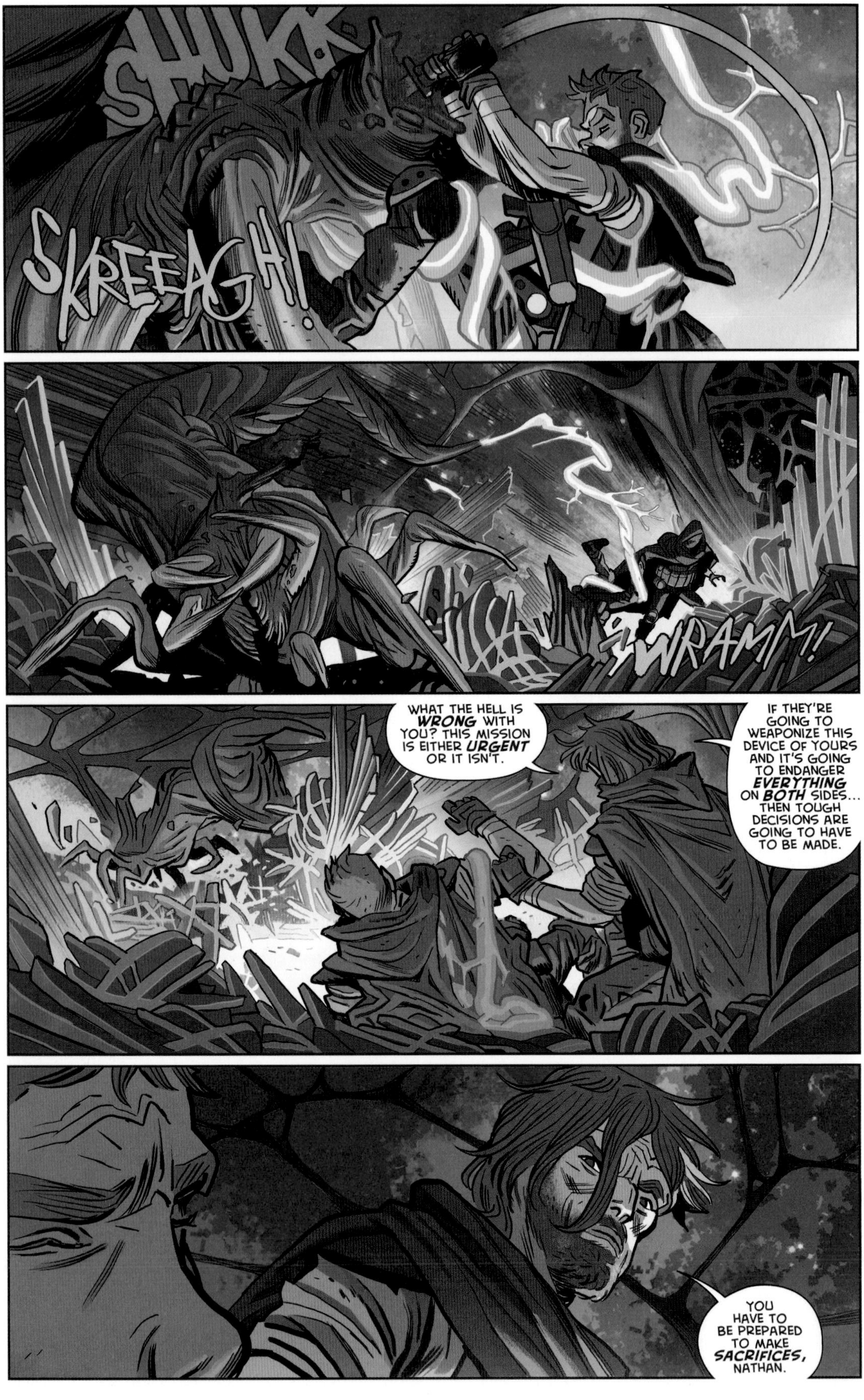
SHUKK
SKREEAGH!
WRAMM!
WHAT THE HELL IS WRONG WITH YOU? THIS MISSION IS EITHER URGENT OR IT ISN'T.
IF THEY'RE GOING TO WEAPONIZE THIS DEVICE OF YOURS AND IT'S GOING TO ENDANGER EVERYTHING ON BOTH SIDES... THEN TOUGH DECISIONS ARE GOING TO HAVE TO BE MADE.
YOU HAVE TO BE PREPARED TO MAKE SACRIFICES, NATHAN.

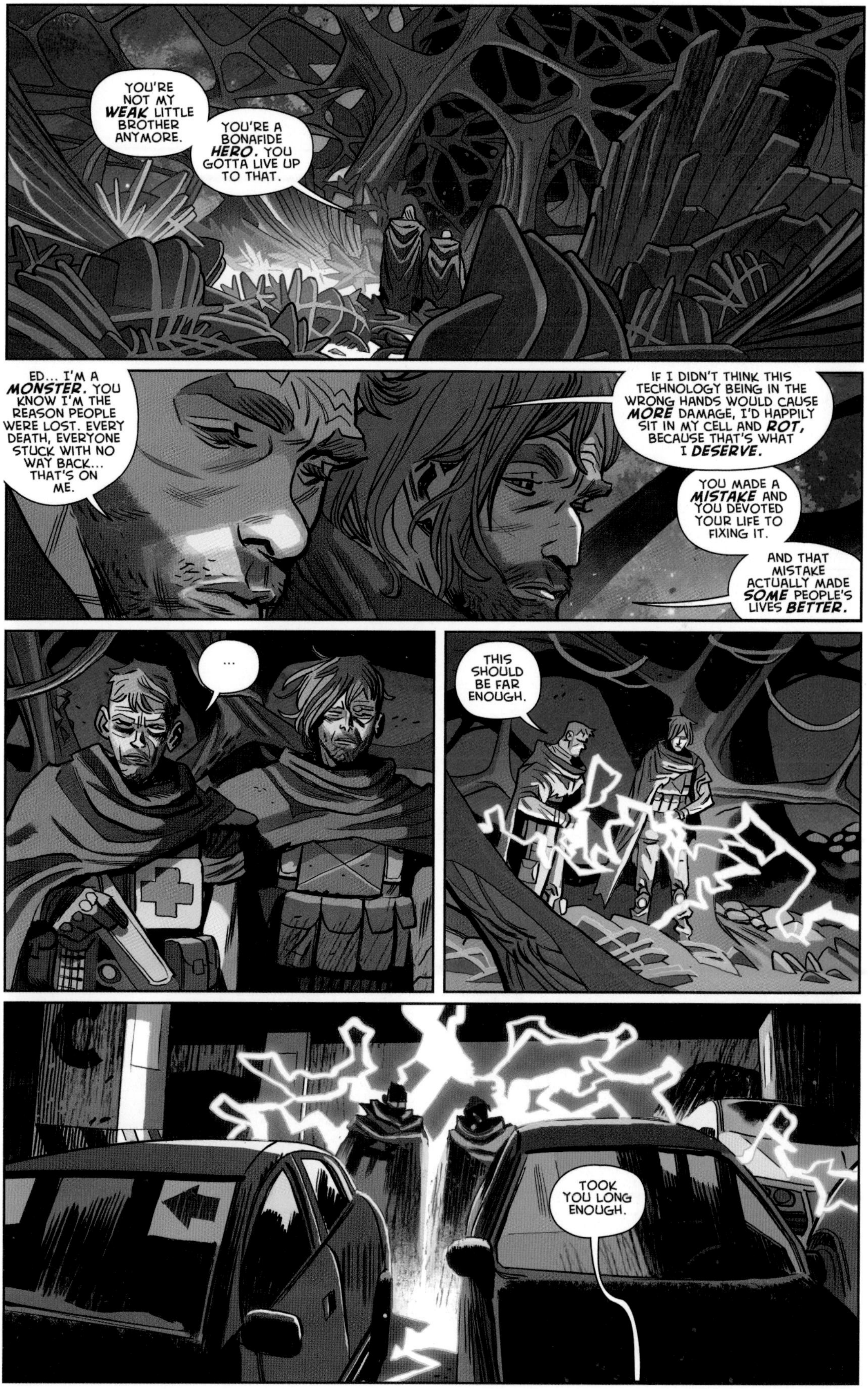

YOU'RE NOT MY WEAK LITTLE BROTHER ANYMORE.
YOU'RE A BONAFIDE HERO. YOU GOTTA LIVE UP TO THAT.
ED... I'M A MONSTER. YOU KNOW I'M THE REASON PEOPLE WERE LOST. EVERY DEATH, EVERYONE STUCK WITH NO WAY BACK... THAT'S ON ME.
IF I DIDN'T THINK THIS TECHNOLOGY BEING IN THE WRONG HANDS WOULD CAUSE MORE DAMAGE, I'D HAPPILY SIT IN MY CELL AND ROT, BECAUSE THAT'S WHAT I DESERVE.
YOU MADE A MISTAKE AND YOU DEVOTED YOUR LIFE TO FIXING IT.
AND THAT MISTAKE ACTUALLY MADE SOME PEOPLE'S LIVES BETTER.
...
THIS SHOULD BE FAR ENOUGH.
TOOK YOU LONG ENOUGH.

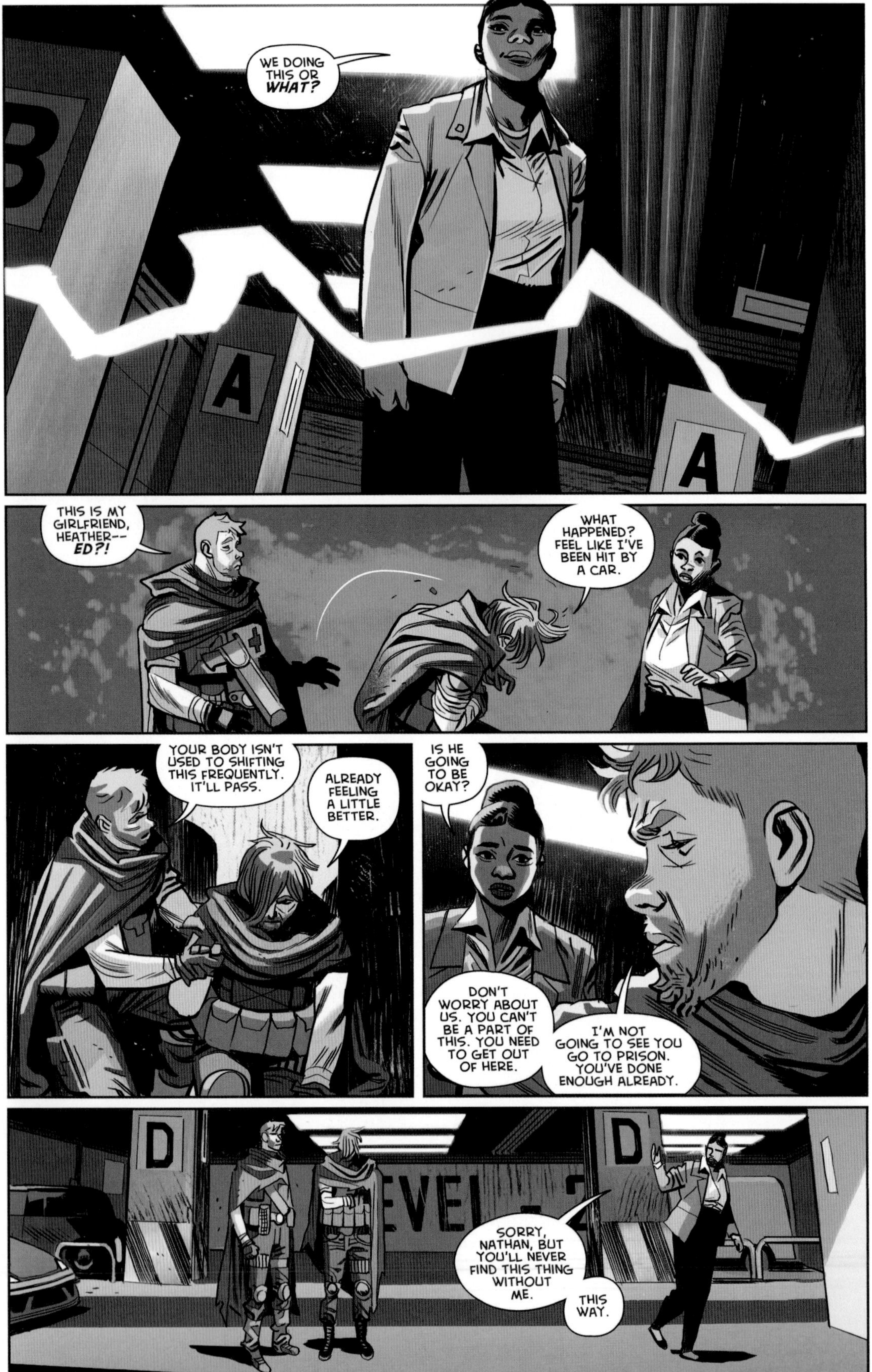
WE DOING THIS OR WHAT?
THIS IS MY GIRLFRIEND, HEATHER-- ED?!
WHAT HAPPENED? FEEL LIKE I'VE BEEN HIT BY A CAR.
YOUR BODY ISN'T USED TO SHIFTING THIS FREQUENTLY. IT'LL PASS.
ALREADY FEELING A LITTLE BETTER.
IS HE GOING TO BE OKAY?
DON'T WORRY ABOUT US. YOU CAN'T BE A PART OF THIS. YOU NEED TO GET OUT OF HERE.
I'M NOT GOING TO SEE YOU GO TO PRISON. YOU'VE DONE ENOUGH ALREADY.
SORRY, NATHAN, BUT YOU'LL NEVER FIND THIS THING WITHOUT ME.
THIS WAY.

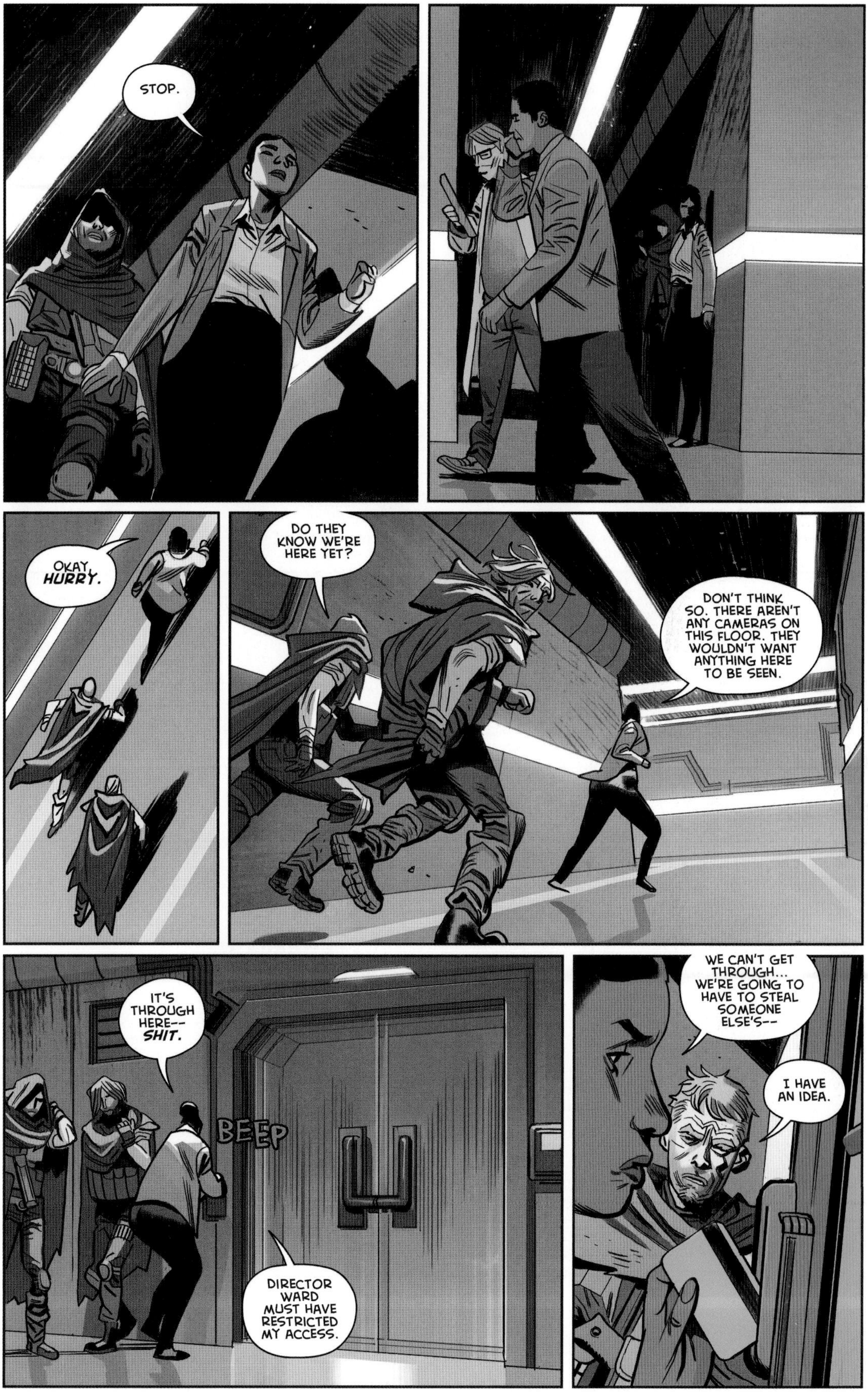
STOP.
OKAY, HURRY.
DO THEY KNOW WE'RE HERE YET?
DON'T THINK SO. THERE AREN'T ANY CAMERAS ON THIS FLOOR. THEY WOULDN'T WANT ANYTHING HERE TO BE SEEN.
IT'S THROUGH HERE-- SHIT.
BEEP
DIRECTOR WARD MUST HAVE RESTRICTED MY ACCESS.
WE CAN'T GET THROUGH... WE'RE GOING TO HAVE TO STEAL SOMEONE ELSE'S--
I HAVE AN IDEA.

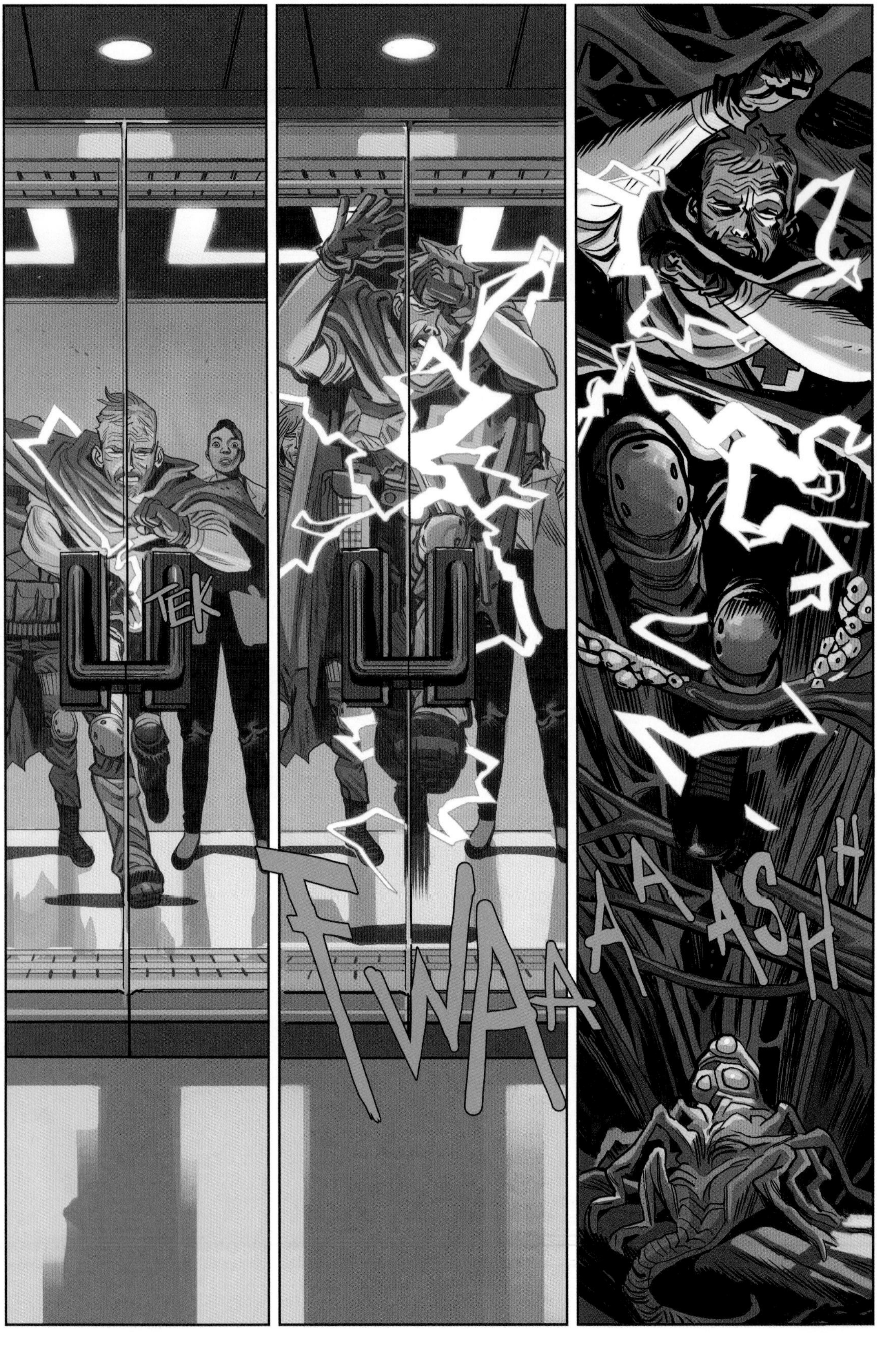
TEK
FWAAAASHH

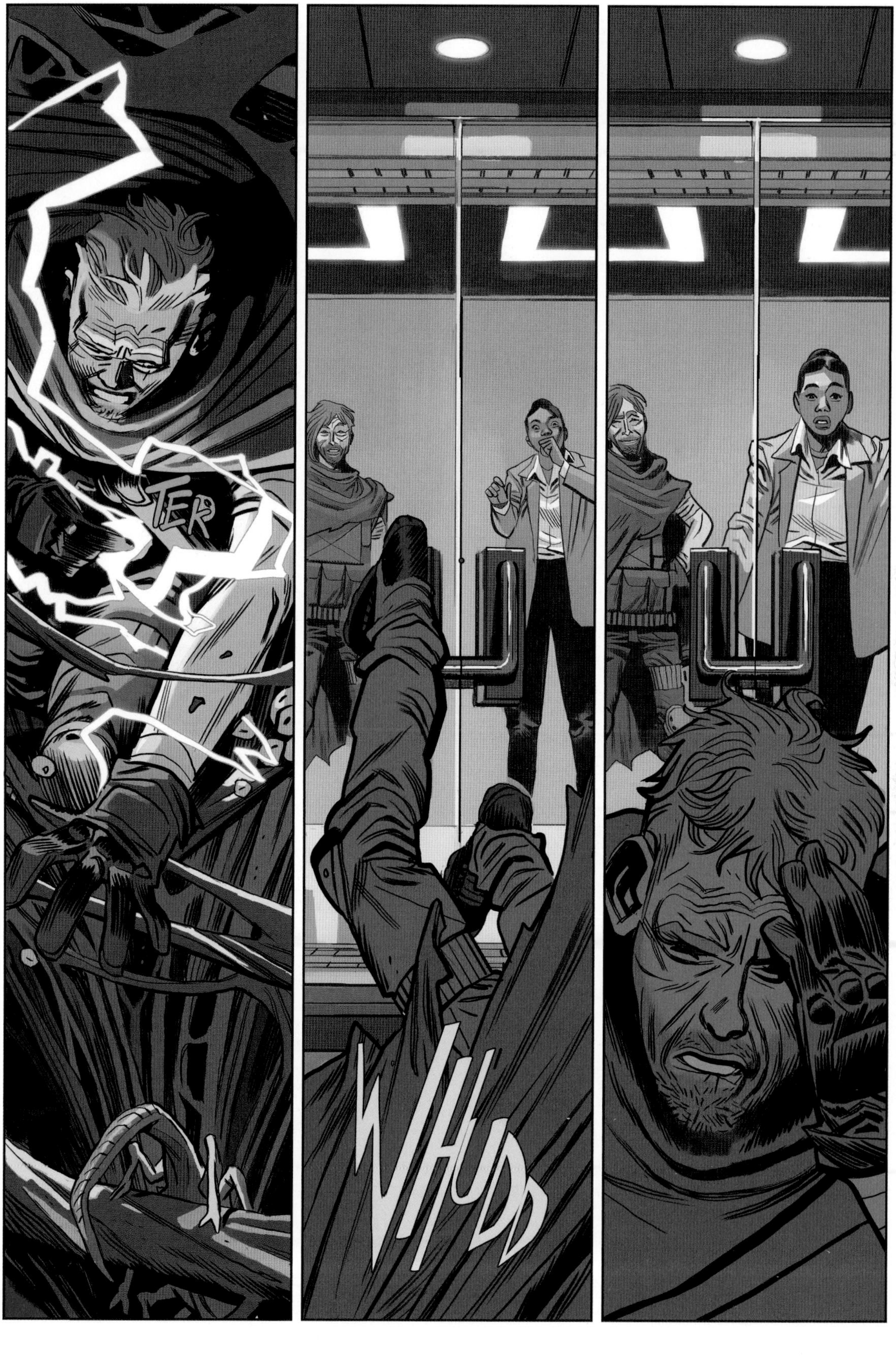
TER
WHUDD

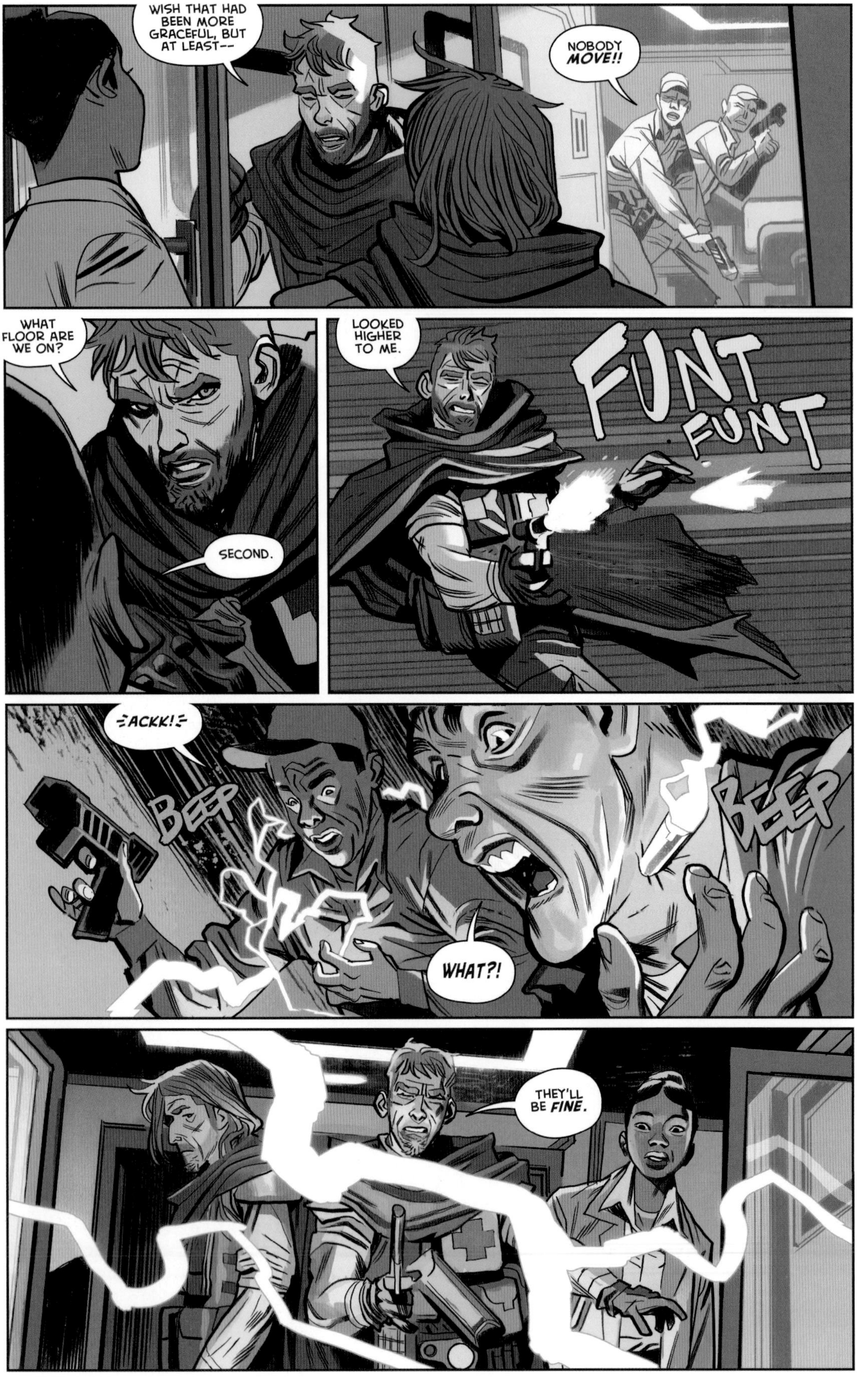
WISH THAT HAD BEEN MORE GRACEFUL, BUT AT LEAST--
NOBODY MOVE!!
WHAT FLOOR ARE WE ON?
SECOND.
LOOKED HIGHER TO ME.
FUNT FUNT
ACKK!
BEEP
BEEP
WHAT?!
THEY'LL BE FINE.

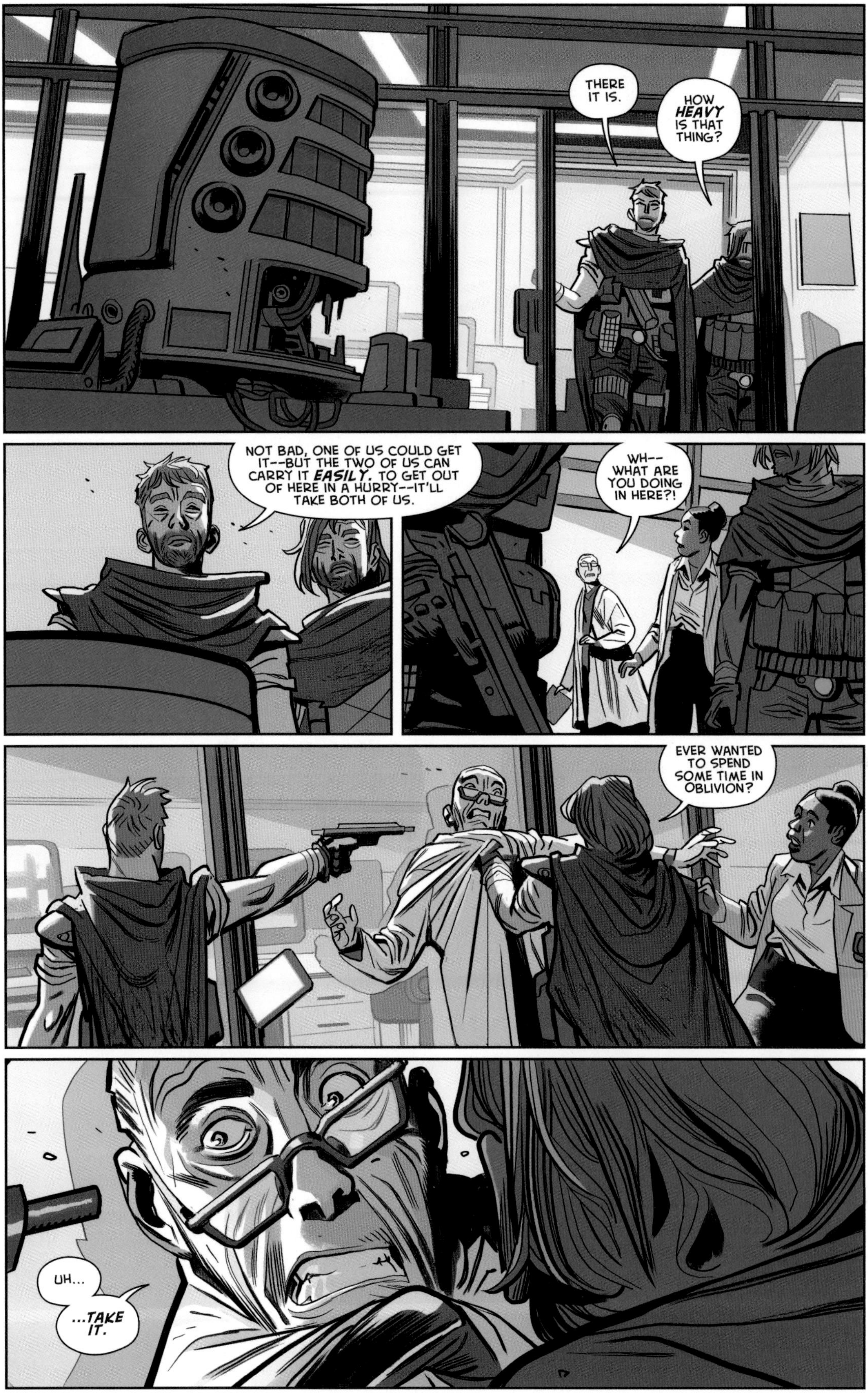
THERE IT IS.
HOW HEAVY IS THAT THING?
NOT BAD, ONE OF US COULD GET IT--BUT THE TWO OF US CAN CARRY IT EASILY. TO GET OUT OF HERE IN A HURRY--IT'LL TAKE BOTH OF US.
WH-- WHAT ARE YOU DOING IN HERE?!
EVER WANTED TO SPEND SOME TIME IN OBLIVION?
UH...
...TAKE IT.

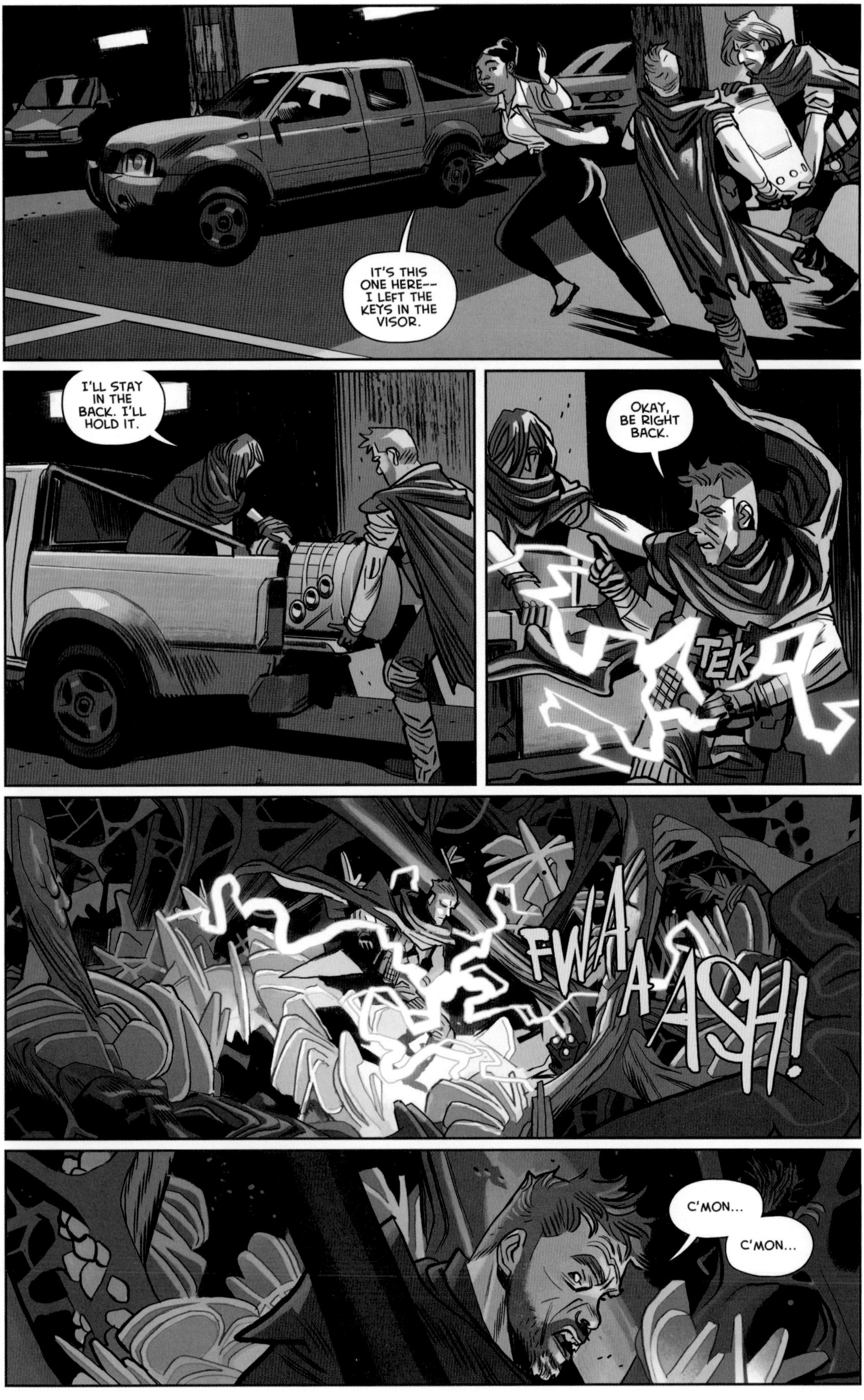
IT'S THIS ONE HERE-- I LEFT THE KEYS IN THE VISOR.
I'LL STAY IN THE BACK. I'LL HOLD IT.
OKAY, BE RIGHT BACK.
TEK
FWAAASH!
C'MON...
C'MON...

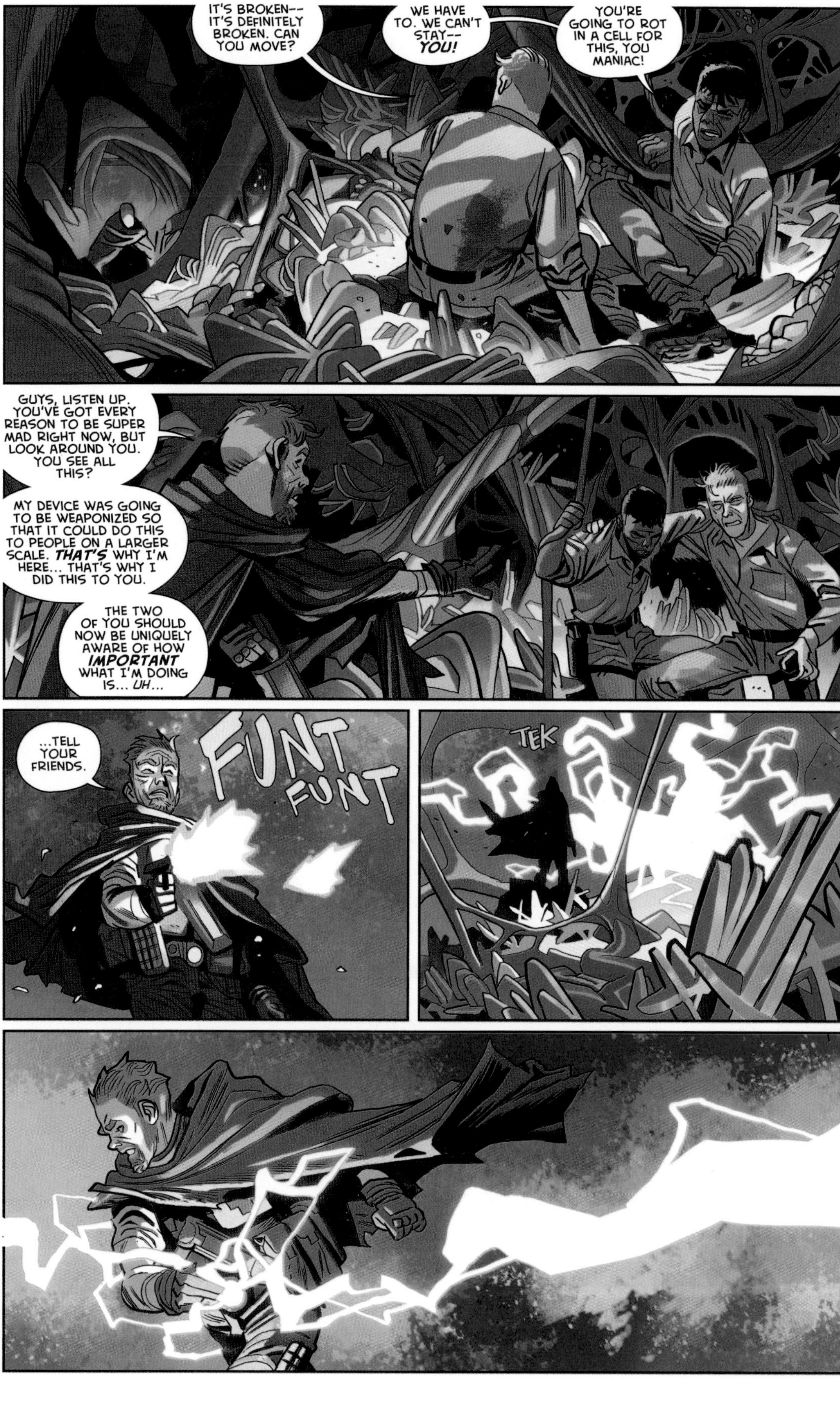
IT'S BROKEN-- IT'S DEFINITELY BROKEN. CAN YOU MOVE?
WE HAVE TO. WE CAN'T STAY-- YOU!
YOU'RE GOING TO ROT IN A CELL FOR THIS, YOU MANIAC!
GUYS, LISTEN UP. YOU'VE GOT EVERY REASON TO BE SUPER MAD RIGHT NOW, BUT LOOK AROUND YOU. YOU SEE ALL THIS?
MY DEVICE WAS GOING TO BE WEAPONIZED SO THAT IT COULD DO THIS TO PEOPLE ON A LARGER SCALE. THAT'S WHY I'M HERE... THAT'S WHY I DID THIS TO YOU.
THE TWO OF YOU SHOULD NOW BE UNIQUELY AWARE OF HOW IMPORTANT WHAT I'M DOING IS... UH...
...TELL YOUR FRIENDS.
FUNT
FUNT
TEK

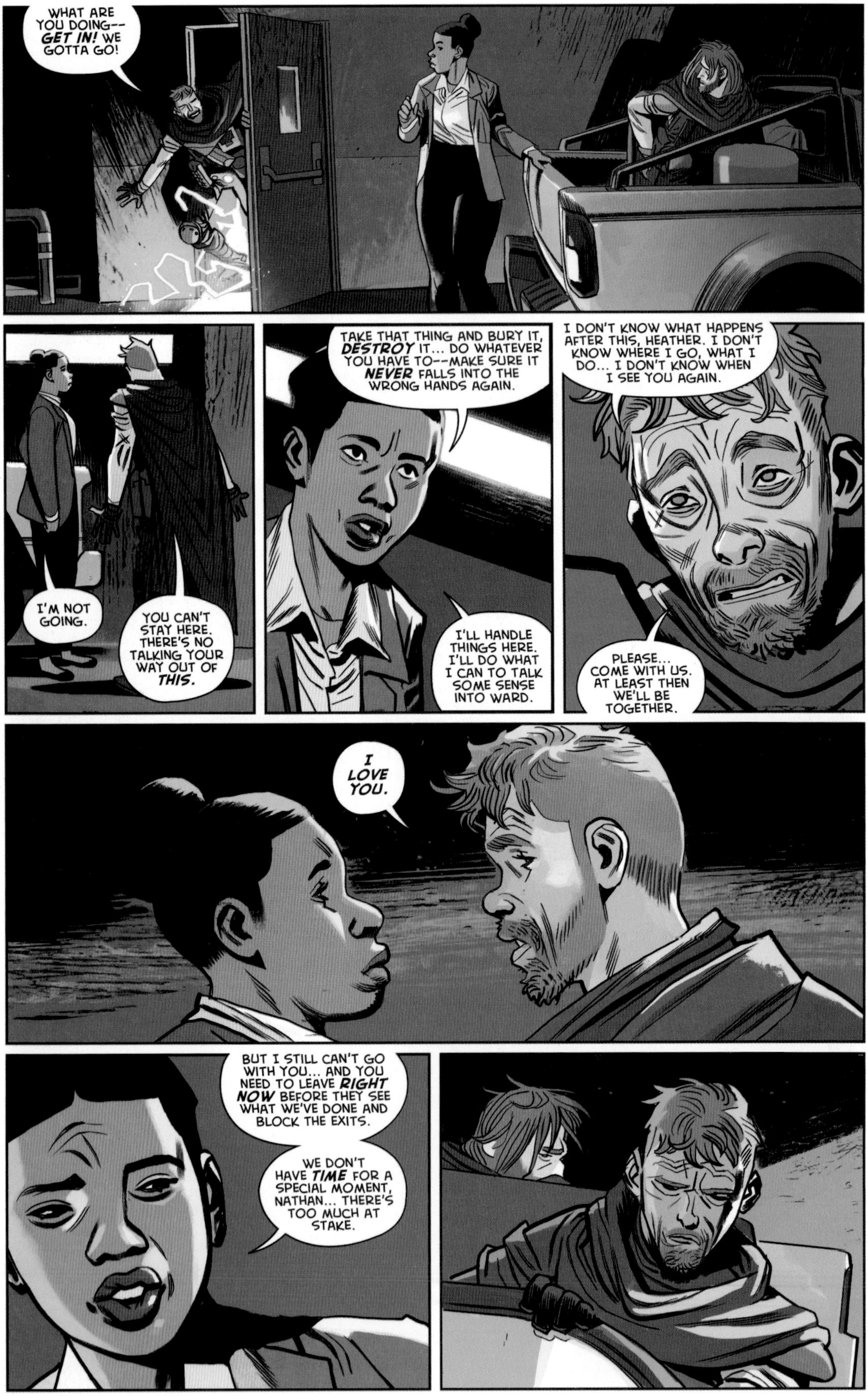
WHAT ARE YOU DOING-- GET IN! WE GOTTA GO!
I'M NOT GOING.
YOU CAN'T STAY HERE. THERE'S NO TALKING YOUR WAY OUT OF THIS.
TAKE THAT THING AND BURY IT, DESTROY IT... DO WHATEVER YOU HAVE TO--MAKE SURE IT NEVER FALLS INTO THE WRONG HANDS AGAIN.
I'LL HANDLE THINGS HERE. I'LL DO WHAT I CAN TO TALK SOME SENSE INTO WARD.
I DON'T KNOW WHAT HAPPENS AFTER THIS, HEATHER. I DON'T KNOW WHERE I GO, WHAT I DO... I DON'T KNOW WHEN I SEE YOU AGAIN.
PLEASE... COME WITH US. AT LEAST THEN WE'LL BE TOGETHER.
I LOVE YOU.
BUT I STILL CAN'T GO WITH YOU... AND YOU NEED TO LEAVE RIGHT NOW BEFORE THEY SEE WHAT WE'VE DONE AND BLOCK THE EXITS.
WE DON'T HAVE TIME FOR A SPECIAL MOMENT, NATHAN... THERE'S TOO MUCH AT STAKE.

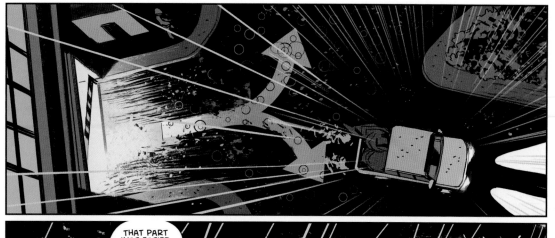

THAT PART WAS EASIER THAN I THOUGHT IT WOULD BE.

THEY WERE FOCUSED ON KEEPING US OUT, NOT IN. LET ME KNOW IF YOU SEE ANYONE FOLLOWING.

HOW DANGEROUS IS THIS THING? DID YOU COMPLETE IT? DOES IT WORK RIGHT NOW?

I REPAIRED AND REBUILT IT. I WAS GOING TO REVERSE THE TRANSFERENCE--BUT AS TIME WENT ON, I REALIZED THAT WOULD PROBABLY JUST MAKE THINGS *WORSE*.

BUT YEAH, IT SHOULD WORK. I EVEN ADDED BATTERIES TO IT SO IT COULD WORK WITHOUT BEING CONNECTED TO A DEDICATED POWER SOURCE.

THAT'S WHY WE HAD TO GET IT BACK-- AT ANY POINT THAT THING COULD BE ACTIVATED AND SEND ANOTHER CHUNK OF THE CITY INTO OBLIVION.

AFTER WE GET IT OUT OF THE CITY, I'LL FIGURE OUT WHAT WE'RE GOING TO DO WITH IT.

LOOK AT ALL THESE PEOPLE... STUCK IN THESE LIVES, UNABLE TO SEE THIS *PRISON* AROUND THEM.

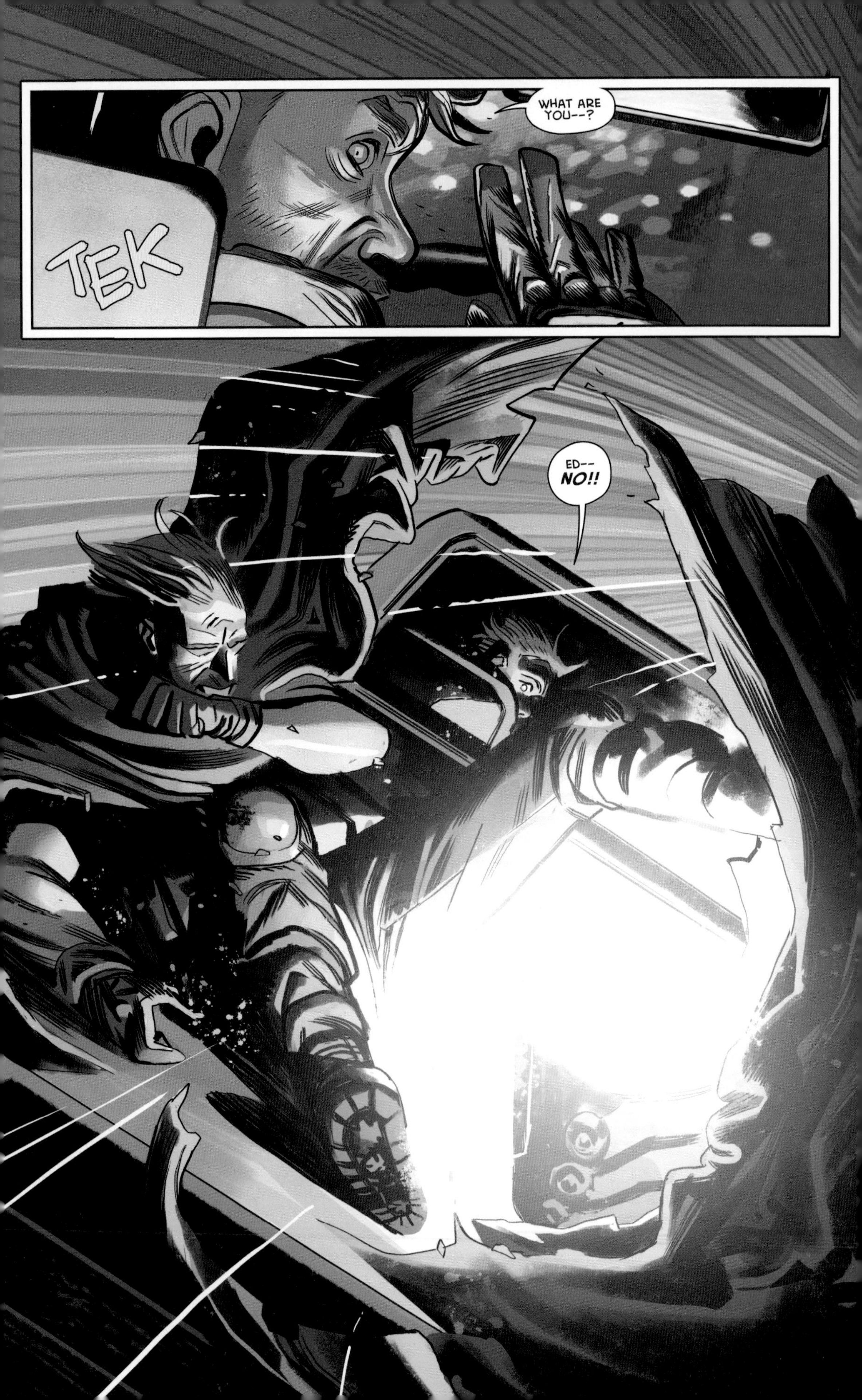
WHAT ARE YOU--?
TEK
ED-- NO!!

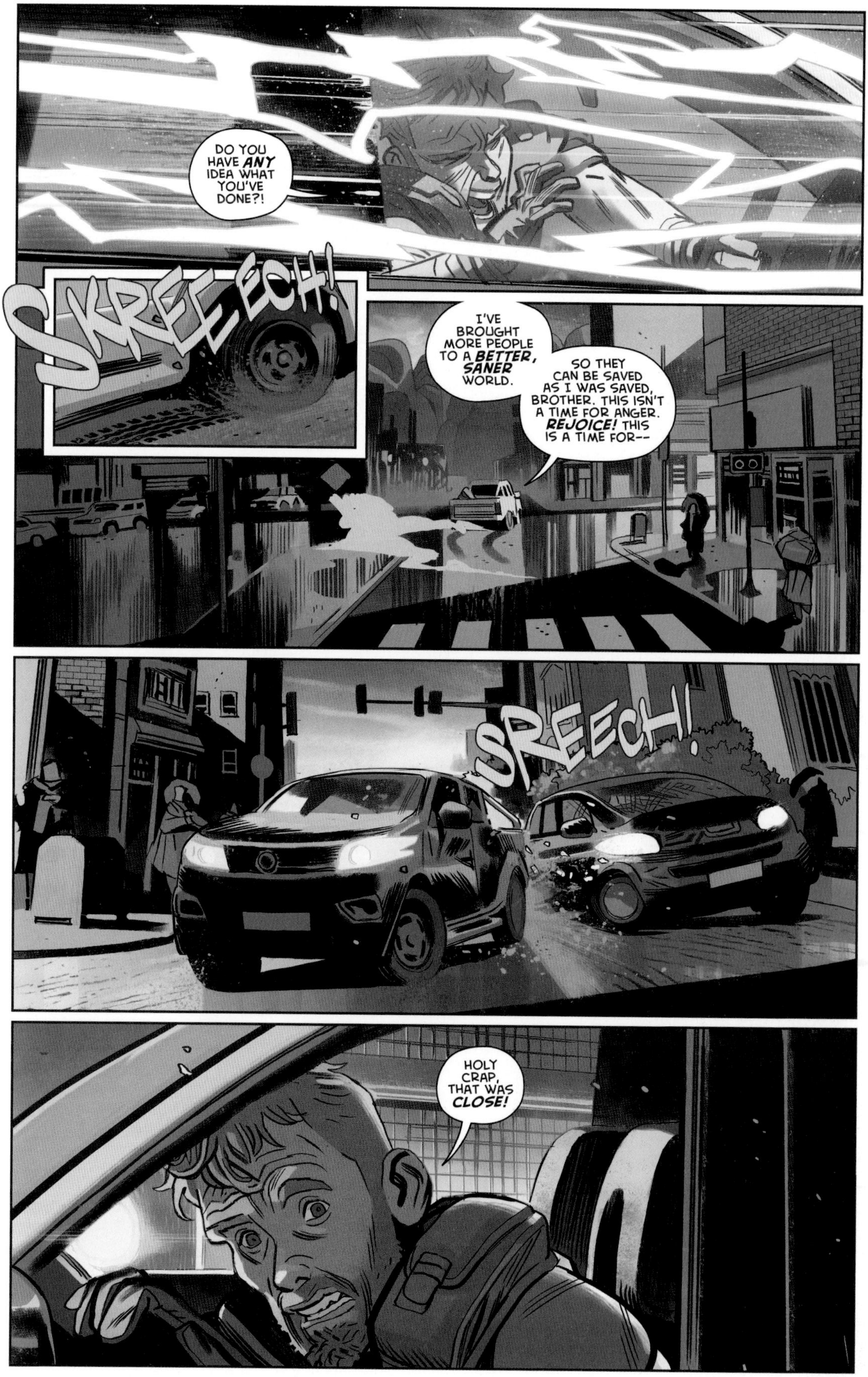
DO YOU HAVE ANY IDEA WHAT YOU'VE DONE?!
SKREEECH!
I'VE BROUGHT MORE PEOPLE TO A BETTER, SANER WORLD.
SO THEY CAN BE SAVED AS I WAS SAVED, BROTHER. THIS ISN'T A TIME FOR ANGER. REJOICE! THIS IS A TIME FOR--
SREECH!
HOLY CRAP, THAT WAS CLOSE!

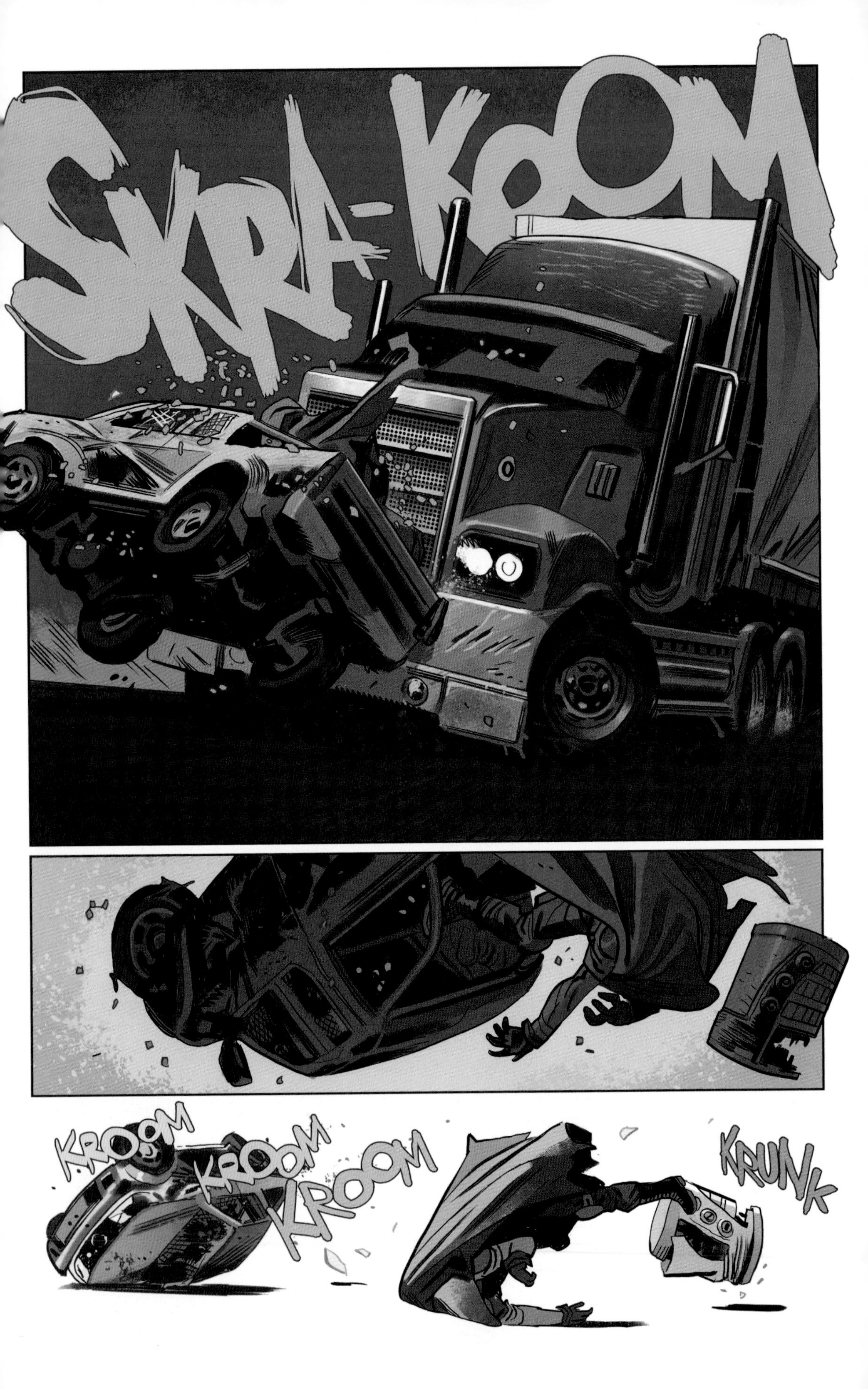
SKRA-KOOM
KROOM
KROOM
KROOM
KRUNK

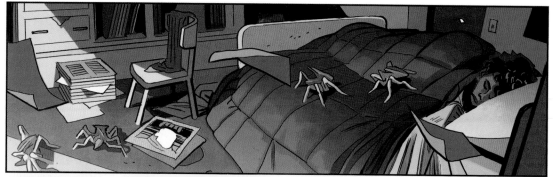

...

YEAAAGH!

OFF--!

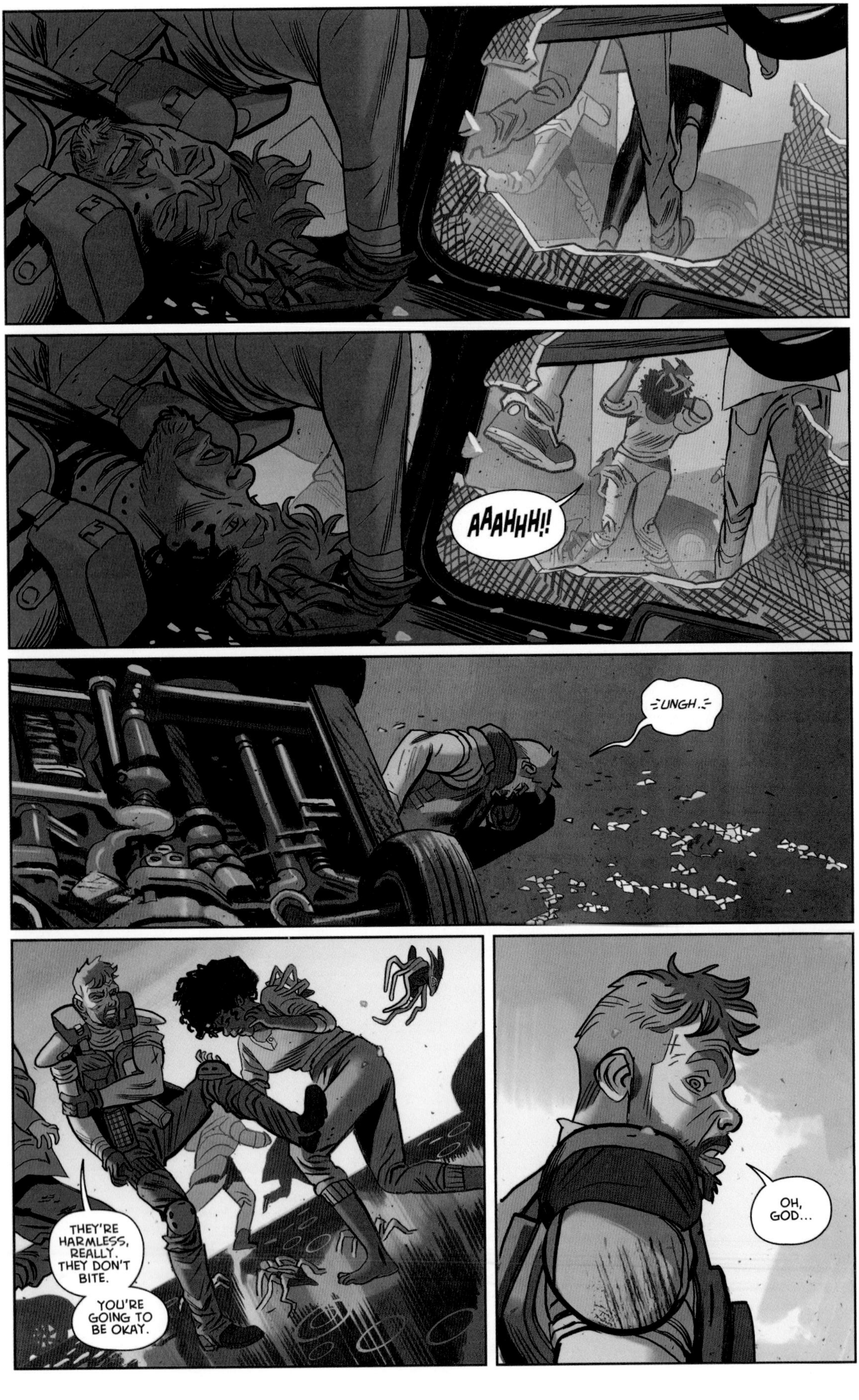
AAAHHH!!
UNGH..
THEY'RE HARMLESS, REALLY. THEY DON'T BITE.
YOU'RE GOING TO BE OKAY.
OH, GOD...

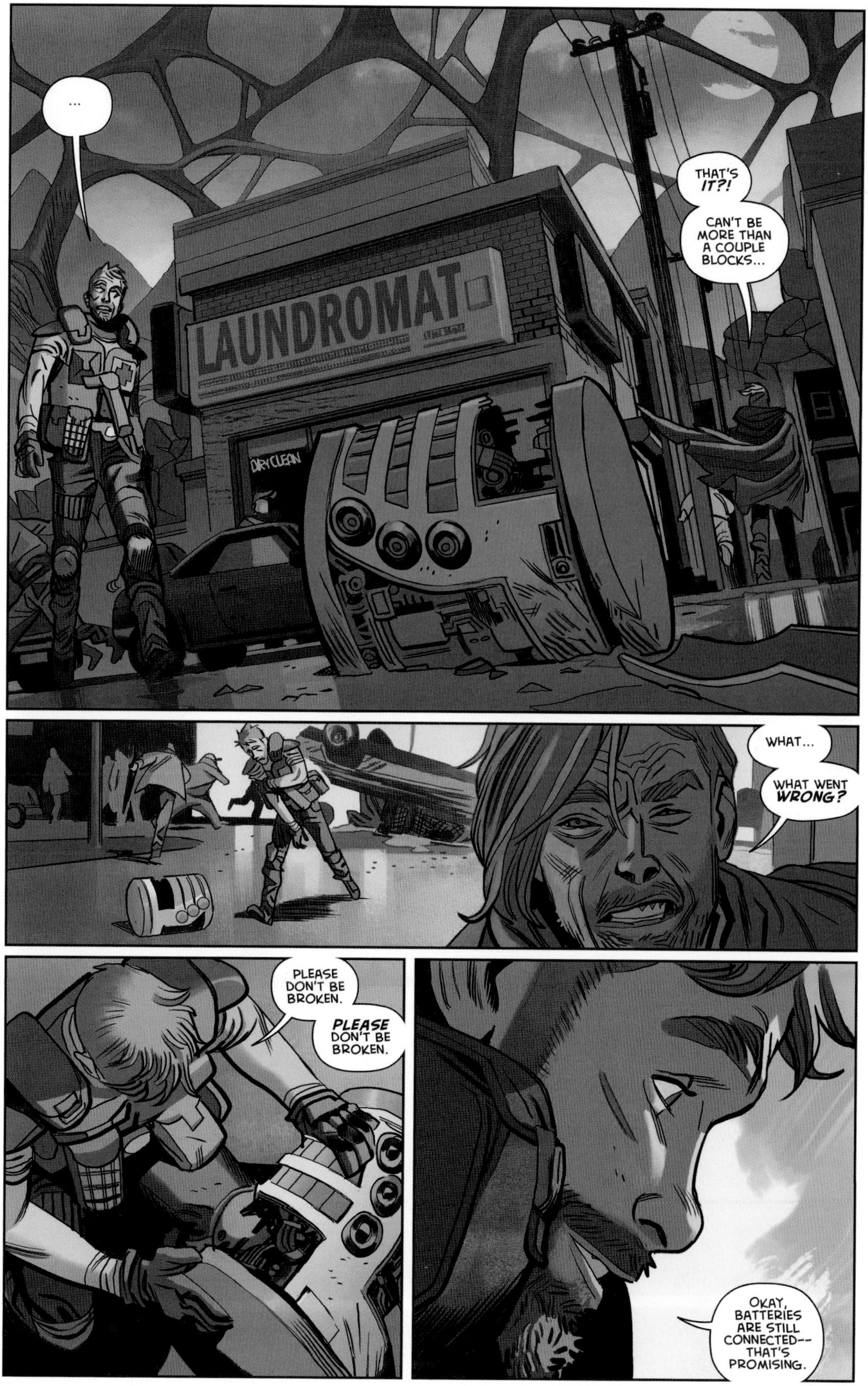
...
THAT'S IT?!
CAN'T BE MORE THAN A COUPLE BLOCKS...
LAUNDROMAT
DRY CLEAN
WHAT...
WHAT WENT WRONG?
PLEASE DON'T BE BROKEN.
PLEASE DON'T BE BROKEN.
OKAY, BATTERIES ARE STILL CONNECTED-- THAT'S PROMISING.

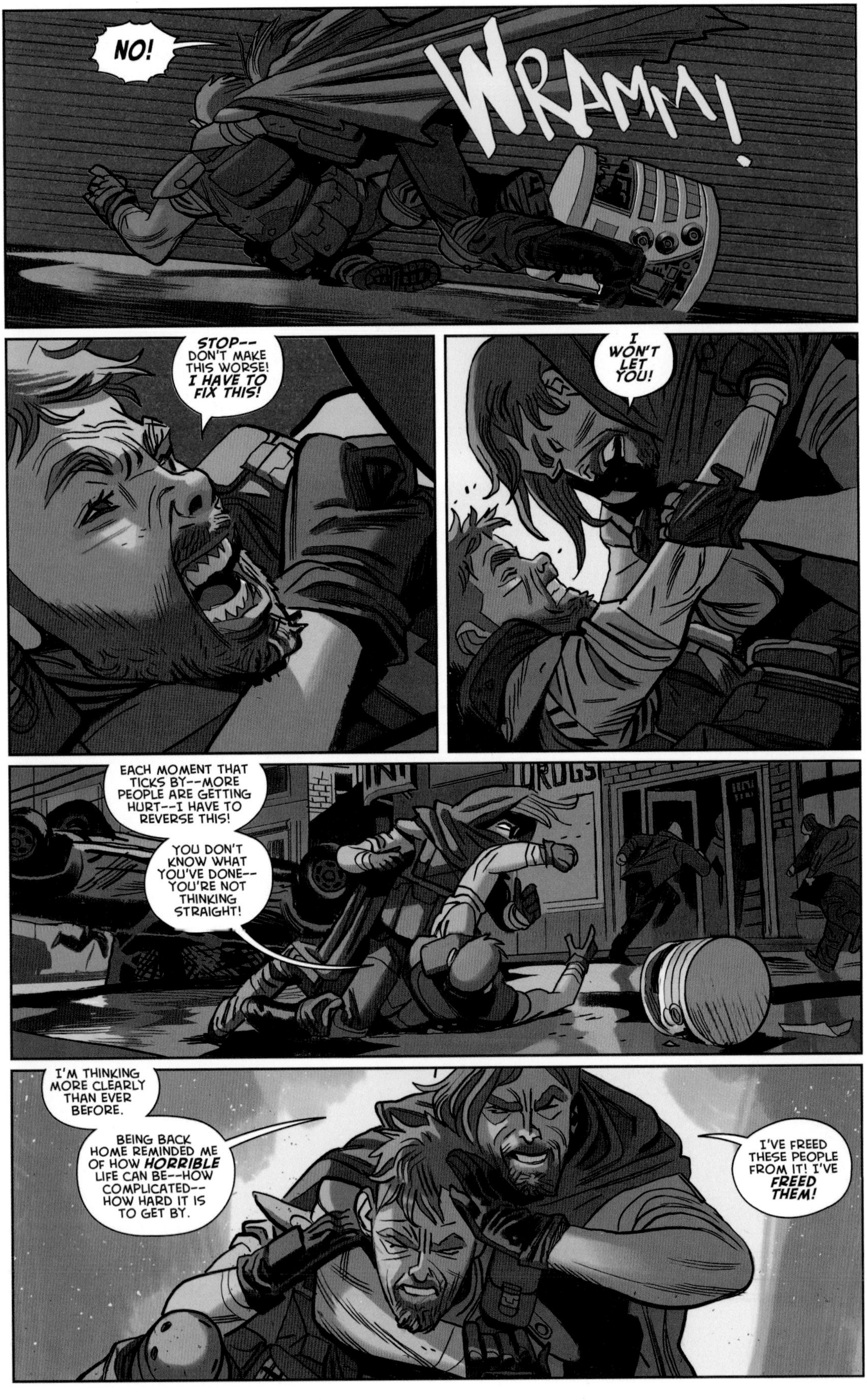
NO!
WRAMM!
STOP-- DON'T MAKE THIS WORSE! I HAVE TO FIX THIS!
I WON'T LET YOU!
EACH MOMENT THAT TICKS BY--MORE PEOPLE ARE GETTING HURT--I HAVE TO REVERSE THIS!
YOU DON'T KNOW WHAT YOU'VE DONE--YOU'RE NOT THINKING STRAIGHT!
DRUGS
I'M THINKING MORE CLEARLY THAN EVER BEFORE.
BEING BACK HOME REMINDED ME OF HOW HORRIBLE LIFE CAN BE--HOW COMPLICATED--HOW HARD IT IS TO GET BY.
I'VE FREED THESE PEOPLE FROM IT! I'VE FREED THEM!

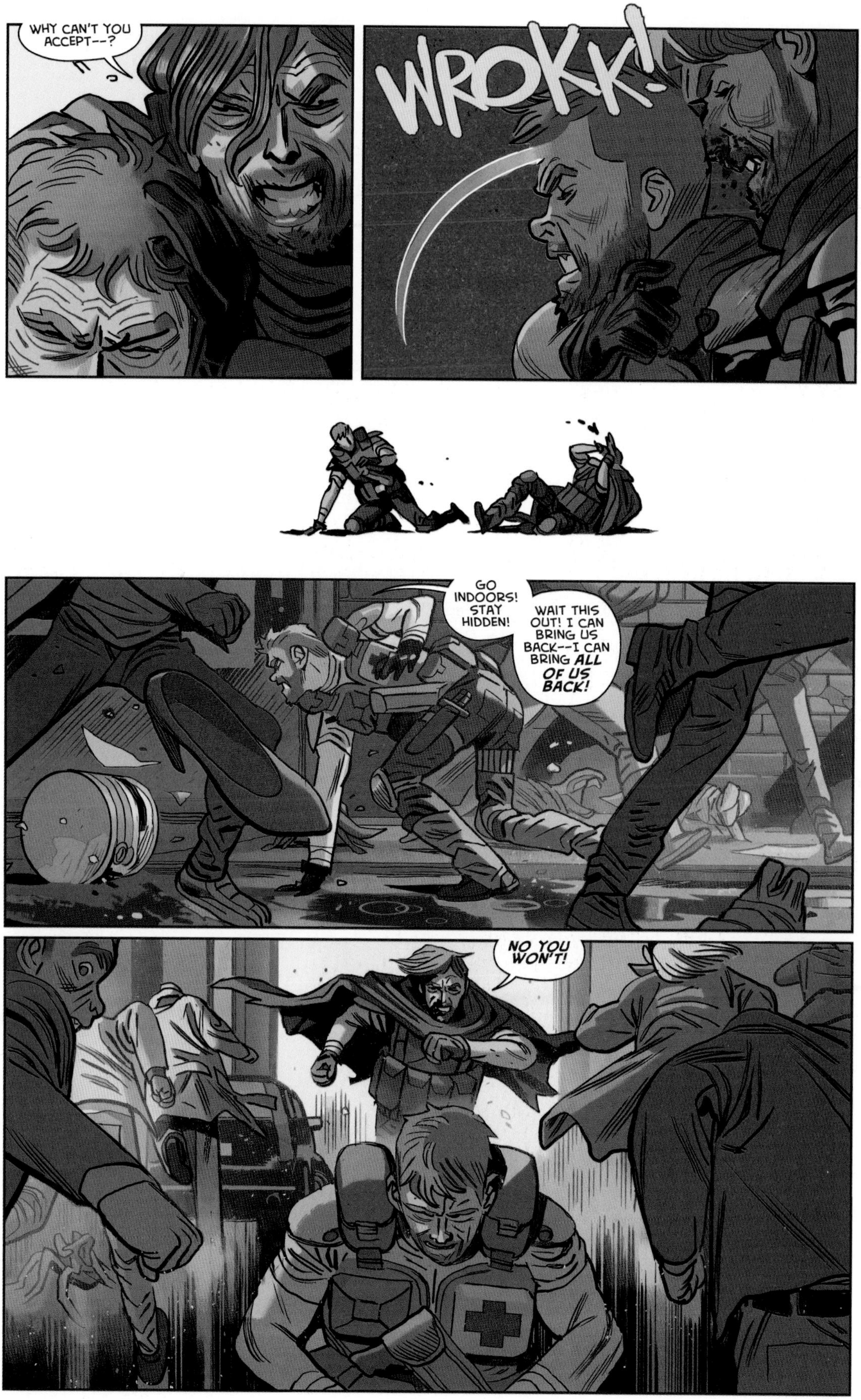
WHY CAN'T YOU ACCEPT--?
WROKK!
GO INDOORS! STAY HIDDEN!
WAIT THIS OUT! I CAN BRING US BACK--I CAN BRING ALL OF US BACK!
NO YOU WON'T!

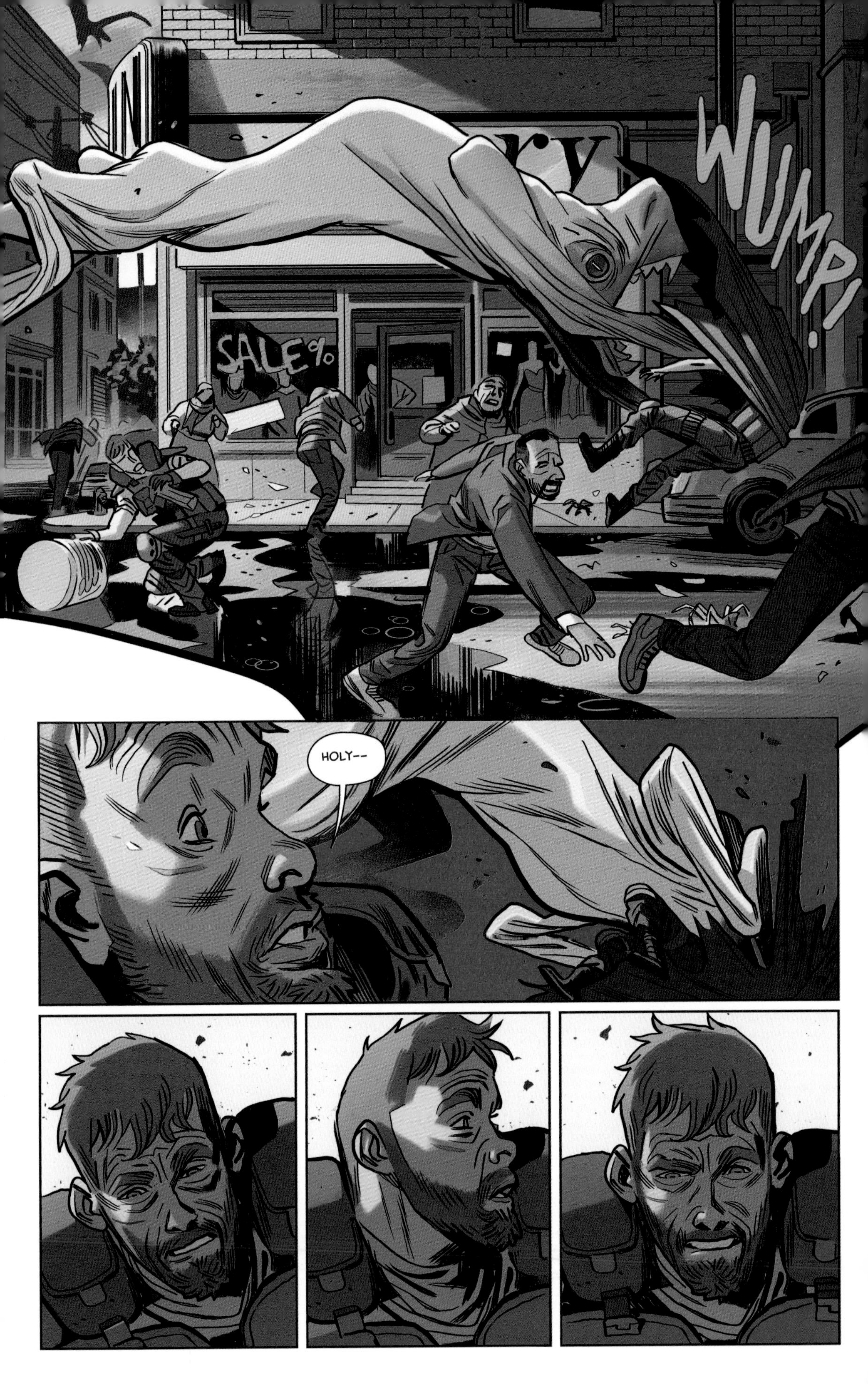
WUMP!
SALE%
HOLY--

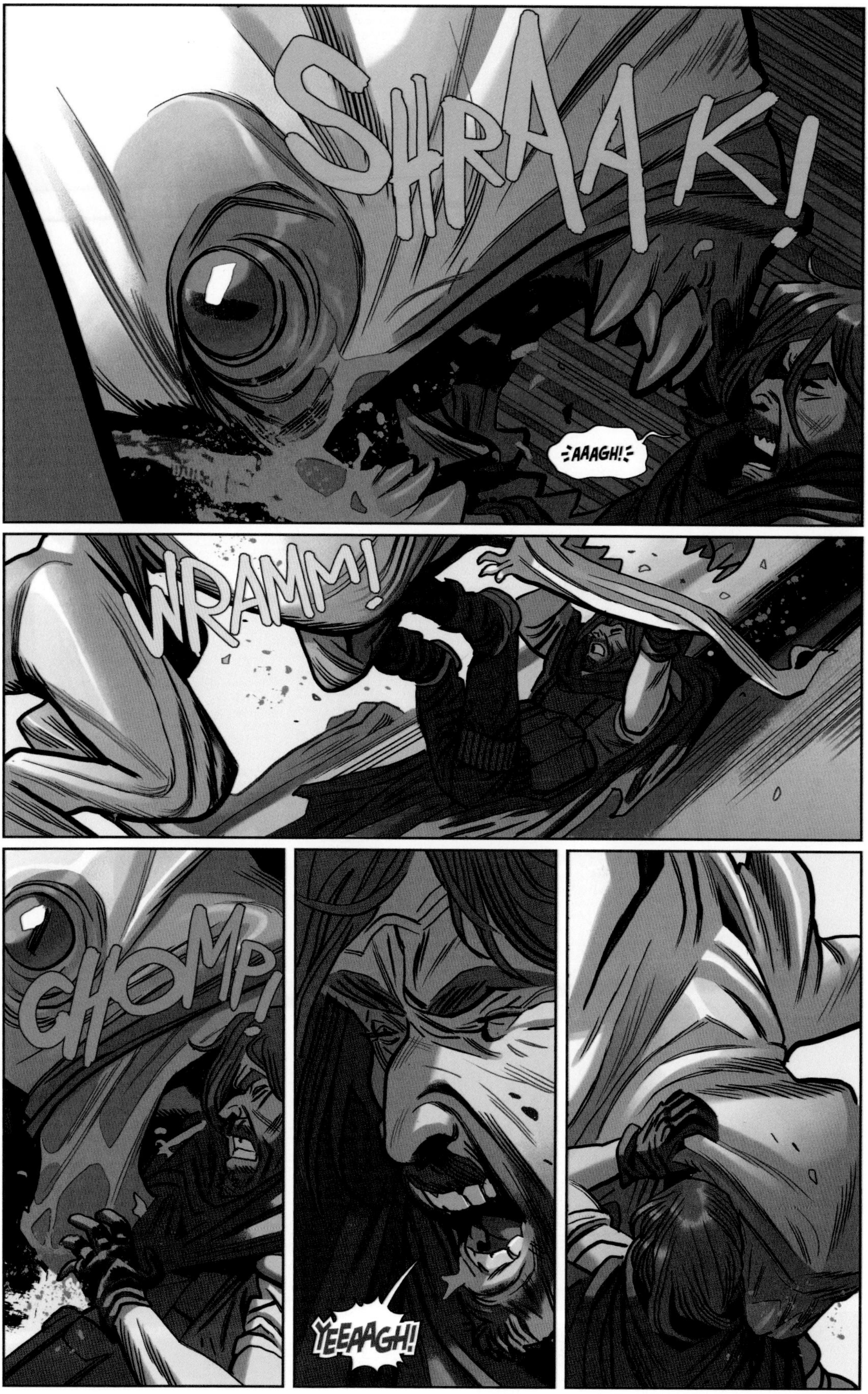
SHRAAK!
AAAGH!
WRAMM!
CHOMP!
YEEAAGH!

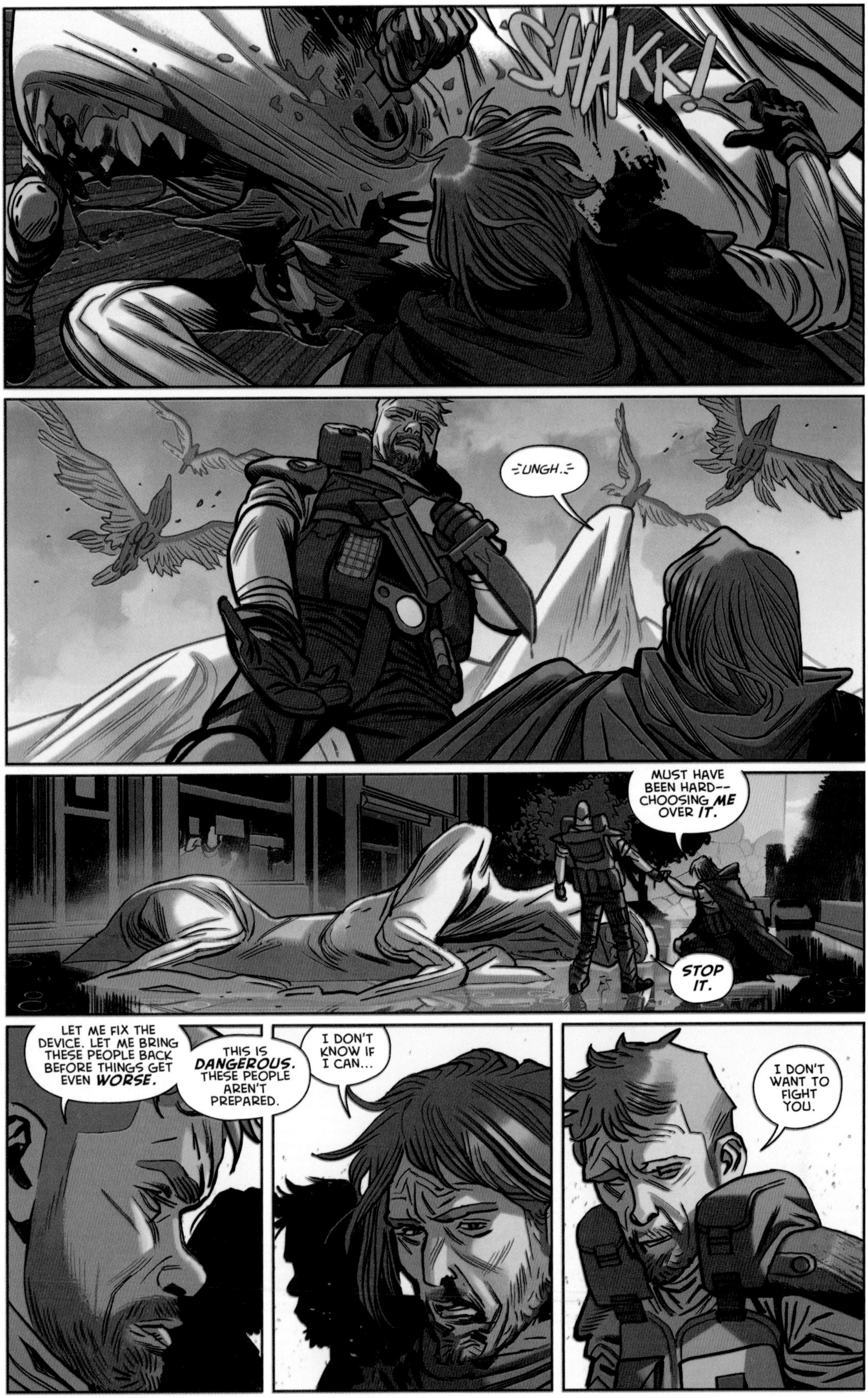
SHAKK!
UNGH.
MUST HAVE BEEN HARD-- CHOOSING ME OVER IT.
STOP IT.
LET ME FIX THE DEVICE. LET ME BRING THESE PEOPLE BACK BEFORE THINGS GET EVEN WORSE.
THIS IS DANGEROUS. THESE PEOPLE AREN'T PREPARED.
I DON'T KNOW IF I CAN...
I DON'T WANT TO FIGHT YOU.

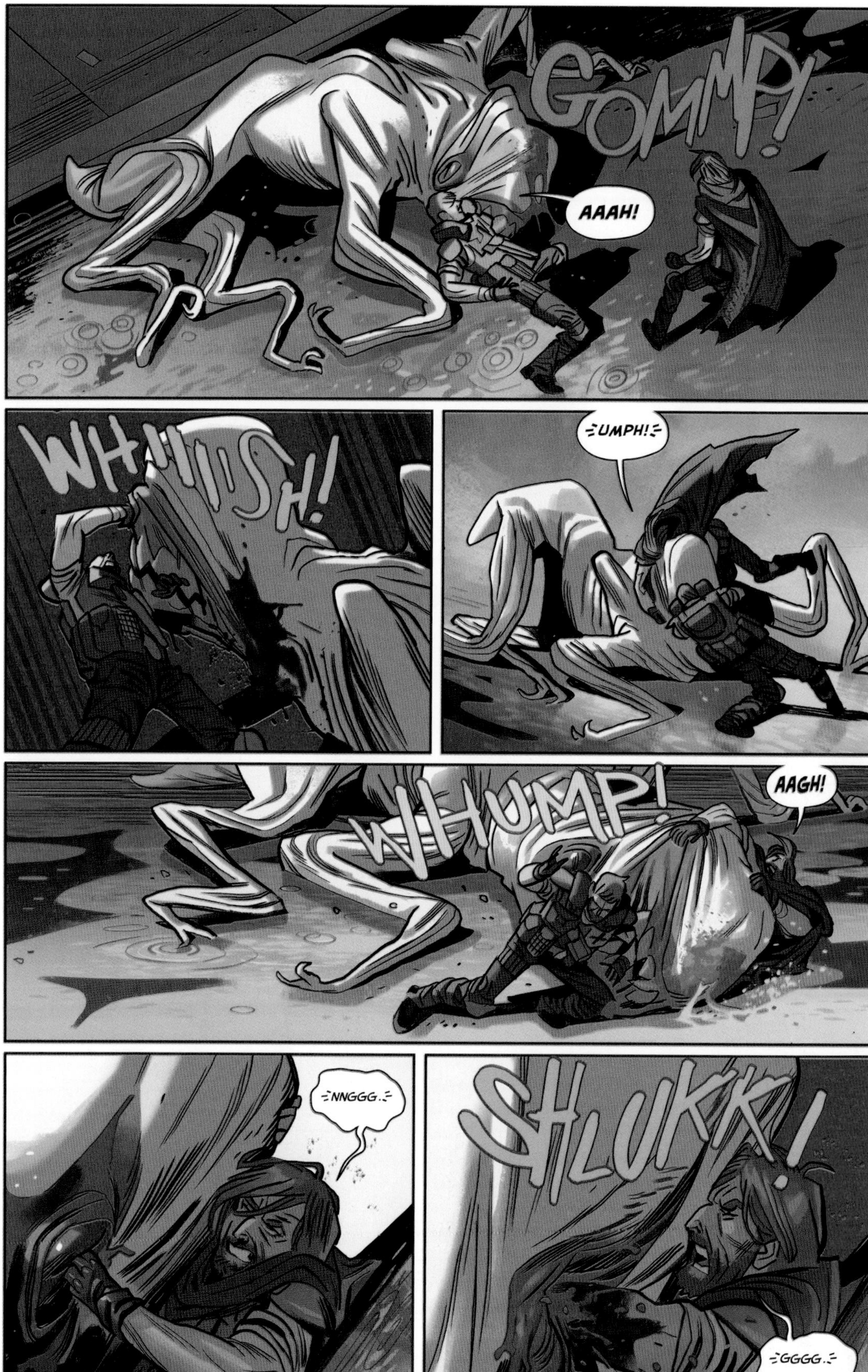
GOMMP!
AAAH!
WHIIIISH!
UMPH!
WHUMP!
AAGH!
NNGGG.
SHLUKK!
GGGG.

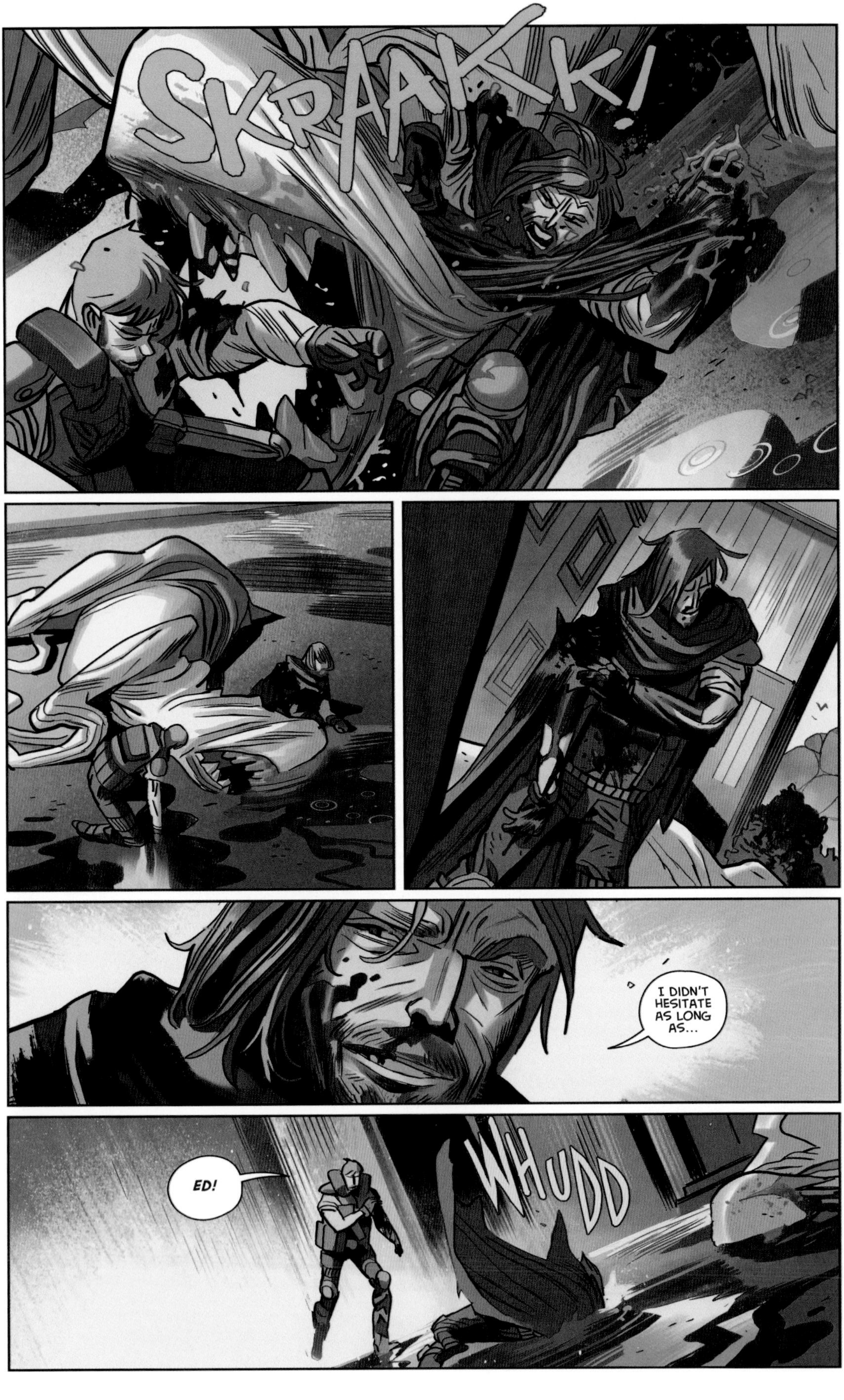
SKRAAKK!
I DIDN'T HESITATE AS LONG AS...
ED!
WHUDD

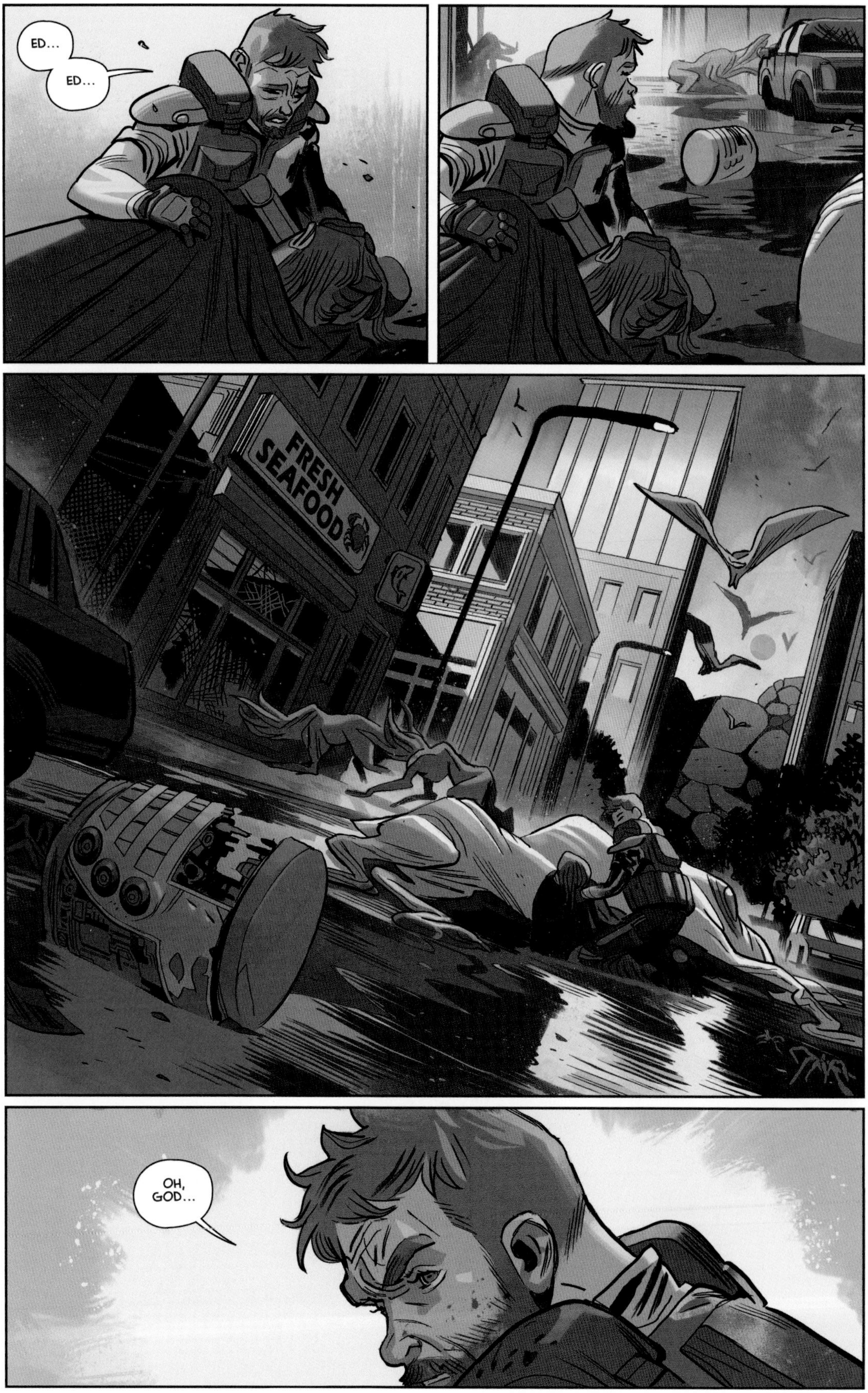
ED...
ED...
FRESH SEAFOOD
OH, GOD...

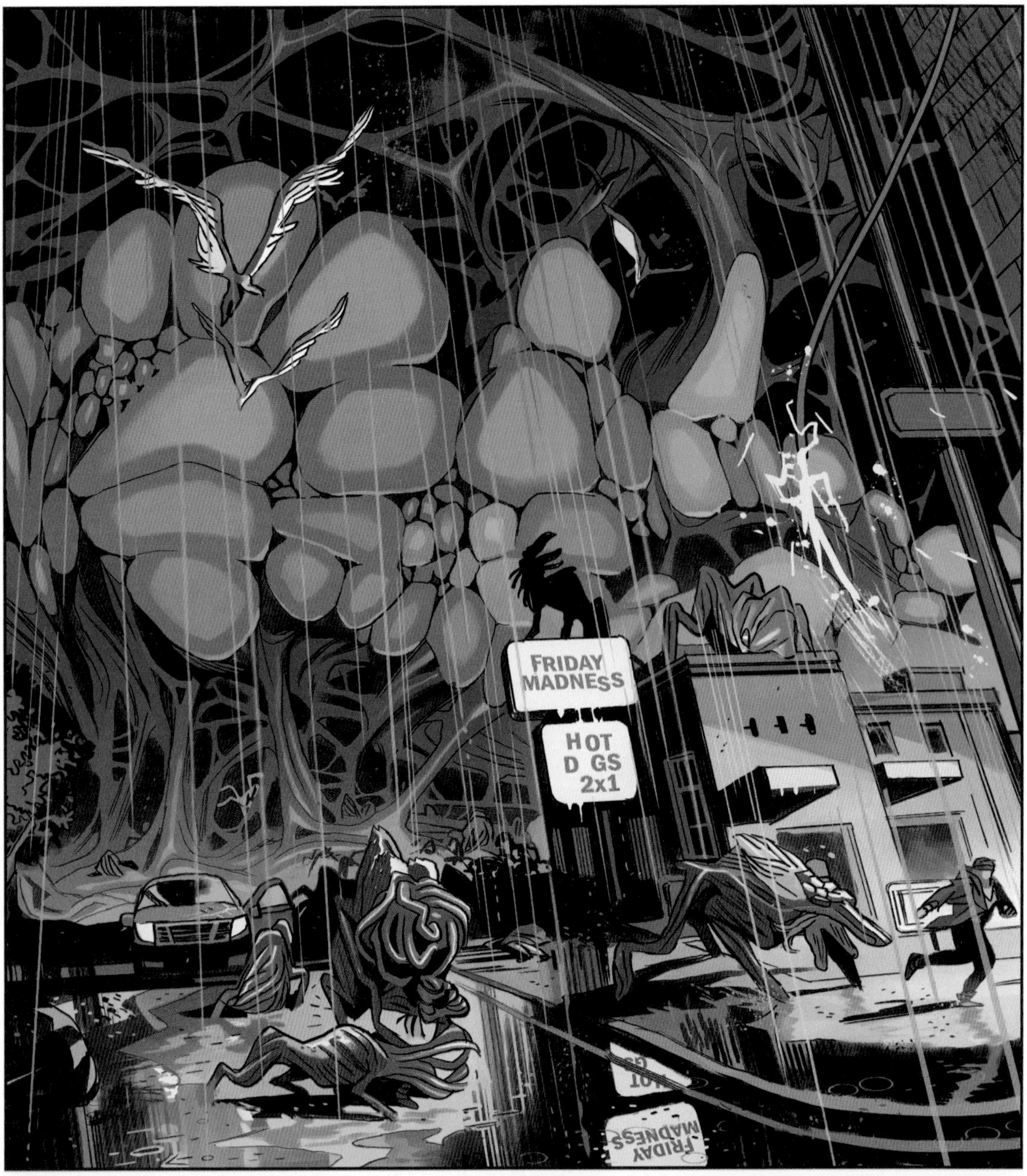
FRIDAY
MADNESS
HOT
D GS
2x1

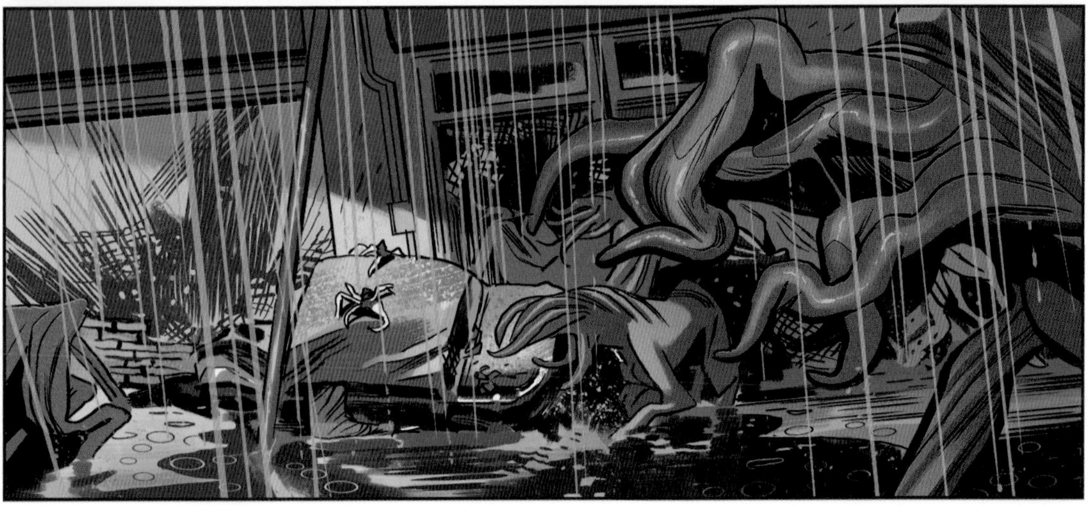

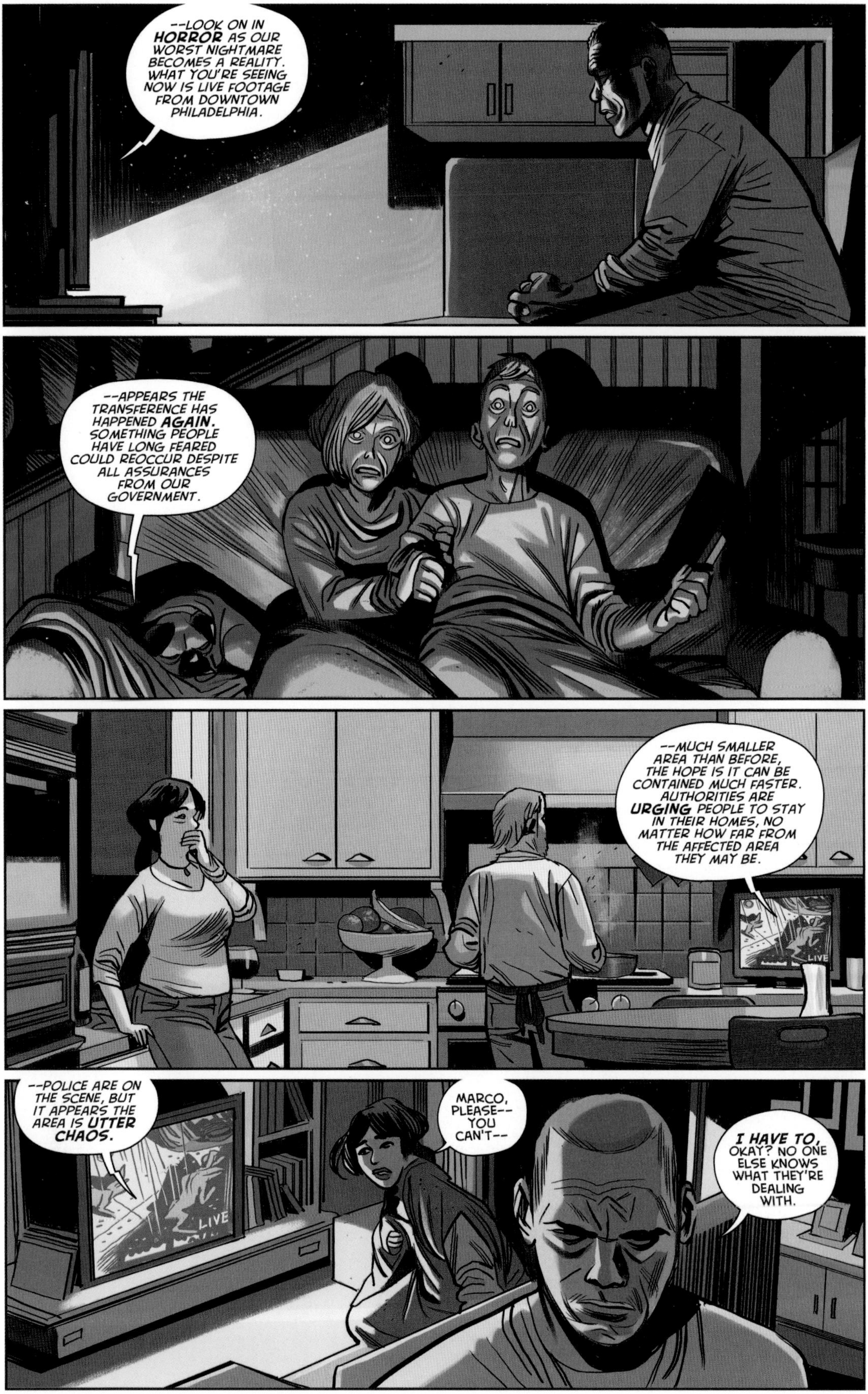
--LOOK ON IN HORROR AS OUR WORST NIGHTMARE BECOMES A REALITY. WHAT YOU'RE SEEING NOW IS LIVE FOOTAGE FROM DOWNTOWN PHILADELPHIA.
--APPEARS THE TRANSFERENCE HAS HAPPENED AGAIN. SOMETHING PEOPLE HAVE LONG FEARED COULD REOCCUR DESPITE ALL ASSURANCES FROM OUR GOVERNMENT.
--MUCH SMALLER AREA THAN BEFORE, THE HOPE IS IT CAN BE CONTAINED MUCH FASTER. AUTHORITIES ARE URGING PEOPLE TO STAY IN THEIR HOMES, NO MATTER HOW FAR FROM THE AFFECTED AREA THEY MAY BE.
LIVE
--POLICE ARE ON THE SCENE, BUT IT APPEARS THE AREA IS UTTER CHAOS.
LIVE
MARCO, PLEASE-- YOU CAN'T--
I HAVE TO, OKAY? NO ONE ELSE KNOWS WHAT THEY'RE DEALING WITH.

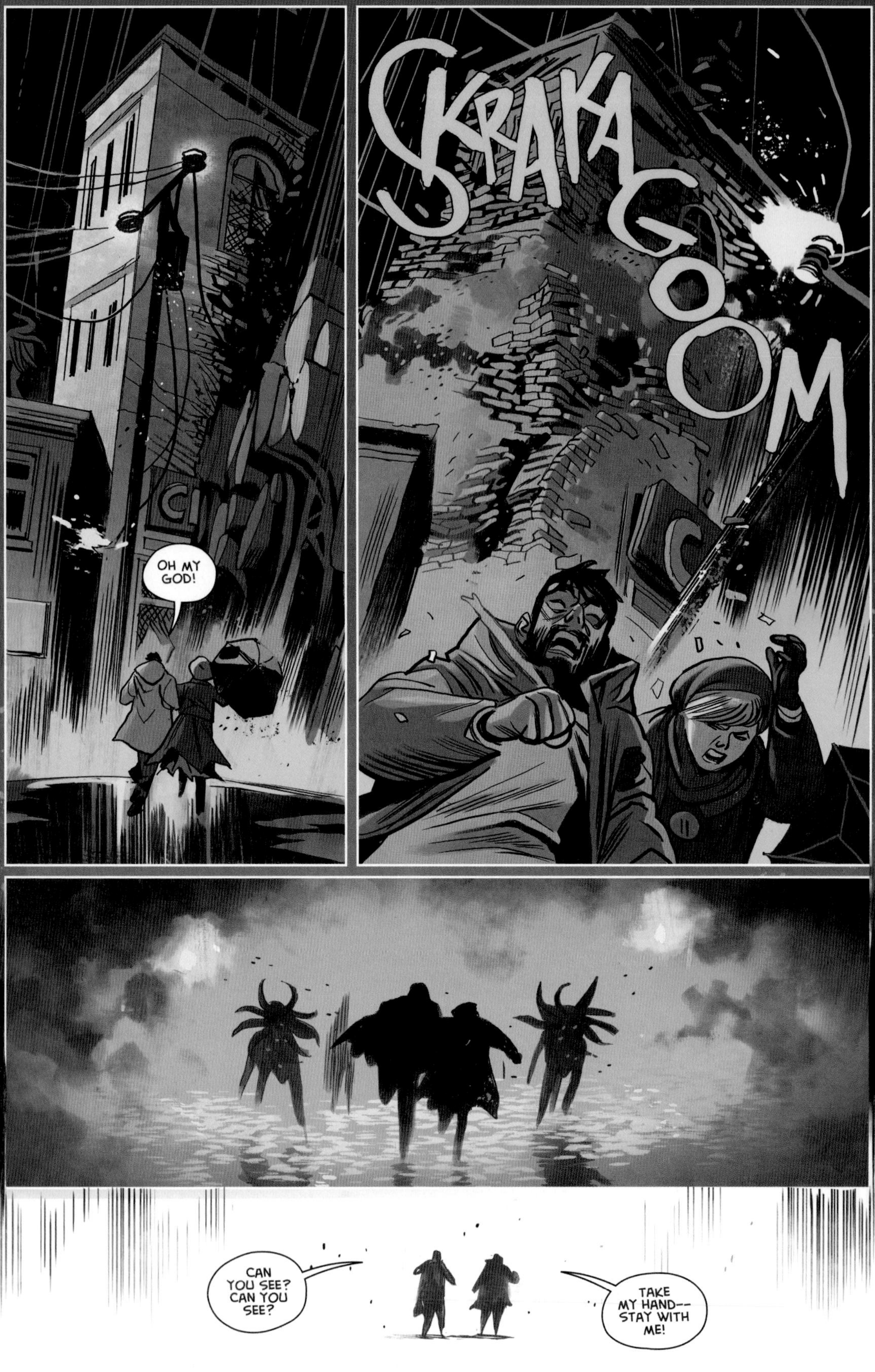
OH MY GOD!
SKRAKAGOOM
CAN YOU SEE? CAN YOU SEE?
TAKE MY HAND-- STAY WITH ME!

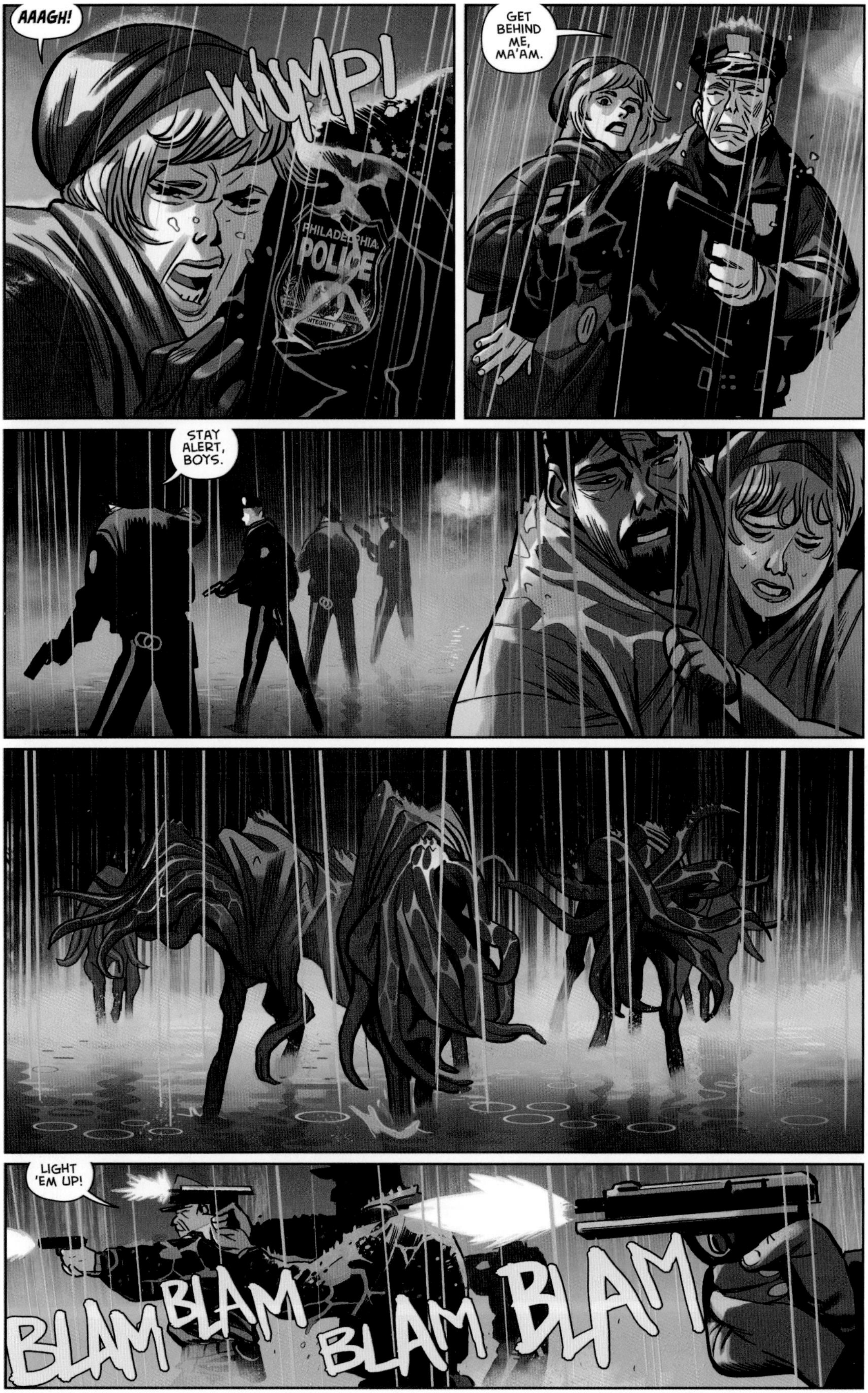
AAAGH!
WUMP!
PHILADELPHIA POLICE
INTEGRITY
GET BEHIND ME, MA'AM.
STAY ALERT, BOYS.
LIGHT 'EM UP!
BLAM BLAM BLAM BLAM

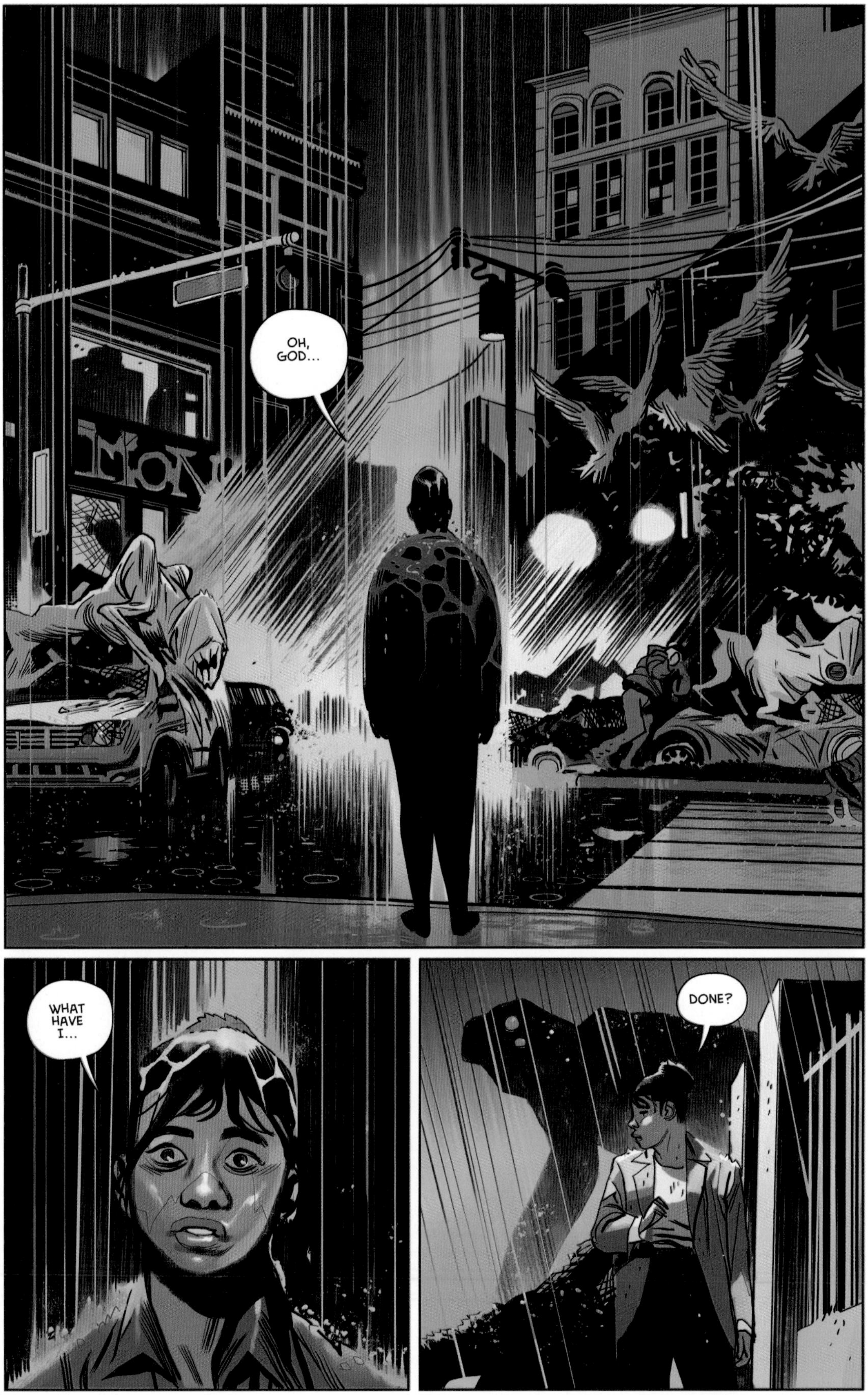
OH, GOD...
WHAT HAVE I...
DONE?

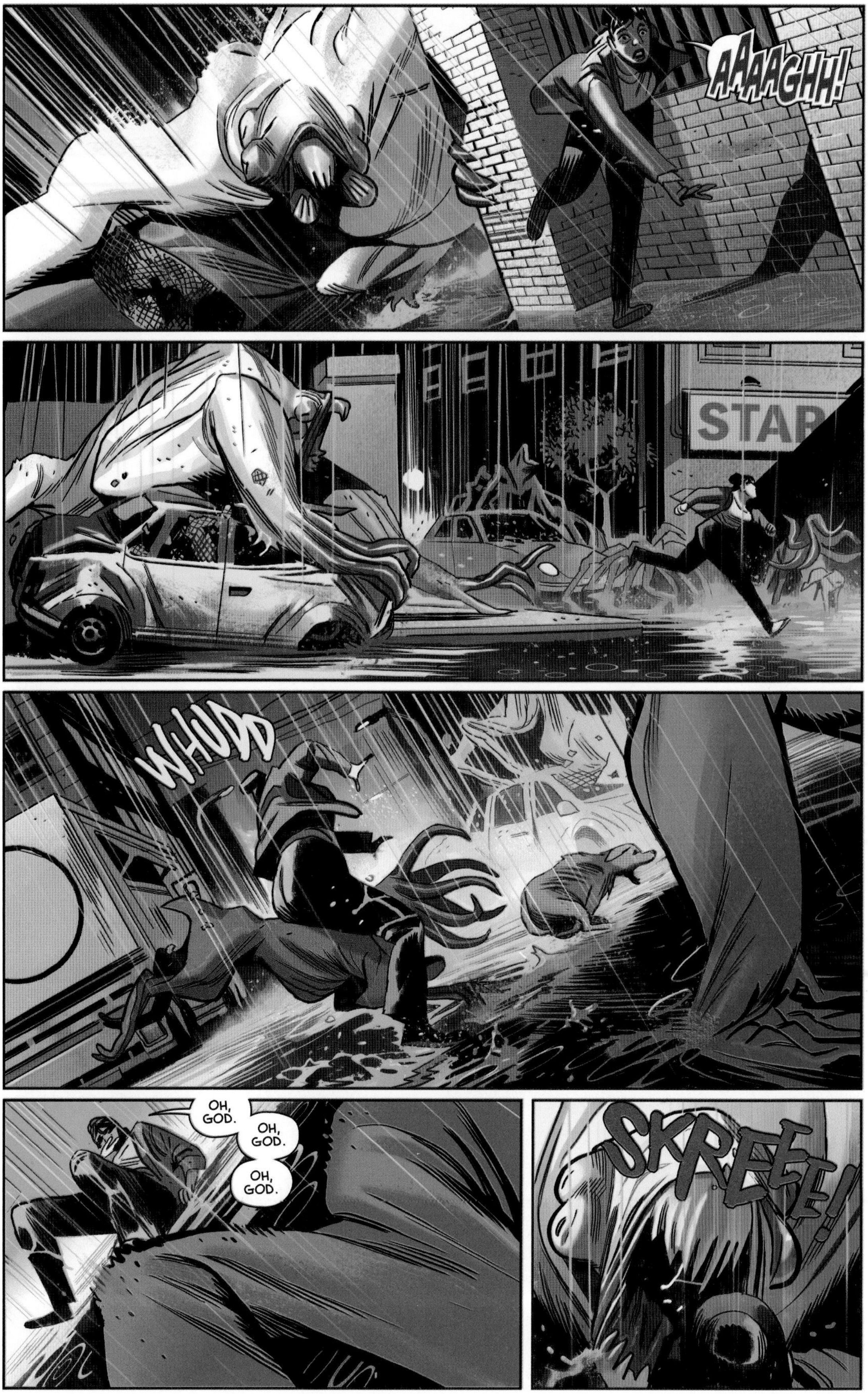

AAAAGHH!
STAR
WHUDD
OH, GOD.
OH, GOD.
OH, GOD.
SKREEEE!

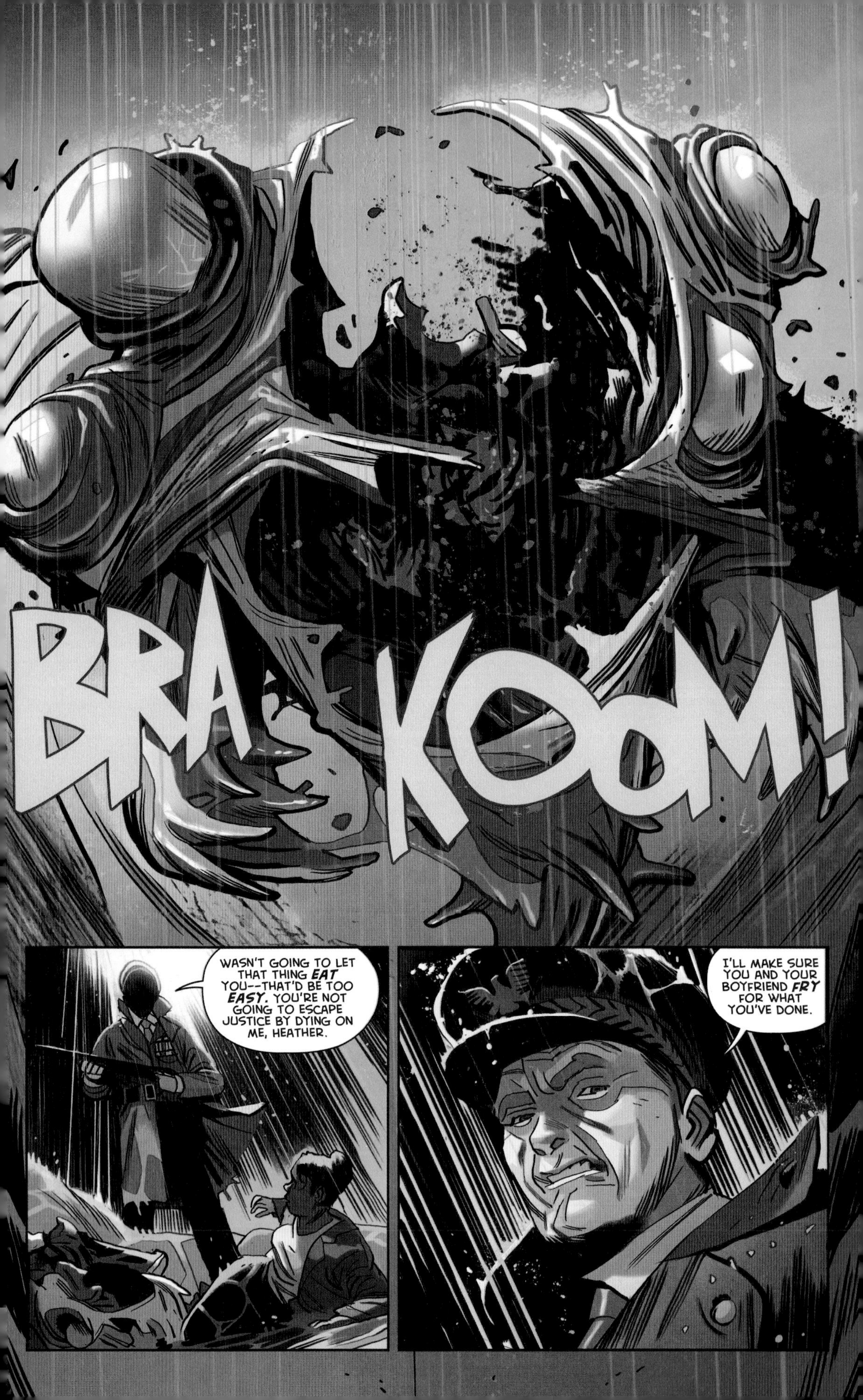
BRA KOOM!
WASN'T GOING TO LET THAT THING EAT YOU--THAT'D BE TOO EASY. YOU'RE NOT GOING TO ESCAPE JUSTICE BY DYING ON ME, HEATHER.
I'LL MAKE SURE YOU AND YOUR BOYFRIEND FRY FOR WHAT YOU'VE DONE.

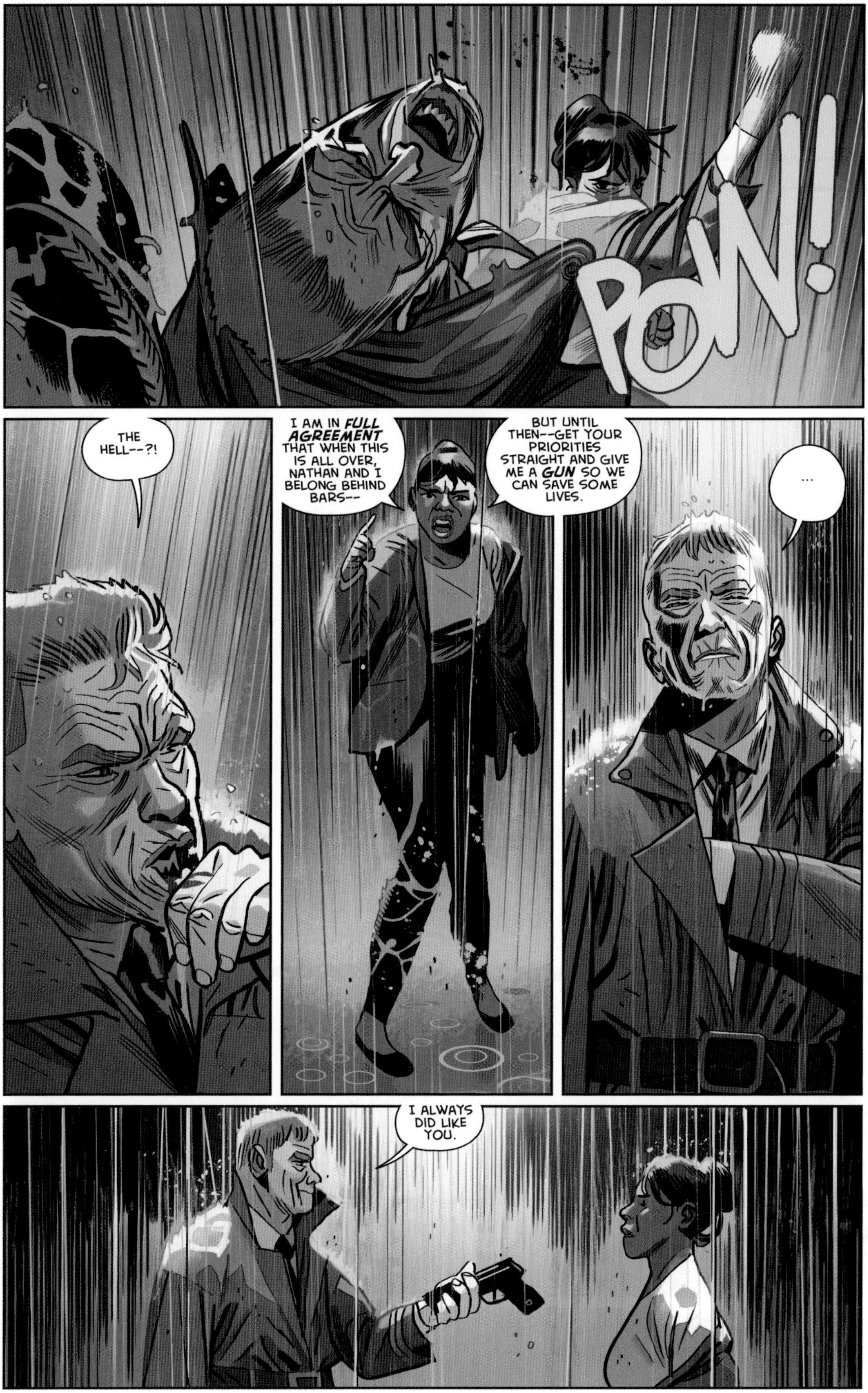
POW!
THE HELL--?!
I AM IN FULL AGREEMENT THAT WHEN THIS IS ALL OVER, NATHAN AND I BELONG BEHIND BARS--
BUT UNTIL THEN--GET YOUR PRIORITIES STRAIGHT AND GIVE ME A GUN SO WE CAN SAVE SOME LIVES.
...
I ALWAYS DID LIKE YOU.

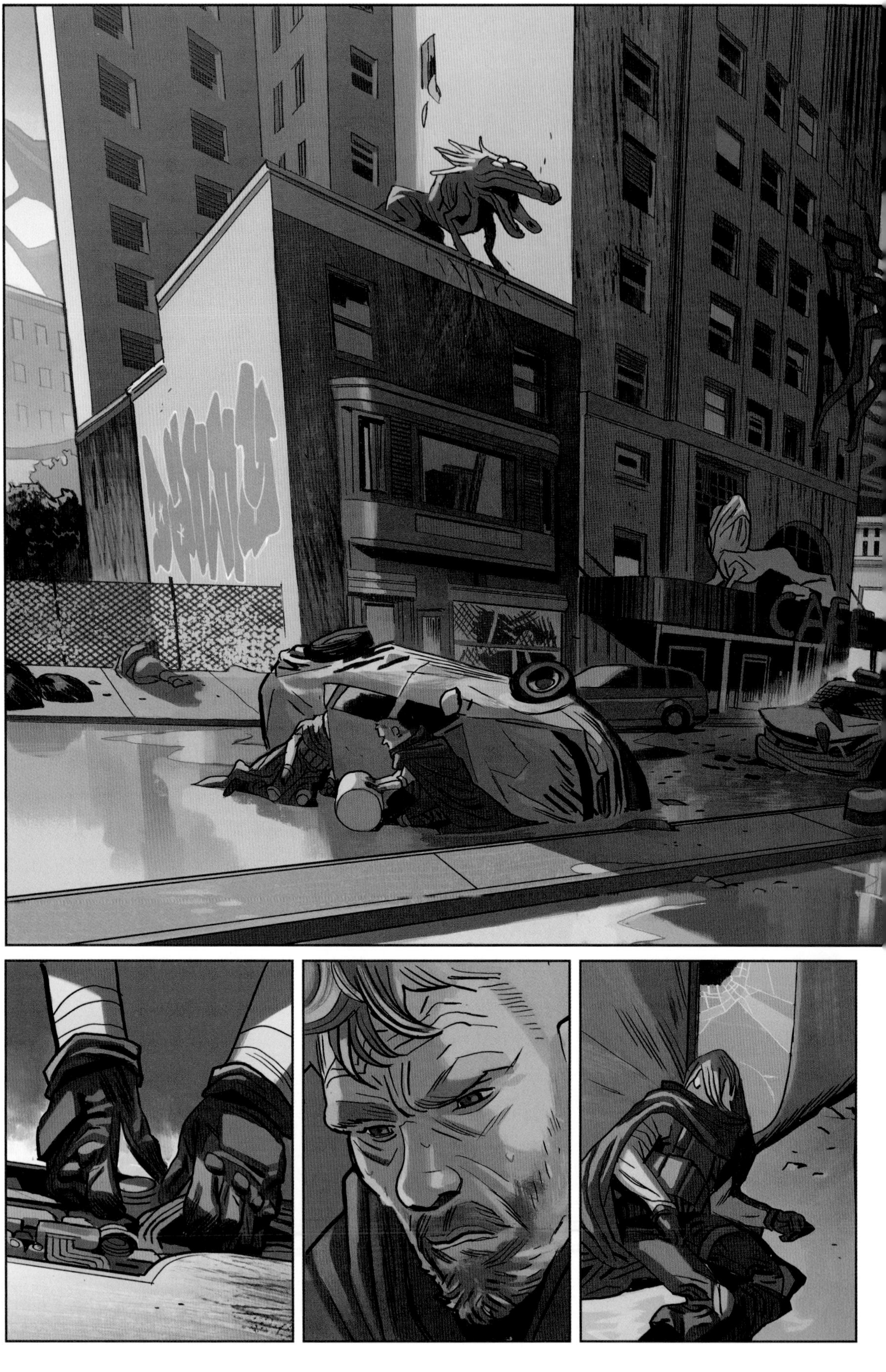

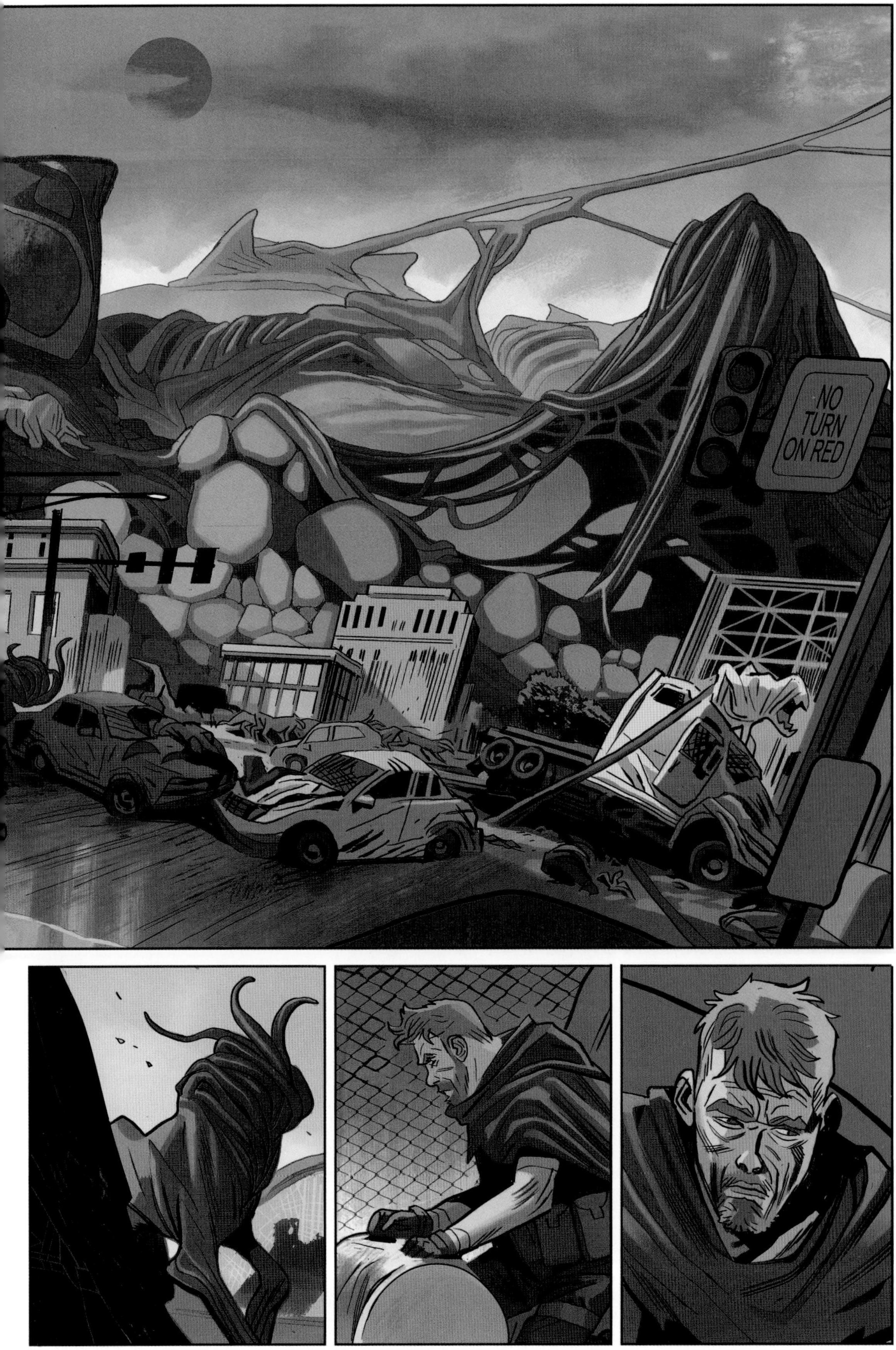
NO TURN ON RED

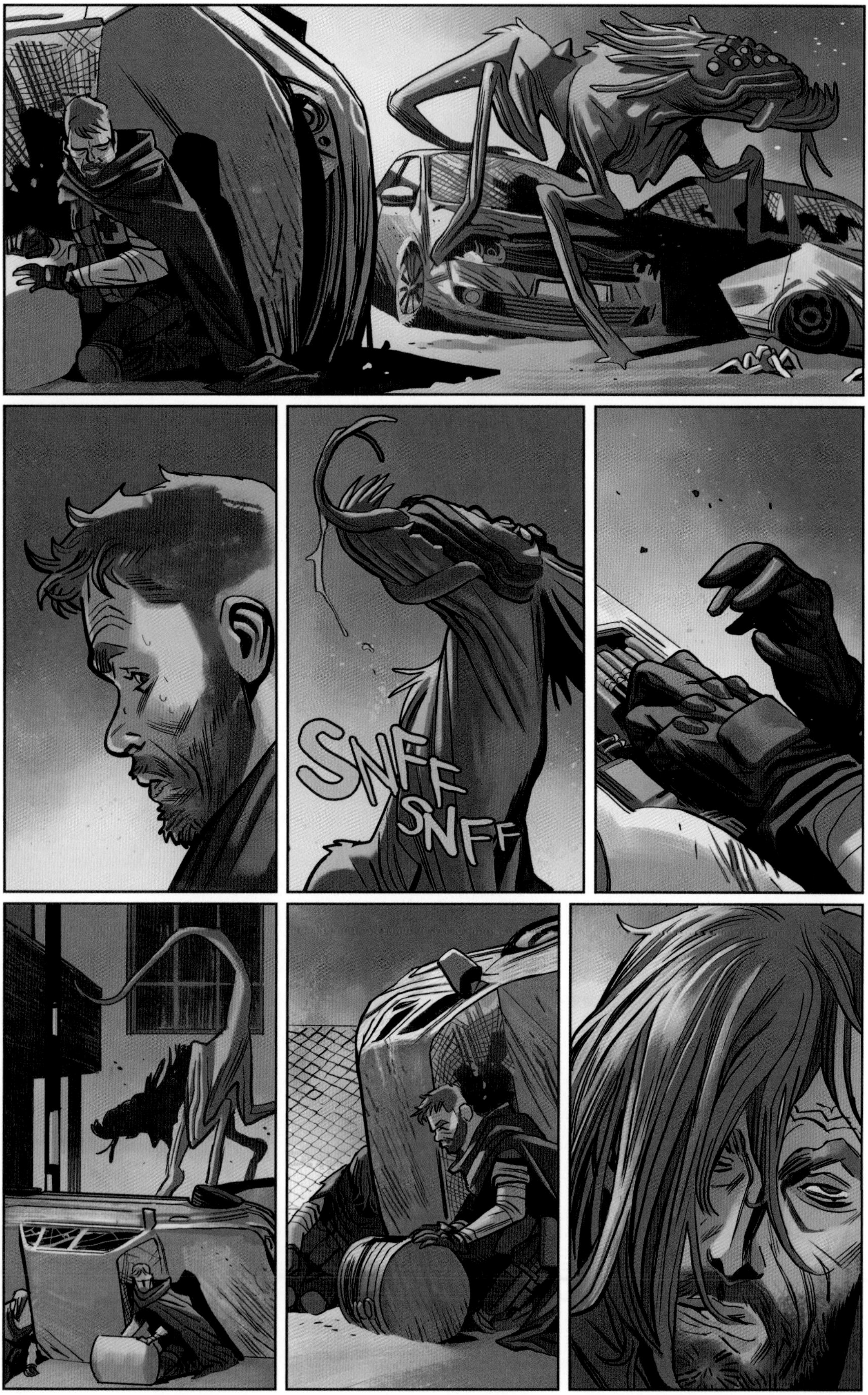
SNFF
SNFF

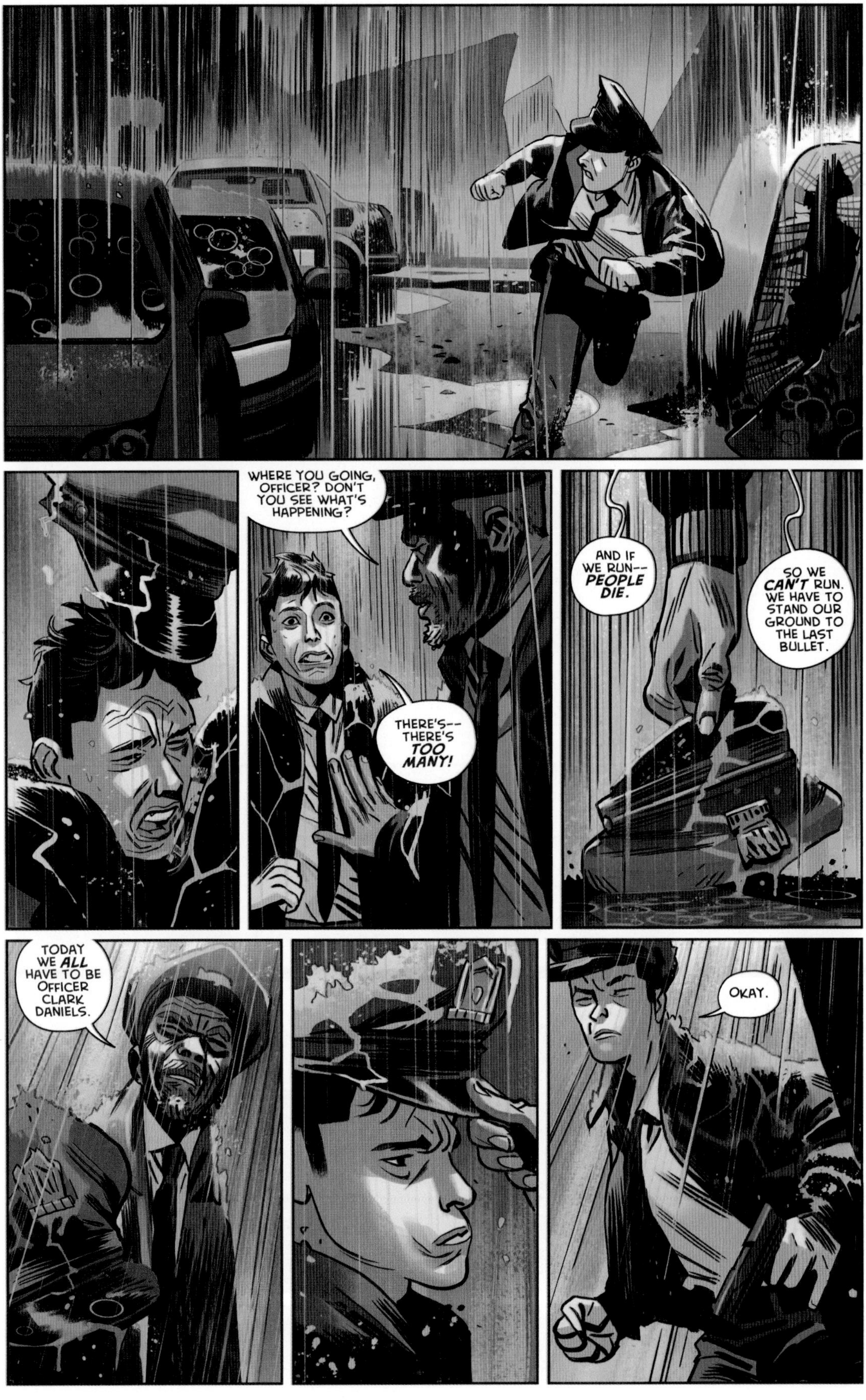

WHERE YOU GOING, OFFICER? DON'T YOU SEE WHAT'S HAPPENING?
THERE'S-- THERE'S TOO MANY!
AND IF WE RUN-- PEOPLE DIE.
SO WE CAN'T RUN. WE HAVE TO STAND OUR GROUND TO THE LAST BULLET.
TODAY WE ALL HAVE TO BE OFFICER CLARK DANIELS.
OKAY.

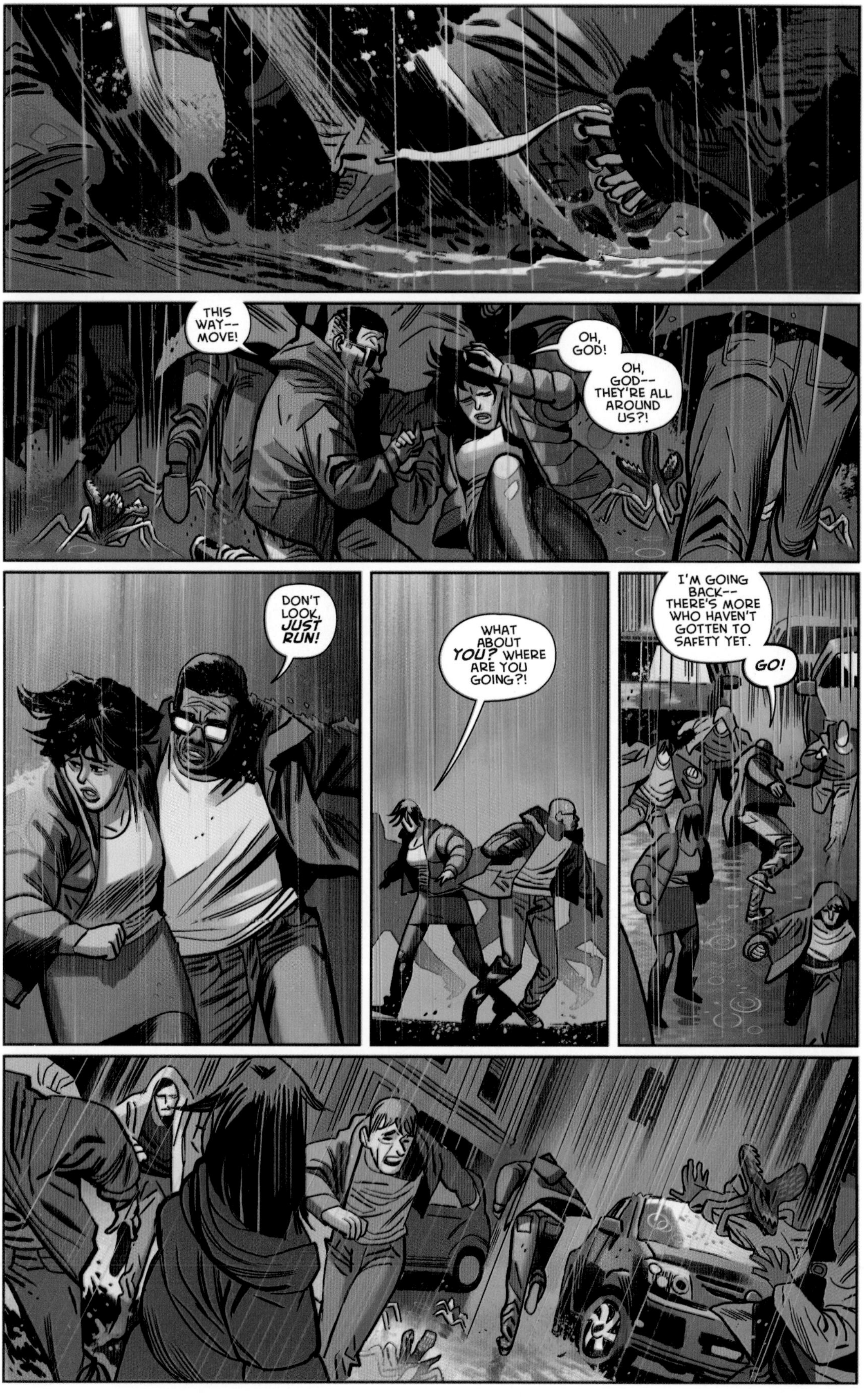
THIS WAY-- MOVE!
OH, GOD!
OH, GOD-- THEY'RE ALL AROUND US?!
DON'T LOOK, JUST RUN!
WHAT ABOUT YOU? WHERE ARE YOU GOING?!
I'M GOING BACK-- THERE'S MORE WHO HAVEN'T GOTTEN TO SAFETY YET.
GO!

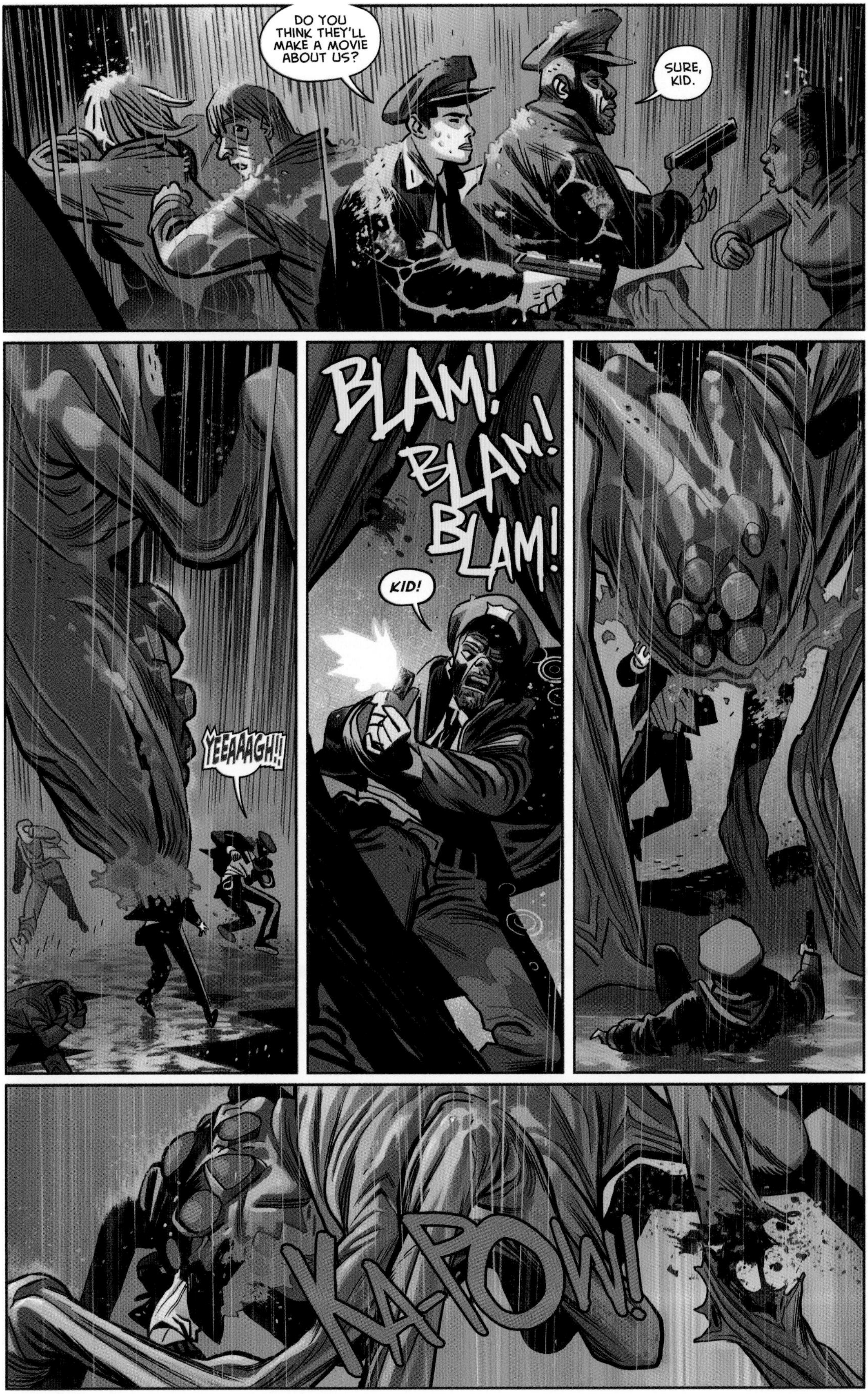
DO YOU THINK THEY'LL MAKE A MOVIE ABOUT US?
SURE, KID.
YEEAAAGH!!
BLAM! BLAM! BLAM!
KID!
KA-POW!

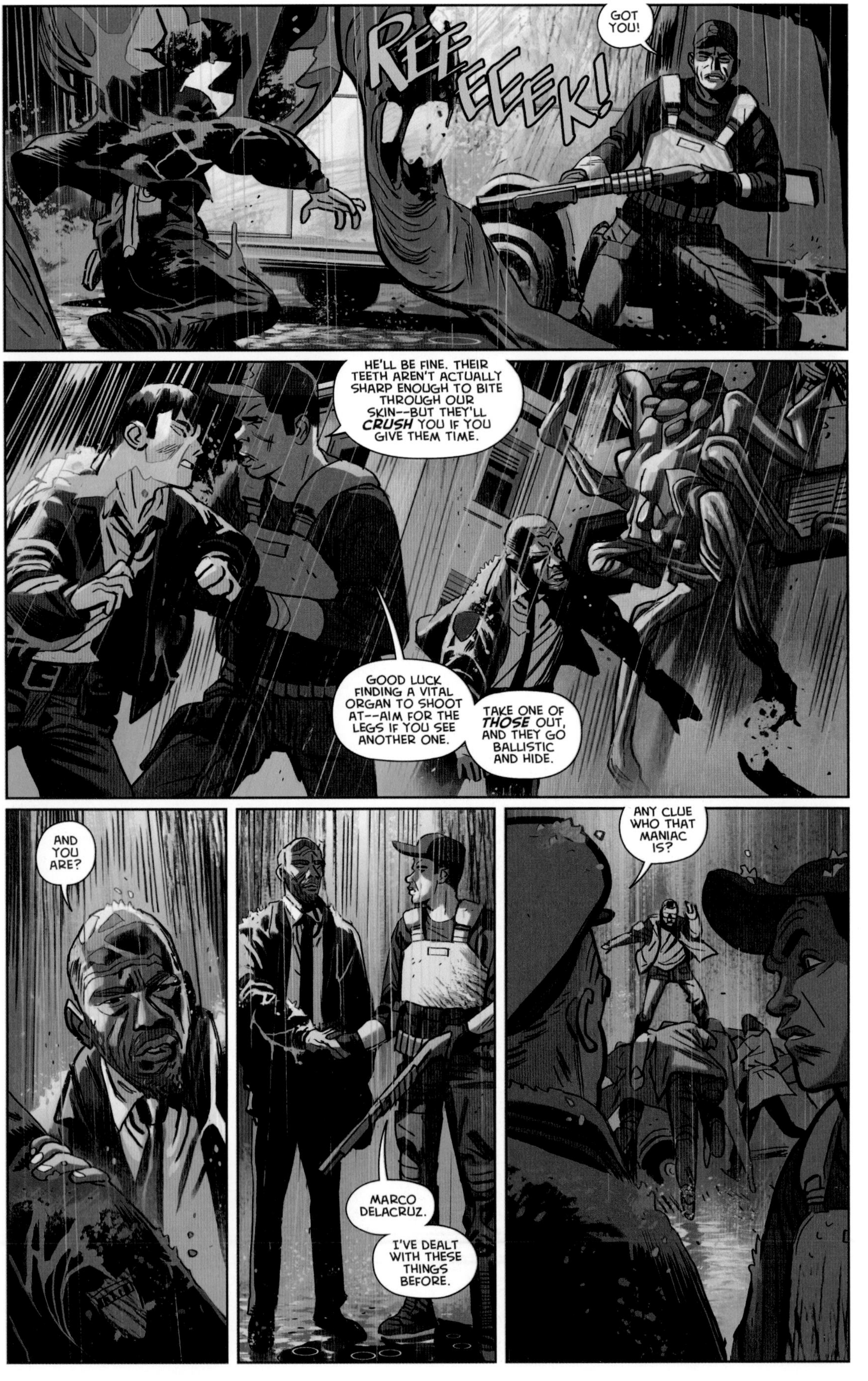
REEEEEEK!
GOT YOU!
HE'LL BE FINE. THEIR TEETH AREN'T ACTUALLY SHARP ENOUGH TO BITE THROUGH OUR SKIN--BUT THEY'LL CRUSH YOU IF YOU GIVE THEM TIME.
GOOD LUCK FINDING A VITAL ORGAN TO SHOOT AT--AIM FOR THE LEGS IF YOU SEE ANOTHER ONE.
TAKE ONE OF THOSE OUT, AND THEY GO BALLISTIC AND HIDE.
AND YOU ARE?
MARCO DELACRUZ.
I'VE DEALT WITH THESE THINGS BEFORE.
ANY CLUE WHO THAT MANIAC IS?

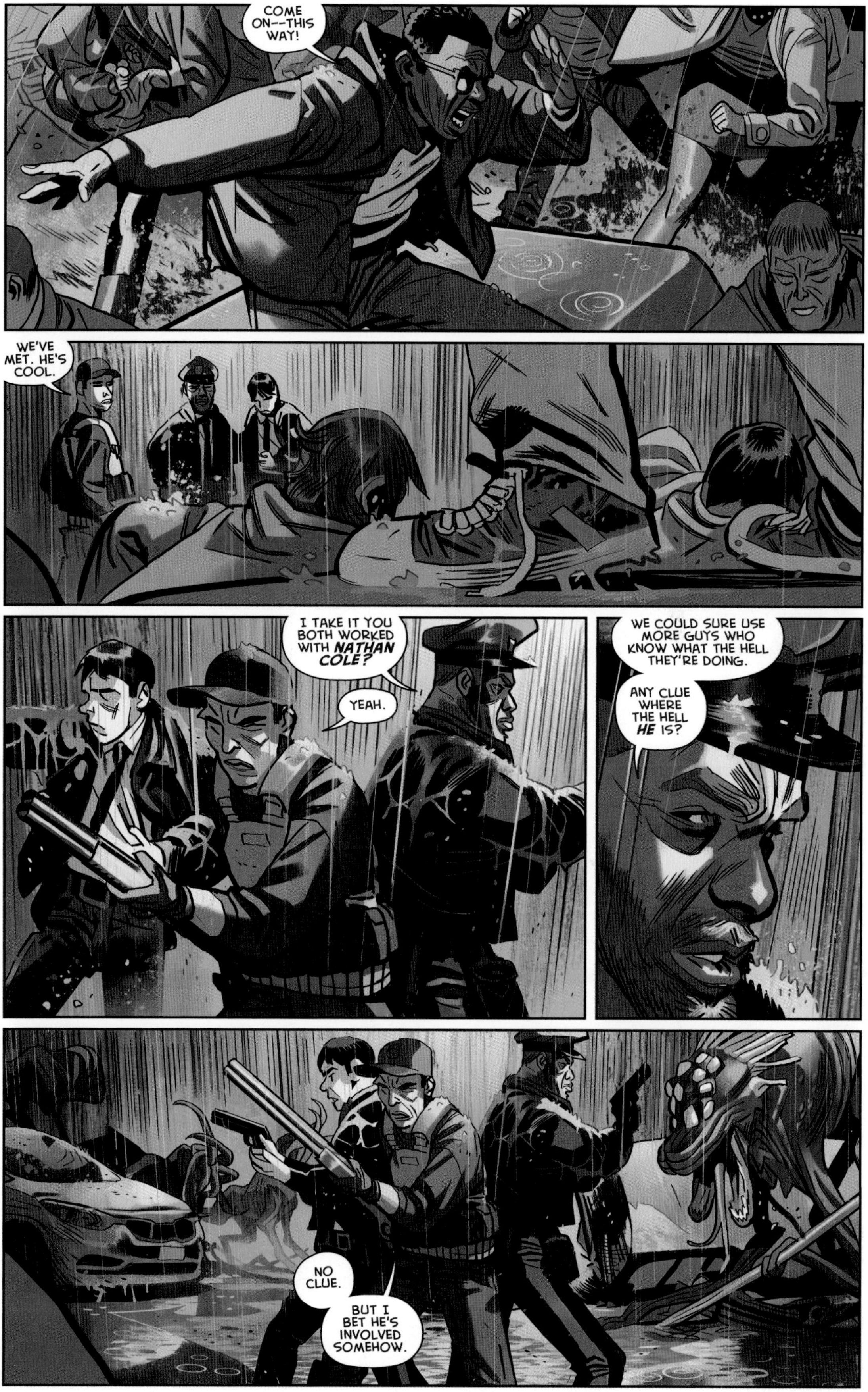
COME ON--THIS WAY!
WE'VE MET. HE'S COOL.
I TAKE IT YOU BOTH WORKED WITH NATHAN COLE?
YEAH.
WE COULD SURE USE MORE GUYS WHO KNOW WHAT THE HELL THEY'RE DOING.
ANY CLUE WHERE THE HELL HE IS?
NO CLUE.
BUT I BET HE'S INVOLVED SOMEHOW.

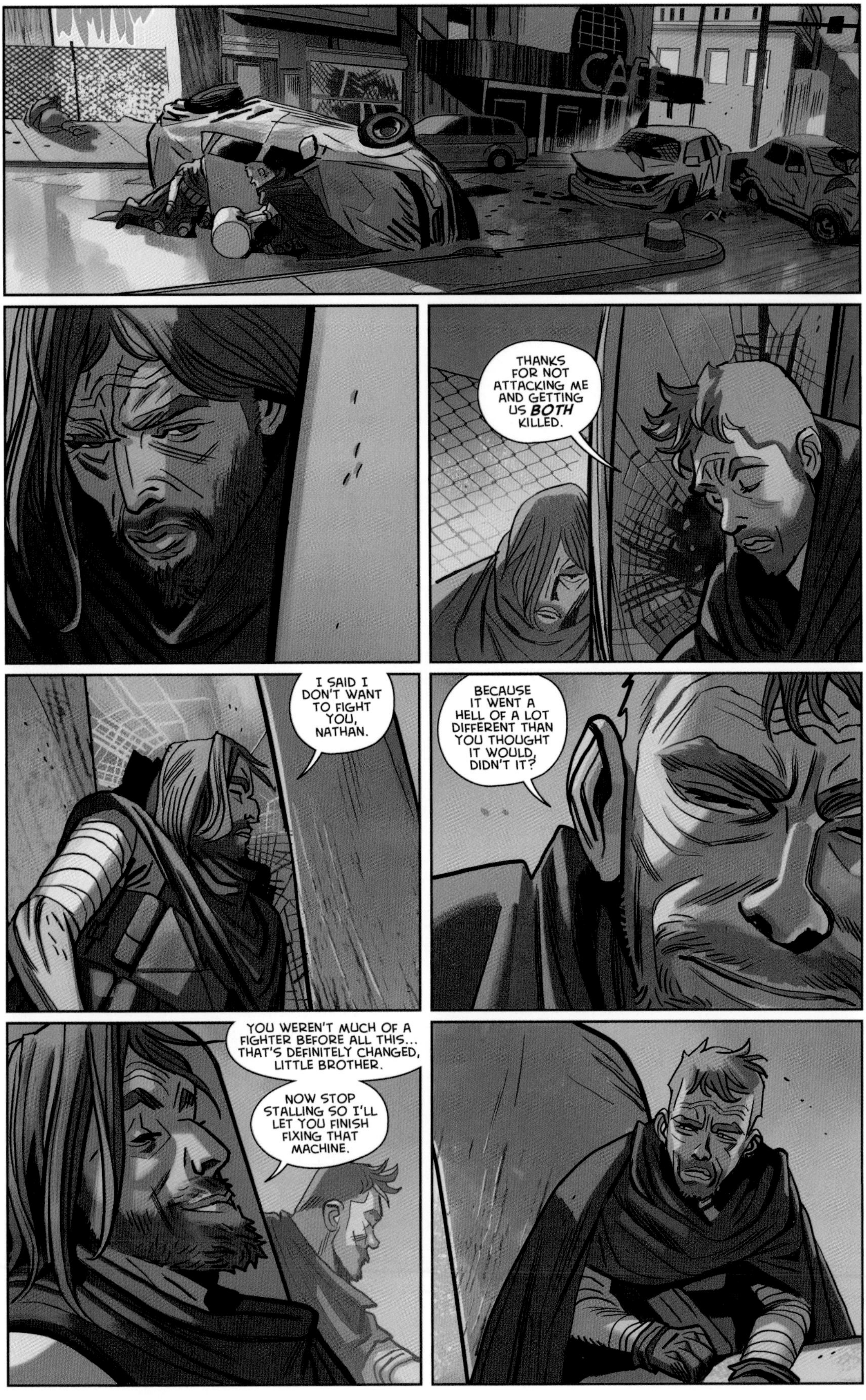
CAFE
THANKS FOR NOT ATTACKING ME AND GETTING US BOTH KILLED.
I SAID I DON'T WANT TO FIGHT YOU, NATHAN.
BECAUSE IT WENT A HELL OF A LOT DIFFERENT THAN YOU THOUGHT IT WOULD, DIDN'T IT?
YOU WEREN'T MUCH OF A FIGHTER BEFORE ALL THIS... THAT'S DEFINITELY CHANGED, LITTLE BROTHER.
NOW STOP STALLING SO I'LL LET YOU FINISH FIXING THAT MACHINE.

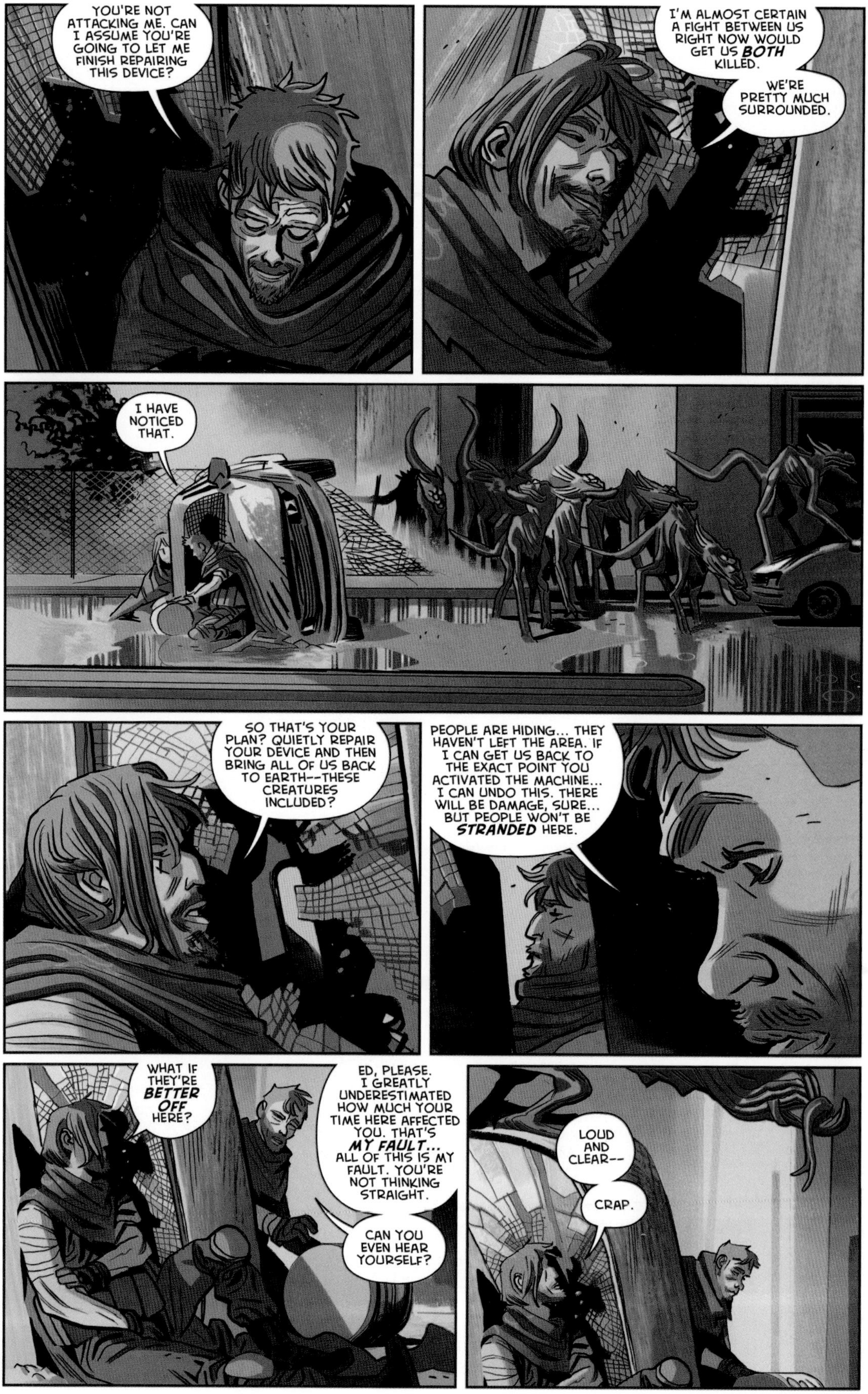
YOU'RE NOT ATTACKING ME. CAN I ASSUME YOU'RE GOING TO LET ME FINISH REPAIRING THIS DEVICE?
I'M ALMOST CERTAIN A FIGHT BETWEEN US RIGHT NOW WOULD GET US *BOTH* KILLED.
WE'RE PRETTY MUCH SURROUNDED.
I HAVE NOTICED THAT.
SO THAT'S YOUR PLAN? QUIETLY REPAIR YOUR DEVICE AND THEN BRING ALL OF US BACK TO EARTH--THESE CREATURES INCLUDED?
PEOPLE ARE HIDING... THEY HAVEN'T LEFT THE AREA. IF I CAN GET US BACK TO THE EXACT POINT YOU ACTIVATED THE MACHINE... I CAN UNDO THIS. THERE WILL BE DAMAGE, SURE... BUT PEOPLE WON'T BE *STRANDED* HERE.
WHAT IF THEY'RE *BETTER OFF* HERE?
ED, PLEASE. I GREATLY UNDERESTIMATED HOW MUCH YOUR TIME HERE AFFECTED YOU. THAT'S *MY FAULT...* ALL OF THIS IS MY FAULT. YOU'RE NOT THINKING STRAIGHT.
CAN YOU EVEN HEAR YOURSELF?
LOUD AND CLEAR--
CRAP.

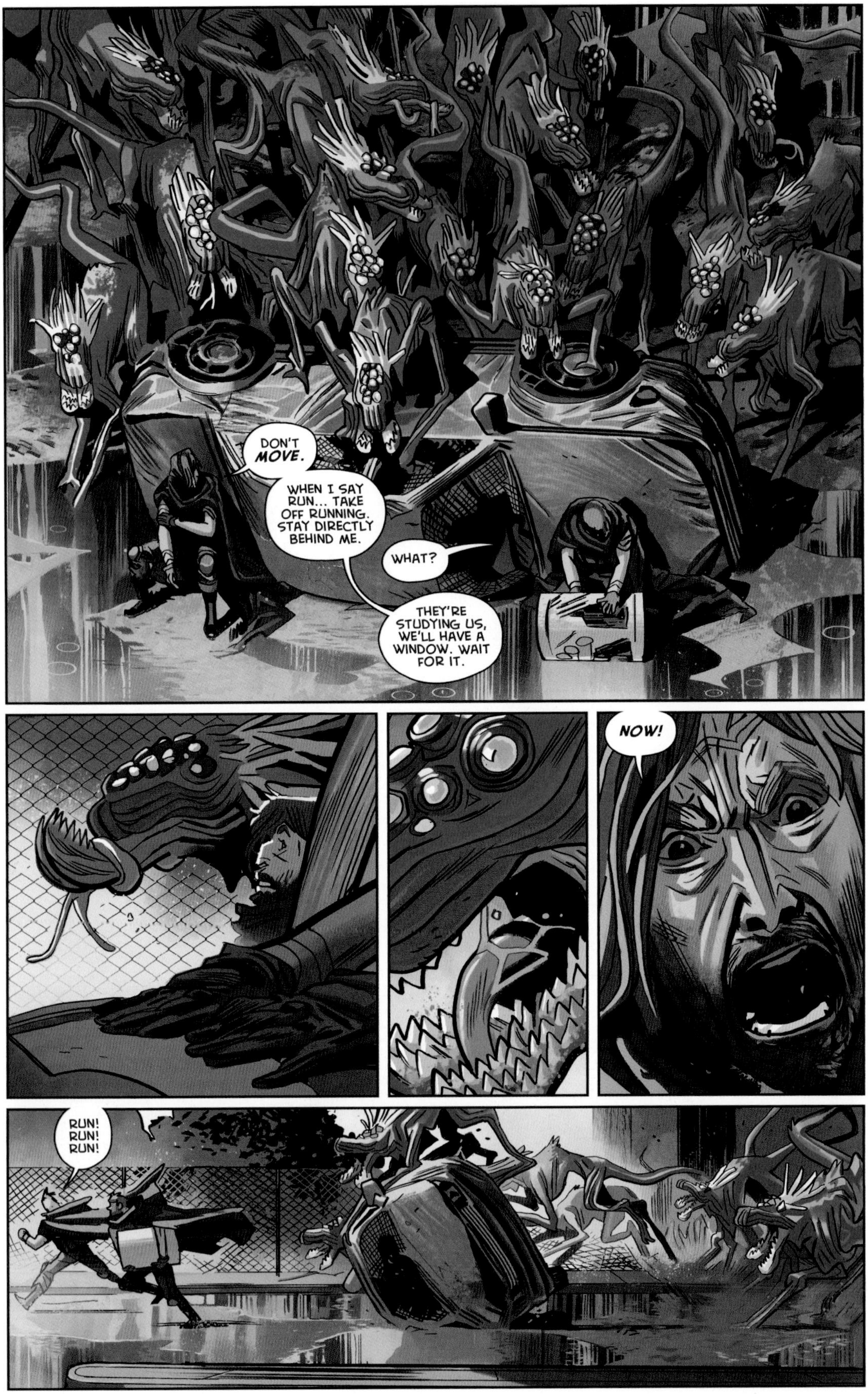
DON'T MOVE.
WHEN I SAY RUN... TAKE OFF RUNNING. STAY DIRECTLY BEHIND ME.
WHAT?
THEY'RE STUDYING US, WE'LL HAVE A WINDOW. WAIT FOR IT.
NOW!
RUN! RUN! RUN!

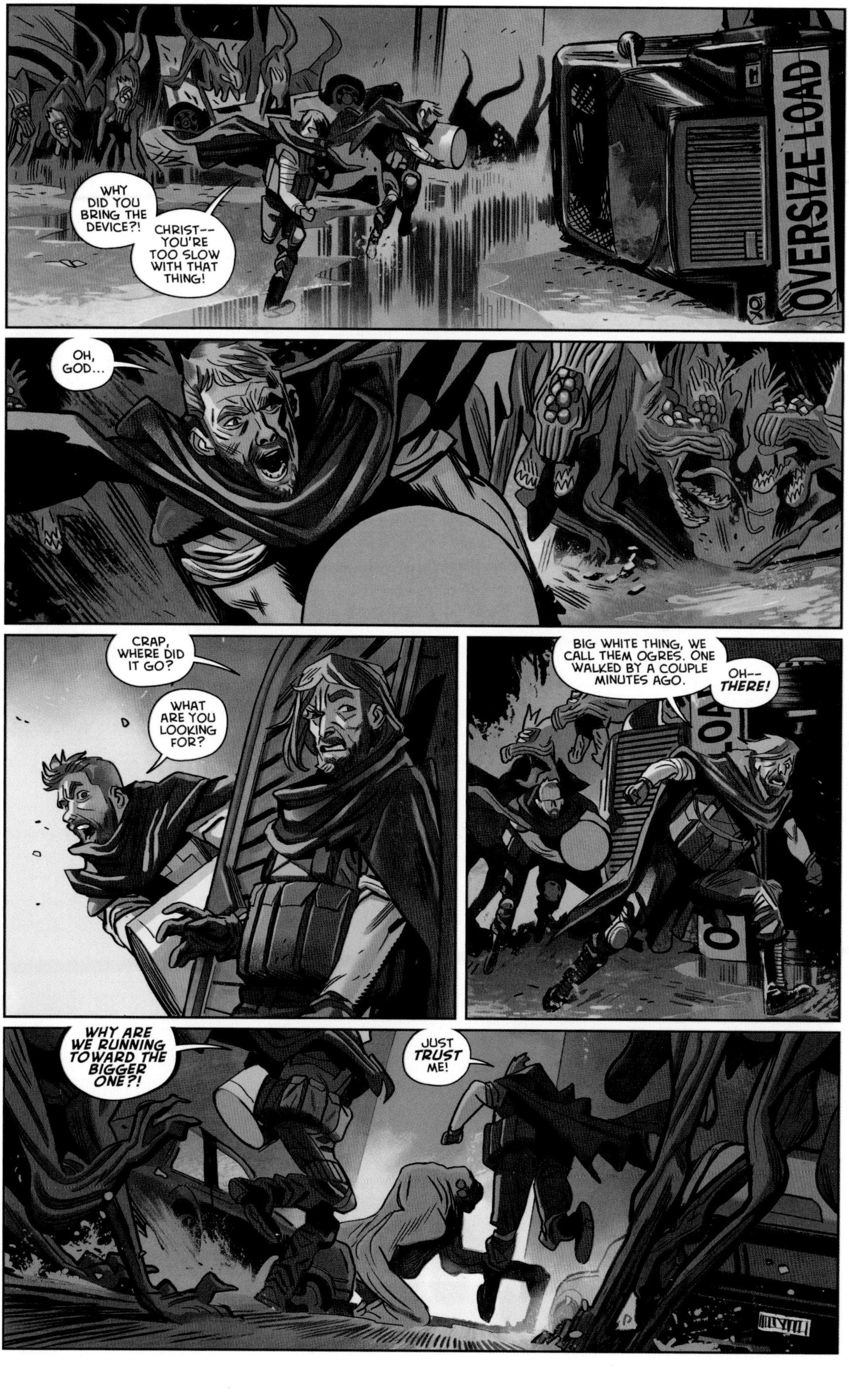
WHY DID YOU BRING THE DEVICE?!
CHRIST-- YOU'RE TOO SLOW WITH THAT THING!
OVERSIZE LOAD
OH, GOD...
CRAP, WHERE DID IT GO?
WHAT ARE YOU LOOKING FOR?
BIG WHITE THING, WE CALL THEM OGRES. ONE WALKED BY A COUPLE MINUTES AGO.
OH-- *THERE!*
WHY ARE WE RUNNING TOWARD THE BIGGER ONE?!
JUST *TRUST* ME!

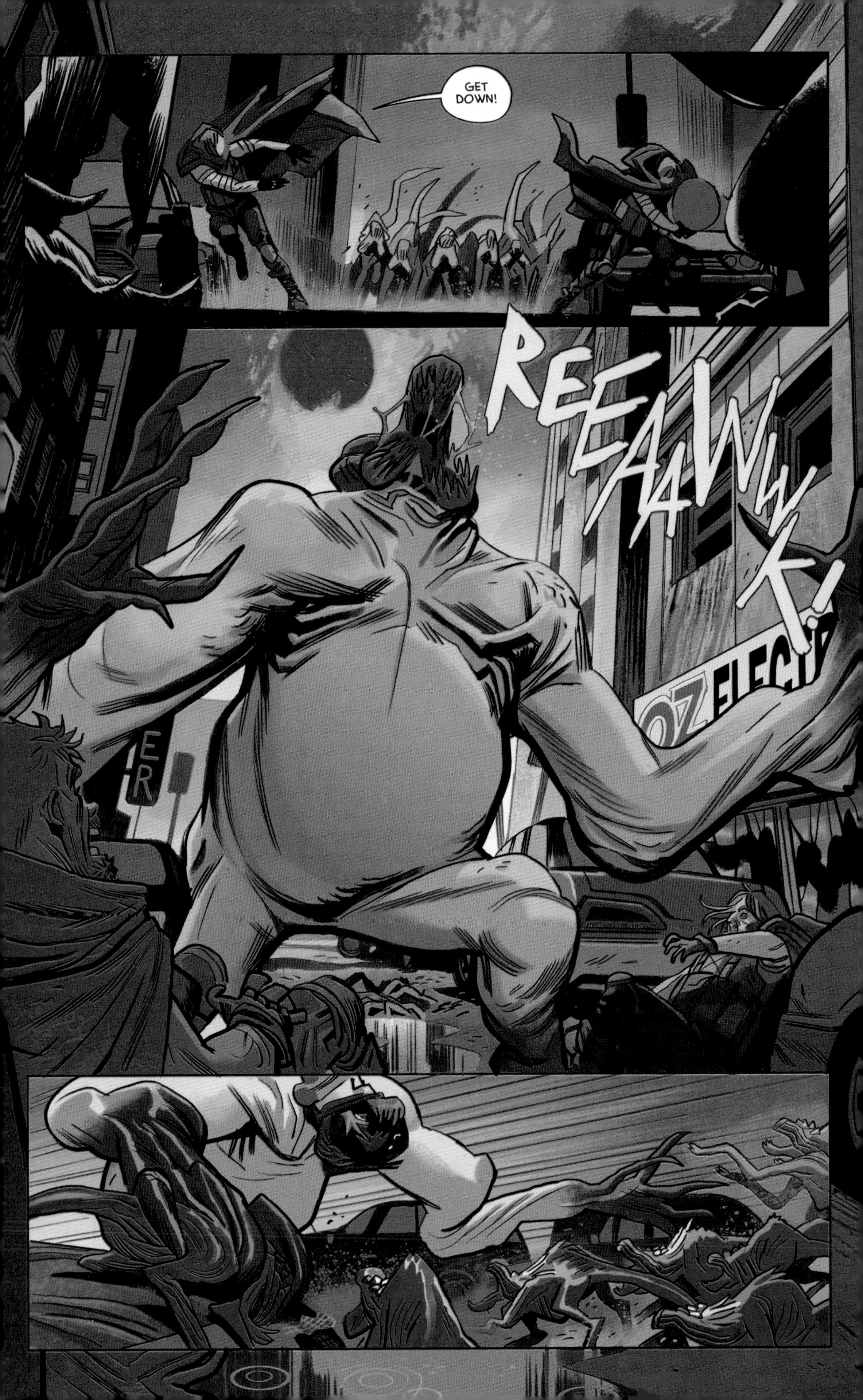
GET DOWN!
REEAAWWK!
OZ ELECT
ER

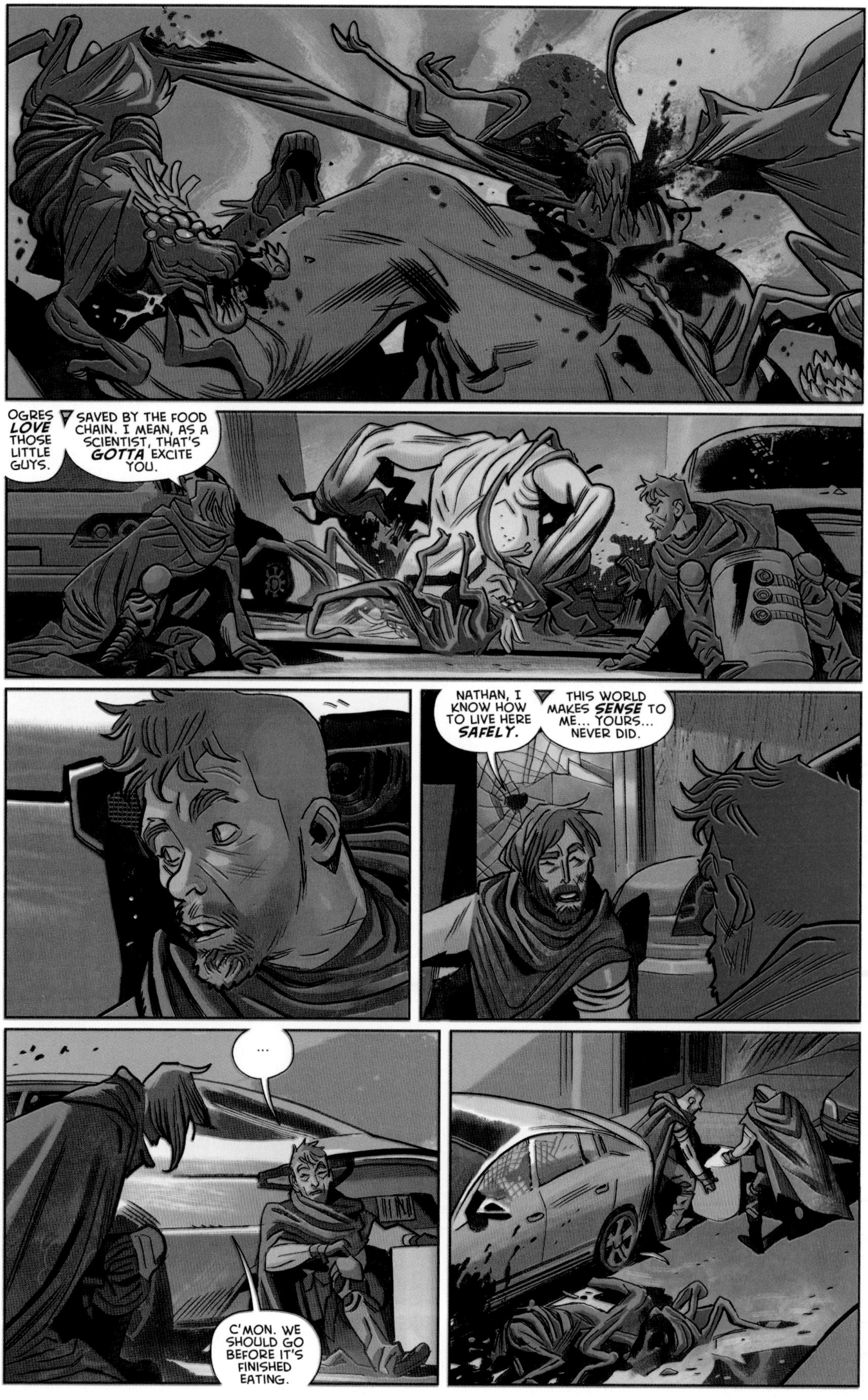
OGRES LOVE THOSE LITTLE GUYS.
SAVED BY THE FOOD CHAIN. I MEAN, AS A SCIENTIST, THAT'S GOTTA EXCITE YOU.
NATHAN, I KNOW HOW TO LIVE HERE SAFELY.
THIS WORLD MAKES SENSE TO ME... YOURS... NEVER DID.
...
C'MON. WE SHOULD GO BEFORE IT'S FINISHED EATING.

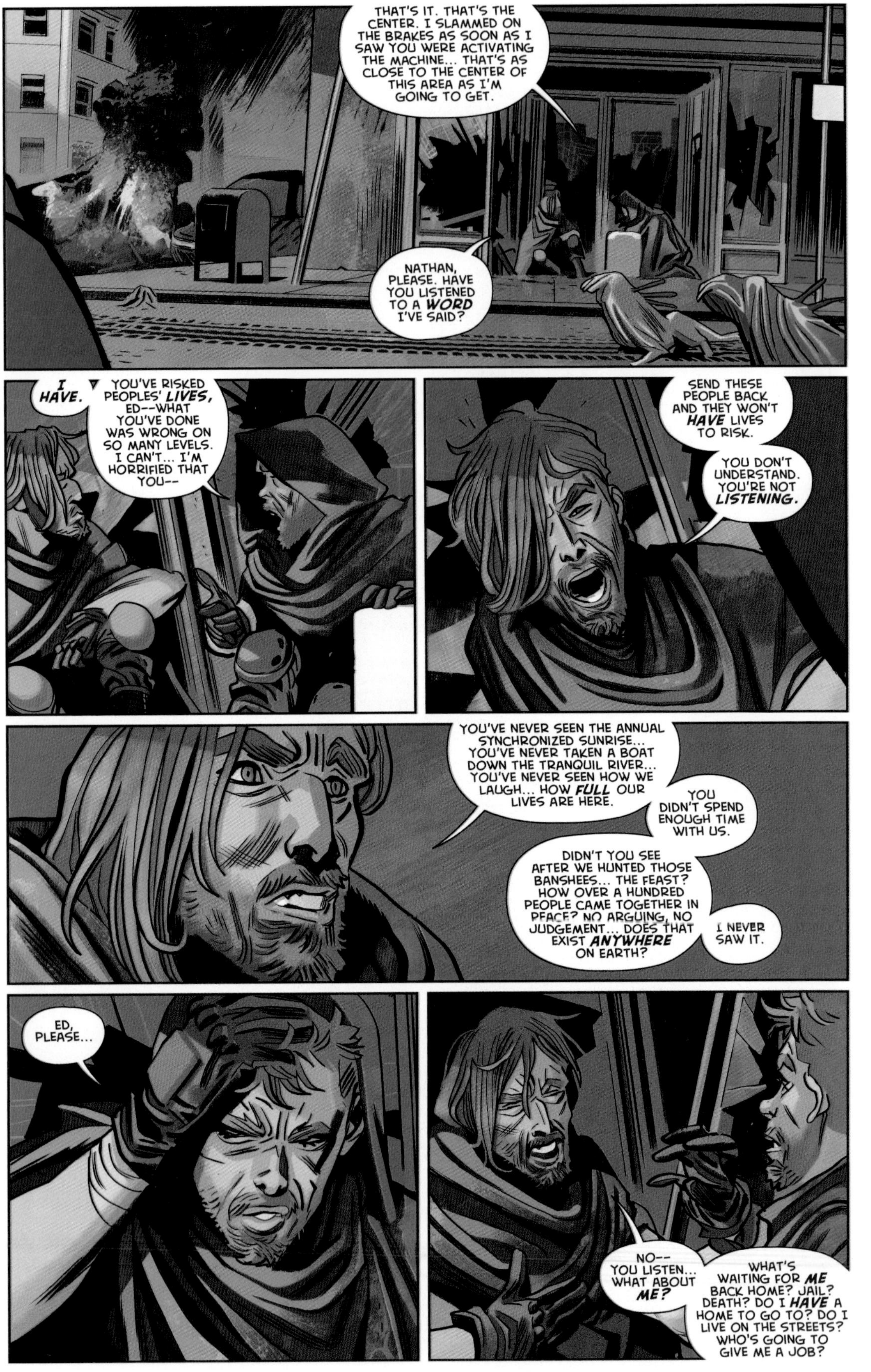
THAT'S IT. THAT'S THE CENTER. I SLAMMED ON THE BRAKES AS SOON AS I SAW YOU WERE ACTIVATING THE MACHINE... THAT'S AS CLOSE TO THE CENTER OF THIS AREA AS I'M GOING TO GET.
NATHAN, PLEASE. HAVE YOU LISTENED TO A WORD I'VE SAID?
I HAVE.
YOU'VE RISKED PEOPLES' LIVES, ED--WHAT YOU'VE DONE WAS WRONG ON SO MANY LEVELS. I CAN'T... I'M HORRIFIED THAT YOU--
SEND THESE PEOPLE BACK AND THEY WON'T HAVE LIVES TO RISK.
YOU DON'T UNDERSTAND. YOU'RE NOT LISTENING.
YOU'VE NEVER SEEN THE ANNUAL SYNCHRONIZED SUNRISE... YOU'VE NEVER TAKEN A BOAT DOWN THE TRANQUIL RIVER... YOU'VE NEVER SEEN HOW WE LAUGH... HOW FULL OUR LIVES ARE HERE.
YOU DIDN'T SPEND ENOUGH TIME WITH US.
DIDN'T YOU SEE AFTER WE HUNTED THOSE BANSHEES... THE FEAST? HOW OVER A HUNDRED PEOPLE CAME TOGETHER IN PEACE? NO ARGUING, NO JUDGEMENT... DOES THAT EXIST ANYWHERE ON EARTH?
I NEVER SAW IT.
ED, PLEASE...
NO-- YOU LISTEN... WHAT ABOUT ME?
WHAT'S WAITING FOR ME BACK HOME? JAIL? DEATH? DO I HAVE A HOME TO GO TO? DO I LIVE ON THE STREETS? WHO'S GOING TO GIVE ME A JOB?

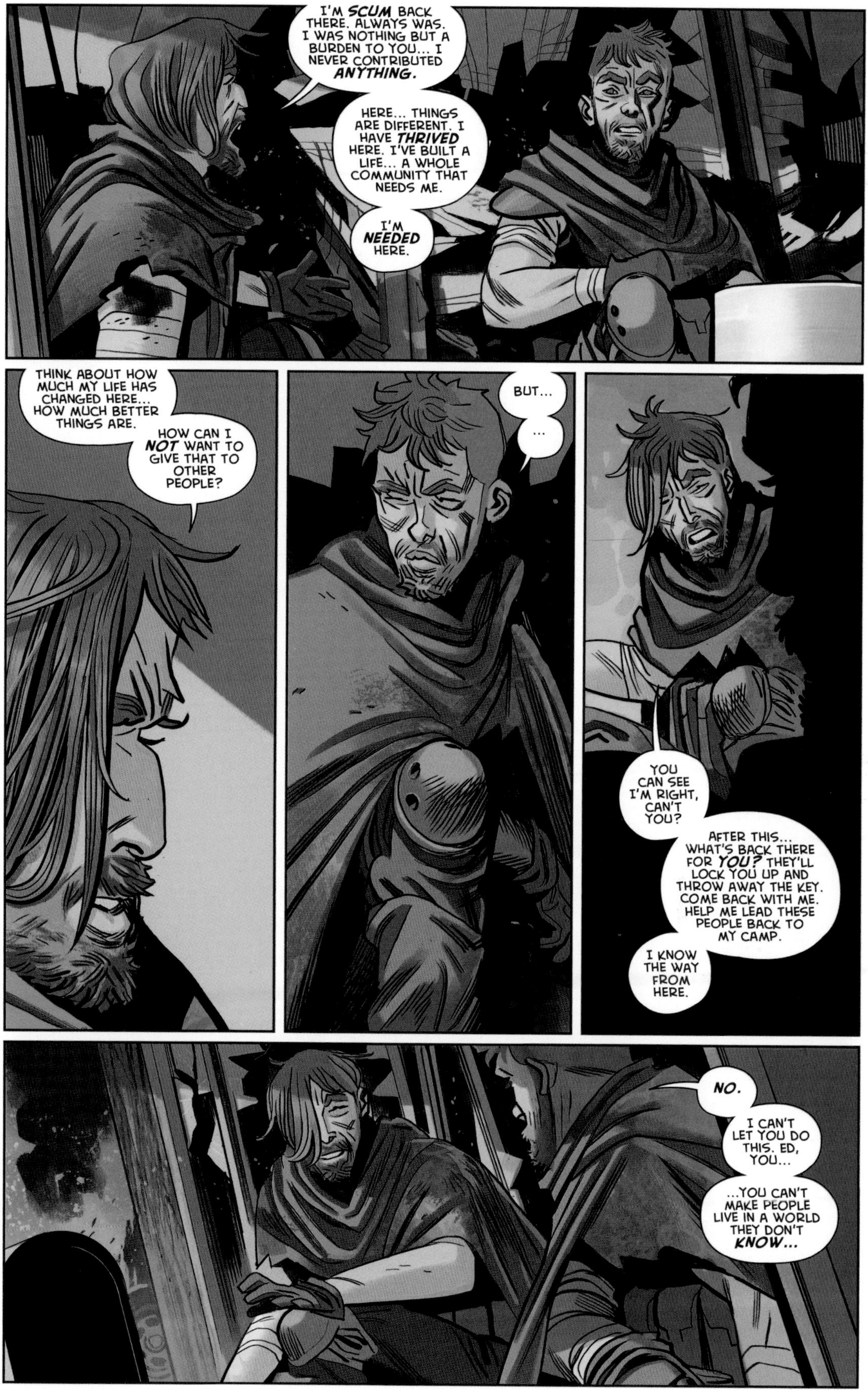
I'M SCUM BACK THERE. ALWAYS WAS. I WAS NOTHING BUT A BURDEN TO YOU... I NEVER CONTRIBUTED ANYTHING.
HERE... THINGS ARE DIFFERENT. I HAVE THRIVED HERE. I'VE BUILT A LIFE... A WHOLE COMMUNITY THAT NEEDS ME.
I'M NEEDED HERE.
THINK ABOUT HOW MUCH MY LIFE HAS CHANGED HERE... HOW MUCH BETTER THINGS ARE.
HOW CAN I NOT WANT TO GIVE THAT TO OTHER PEOPLE?
BUT...
...
YOU CAN SEE I'M RIGHT, CAN'T YOU?
AFTER THIS... WHAT'S BACK THERE FOR YOU? THEY'LL LOCK YOU UP AND THROW AWAY THE KEY. COME BACK WITH ME. HELP ME LEAD THESE PEOPLE BACK TO MY CAMP.
I KNOW THE WAY FROM HERE.
NO.
I CAN'T LET YOU DO THIS. ED, YOU...
...YOU CAN'T MAKE PEOPLE LIVE IN A WORLD THEY DON'T KNOW...

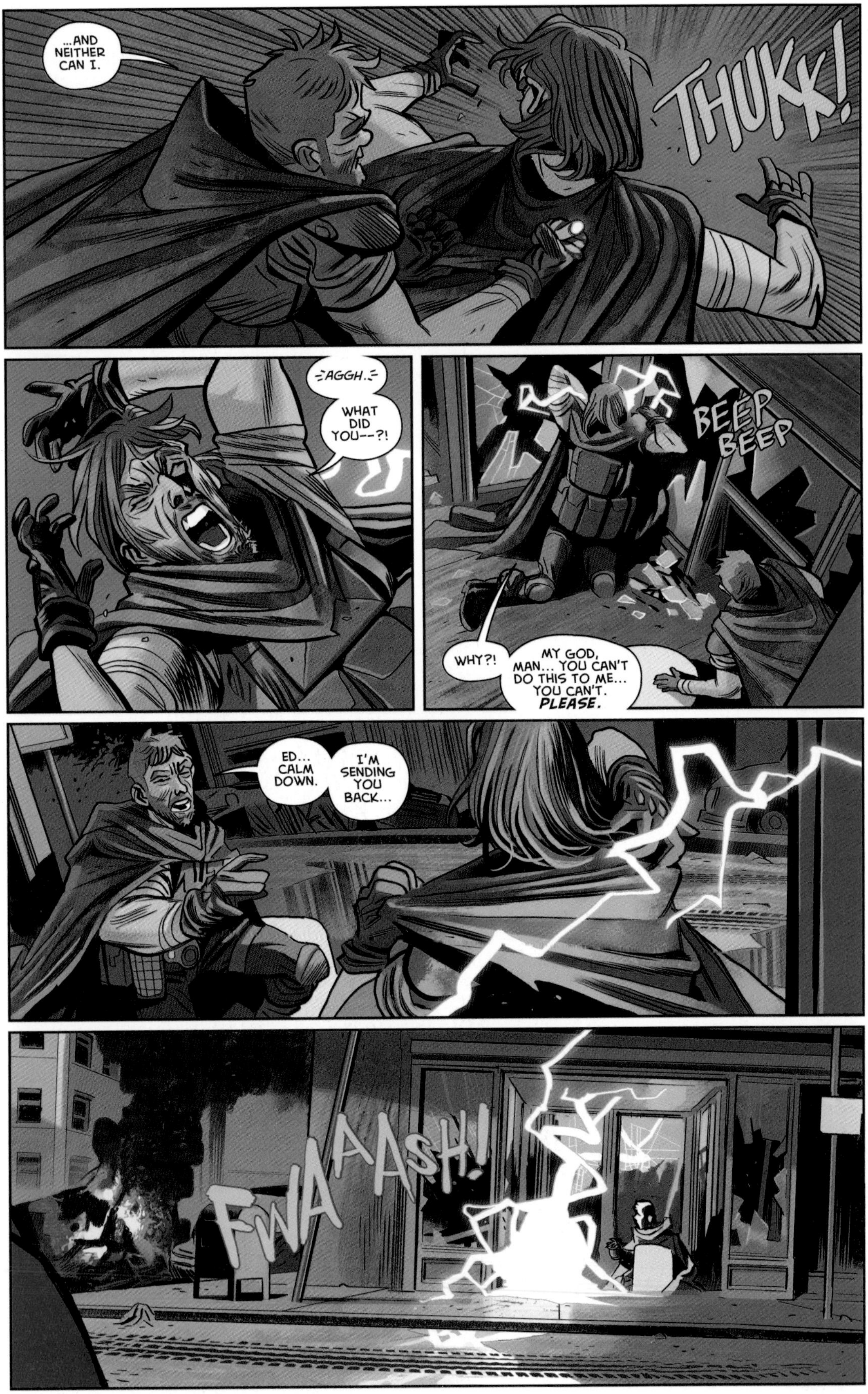
...AND NEITHER CAN I.
THUKK!
AGGH.
WHAT DID YOU--?!
BEEP BEEP
WHY?!
MY GOD, MAN... YOU CAN'T DO THIS TO ME... YOU CAN'T. PLEASE.
ED... CALM DOWN.
I'M SENDING YOU BACK...
FWAAASH!

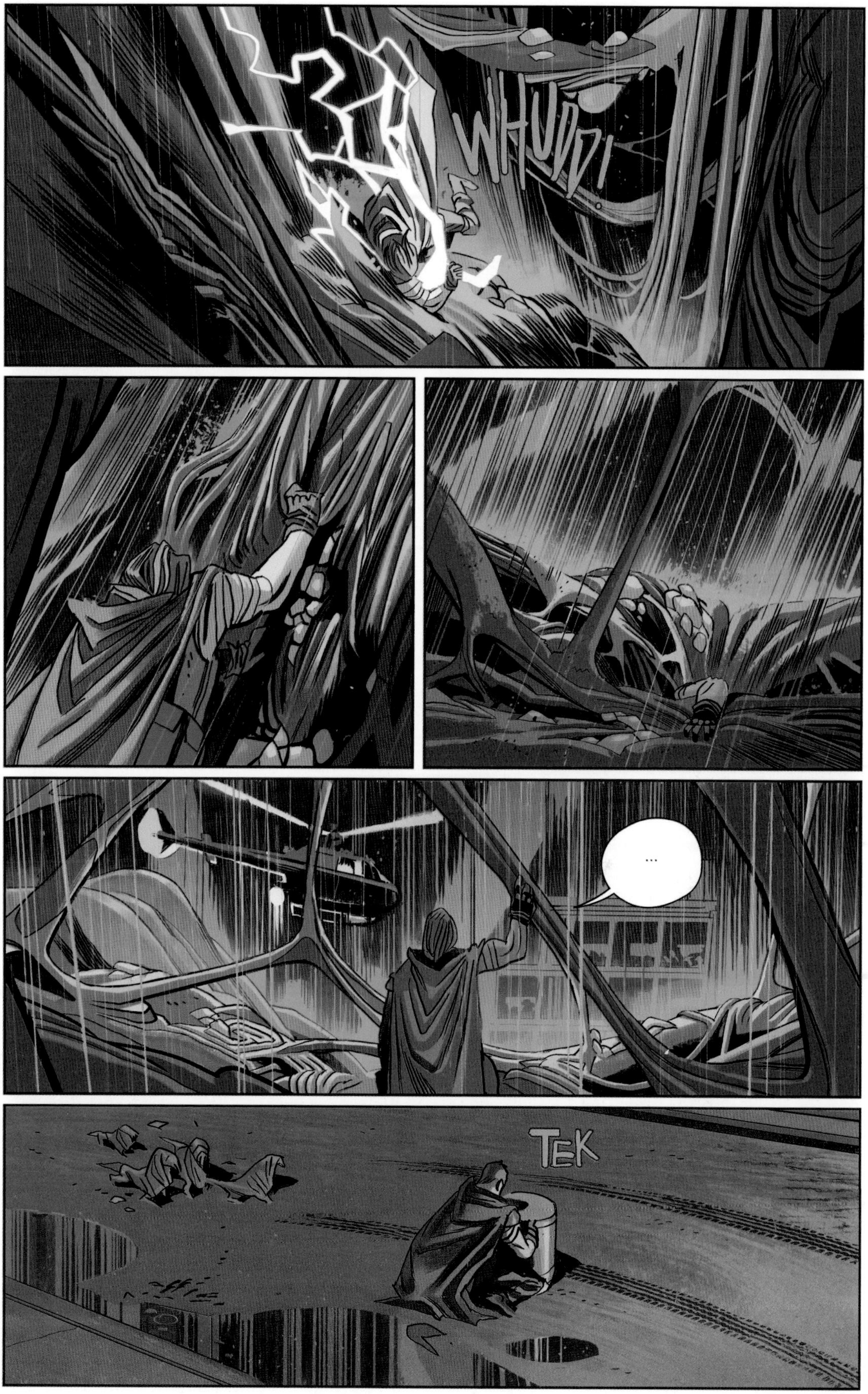
WHUDD!
...
TEK

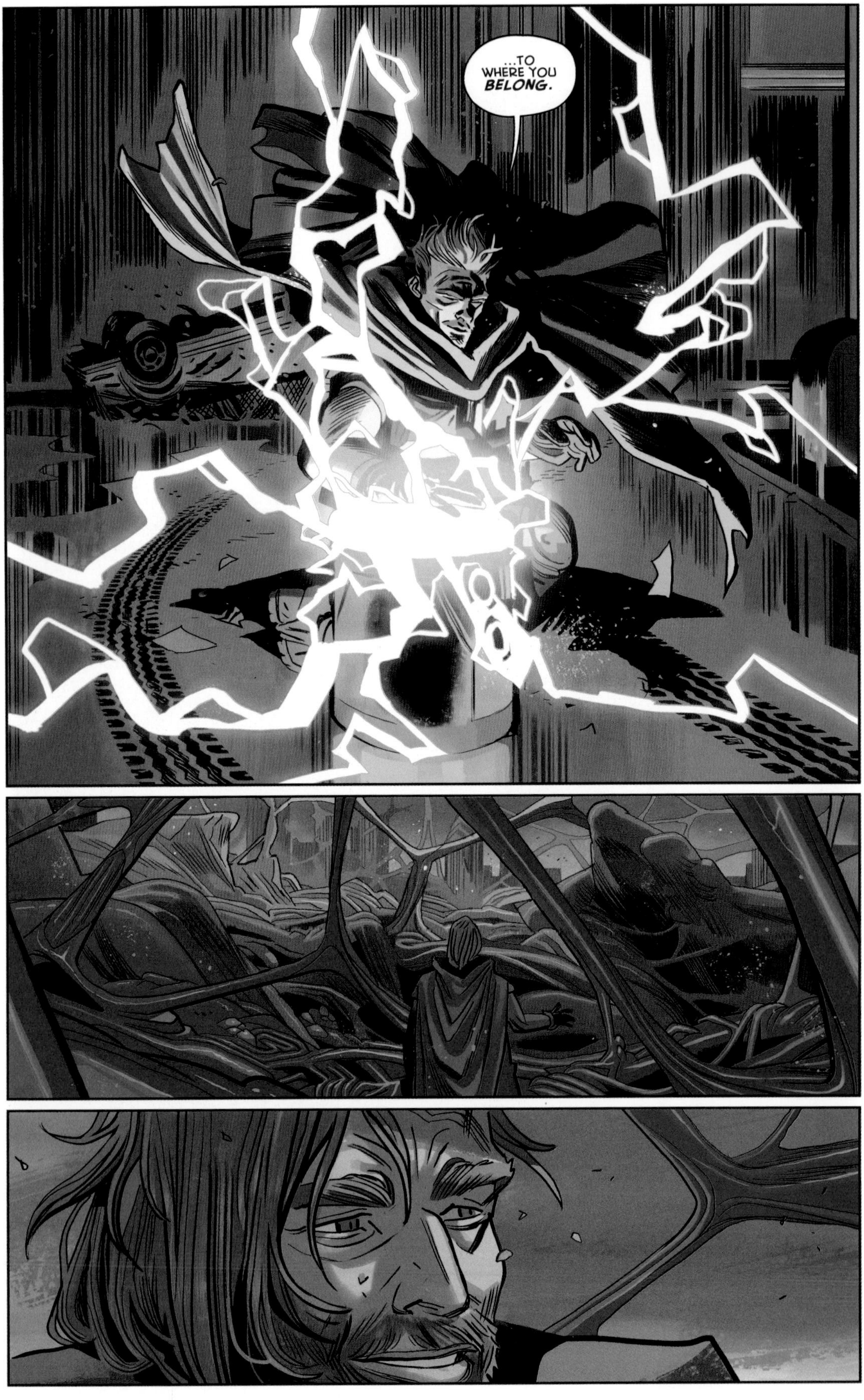
...TO WHERE YOU BELONG.

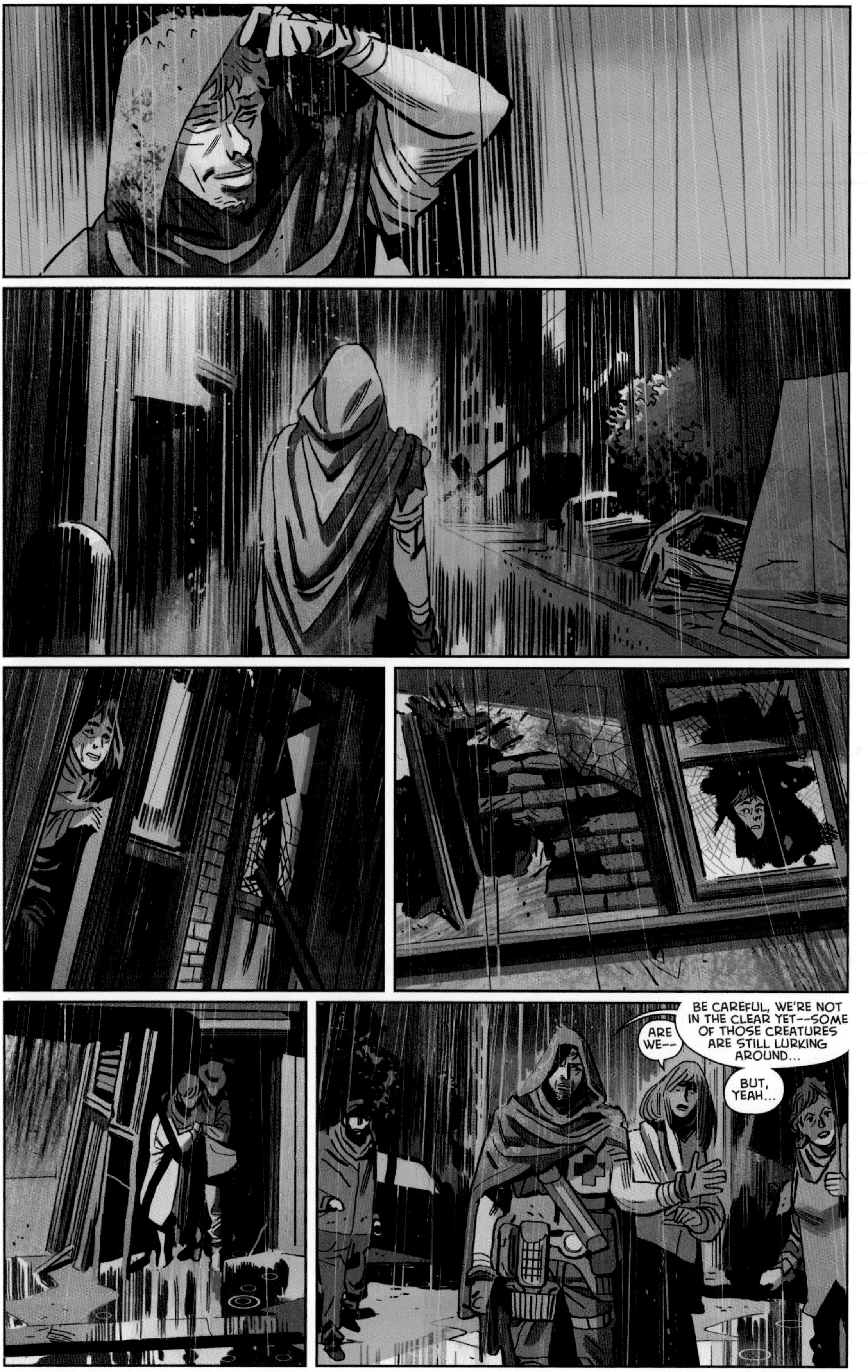
ARE WE--
BE CAREFUL, WE'RE NOT IN THE CLEAR YET--SOME OF THOSE CREATURES ARE STILL LURKING AROUND...
BUT, YEAH...

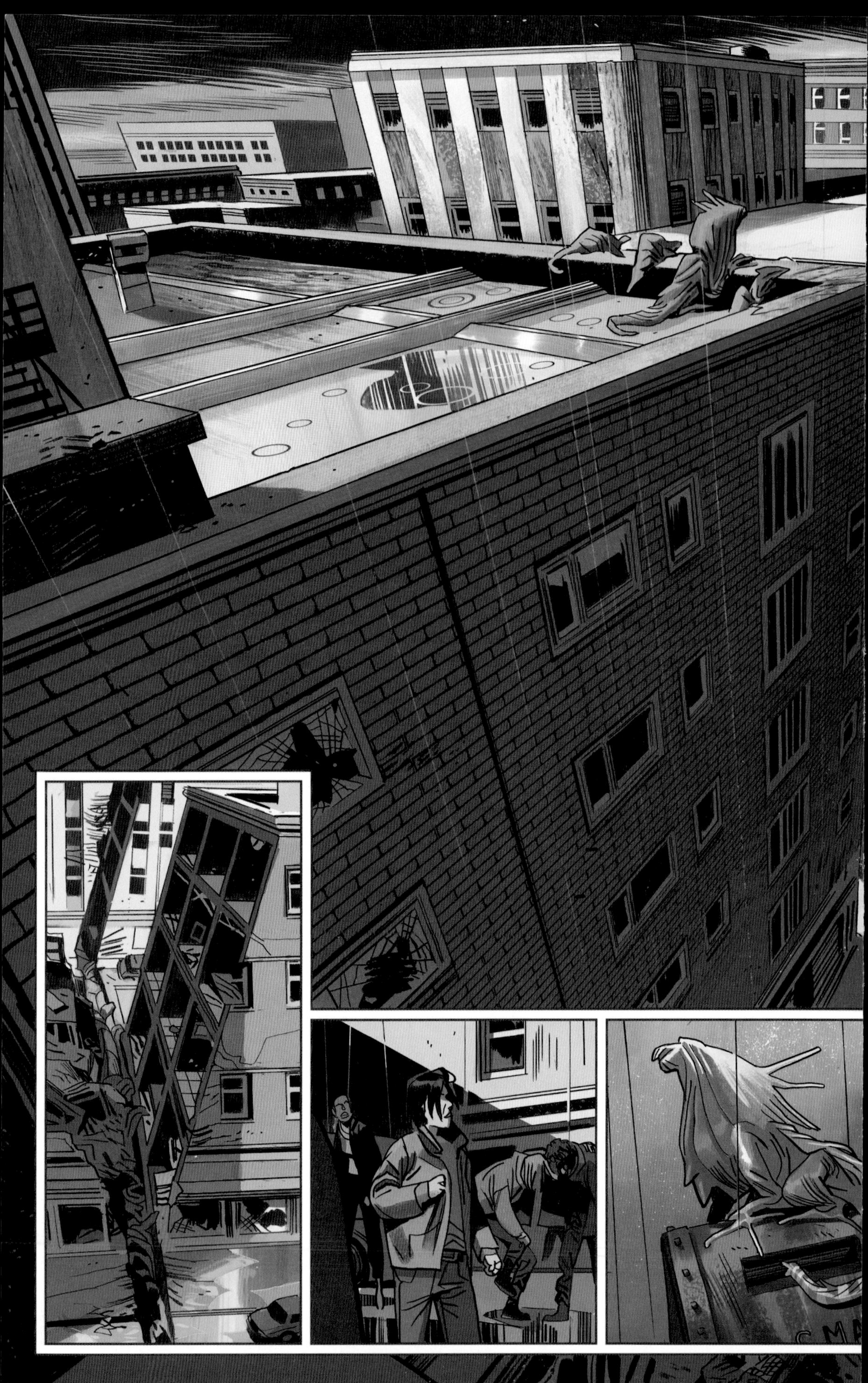

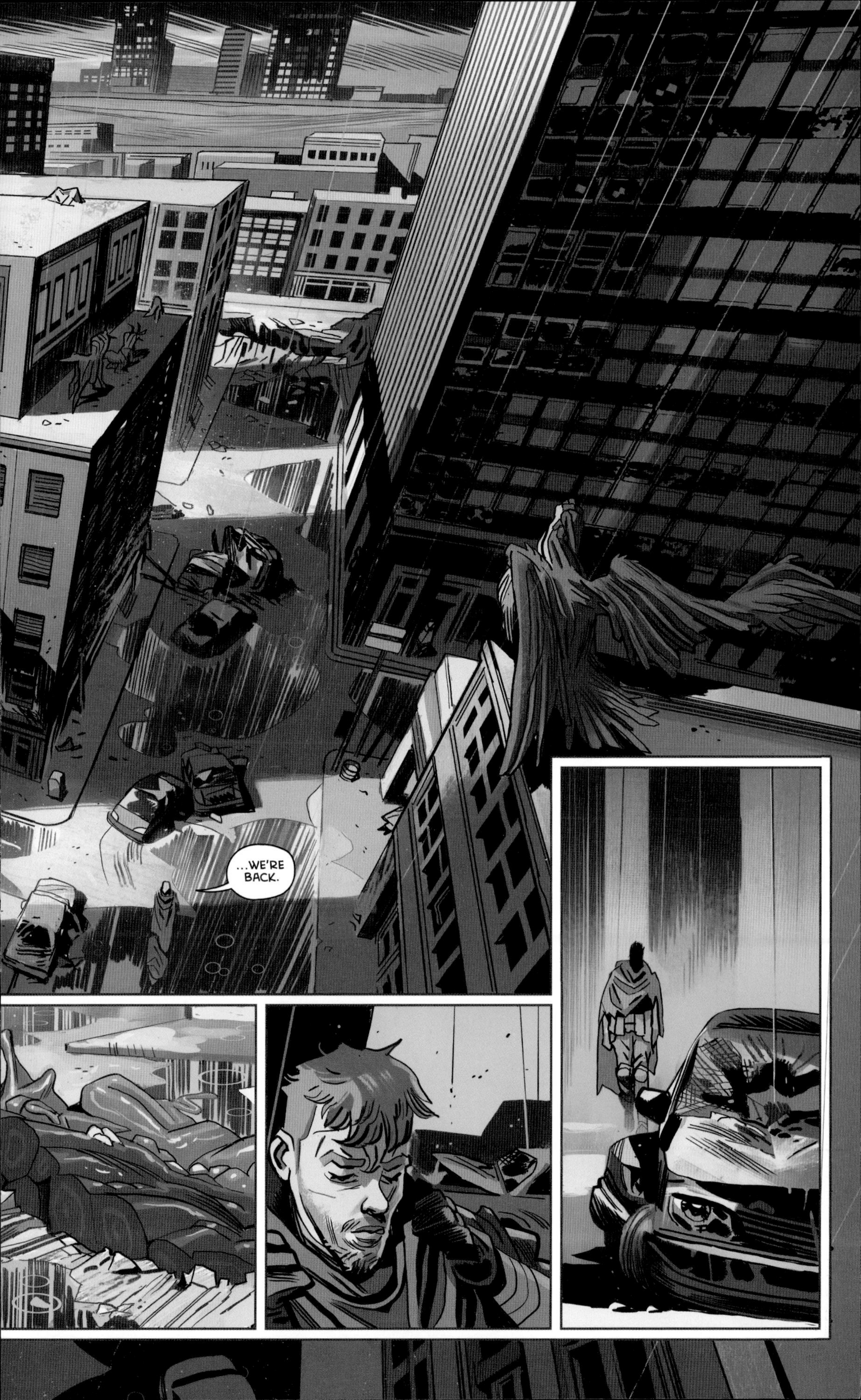
...WE'RE BACK.

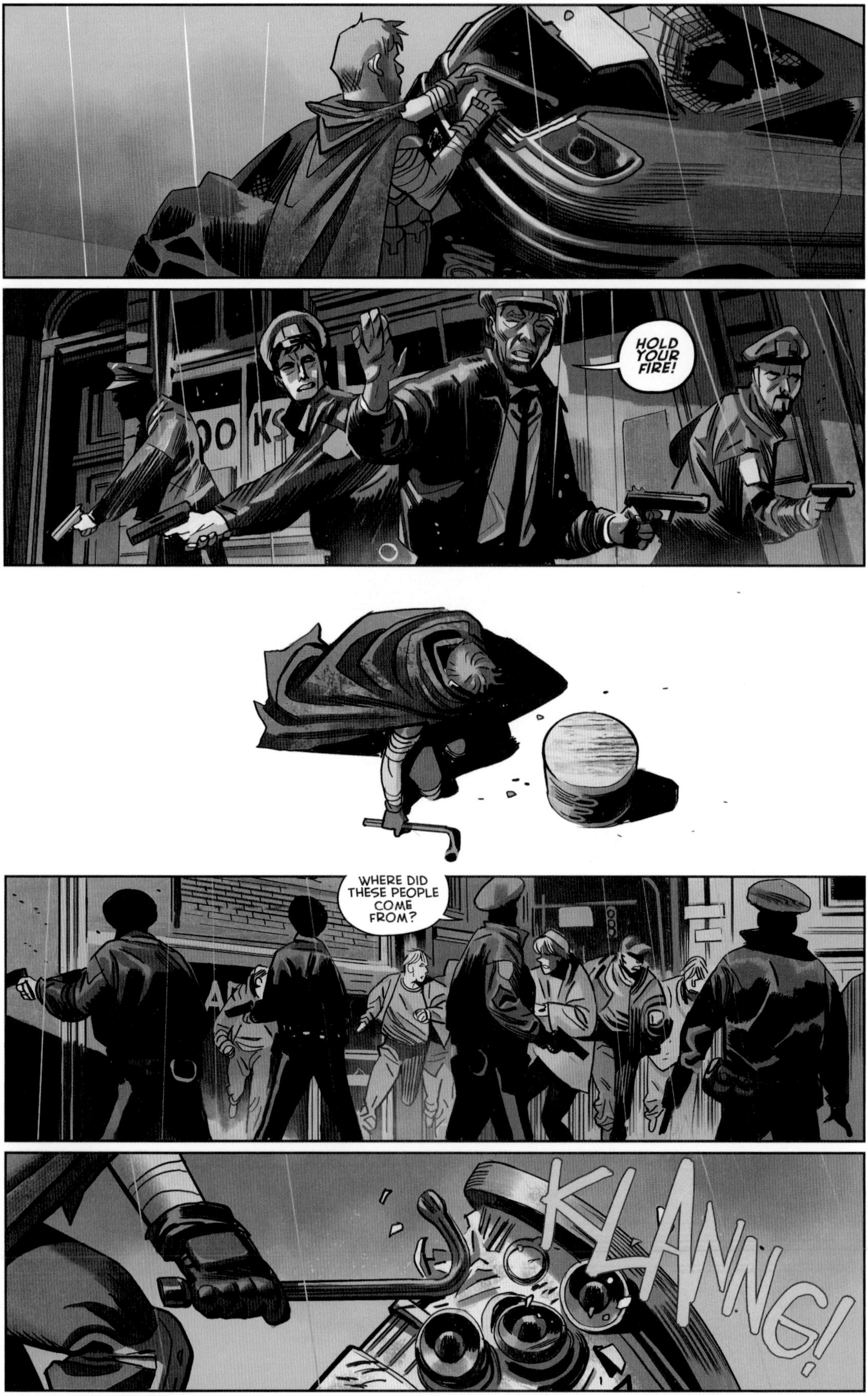
HOLD YOUR FIRE!
WHERE DID THESE PEOPLE COME FROM?
KLANNG!

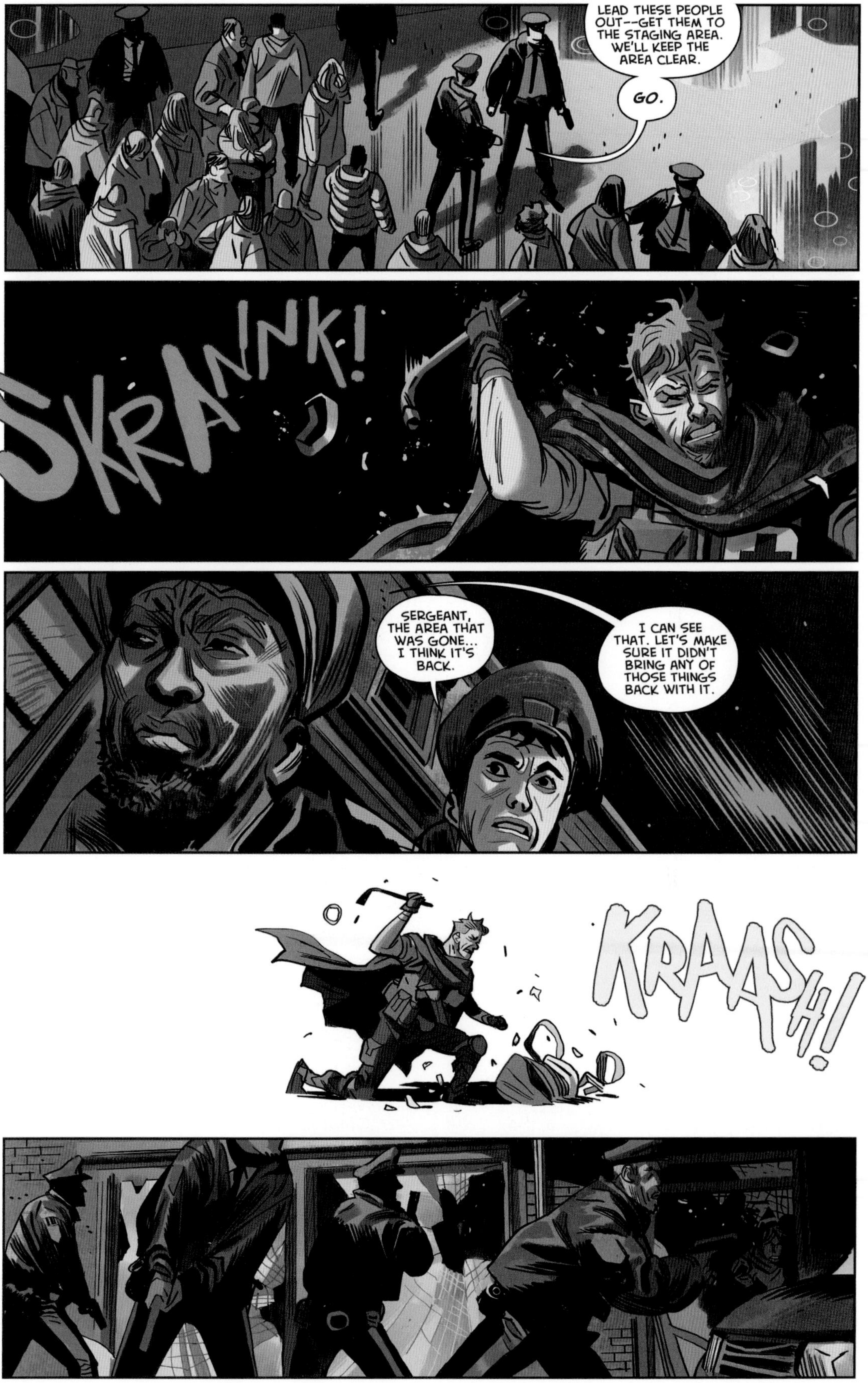

LEAD THESE PEOPLE OUT--GET THEM TO THE STAGING AREA. WE'LL KEEP THE AREA CLEAR.
GO.
SKRANNK!
SERGEANT, THE AREA THAT WAS GONE... I THINK IT'S BACK.
I CAN SEE THAT. LET'S MAKE SURE IT DIDN'T BRING ANY OF THOSE THINGS BACK WITH IT.
KRAASH!

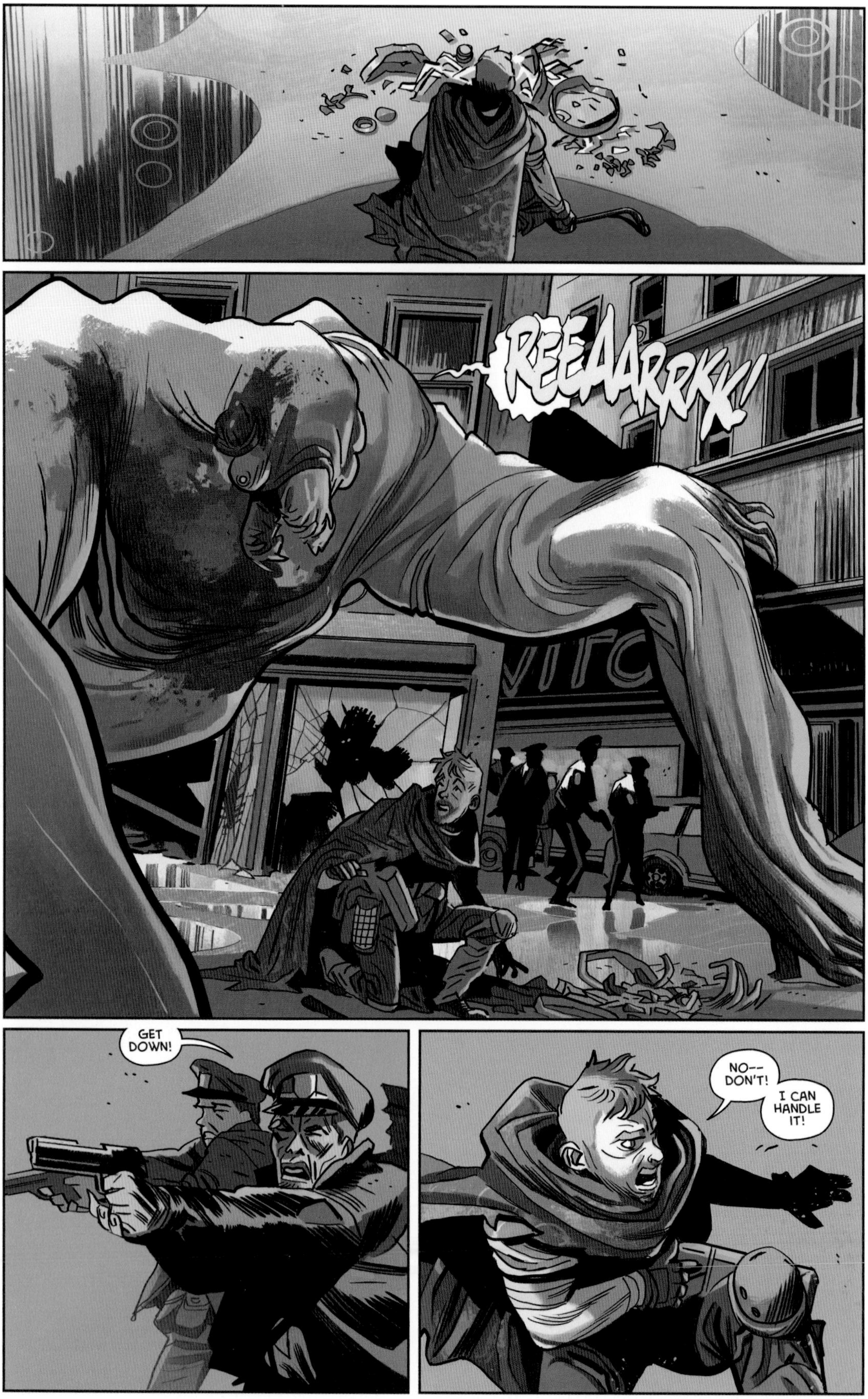
REEAARRKK!
GET DOWN!
NO-- DON'T!
I CAN HANDLE IT!

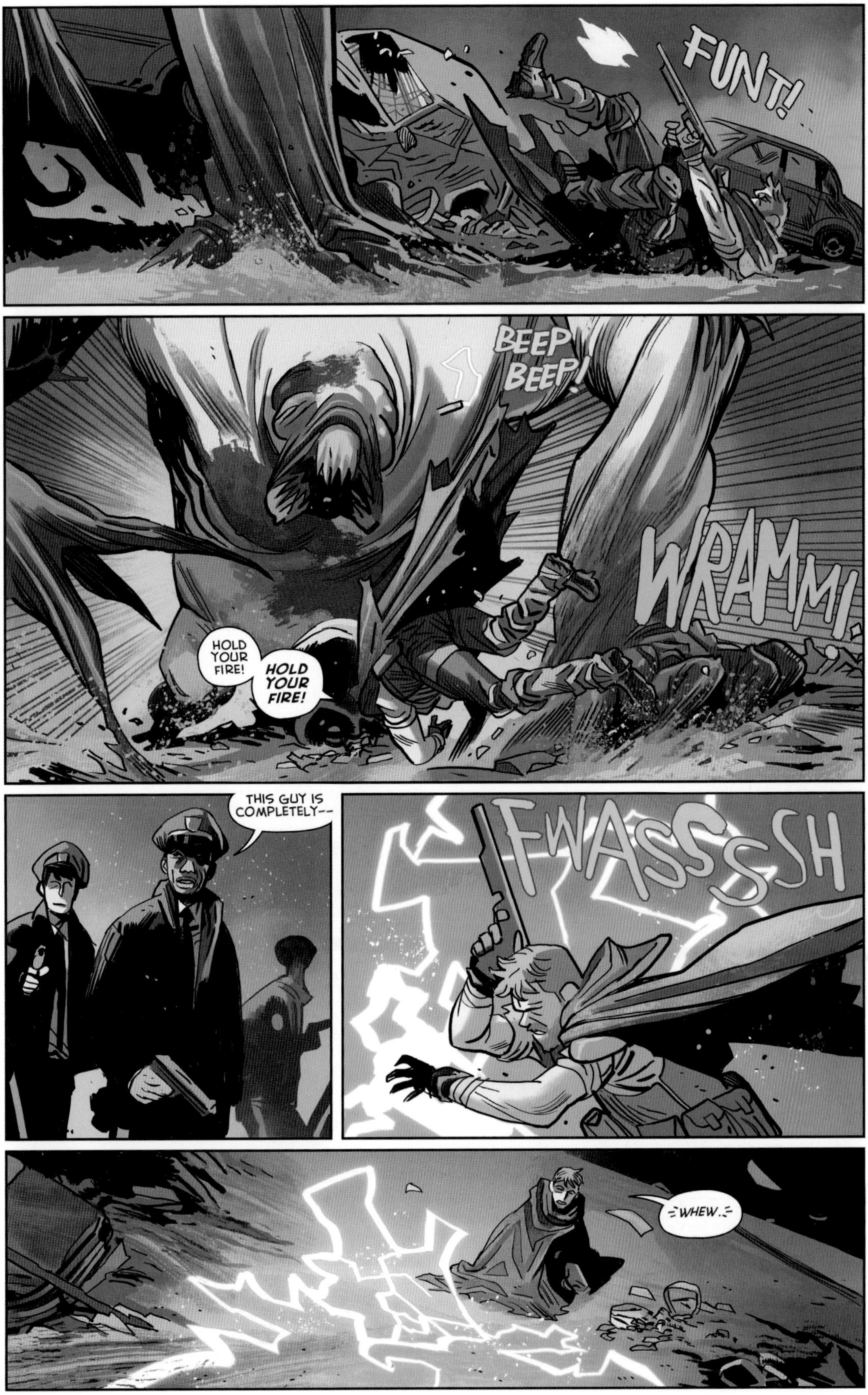
FUNT!
BEEP BEEP!
WRAMM!
HOLD YOUR FIRE!
HOLD YOUR FIRE!
THIS GUY IS COMPLETELY--
FWASSSSH
WHEW.

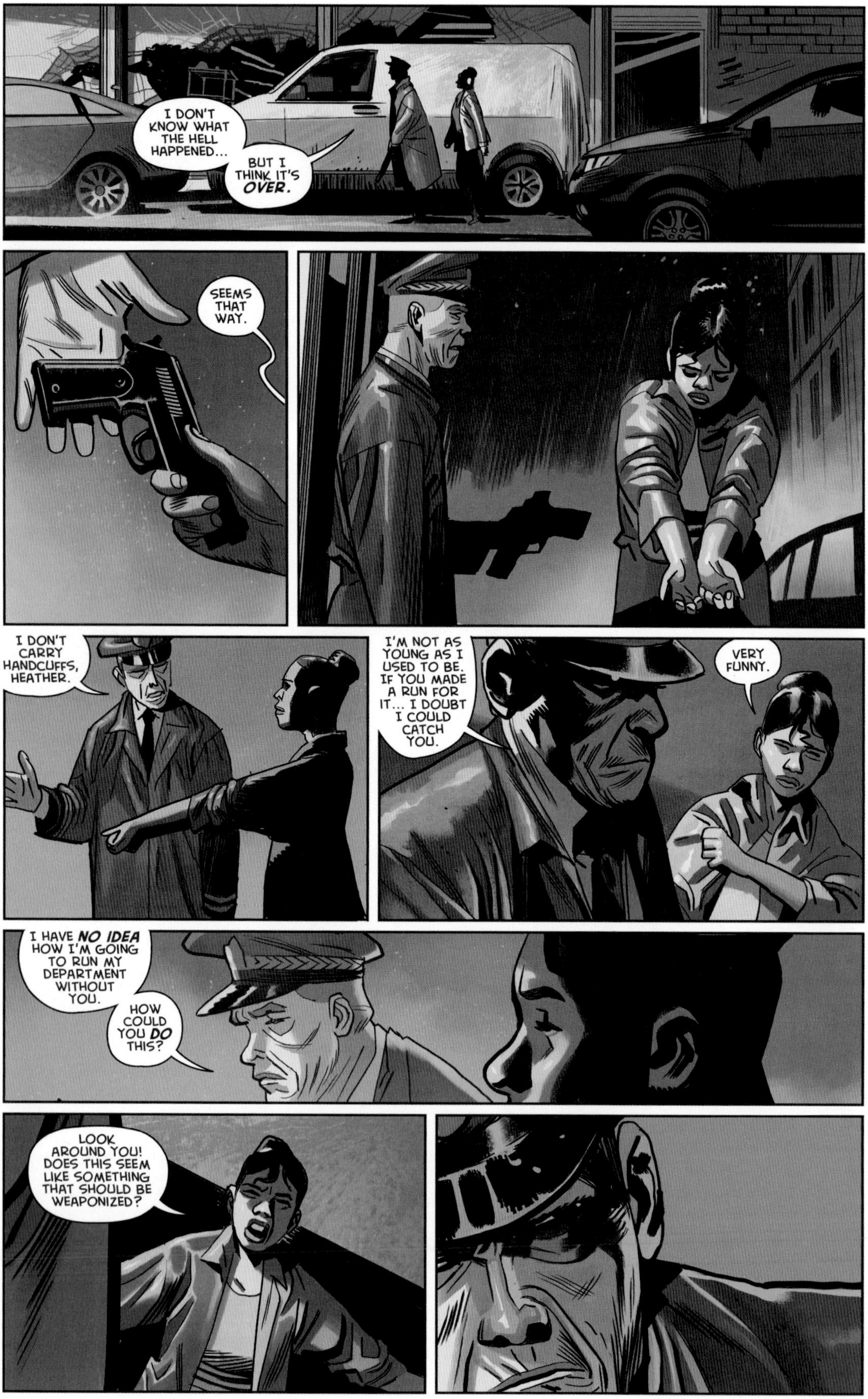
I DON'T KNOW WHAT THE HELL HAPPENED...
BUT I THINK IT'S *OVER.*
SEEMS THAT WAY.
I DON'T CARRY HANDCUFFS, HEATHER.
I'M NOT AS YOUNG AS I USED TO BE. IF YOU MADE A RUN FOR IT... I DOUBT I COULD CATCH YOU.
VERY FUNNY.
I HAVE *NO IDEA* HOW I'M GOING TO RUN MY DEPARTMENT WITHOUT YOU.
HOW COULD YOU *DO* THIS?
LOOK AROUND YOU! DOES THIS SEEM LIKE SOMETHING THAT SHOULD BE WEAPONIZED?

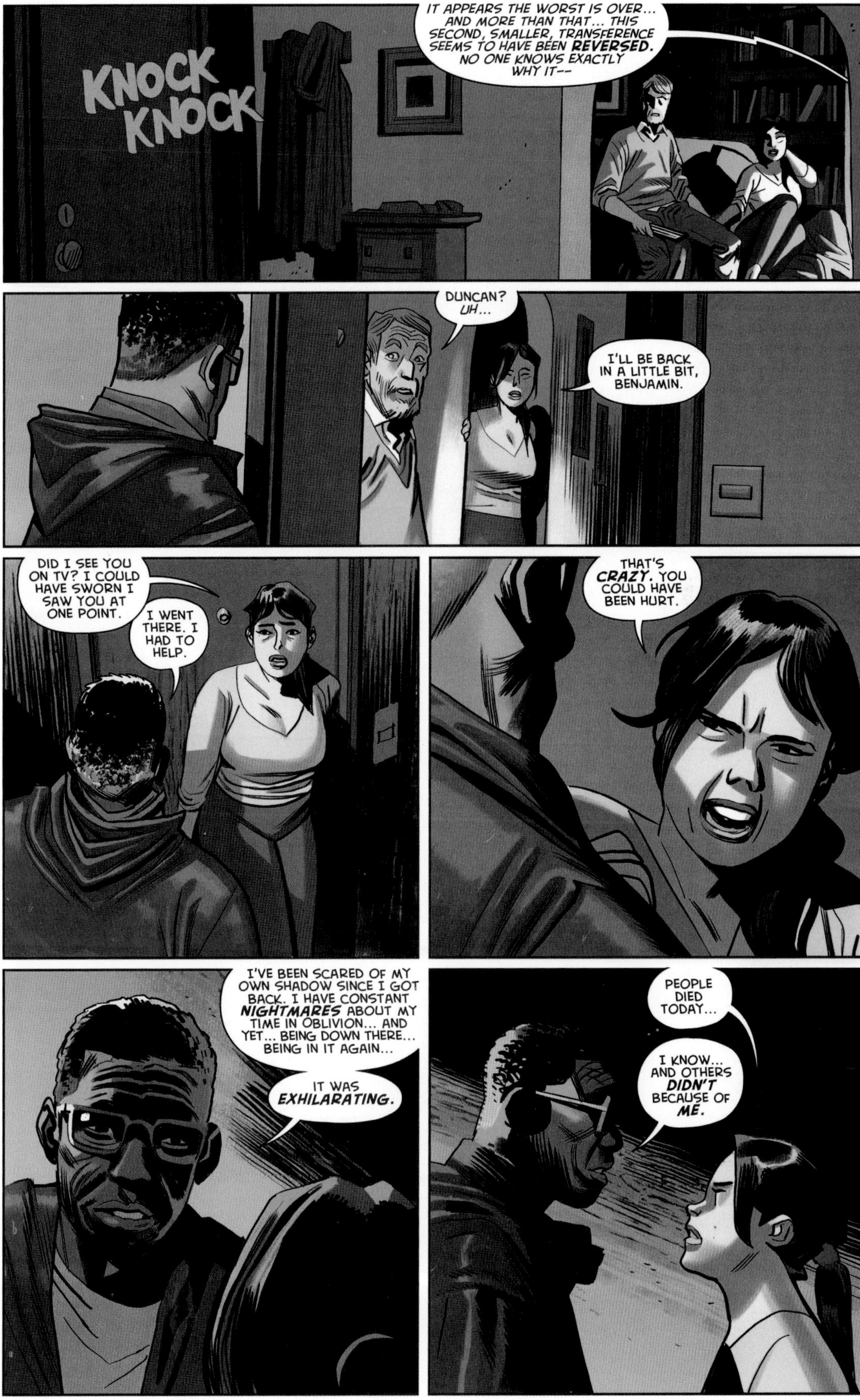
KNOCK KNOCK
IT APPEARS THE WORST IS OVER... AND MORE THAN THAT... THIS SECOND, SMALLER, TRANSFERENCE SEEMS TO HAVE BEEN REVERSED. NO ONE KNOWS EXACTLY WHY IT--
DUNCAN? UH...
I'LL BE BACK IN A LITTLE BIT, BENJAMIN.
DID I SEE YOU ON TV? I COULD HAVE SWORN I SAW YOU AT ONE POINT.
I WENT THERE. I HAD TO HELP.
THAT'S CRAZY. YOU COULD HAVE BEEN HURT.
I'VE BEEN SCARED OF MY OWN SHADOW SINCE I GOT BACK. I HAVE CONSTANT NIGHTMARES ABOUT MY TIME IN OBLIVION... AND YET... BEING DOWN THERE... BEING IN IT AGAIN...
IT WAS EXHILARATING.
PEOPLE DIED TODAY...
I KNOW... AND OTHERS DIDN'T BECAUSE OF ME.

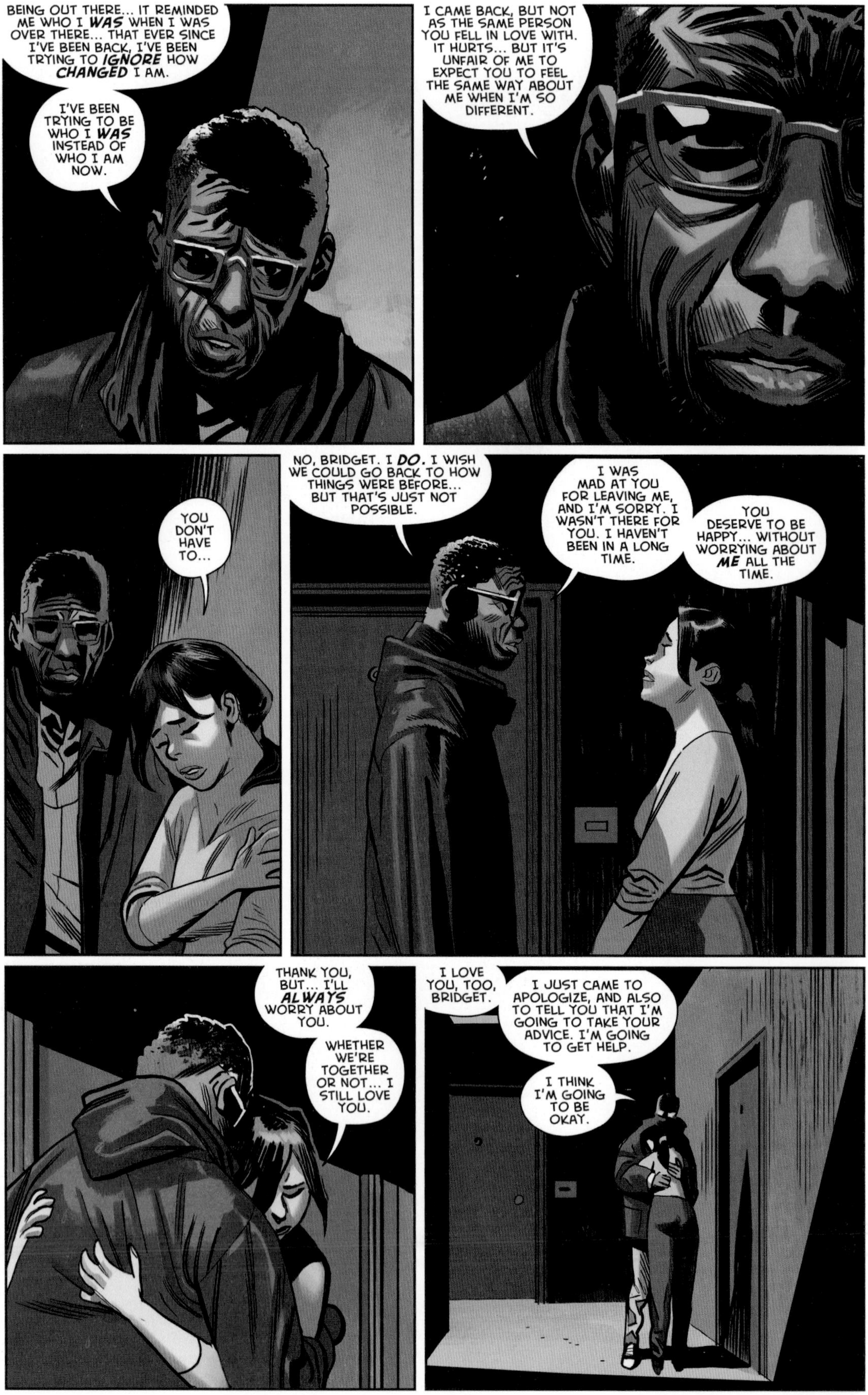
BEING OUT THERE... IT REMINDED ME WHO I WAS WHEN I WAS OVER THERE... THAT EVER SINCE I'VE BEEN BACK, I'VE BEEN TRYING TO IGNORE HOW CHANGED I AM.
I'VE BEEN TRYING TO BE WHO I WAS INSTEAD OF WHO I AM NOW.
I CAME BACK, BUT NOT AS THE SAME PERSON YOU FELL IN LOVE WITH. IT HURTS... BUT IT'S UNFAIR OF ME TO EXPECT YOU TO FEEL THE SAME WAY ABOUT ME WHEN I'M SO DIFFERENT.
YOU DON'T HAVE TO...
NO, BRIDGET. I DO. I WISH WE COULD GO BACK TO HOW THINGS WERE BEFORE... BUT THAT'S JUST NOT POSSIBLE.
I WAS MAD AT YOU FOR LEAVING ME, AND I'M SORRY. I WASN'T THERE FOR YOU. I HAVEN'T BEEN IN A LONG TIME.
YOU DESERVE TO BE HAPPY... WITHOUT WORRYING ABOUT ME ALL THE TIME.
THANK YOU, BUT... I'LL ALWAYS WORRY ABOUT YOU.
WHETHER WE'RE TOGETHER OR NOT... I STILL LOVE YOU.
I LOVE YOU, TOO, BRIDGET.
I JUST CAME TO APOLOGIZE, AND ALSO TO TELL YOU THAT I'M GOING TO TAKE YOUR ADVICE. I'M GOING TO GET HELP.
I THINK I'M GOING TO BE OKAY.

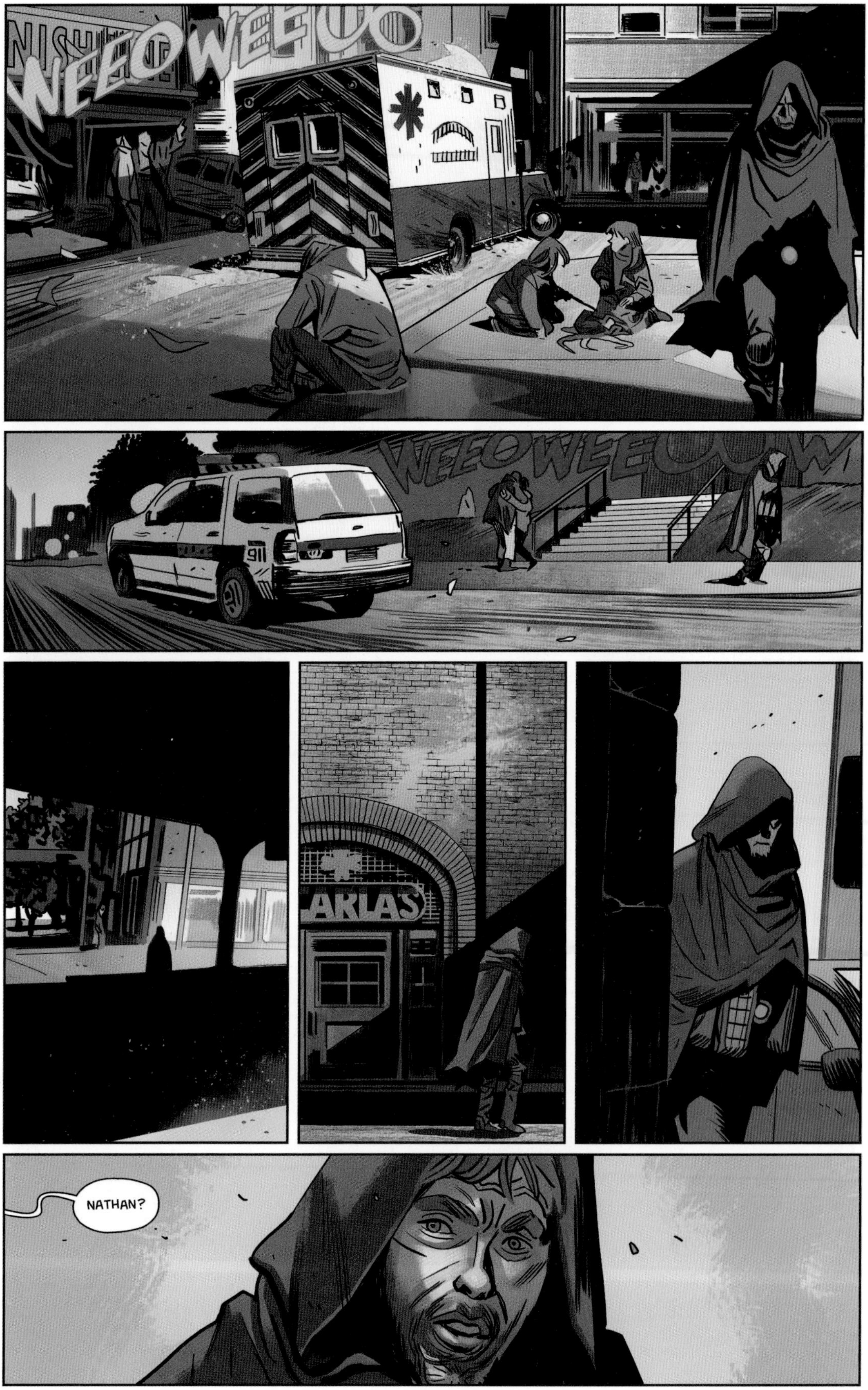

WEEOWEEOO
WEEOWEEOOW
911
CARLA'S
NATHAN?

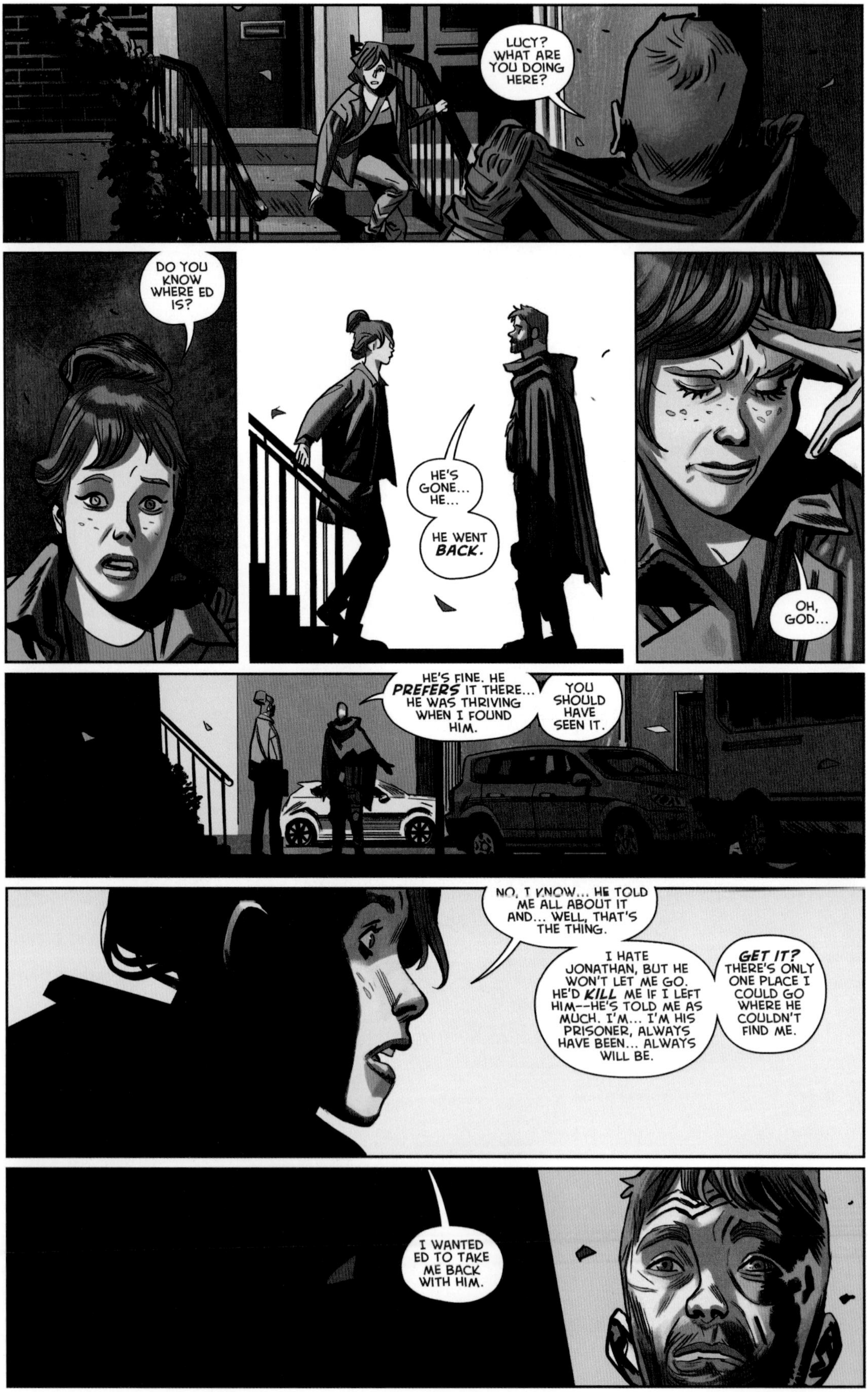
LUCY? WHAT ARE YOU DOING HERE?
DO YOU KNOW WHERE ED IS?
HE'S GONE... HE...
HE WENT BACK.
OH, GOD...
HE'S FINE. HE PREFERS IT THERE... HE WAS THRIVING WHEN I FOUND HIM.
YOU SHOULD HAVE SEEN IT.
NO, I KNOW... HE TOLD ME ALL ABOUT IT AND... WELL, THAT'S THE THING.
I HATE JONATHAN, BUT HE WON'T LET ME GO. HE'D KILL ME IF I LEFT HIM--HE'S TOLD ME AS MUCH. I'M... I'M HIS PRISONER, ALWAYS HAVE BEEN... ALWAYS WILL BE.
GET IT? THERE'S ONLY ONE PLACE I COULD GO WHERE HE COULDN'T FIND ME.
I WANTED ED TO TAKE ME BACK WITH HIM.

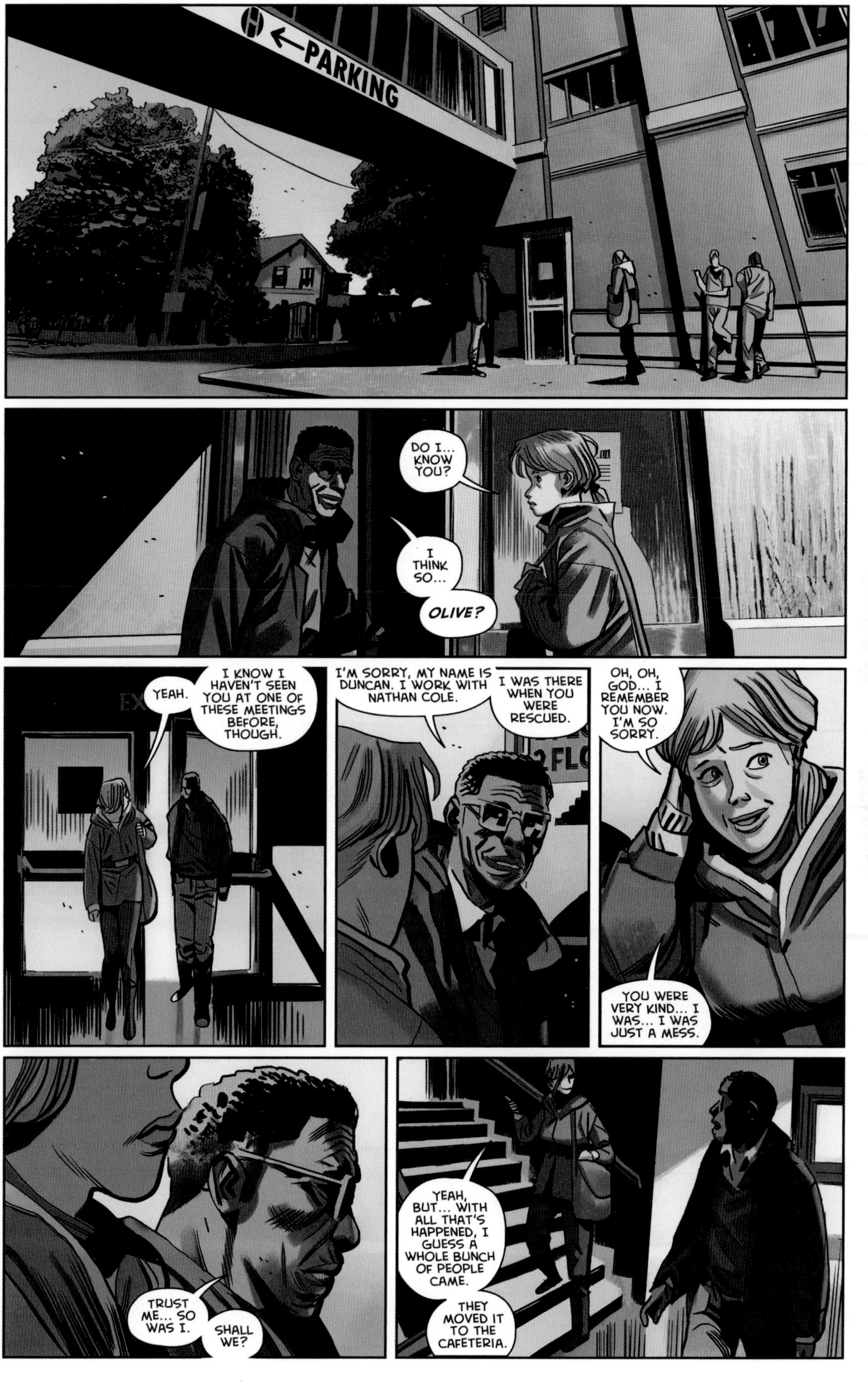

PARKING
DO I... KNOW YOU?
I THINK SO...
OLIVE?
YEAH.
I KNOW I HAVEN'T SEEN YOU AT ONE OF THESE MEETINGS BEFORE, THOUGH.
I'M SORRY, MY NAME IS DUNCAN. I WORK WITH NATHAN COLE.
I WAS THERE WHEN YOU WERE RESCUED.
OH, OH, GOD... I REMEMBER YOU NOW. I'M SO SORRY.
YOU WERE VERY KIND... I WAS... I WAS JUST A MESS.
TRUST ME... SO WAS I.
SHALL WE?
YEAH, BUT... WITH ALL THAT'S HAPPENED, I GUESS A WHOLE BUNCH OF PEOPLE CAME.
THEY MOVED IT TO THE CAFETERIA.

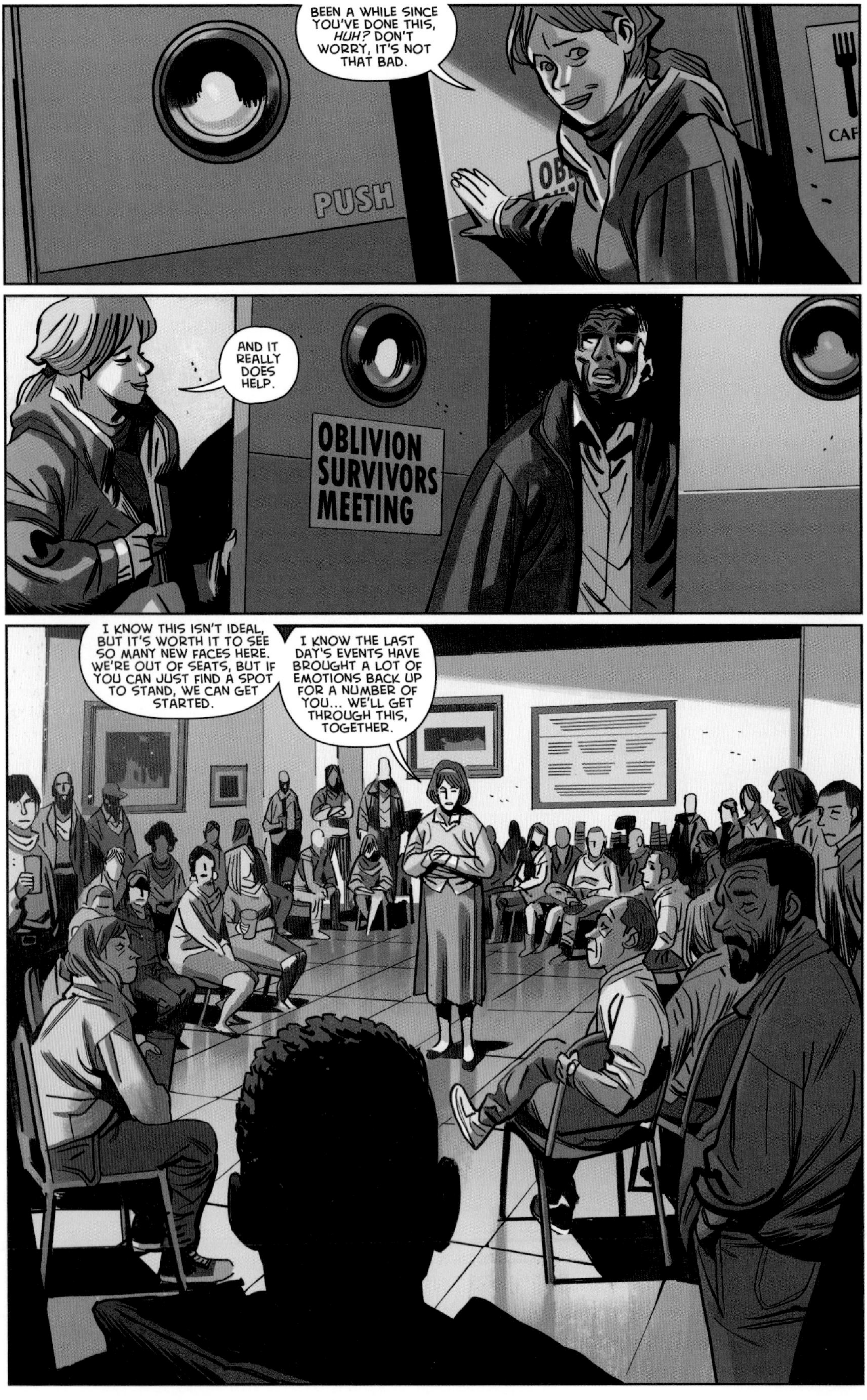
BEEN A WHILE SINCE YOU'VE DONE THIS, *HUH?* DON'T WORRY, IT'S NOT THAT BAD.
PUSH
AND IT REALLY DOES HELP.
OBLIVION SURVIVORS MEETING
I KNOW THIS ISN'T IDEAL, BUT IT'S WORTH IT TO SEE SO MANY NEW FACES HERE. WE'RE OUT OF SEATS, BUT IF YOU CAN JUST FIND A SPOT TO STAND, WE CAN GET STARTED.
I KNOW THE LAST DAY'S EVENTS HAVE BROUGHT A LOT OF EMOTIONS BACK UP FOR A NUMBER OF YOU... WE'LL GET THROUGH THIS, TOGETHER.

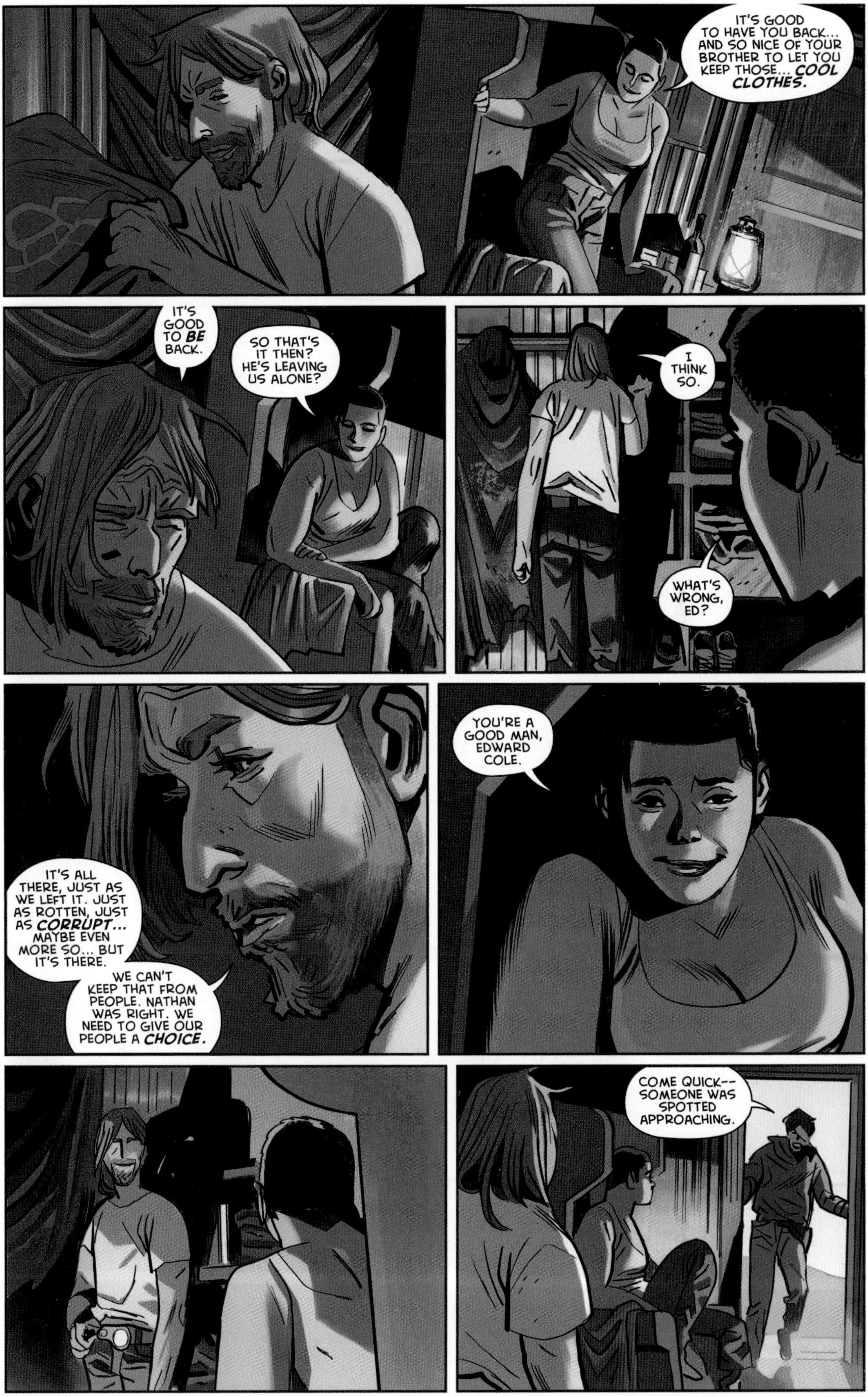

IT'S GOOD TO HAVE YOU BACK... AND SO NICE OF YOUR BROTHER TO LET YOU KEEP THOSE... COOL CLOTHES.
IT'S GOOD TO BE BACK.
SO THAT'S IT THEN? HE'S LEAVING US ALONE?
I THINK SO.
WHAT'S WRONG, ED?
IT'S ALL THERE, JUST AS WE LEFT IT. JUST AS ROTTEN, JUST AS CORRUPT... MAYBE EVEN MORE SO... BUT IT'S THERE.
WE CAN'T KEEP THAT FROM PEOPLE. NATHAN WAS RIGHT. WE NEED TO GIVE OUR PEOPLE A CHOICE.
YOU'RE A GOOD MAN, EDWARD COLE.
COME QUICK-- SOMEONE WAS SPOTTED APPROACHING.

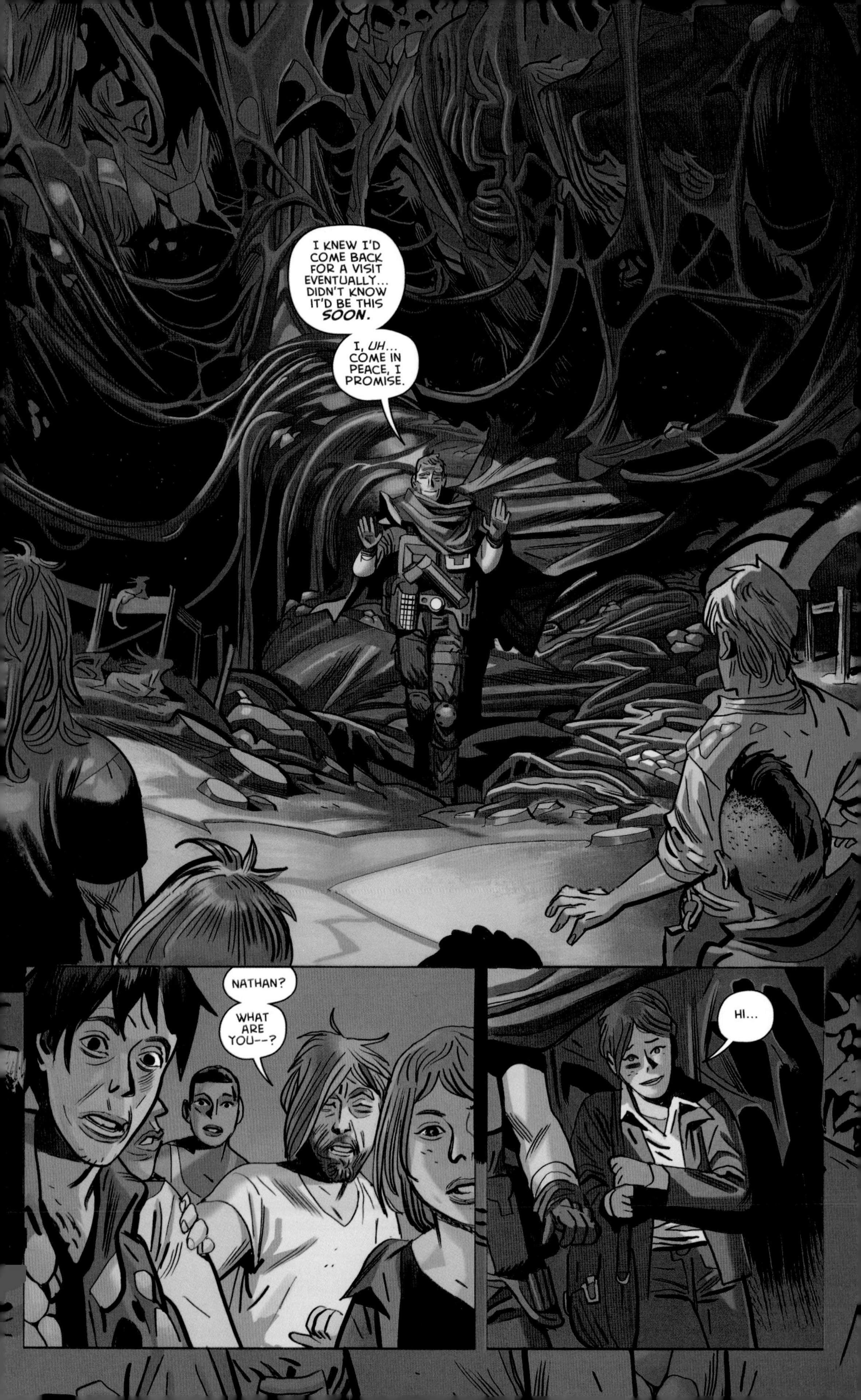
I KNEW I'D COME BACK FOR A VISIT EVENTUALLY... DIDN'T KNOW IT'D BE THIS SOON.
I, UH... COME IN PEACE, I PROMISE.
NATHAN?
WHAT ARE YOU--?
HI...

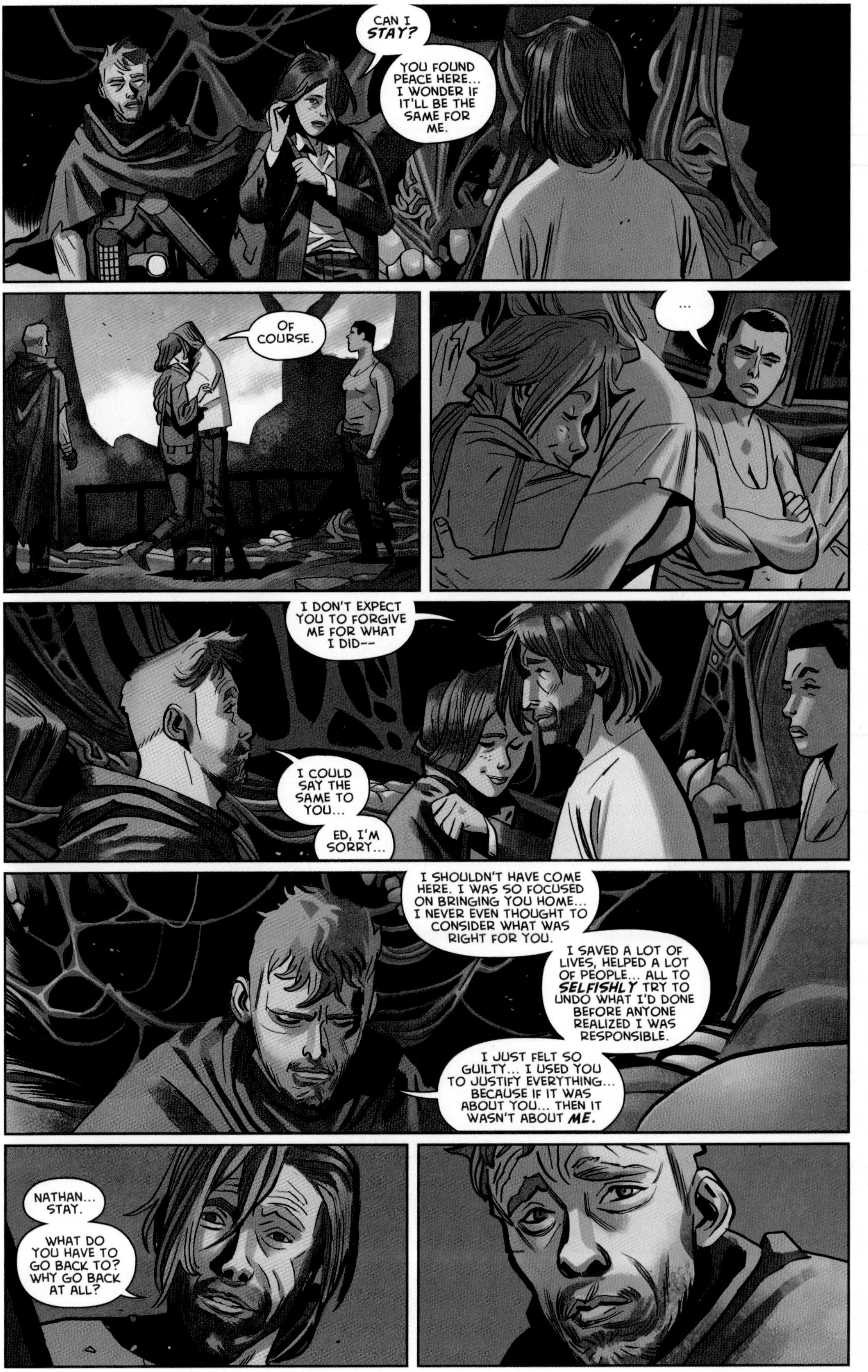
CAN I STAY?
YOU FOUND PEACE HERE... I WONDER IF IT'LL BE THE SAME FOR ME.
OF COURSE.
...
I DON'T EXPECT YOU TO FORGIVE ME FOR WHAT I DID--
I COULD SAY THE SAME TO YOU...
ED, I'M SORRY...
I SHOULDN'T HAVE COME HERE. I WAS SO FOCUSED ON BRINGING YOU HOME... I NEVER EVEN THOUGHT TO CONSIDER WHAT WAS RIGHT FOR YOU.
I SAVED A LOT OF LIVES, HELPED A LOT OF PEOPLE... ALL TO SELFISHLY TRY TO UNDO WHAT I'D DONE BEFORE ANYONE REALIZED I WAS RESPONSIBLE.
I JUST FELT SO GUILTY... I USED YOU TO JUSTIFY EVERYTHING... BECAUSE IF IT WAS ABOUT YOU... THEN IT WASN'T ABOUT ME.
NATHAN... STAY.
WHAT DO YOU HAVE TO GO BACK TO? WHY GO BACK AT ALL?

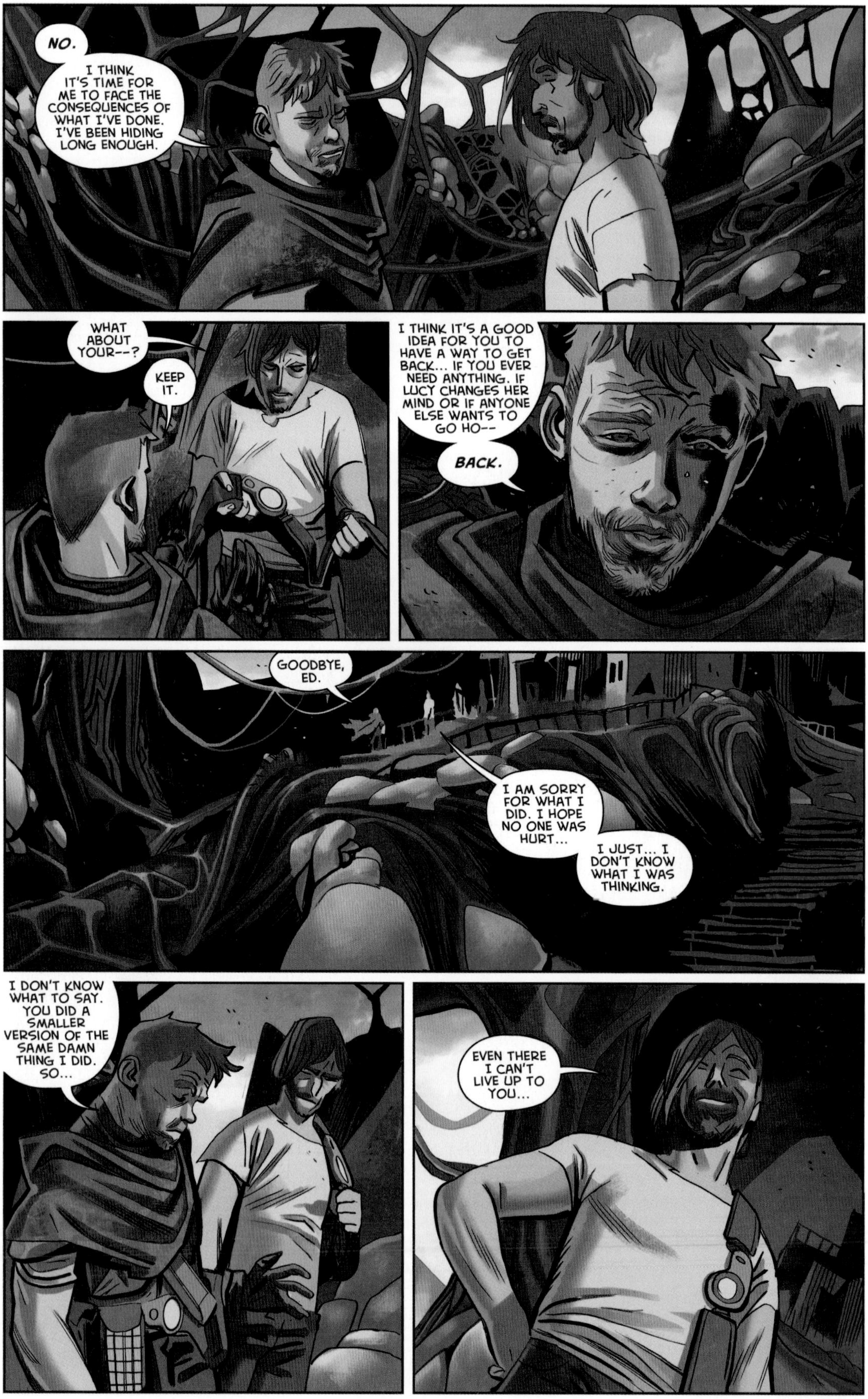
NO.
I THINK IT'S TIME FOR ME TO FACE THE CONSEQUENCES OF WHAT I'VE DONE. I'VE BEEN HIDING LONG ENOUGH.
WHAT ABOUT YOUR--?
KEEP IT.
I THINK IT'S A GOOD IDEA FOR YOU TO HAVE A WAY TO GET BACK... IF YOU EVER NEED ANYTHING. IF LUCY CHANGES HER MIND OR IF ANYONE ELSE WANTS TO GO HO--
BACK.
GOODBYE, ED.
I AM SORRY FOR WHAT I DID. I HOPE NO ONE WAS HURT...
I JUST... I DON'T KNOW WHAT I WAS THINKING.
I DON'T KNOW WHAT TO SAY. YOU DID A SMALLER VERSION OF THE SAME DAMN THING I DID. SO...
EVEN THERE I CAN'T LIVE UP TO YOU...

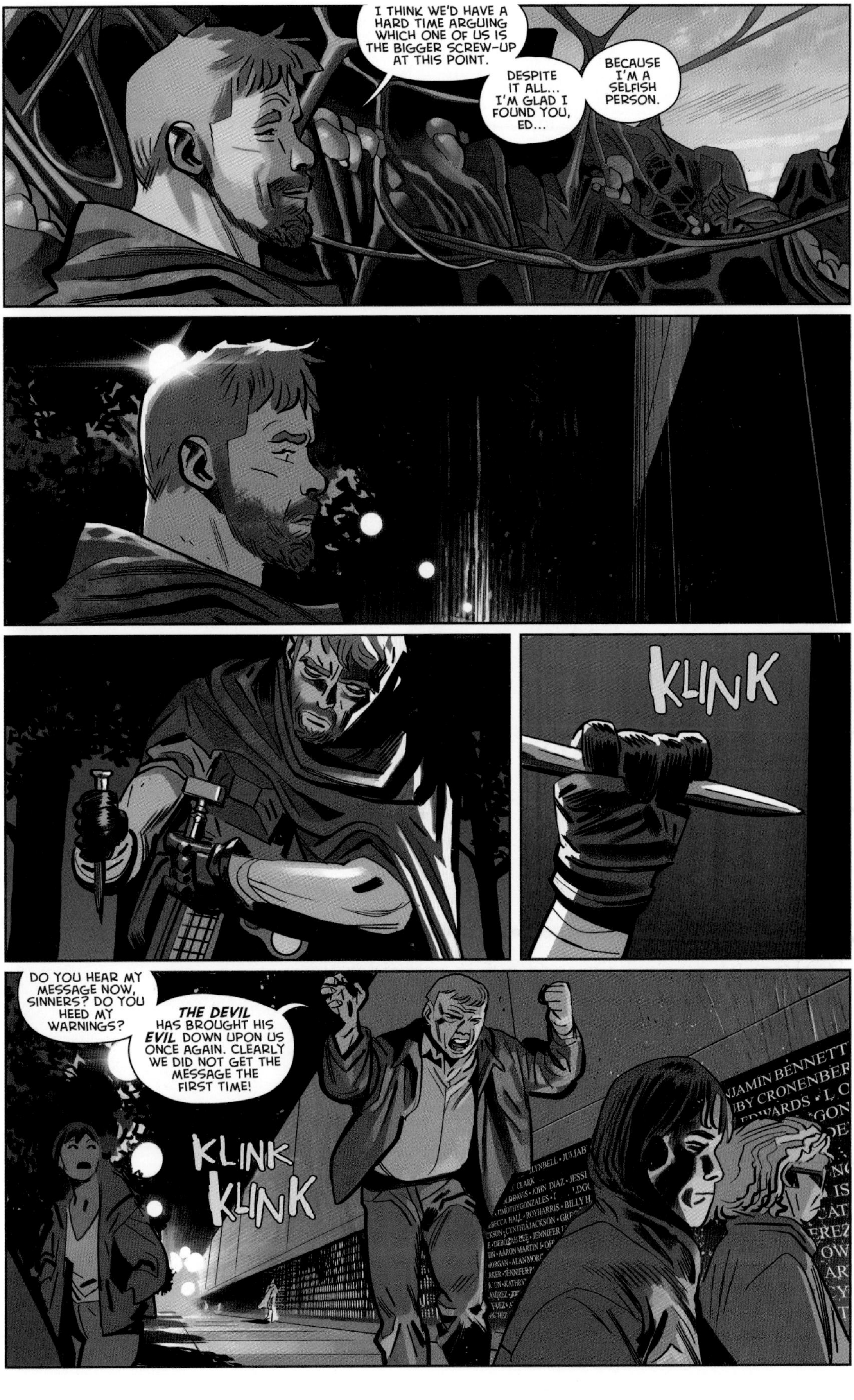
I THINK WE'D HAVE A HARD TIME ARGUING WHICH ONE OF US IS THE BIGGER SCREW-UP AT THIS POINT.
DESPITE IT ALL... I'M GLAD I FOUND YOU, ED...
BECAUSE I'M A SELFISH PERSON.
KLINK
DO YOU HEAR MY MESSAGE NOW, SINNERS? DO YOU HEED MY WARNINGS?
THE DEVIL HAS BROUGHT HIS EVIL DOWN UPON US ONCE AGAIN. CLEARLY WE DID NOT GET THE MESSAGE THE FIRST TIME!
KLINK
KLINK

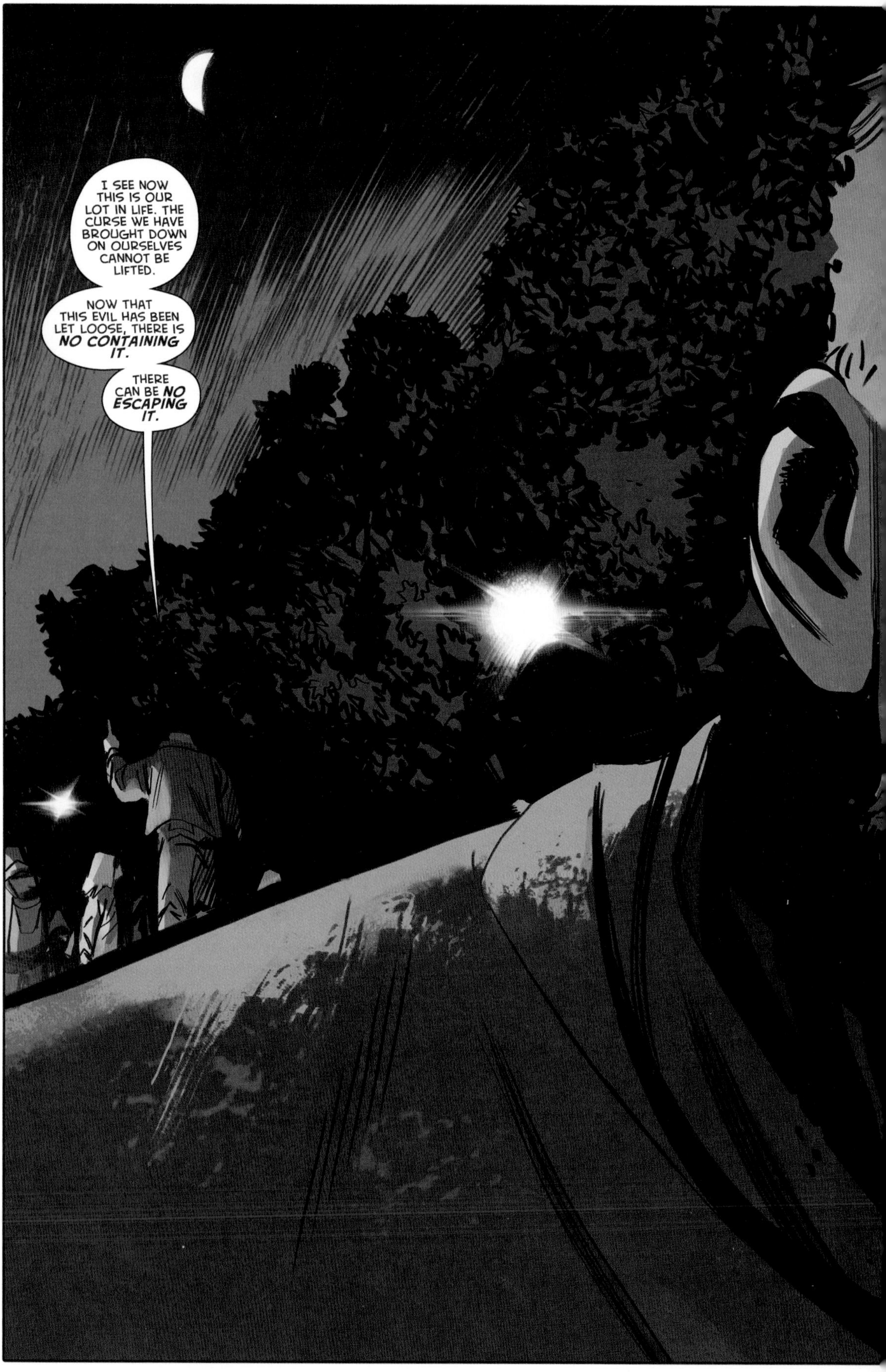
I SEE NOW THIS IS OUR LOT IN LIFE. THE CURSE WE HAVE BROUGHT DOWN ON OURSELVES CANNOT BE LIFTED.
NOW THAT THIS EVIL HAS BEEN LET LOOSE, THERE IS NO CONTAINING IT.
THERE CAN BE NO ESCAPING IT.

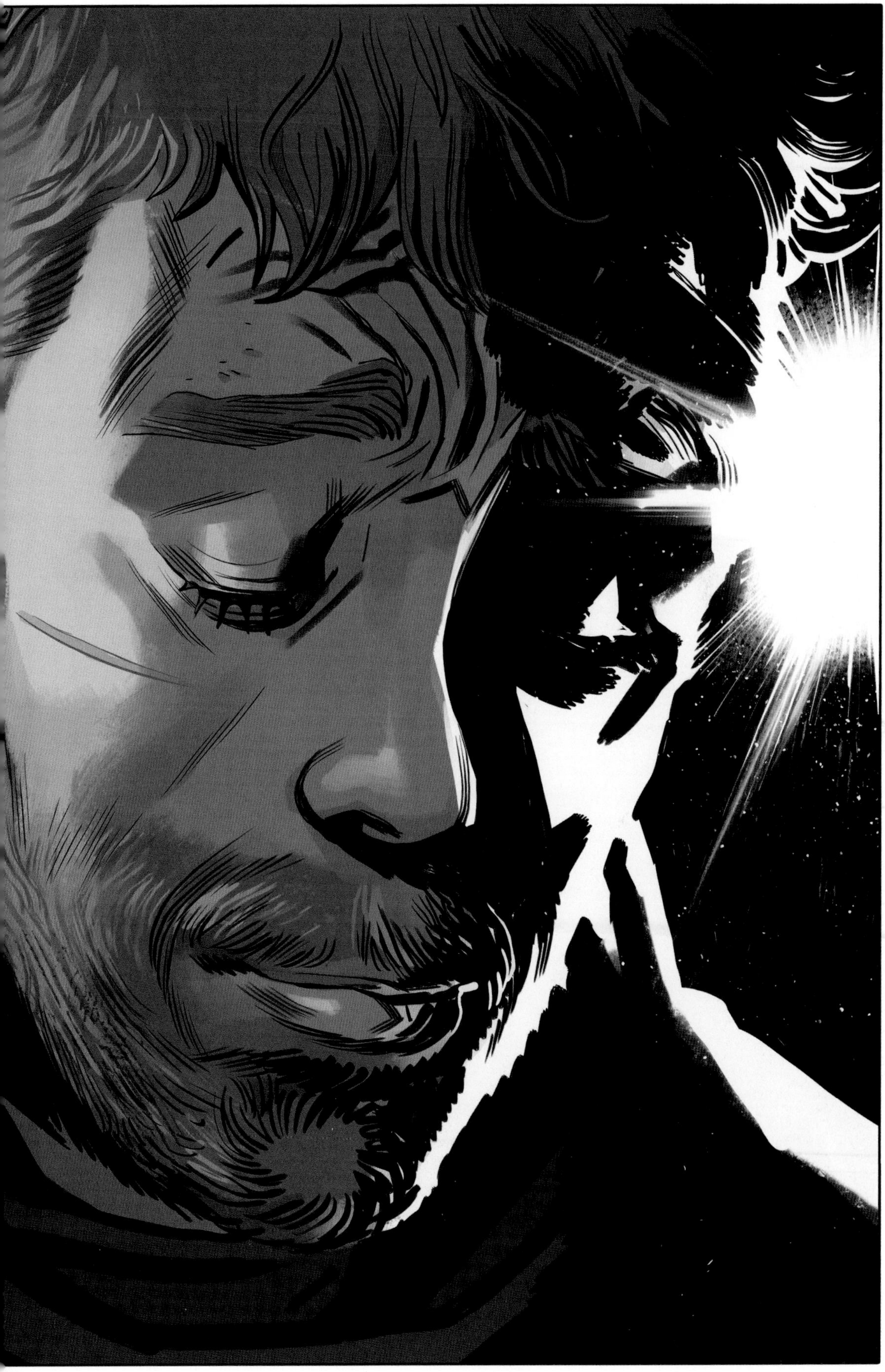

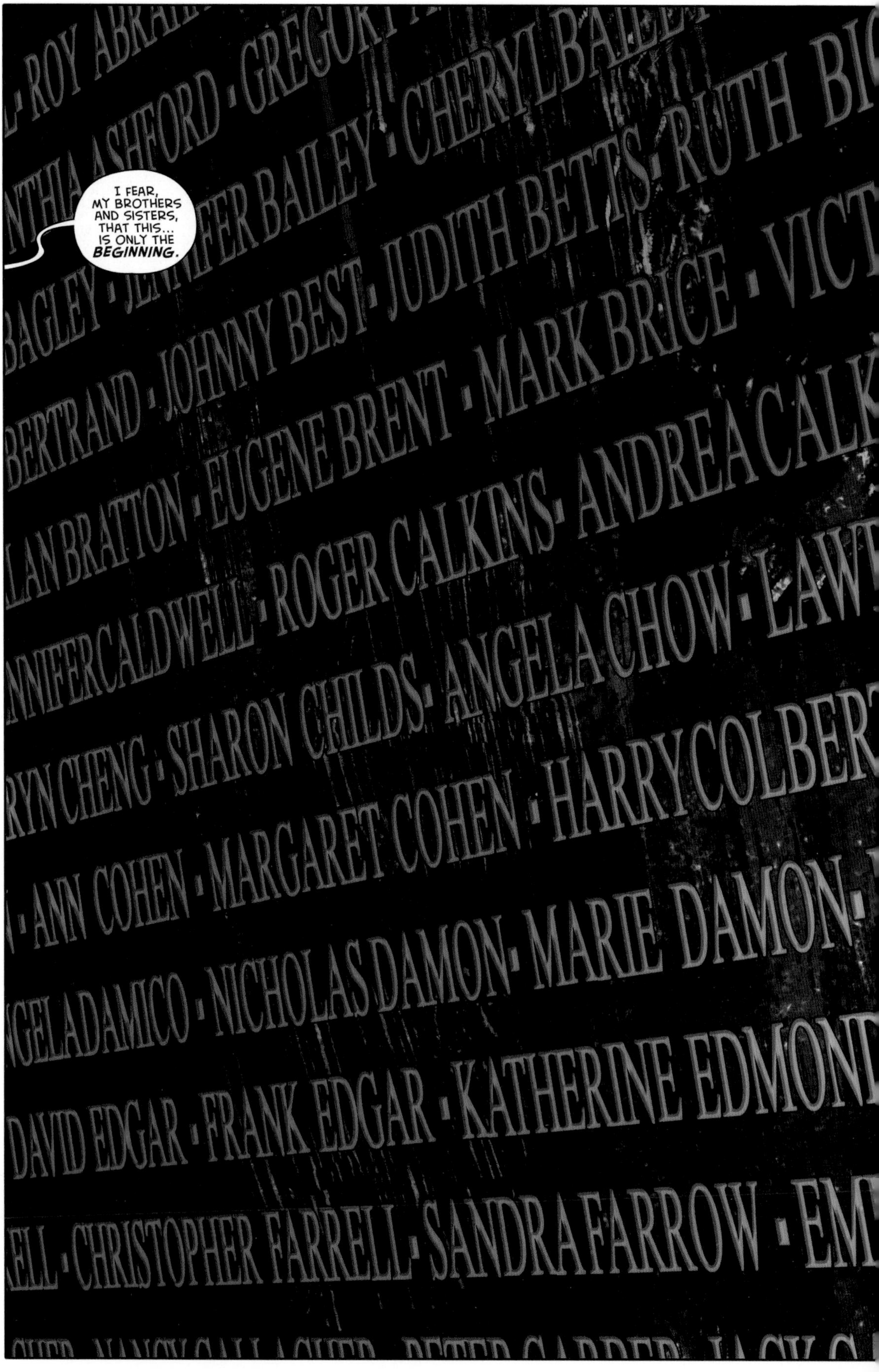
I FEAR, MY BROTHERS AND SISTERS, THAT THIS... IS ONLY THE *BEGINNING.*
ROY
ASHFORD
JENNIFER BAILEY · CHERYL BAILEY
JOHNNY BEST · JUDITH BETTS · RUTH
BERTRAND · JOHNNY BEST · MARK BRICE
ALAN BRATTON · EUGENE BRENT · MARK BRICE
ROGER CALKINS · ANDREA
SHARON CHILDS · ANGELA CHOW
MARGARET COHEN · HARRY COLBERT
ANN COHEN · MARGARET COHEN
NICHOLAS DAMON · MARIE DAMON
DAVID EDGAR · FRANK EDGAR · KATHERINE
CHRISTOPHER FARRELL · SANDRA FARROW

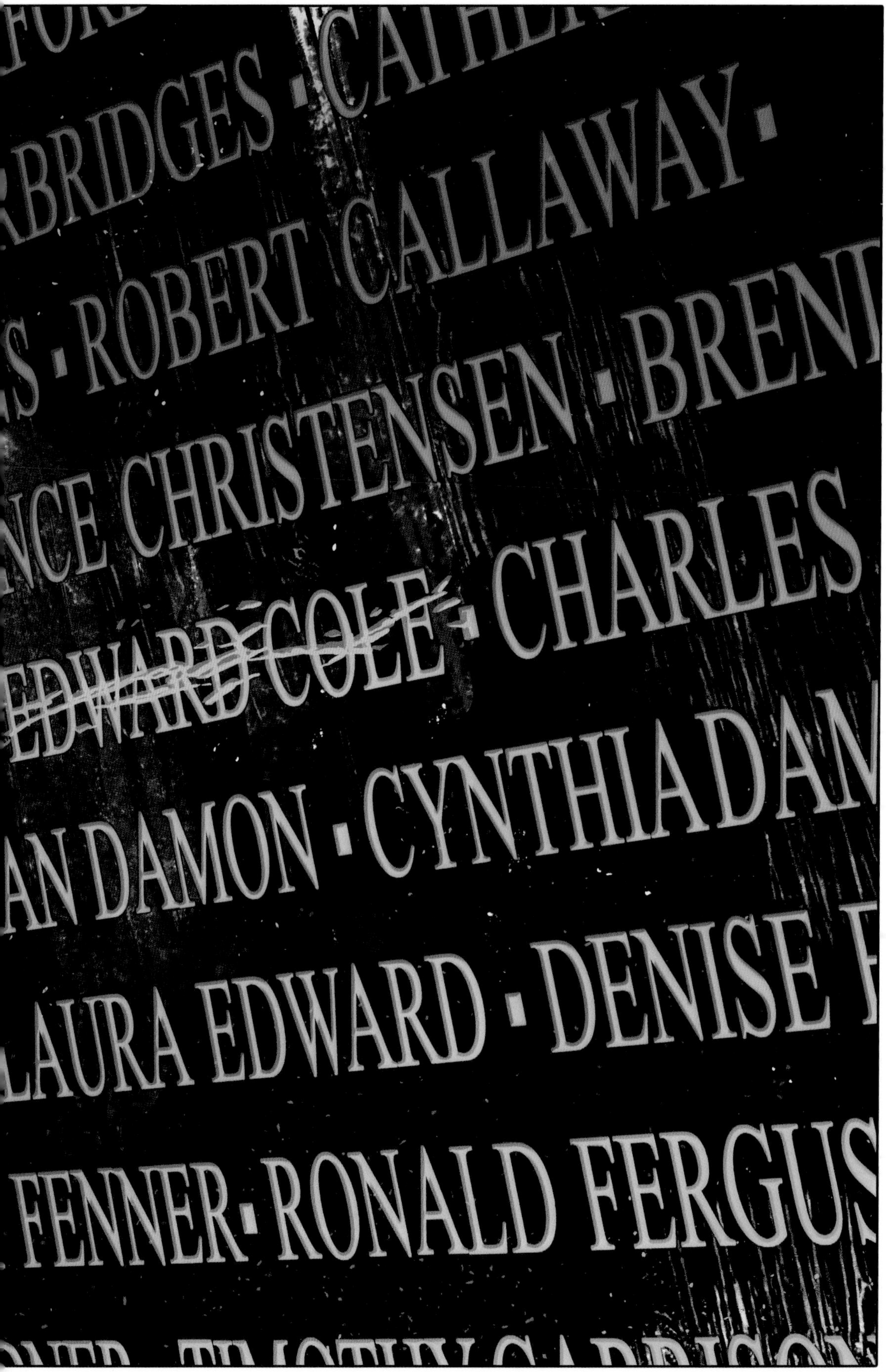
BRIDGES · CATHE
ROBERT CALLAWAY ·
NCE CHRISTENSEN · BREN
EDWARD COLE · CHARLES
AN DAMON · CYNTHIA DAN
LAURA EDWARD · DENISE
FENNER · RONALD FERGUS

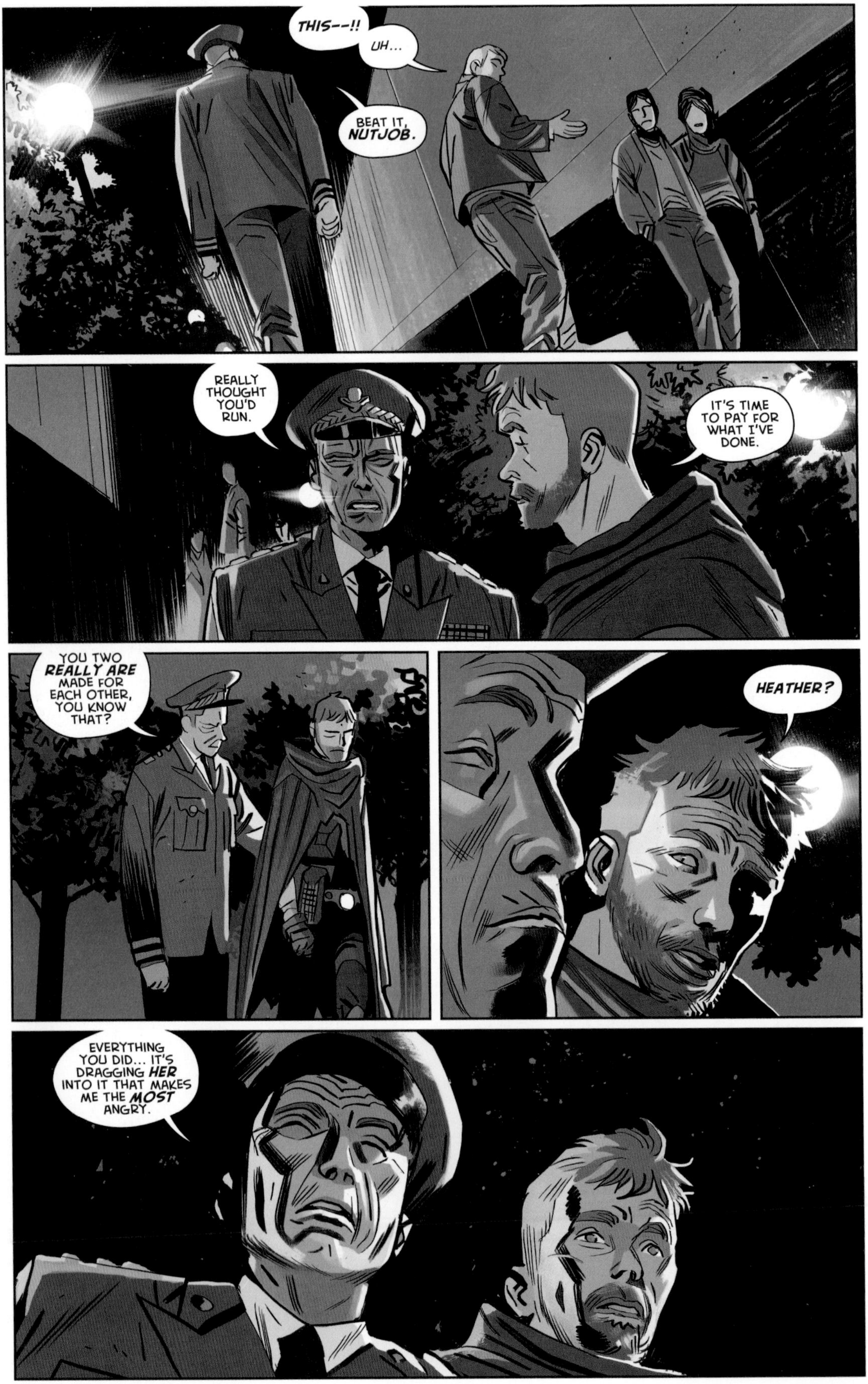
THIS--!!
UH...
BEAT IT, NUTJOB.
REALLY THOUGHT YOU'D RUN.
IT'S TIME TO PAY FOR WHAT I'VE DONE.
YOU TWO REALLY ARE MADE FOR EACH OTHER, YOU KNOW THAT?
HEATHER?
EVERYTHING YOU DID... IT'S DRAGGING HER INTO IT THAT MAKES ME THE MOST ANGRY.

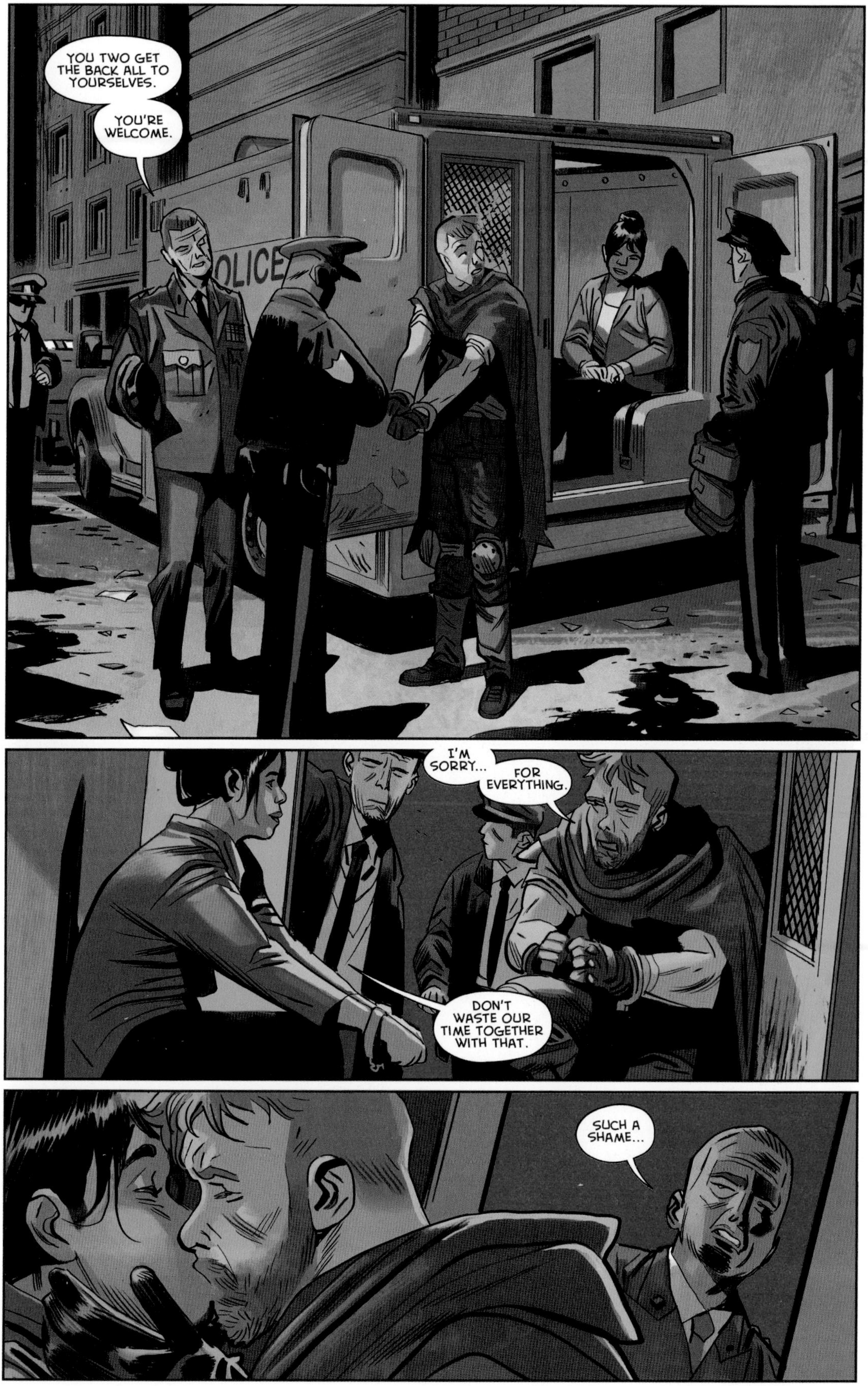
YOU TWO GET THE BACK ALL TO YOURSELVES.
YOU'RE WELCOME.
POLICE
I'M SORRY...
FOR EVERYTHING.
DON'T WASTE OUR TIME TOGETHER WITH THAT.
SUCH A SHAME...

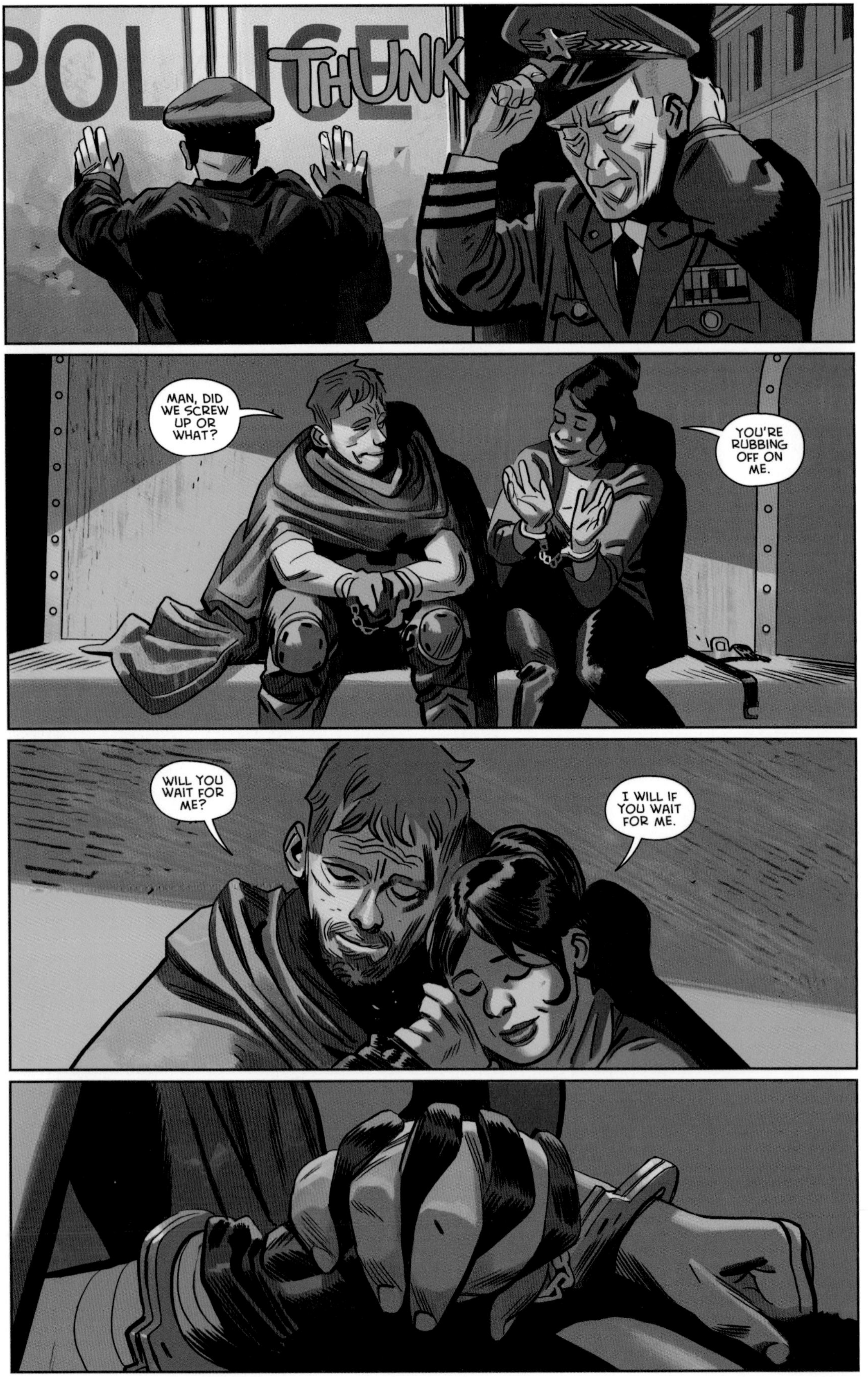
POLICE
THUNK
MAN, DID WE SCREW UP OR WHAT?
YOU'RE RUBBING OFF ON ME.
WILL YOU WAIT FOR ME?
I WILL IF YOU WAIT FOR ME.

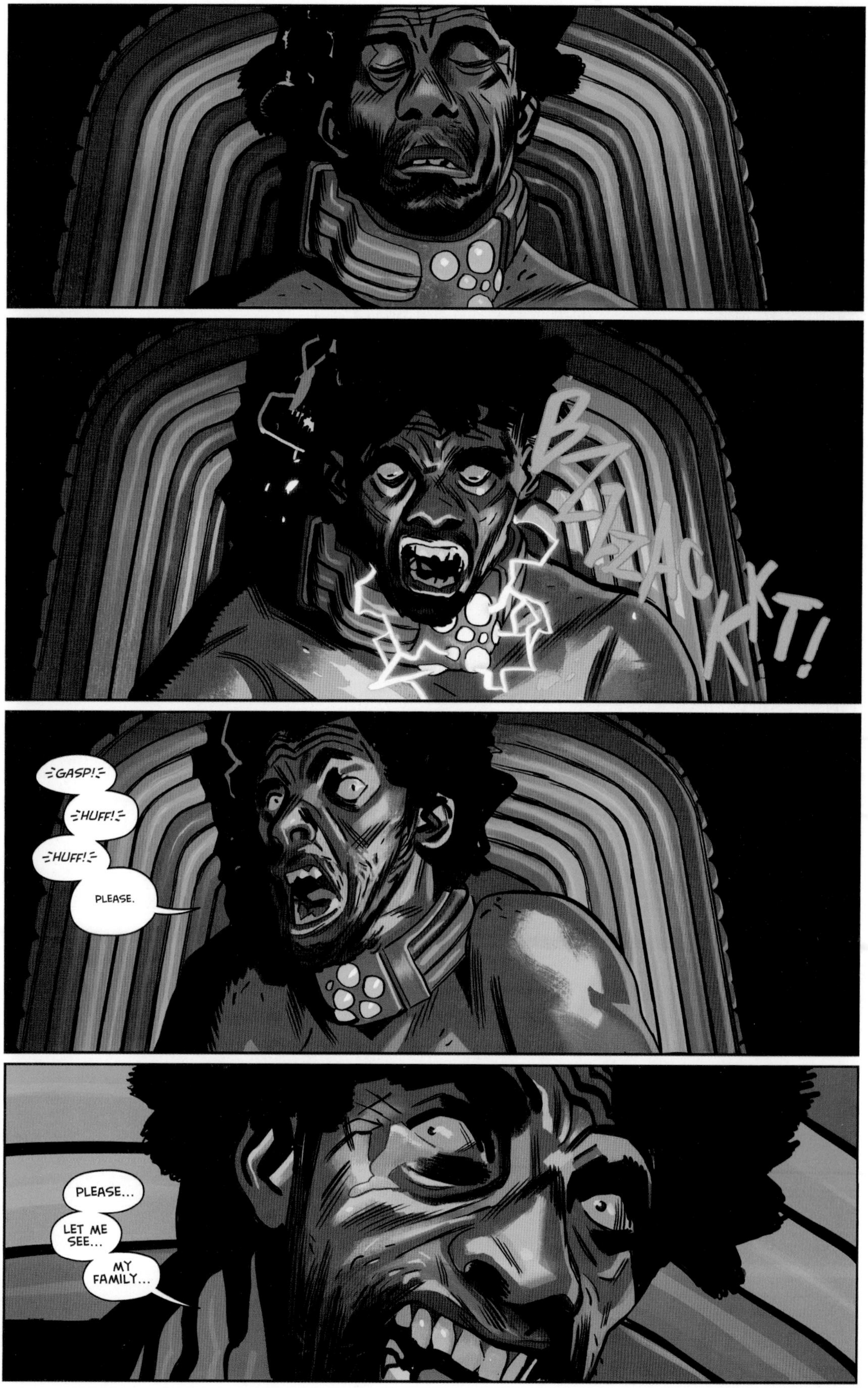
BZZZACKKT!
GASP!
HUFF!
HUFF!
PLEASE.
PLEASE...
LET ME SEE...
MY FAMILY...

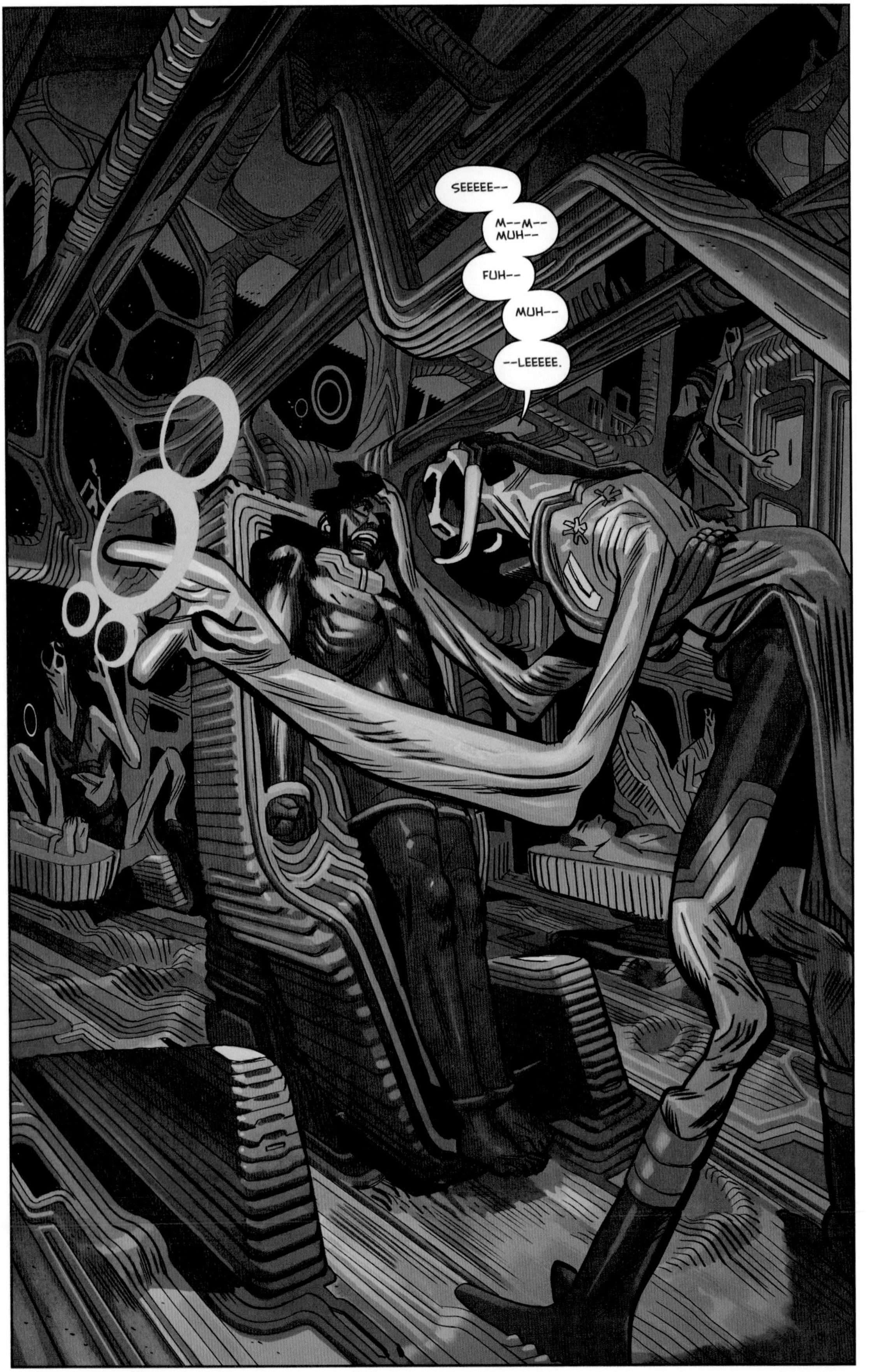
SEEEEE--
M--M--
MUH--
FUH--
MUH--
--LEEEEE.

TO BE CONTINUED...

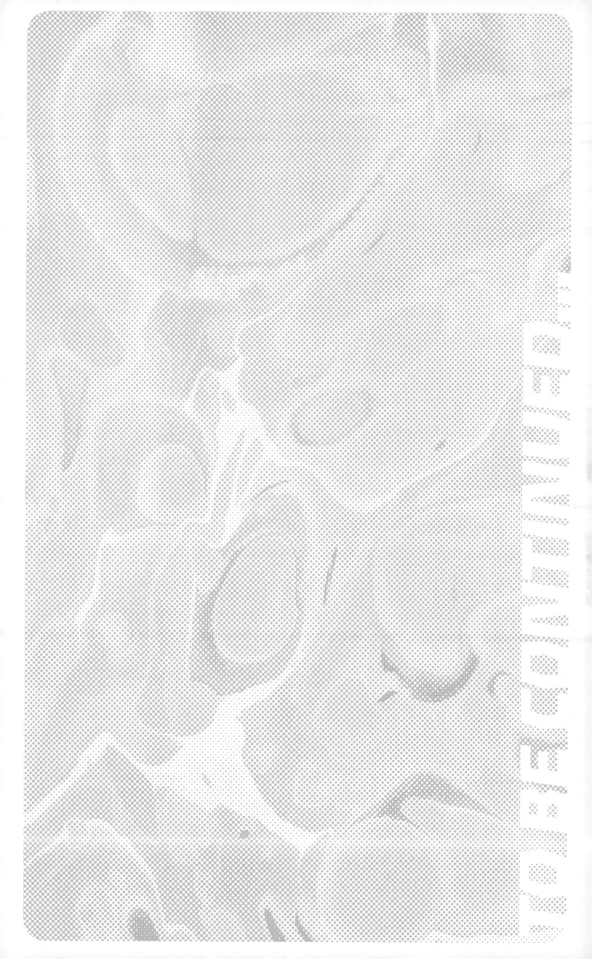

FOR MORE TALES FROM **ROBERT KIRKMAN** AND **SKYBOUND**

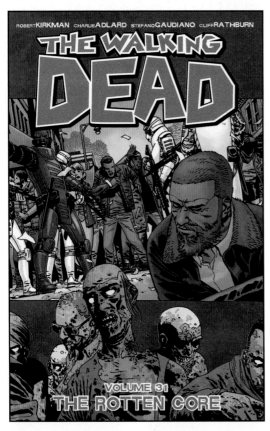

ROBERT KIRKMAN CHARLIE ADLARD STEFANO GAUDIANO CLIFF RATHBURN
THE WALKING DEAD
VOLUME 31
THE ROTTEN CORE

VOL. 1: DAYS GONE BYE TP
ISBN: 978-1-58240-672-5
$14.99

VOL. 2: MILES BEHIND US TP
ISBN: 978-1-58240-775-3
$14.99

VOL. 3: SAFETY BEHIND BARS TP
ISBN: 978-1-58240-805-7
$14.99

VOL. 4: THE HEART'S DESIRE TP
ISBN: 978-1-58240-530-8
$14.99

VOL. 5: THE BEST DEFENSE TP
ISBN: 978-1-58240-612-1
$14.99

VOL. 6: THIS SORROWFUL LIFE TP
ISBN: 978-1-58240-684-8
$14.99

VOL. 7: THE CALM BEFORE TP
ISBN: 978-1-58240-828-6
$14.99

VOL. 8: MADE TO SUFFER TP
ISBN: 978-1-58240-883-5
$14.99

VOL. 9: HERE WE REMAIN TP
ISBN: 978-1-60706-022-2
$14.99

VOL. 10: WHAT WE BECOME TP
ISBN: 978-1-60706-075-8
$14.99

VOL. 11: FEAR THE HUNTERS TP
ISBN: 978-1-60706-181-6
$14.99

VOL. 12: LIFE AMONG THEM TP
ISBN: 978-1-60706-254-7
$14.99

VOL. 13: TOO FAR GONE TP
ISBN: 978-1-60706-329-2
$14.99

VOL. 14: NO WAY OUT TP
ISBN: 978-1-60706-392-6
$14.99

VOL. 15: WE FIND OURSELVES TP
ISBN: 978-1-60706-440-4
$14.99

VOL. 16: A LARGER WORLD TP
ISBN: 978-1-60706-559-3
$14.99

VOL. 17: SOMETHING TO FEAR TP
ISBN: 978-1-60706-615-6
$14.99

VOL. 18: WHAT COMES AFTER TP
ISBN: 978-1-60706-687-3
$14.99

VOL. 19: MARCH TO WAR TP
ISBN: 978-1-60706-818-1
$14.99

VOL. 20: ALL OUT WAR PART ONE TP
ISBN: 978-1-60706-882-2
$14.99

VOL. 21: ALL OUT WAR PART TWO TP
ISBN: 978-1-63215-030-1
$14.99

VOL. 22: A NEW BEGINNING TP
ISBN: 978-1-63215-041-7
$14.99

VOL. 23: WHISPERS INTO SCREAMS TP
ISBN: 978-1-63215-258-9
$14.99

VOL. 24: LIFE AND DEATH TP
ISBN: 978-1-63215-402-6
$14.99

VOL. 25: NO TURNING BACK TP
ISBN: 978-1-63215-659-4
$14.99

VOL. 26: CALL TO ARMS TP
ISBN: 978-1-63215-917-5
$14.99

VOL. 27: THE WHISPERER WAR TP
ISBN: 978-1-5343-0052-1
$14.99

VOL. 28: A CERTAIN DOOM TP
ISBN: 978-1-5343-0244-0
$14.99

VOL. 29: LINES WE CROSS TP
ISBN: 978-1-5343-0497-0
$16.99

VOL. 30: NEW WORLD ORDER TP
ISBN: 978-1-5343-0884-8
$16.99

VOL. 31: THE ROTTEN CORE TP
ISBN: 978-1-5343-1052-0
$16.99

BOOK ONE HC
ISBN: 978-1-58240-619-0
$34.99

BOOK TWO HC
ISBN: 978-1-58240-698-5
$34.99

BOOK THREE HC
ISBN: 978-1-58240-825-5
$34.99

BOOK FOUR HC
ISBN: 978-1-60706-000-0
$34.99

BOOK FIVE HC
ISBN: 978-1-60706-171-7
$34.99

BOOK SIX HC
ISBN: 978-1-60706-327-8
$34.99

BOOK SEVEN HC
ISBN: 978-1-60706-439-8
$34.99

BOOK EIGHT HC
ISBN: 978-1-60706-593-7
$34.99

BOOK NINE HC
ISBN: 978-1-60706-798-6
$34.99

BOOK TEN HC
ISBN: 978-1-63215-034-9
$34.99

BOOK ELEVEN HC
ISBN: 978-1-63215-271-8
$34.99

BOOK TWELVE HC
ISBN: 978-1-63215-451-4
$34.99

BOOK THIRTEEN HC
ISBN: 978-1-63215-916-8
$34.99

BOOK FOURTEEN HC
ISBN: 978-1-5343-0329-4
$34.99

BOOK FIFTEEN HC
ISBN: 978-1-5343-0850-3
$34.99

BIRTHRIGHT
WILLIAMSON BRESSAN LUCAS
VOLUME SEVEN
BLOOD BROTHERS

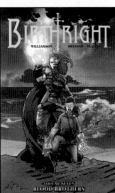

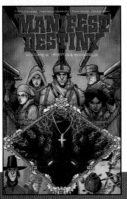

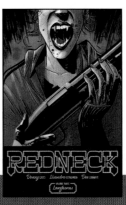

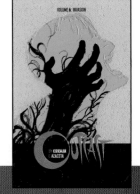

VOL. 1: HOMECOMING TP
ISBN: 978-1-63215-231-2
$9.99

VOL. 2: CALL TO ADVENTURE TP
ISBN: 978-1-63215-446-0
$12.99

VOL. 3: ALLIES AND ENEMIES TP
ISBN: 978-1-63215-683-9
$12.99

VOL. 4: FAMILY HISTORY TP
ISBN: 978-1-63215-871-0
$12.99

VOL. 5: BELLY OF THE BEAST TP
ISBN: 978-1-5343-0218-1
$12.99

VOL. 6: FATHERHOOD TP
ISBN: 978-1-53430-498-7
$14.99

VOL. 7: BLOOD BROTHERS TP
ISBN: 978-1-5343-1053-7
$14.99

MANIFEST DESTINY

VOL. 1: FLORA & FAUNA TP
ISBN: 978-1-60706-982-9
$9.99

VOL. 2: AMPHIBIA & INSECTA TP
ISBN: 978-1-63215-052-3
$14.99

VOL. 3: CHIROPTERA & CARNIFORMAVES TP
ISBN: 978-1-63215-397-5
$14.99

VOL. 4: SASQUATCH TP
ISBN: 978-1-63215-890-1
$14.99

VOL. 5: MNEMOPHOBIA & CHRONOPHOBIA TP
ISBN: 978-1-5343-0230-3
$16.99

VOL. 6: FORTIS & INVISIBILIA TP
ISBN: 978-1-5343-0513-7
$16.99

REDNECK
Longhorns

VOL. 1: DEEP IN THE HEART TP
ISBN: 978-1-5343-0331-7
$16.99

VOL. 2: THE EYES UPON YOU TP
ISBN: 978-1-5343-0665-3
$16.99

VOL. 3: LONGHORNS TP
ISBN: 978-1-5343-1050-6
$16.99

VOLUME 6: INVASION
BY KIRKMAN & AZACETA
OUTCAST

VOL. 1: A DARKNESS SURROUNDS HIM TP
ISBN: 978-1-63215-053-0
$9.99

VOL. 2: A VAST AND UNENDING RUIN TP
ISBN: 978-1-63215-448-4
$14.99

VOL. 3: THIS LITTLE LIGHT TP
ISBN: 978-1-63215-693-8
$14.99

VOL. 4: UNDER DEVIL'S WING TP
ISBN: 978-1-5343-0050-7
$14.99

VOL. 5: THE NEW PATH TP
ISBN: 978-1-5343-0249-5
$16.99

VOL. 6: INVASION TP
ISBN: 978-1-5343-0751-3
$16.99